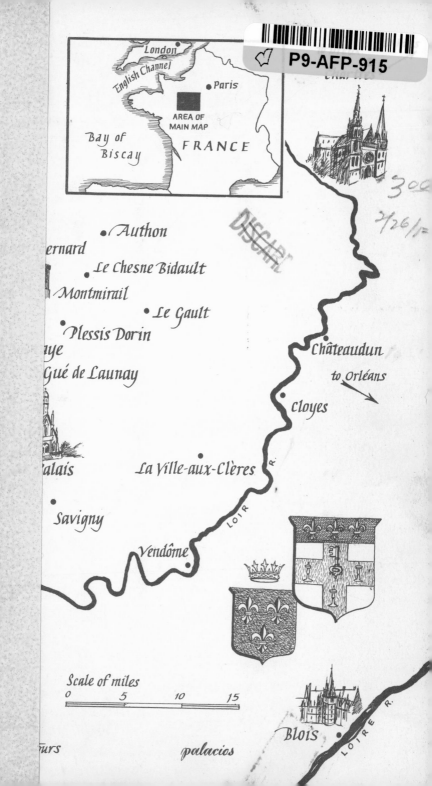

London

English Channel

•Paris

AREA OF
MAIN MAP

Bay of
Biscay

FRANCE

300
7/26/17

DISCARD

•Authon

ernard

Le Chesne Bidault

Montmirail

•Le Gault

•Plessis Dorin

aye

Gué de Launay

Châteaudun

to Orléans

Cloyes

La Ville-aux-Clères

LOIR R.

Savigny

LOIR

Vendôme

Scale of miles

0   5   10   15

Blois

LOIRE R.

urs   palacios

THE GLASS-BLOWERS

DAPHNE DU MAURIER

The Glass-Blowers

DOUBLEDAY & COMPANY, INC., GARDEN CITY, NEW YORK

R
007
147
354

12/03/91

*To my forebears, the master glass-blowers of
la Brûlonnerie, Chérigny, la Pierre and
le Chesne-Bidault.*

ACKNOWLEDGMENTS

I WISH TO THANK the following for their great help in making known to me the many facts relating to my forebears, the Bussons, during the hundred years from 1747–1845, as well as the historical events in the départements of Sarthe and Loir-et-Cher during the revolutionary period:

Mademoiselle Madeleine Fargeaud of Paris

Mr. Robert Glass of Paris

Mrs. St. George Saunders of London

Professeur R. Bouis of Blois, author of *Les Elections à la Convention Nationale dans le Département de Loir-et-Cher*, etc.

Monsieur André Bouton of Le Mans, author of *Les Francs-Maçons Manceaux et la Révolution Française*

Monsieur Paul Cordonnier of Le Mans, author of *L'Invasion et la Déroute de l'Armée Vendéene au Mans*, etc.

Madame Marthe of la Pierre, Coudrecieux

CONTENTS

PROLOGUE

ONE DAY IN THE June of 1844 Madame Sophie Duval, née Busson, eighty years of age and mother of the mayor of Vibraye, a small commune in the département of Sarthe, rose from her chair in the salon of her property at le Gué de Launay, chose her favourite walking-stick from a stand in the hall, and calling to her dog made her way, as was her custom at this hour of the afternoon every Tuesday, down the short approach drive to the entrance gate.

She walked briskly, with the quick step of one who did not suffer, or perhaps refused to suffer, any of the inconveniences of old age; and her bright blue eyes—the noticeable feature of her otherwise unremarkable face—looked keenly to right and left, pin-pointing signs of negligence on the part of the gardener: the gravel under her feet not raked this morning as it should have been, the careless staking of a lily, the grass verges of the formal flower-bed raggedly clipped.

These matters would be corrected at their proper time, either by her son the mayor or by herself; for although Pierre-François had been mayor of Vibraye for some fourteen years, and was approaching his forty-seventh birthday, he knew very well that the house and grounds at le Gué de Launay were his mother's property, that in all matters referring to their upkeep and maintenance she must be the final judge and arbitrator. This small estate which Madame Duval and her husband had settled upon for their retirement at the turn of the century was no great domain, a few acres of ground only, and the house was of medium size; but it was their own, bought and paid for by themselves, so giving them both the status of land-owners and making them the proud equal of any outdated seigneur who still boasted that he held a property by right of birth.

Madame Duval adjusted the widow's cap upon her crown of white hair, set in pin-curls high on her forehead. As she arrived at the end of the approach drive she heard the sound she was expecting, the click of the fastened iron gate and the rasp of the hinge as it swung open, while the gardener—later to be reprimanded—who also served as odd-man, groom and messenger, came towards her with the mail he had fetched from Vibraye.

Her son the mayor usually brought the letters back with him of an evening, if there were any to bring, but once a week, every Tuesday, there came the very special letter written to Madame Duval from her married daughter in Paris, Madame Rosiau; and since this was the most precious moment of her week the old lady could not bear to wait for it. She had given special orders to the gardener for many months now, ever since the Rosiaus had left Mamers for Paris, to go himself on foot the few kilometres to Vibraye, and enquire for the letters addressed to le Gué de Launay, and give them into her hands.

This he now did, doffing his hat, and placing uppermost in her hands the expected letter, with his customary remark, "Now Madame is content". "Thank you, Joseph," she replied. "Find your way to the kitchen and see if there is some coffee for you"— as though the gardener, who had worked for her at le Gué de Launay for thirty years, was looking for the kitchen for the first time. She waited until he was out of sight before she followed him, for it was part of the ritual to be preceded by the servant and walk herself, with measured step, at a certain distance in the rear, the unopened envelope clutched tightly to her, the dog at her heels; and then up the steps and into the house, and to the salon, where she would seat herself once more in her chair by the window, and give herself up to the long-awaited pleasure of the weekly letter.

The tie between mother and daughter was close, as it had been once, so many years ago, between Sophie Duval and her own mother Magdaleine. Sons, even if they lived under one's roof, had their own preoccupations, their business, their wives, political interests; but a daughter, even if she took to herself a husband as Zoë had done, and a very able doctor at that, remained always part of the mother, a nestling, intimate and confiding, a sharer of ills and joys, using the same family expressions long forgotten by the sons. The pains of the daughter were the pains the mother herself knew, or had known: the trifling differences between husband and wife that occurred from time to time had all been endured by Madame Duval in days gone by, along with housekeeping troubles, high prices in the market, sudden illnesses, the dismissal of a servant, the numerous trifles that went with a woman's day.

This letter was the answer to the one she had written over a week ago on her daughter's birthday. Zoë had been fifty-one on the 27th of May. It seemed scarcely credible. Over half a century had passed since she had held that scrap of humanity in her arms—her third child, and the first to survive infancy—and how well she remembered that summer's day too, with the window wide open to the orchard, the pungent smoke from the glass-foundry chimney filling the languid air, and the sound and clatter of the workmen as they crossed from the furnace-house to the yard drowning her own cries in labour.

What a moment to bring a child into the world, that summer of '93, the first year of the Republic; with the Vendée in revolt, the country at war, the traitorous Girondins endeavouring to bring down the Convention, the patriot Marat to be assassinated by an hysterical girl, and the unhappy ex-Queen Marie Antoinette confined in the Temple and later guillotined for all the misery she had brought upon France.

So many bitter and exciting days. Such exultation, triumph, and despair. All part of history now, forgotten by most people, over-shadowed by the achievements of the Emperor and his era. Only remembered by herself when she learnt of the death of a contemporary, and so was reminded suddenly, as though it were yesterday, that this same contemporary just laid to rest in the cemetery at Vibraye had been a member of the National Guard under her brother Michel, that the pair of them, with her husband François, had led the foundry workmen on the march in November '90 to sack the château of Charbonnières.

It did not do to speak of these things in front of her son the mayor. After all, he was a loyal subject of King Louis-Philippe, and hardly liked to be reminded of the part his father and uncle had played in the troubled days of the Revolution before he was born; though heaven knows it tempted her sometimes to do so, when he showed himself more than usually pompous and full of bourgeois principle.

Madame Duval opened her letter and straightened out the closely-written pages, crossed and re-crossed in her daughter's cramped hand. Thank God she did not need spectacles, despite her eighty years. "My very dear Maman. . . ."

First, Zoë's grateful thanks for the birthday gift (a patchwork quilt, worked at home during the winter and spring), followed by the usual small items of family news, her husband the doctor producing a paper on asthma to be read before the medical authorities, her daughter Clementine making excellent progress with piano lessons under a good master, and then—the handwriting becoming more careless because of excitement—the main content of the letter, reserved as a final surprise.

"We spent Sunday evening with near neighbours of ours in the Faubourg St. Germain," she wrote, "and as usual there was quite a gathering of doctors and scientists, and much interesting conversation. We were both impressed by the fluent talk and engaging manners of a stranger to our particular circle, an inventor who has apparently patented a portable lamp and expects to make his fortune from it. We were introduced, and imagine my surprise when we learnt that his name was Louis-Mathurin Busson, that he had been born and brought up in England of émigré parents, had come to Paris at some period after the Restoration of the monarchy when he was quite a young man, in company with his mother, now dead, and his surviving brother and sister, and had since lived—chiefly by his wits, I gathered, and his powers as an inventor—between the two countries, sometimes in London, sometimes in Paris, with business in both cities. He is married to an Englishwoman, has a young family, a house in the rue de la Pompe, and a laboratory in the Faubourg Poissonnière. Now, all this might have passed me by but for the singularity of the two names Busson and Mathurin, and the mention of émigré parents. I was careful not to commit myself immediately, or acquaint him of the fact that your maiden name was Busson and Mathurin a family first name, but when I casually enquired if his father, the émigré, had followed any particular profession or had been a man of leisure he answered me at once, and with great pride, 'Oh yes, indeed. He was a gentleman glass-blower, and owned several foundries before the Revolution. At one time he was first engraver in crystal at St. Cloud, the royal foundry patronised by the Queen herself. Naturally, at the outbreak of the Revolution he followed the example of the clergy and the aristocracy and emigrated to England with his young bride, my mother, and suffered much penury in consequence. His full name was Robert-Mathurin Busson du Maurier, and he died tragically and suddenly in 1802, after the Peace of Amiens, on returning to France in the hopes of restoring the family fortunes. My poor mother, left behind in England with her young children, little guessed, when she said good-bye to him, that it was for the last time. I was five years old then, and have no recollection of him, but my mother brought us up to understand that he was a man of tremendous principle and integrity, and of course a Royalist to his finger-tips.'

"Maman . . . I nodded my head, and made some remark or other, while I tried to collect my thoughts. I am right, am I not? This man, this inventor, must be my cousin, son of your beloved brother my uncle Robert. But what is all this talk of his being called du Maurier, leaving a family in England and dying in 1802, when you and I know perfectly well that he died in 1811, and was a widower anyway, with his son Jacques a corporal in the Grande Armée? Why, I was eighteen years old when uncle Robert died, a schoolmaster in Tours, yet here is this inventor, Monsieur Busson, who must be his son, giving a very different account of his father from the one you gave us, and apparently in complete ignorance of his father's true end, or of your existence.

"I asked if he had relatives. He said he believed not. They had all been guillotined during the Terror, and the château Maurier and the glass-foundries destroyed. He had made no enquiries. It was better not. What was past was past. Then my hostess interrupted us, and we were parted. I did not speak to him again. But I have discovered his address—31, rue de la Pompe, in Passy

—should you wish me to get in touch with him. Maman, what would you have me do?"

Madame Duval laid her daughter's letter aside, and stared out of the window. So . . . It had happened at last. It had taken more than thirty years, but it had happened. What Robert had believed would never be.

"Those children will be brought up in England, and make their life there," he had told her. "What should bring them to France, especially if they believe their father dead? No, that phase of my life, like all the others, is over and done with."

Madame Duval picked up the letter and read it through once again. Two courses were open to her. The first, to write to her daughter Zoë and tell her to make no further attempt to get in touch with the man who had declared himself to be Louis-Mathurin Busson. The second, to go herself to Paris immediately, to call upon Monsieur Busson at 31, rue de la Pompe and acknowledge their relationship, and so see at last, before she died, her brother's child.

The first course she dismissed almost as soon as it entered her head. By following it she would deny all family feeling, and so go against everything she held most dear. The second course must be embarked upon forthwith, or as soon as it could be put into practice.

That evening, when her son the mayor returned from Vibraye, Madame Duval told him her news, and it was arranged that she should travel to Paris within the week to stay with her daughter in the Faubourg St. Germain. All attempts on the part of her son to dissuade her were useless. She remained firm. "If this man is an impostor I shall know it directly I set eyes on him," she said. "If not, then I shall have done my duty."

The night before she left for Paris, she went to the cabinet in the corner of the salon, unlocked it with the key she wore in a locket round her neck, and took out a leather case. This case she packed carefully amongst the few clothes she took with her.

It was about four o'clock on the Sunday of the following week when Madame Duval and her daughter Madame Rosiau called at 31, rue de la Pompe, in Passy. The house was well placed, on the corner of the rue de la Pompe and the rue de la Tour, opposite a boys' school, with a garden behind and a long avenue leading directly to the Bois de Boulogne.

A cheerful femme de ménage opened the door, took their cards, and showed the visitors into a pleasant room facing the garden, from where they could hear the cries of children at play. In a moment or two a figure stepped through the long windows giving on to the garden, and Madame Rosiau, with a brief word of explanation and apology for the intrusion, introduced her mother to the inventor.

One look was enough. The blue eyes, the light hair, the tilt of the head, the quick courteous smile, showing an instant wish to please combined with a desire to turn the occasion to his own advantage if it were possible—here was Robert in the flesh as she remembered him, forty, fifty, sixty years ago.

Madame Duval took his extended hand in both of hers and held it, her eyes, the mirror of his own, dwelling at length upon his face. "Forgive me," she said, "but I have every reason to believe that you are my nephew, and the son of my eldest brother Robert-Mathurin."

"Your nephew?" He looked from one to the other in astonishment. "I'm afraid I don't understand. I met Madame . . . Madame Rosiau for the first time nearly two weeks ago. I had not the pleasure of her acquaintance before, and . . ."

"Yes, yes," interrupted Madame Duval. "I know just how you met, but she was too overwhelmed when she learnt your name, and your history, to tell you that her mother's maiden name was Busson, that her uncle was Robert-Mathurin Busson, a master glass-engraver who emigrated . . . I am, in short, her mother, and your aunt Sophie, and have been waiting for this moment for nearly half a century."

They led her to a chair and made her sit down, and she wiped the tears from her eyes—so foolish, she told him, to break down, and how Robert would have mocked her. In a few minutes she was composed, and sufficiently mistress of herself to seize upon the fact that, although her nephew expressed himself delighted to find that he had relatives, he was at the same time a trifle disconcerted that his aunt and his cousin were not great ladies, but ordinary provincial folk with no claim to vast estates or ruined châteaux.

"But the name Busson," he insisted. "I was brought up to understand that we were descended from an aristocratic Breton family going back to the fourteenth century, that my father became a gentleman glass-engraver merely for his own amusement, that our motto—Abret ag Aroag, First and Foremost—belonged to the old knights of Brittany. Do you mean to tell me none of this is true?"

Madame Duval considered her nephew with a sceptical eye. "Your father Robert was first and foremost the most incorrigible farceur I have ever known," she said drily, "and if he told these tales in England no doubt it suited his purpose at the time."

"But the château Maurier," protested the inventor, "the château Maurier that was burnt to the ground by the peasants during the Revolution?"

"A farmhouse," replied his aunt, "unchanged since your father was born there in 1749. We have cousins there still."

Her nephew stared at her aghast. "There must be some misunderstanding," he said. "My mother can have known nothing of this. Unless . . ." He broke off, at a loss how to continue, and she understood from his expression that her blunt words had shattered an illusion held since childhood, that his self-confidence was shaken, that he might now even doubt himself and his own powers for the future.

"Tell me one thing," she asked. "Was she a good mother to you?"

"Oh, yes," he replied, "the best in the world. And she had a hard struggle, I can tell you, with my father gone. But she had wonderful friends amongst the French colony. A fund was started to help us. We received the best of educations in one of the schools founded by the Abbé Carron, along with the children of other émigrés, the de Polignacs, the de Labourdomains, etc." A note of pride crept into his voice, and he did not notice his aunt flinch as he pronounced names reviled and detested by herself and her brothers over fifty years before.

"My sister," he continued, "is companion to the daughter of the Duke of Palmella in Lisbon. My brother James is in business in Hamburg. I myself, with the help of influential friends, intend placing upon the markets of the world a lamp of my own invention. Indeed, we none of us have anything to be ashamed of, we have great hopes . . ." Once again he broke off in mid-sentence. There was a speculative look in his eye strangely reminiscent of his father. This aunt from the provinces was, alas, no aristocrat, but had she money tucked away in a stocking?

Madame Duval could read his thoughts as once she had read her brother Robert's. "You are an optimist, like your father," she told him. "So much the better. It makes life comparatively easy."

He smiled. The look of speculation vanished. The charm returned, Robert's charm, winning, endearing, that could never be withstood.

"Tell me about him," he said. "I must know everything. From the very beginning. Even if he was born in a farmhouse, as you say, and not a château. And far from being a nobleman was in reality . . ."

"An adventurer?" she finished for him.

At that moment her nephew's wife came in from the garden, followed by the three children. The femme de ménage brought in tea. Conversation became general. Madame Rosiau, who felt that her mother had already been far too indiscreet, pressed the wife of her newly found cousin to comparisons between life in London and in Paris. The inventor produced a model of his portable lamp that was to make all their fortunes. Madame Duval remained silent, watching each of the children in turn for a family likeness. Yes, the little girl Isobel, pert and quick, was something like her own young sister Edmé at the same age. The second boy, Eugène, or Gyggy, reminded her of nobody. But the eldest, George, nicknamed Kicky, a lad of ten, was her brother Pierre in miniature, the same dreamy reflective eyes, the same way of standing with his feet crossed, his hands in his pockets.

"And you, Kicky," she said, "what do you intend to do when you grow up?"

"My father hopes I'll become a chemist," he said, "but I doubt if I'd pass the exams. I like to draw best of all."

"Show me your drawings," she whispered.

He ran out of the room, pleased at her interest, and returned in a moment with a portfolio full of sketches. She examined them carefully, one by one.

"You have talent," she said. "One day you'll put it to good purpose. It's in your blood."

Madame Duval then turned to her nephew the inventor, interrupting the flow of conversation. "I wish to make a gift to your son George," she announced. "It must be his, by right of inheritance." She felt in the lining pocket of her voluminous cape, and drew forth a package which she proceeded to unwrap. The paper dropped to the floor. From a leather case she produced a crystal tumbler, engraved with the fleur-de-lys, and with the interlaced letters L.R.XV.

"This glass was made in the foundry of la Pierre, Coudrecieux," she said, "engraved by my father, Mathurin Busson, on the occasion of the visit of King Louis XV. It has had a chequered history, but has been in my safekeeping for many years. My father used to say that as long as it remained unbroken, treasured in the family, the creative talent of the Bussons would continue, in some form or other, through the succeeding generations."

Silently, her newly found nephew and his wife and children gazed upon the glass. Then Madame Duval replaced it in the leather case. "There," she said to the boy George, "remain true to your talent, and the glass will bring you luck. Abuse your talent, or neglect it, as my brother did, and the luck will run out of the glass."

She gave him the leather case and smiled, then turned to her nephew the inventor. "I shall return home to le Gué de Launay tomorrow," she told him. "Perhaps we shall not see each other again. I will write to you, though, and tell you, as best as I can, the story of your family. A glass-blower, remember, breathes life into a vessel, giving it shape and form and sometimes beauty; but he can, with that same breath, shatter and destroy it. If what I write displeases you, it will not matter. Throw my letters in the fire unread, and keep your illusions. For myself, I have always preferred to know the truth."

Madame Duval nodded to her daughter Madame Rosiau and,

rising from her chair, embraced her nephew and her nephew's children.

The next day she left Paris and returned home. She said little about her visit to her son the mayor of Vibraye, beyond remarking that looking upon her nephew and his children for the first and perhaps the last time had revived old memories. During the weeks that followed, instead of giving orders at le Gué de Launay and inspecting her fruit-trees, vegetables and flowers, she spent all her time at her bureau in the salon, covering sheet after sheet of writing-paper in her formal, upright hand.

PART ONE

La Reyne d'Hongrie

ONE

"IF YOU MARRY into glass," Pierre Labbé warned my mother, his daughter Magdaleine, in 1747, "you will say good-bye to everything familiar, and enter a closed world."

She was twenty-two years old, and her prospective bridegroom, Mathurin Busson, master glass-maker from the neighbouring village of Chenu, was a childhood sweetheart, four years older than herself. They had never had eyes for anyone but each other from the day they met, and my father, the son of a merchant in glass, orphaned at an early age, had been apprenticed with his brother Michel to the glass-house known as la Brûlonnerie, in the Vendôme, between Busloup and la Ville-aux-Clercs. Both brothers showed great promise, and my father Mathurin had risen rapidly to the rank of master glass-maker, working directly under Robert Brossard the proprietor, who was a member of one of the four great glass-making families in France.

"I have no doubt Mathurin Busson will succeed in everything he undertakes," continued Pierre Labbé, who was himself bailiff at St. Christophe and law-officer to the district, and a man of some importance. "He is steady, hard-working, and a very fine craftsman; but it is breaking with tradition for a glass-maker to marry outside his own community. As his bride you will find it hard to adapt yourself to their way of life."

He knew what he was talking about. So did she. She was not afraid. The glass world was unique, a law unto itself. It had its own rules and customs, and a separate language too, handed down not only from father to son but from master to apprentice, instituted heaven knows how many centuries ago wherever the glass-makers settled—in Normandy, in Lorraine, by the Loire— but always, naturally, by forests, for wood was the glass-foundry's food, the mainstay of its existence.

The laws, customs, and privileges of the glass-makers were more strictly observed than the feudal rights of the aristocracy; they had more justice, too, and they made more sense. Theirs was indeed a closed community, with every man, woman and child knowing his place within the walls, from the director himself, who worked beside his men, sharing their labour, wearing the same apparel, yet looked upon by all as lord and master, to the little child of six or seven who fetched and carried, taking his shift with his elders, seizing his chance to approach the foundry fire.

"What I do," said Magdaleine Labbé, my mother, "I do with my eyes open, without any vain ideas of an easy life, or believing I can sit back and be waited upon. Mathurin has already disabused me about that."

Nevertheless, as she stood beside her bridegroom on that 18th day of September in the year 1747, in the church of her native village of St. Christophe in the Touraine, and looked from her own relatives—her wealthy uncle Georget, her lawyer uncle Thiezie, her own father in his bailiff's dress—to the opposite side of the nave, where her bridegroom's relatives were assembled, and a number of his workmen and their wives, all glass-makers, all watching her with suspicion, almost with hostility, she certainly experienced—so she told us children years afterwards—a brief moment of doubt; she refused to call it fear.

"I felt," she said, "as a white man must feel when he is surrounded for the first time by American Indians, and knows that by sundown he must enter their encampment, never to return."

The workmen from the glass-house were certainly not in war-paint, but their uniform of black coat and breeches and black flat hat, worn on saints' days and holidays, set them apart from my mother's relatives, giving them the appearance of a religious sect.

Nor did they mix with the rest of the company afterwards at the wedding breakfast, which, because Pierre Labbé was a man of standing in St. Christophe, was necessarily a big event, with almost everyone in the neighbourhood present. They stood aside in a group of their own, too proud, perhaps, to exchange the usual quips and compliments with the rest of the guests, laughing and joking amongst themselves and making a great deal of noise about it too.

The only one to be perfectly at ease was Monsieur Brossard, my father's employer, but then, he was not only a seigneur by birth but the proprietor of three or four other glass-houses besides la Brûlonnerie, and it was a great condescension on his part to be present at the wedding. He did so because of the regard he had for my father: he had already promised him, within the year, the directorship of la Brûlonnerie.

The wedding was held at midday, so that the happy pair and their cortège could reach their destination the other side of Vendôme before midnight. When the last toast had been given my mother had to take off her finery and put on a travelling dress, then mount one of the foundry waggons with the rest of them, and so drive away to her new home in the forest of Fréteval. Monsieur Brossard did not accompany them. He was bound in the opposite direction. My father Mathurin and my mother Magdaleine, with his sister Françoise and her husband Louis Déméré—a master glass-maker like himself—seated themselves in the front of the waggon beside the driver, and behind them, in order of precedence, came the various craftsmen with their wives: the souffleurs, or blowers, the melters, and the flux-burners. The stokers, along with the driers, came in the second waggon, and a crowd of apprentices filled the third, with my father's brother Michel in charge.

During the first half of the journey, my mother Magdaleine said, she listened to the singing, for all glass-makers are musicians after their own fashion, and play some instrument or other, and have the special songs of their trade. When they ceased singing they began to discuss the plans for the day ahead, and the week's work. None of it as yet made sense to her, the newcomer, and when darkness fell she was so worn out with excitement and expectation, and the motion of the waggon, that she fell asleep on her bridegroom's shoulder, and did not wake up until they were past Vendôme and entering the forest of Fréteval.

She awoke suddenly, for the waggon had left the road, and she was aware of an immense darkness all about her, seemingly impenetrable. Even the stars were lost, for the interlaced branches of the forest trees made a vault where the sky had been. The silence was as deep as the darkness. The waggon wheels made no sound on the muddied track. As they lurched on into even greater depths of forest she was reminded once more of her fancy of an approach to an Indian encampment.

Then of a sudden she saw the fires of the charcoal-burners, and smelt, for the first time, the bitter-sweet smell of blackened wood and ashes that would remain with her throughout the whole of her married life—the smell that all of us were to know as children and inhale with our first breath, that would become synonymous with our very existence.

The silence ceased. Figures came out of the forest clearing and ran towards the waggons. There was sudden shouting, sudden laughter. "Then indeed," my mother Magdaleine said, "I thought I was amongst the Indians, for the charcoal-burners, their faces blackened with the smoke, their long hair falling about their shoulders, had their huts as outposts to the glass-house itself, and they were the first to greet me, the bride. What I took to be an assault upon all of us in the waggon was in reality their welcome."

This astonished us as children, for we grew up beside the charcoal-burners, called them by their Christian names, watched them at work, visited them in their log huts when they were ill; but to my mother, the bailiff's daughter from St. Christophe, gently nurtured, educated and well-spoken, the rude shouts of these wild men of the woods at midnight must have sounded like devils in hell.

They had to look at her, of course, by the light of their flaring torches, and then with a friendly laugh and a wave of his hand my father Mathurin bade them goodnight, and the waggon plunged on again out of the clearing into the forest, and along the remainder of the track to the glass-house itself. La Brûlonnerie, in those days, consisted of the big furnace house itself, surrounded by the work-buildings, the potting rooms, store-rooms and drying-rooms, and behind these the living quarters of the workmen; while further across the big yard were the small houses for the masters. The first thought to strike my mother was that the furnace chimney was on fire. Tongues of flame shot into the air, with sparks flying in all directions; a belching volcano could not be more malevolent.

"We have arrived just in time," she said abruptly.

"In time for what?" asked my father.

"To put out the fire," she said, pointing to the chimney. A moment later she realised her mistake, and could have bitten out her tongue for making a fool of herself before she had even set foot within the glass-house precincts. Of course her remark was repeated, amidst laughter, to everyone else within the waggon, and so back to the other waggons. Her arrival, instead of being a dignified affair with the workmen standing aside to let her pass, became a triumphant procession into the furnace-house itself, hemmed about with grinning faces, so that she could see for herself the "fire" upon which the livelihood of them all depended.

"There I stood," she told us, "on the threshold of the great vaulted space, some ninety feet long, with the two furnaces in the centre, enclosed, of course, so that I could not see the fire. It was the rest period, between midnight and one-thirty, and some of the workmen were sleeping, wherever they could find space upon the floor, and as close to the furnaces as possible, little children amongst them, while the rest were drinking great jugfuls of strong black coffee brewed by the women, and the stokers, naked to the waist, stood ready to feed the two fires before the next shift. I thought I had entered an inferno, and that the curled-up bodies of the children were sacrifices, to be shovelled into the pots and melted. The men stopped drinking their coffee and stared at me, and the women too, and they all waited to see what I would do."

"And what did you do?" we asked, for this was a favourite story, one which we never tired of hearing.

"There was only one thing I could do," she told us. "I took off my travelling-cloak and walked over to the women, and asked them if I could help with the coffee. They were so surprised at my boldness that they handed a jug to me without a word. It was not much of a start to a bridal night, perhaps, but nobody afterwards ever called me too delicate for work, or mocked at me for being a bailiff's daughter."

I do not think they would have mocked my mother whatever she had done. She had a look in her eye, our father told us, even in those days, when she was twenty-two, that would silence anyone who thought to take a liberty. She was immensely tall for a woman, five foot ten or thereabouts, with square shoulders, dwarfing the other foundry women; she even made my father, who was of medium height, look small. She dressed her blonde hair high, which added to her stature, and she kept this style throughout her life; I believe it was her secret vanity.

"Such was my introduction to glass," she told us. "The next morning another shift began, and I watched my bridegroom dress in his working blouse and go off to the furnace-house, leaving me to get accustomed to the smell of the wood-smoke, with work-sheds all about me, and nothing outside the foundry fence but forest for ever and ever."

When her sister-in-law Françoise Démére came to the house at mid-morning to help her unpack she found everything put away and the linen sorted, and my mother Magdaleine gone across to the workshops to talk to the flux-burner, the craftsman who prepared the potash. She wanted to see how the ash was sieved and mixed with the lime, and then placed in the cauldron to boil, before being passed on to the melter.

My aunt Démére was shocked. Her husband, my uncle Démére, was one of the most important men in the foundry. He was a master-melter, that is to say he prepared the mixture for the pots, and saw to it that the pots were filled with the right amount for the furnaces before the day's melt, and never, since they had been married, had my aunt Démére watched the potash being prepared by the flux-burner.

"The first duty of a master's wife is to have food ready for her husband between shifts," she told my mother, "and then to attend to any women or children directly employed by her husband who may be sick. The work in the furnace-house, or outside it, is nothing to do with us."

My mother Magdaleine was silent for a moment. She had sense enough not to argue with someone well versed in glass-house law. "Mathurin's dinner will be ready for him when he comes in," she said at last, "and if I broke one of the rules I'm sorry for it."

"It is not a question of rule," replied my aunt Déméré, "but a matter of principle."

During the next few days my mother remained within doors, where she could not cause gossip, but later in the week curiosity became too strong for her, and she made another break with tradition. She went down to the stamping mill, as they called it, where the blocks of quartz were ground to powder which, after sieving, formed the core of the glass. Before the quartz was ground it had to be sorted and freed from all impurities, and this was one of the tasks of the women, who knelt by the stream, sorting the quartz on large flat boards. My mother Magdaleine went straight to the woman who seemed to be in charge, introduced herself, and asked if she might take her place in the line and learn how the work was done.

They must have been too overcome by her manner and her appearance to say much, but they let her sort the quartz side by side with them until midday, when the ringer-boy sounded the great bell, and those amongst the women who expected their husbands back from morning shift went home. By this time, of course, word had gone round what had happened, for news spreads fast in a glass-house, and when my father came back to the house, and changed from his working-blouse into his Sunday coat and breeches, she sensed that something was wrong. He looked grave too.

"I have to see Monsieur Brossard," he told her, "on account of your behaviour this morning. It seems that he has heard all about it, and demands an explanation."

Here was an issue, my mother Magdaleine told us, upon which the whole of their future might depend, and it had to come up during their first week of married life.

"Did I do anything wrong by working with the women?" she asked him.

"No," he answered, "but a master's wife is on a different footing from the workmen's wives. She is not expected to do manual work, and only loses face by doing so."

Once again my mother did not argue the point. But she too

changed her dress, and when my father left the house to see
Monsieur Brossard she went with him.

Monsieur Brossard received them in the entrance lodge, which
he reserved for his own use when he visited the glass-house. He
never spent more than a few days in any place, and was proceed-
ing to another of his foundries later that evening. His manner
was more distant than it had been at the wedding, my mother
said, when he had given the toast to the bride and kissed her
cheek. Now he was the proprietor of la Brûlonnerie, and my
father Mathurin one of the master glass-makers in his employ.

"You know why I have sent for you, Monsieur Busson," he
said. He had called my father Mathurin at the wedding, but
in the glass-house precincts formality between proprietor and
master was strictly observed.

"Yes, Monsieur Brossard," replied my father, "and I have come
to apologise for what was observed down by the stamping mill
this morning. My wife let her curiosity overcome her sense of
propriety, and what is due to my position. As you know, she
has only lived amongst us for a week."

Monsieur Brossard nodded, and turned to my mother.

"You will soon learn our ways," he said, "and come to understand our traditions. If you are in any quandary as to procedure,
and your husband is at work, you have only to ask your sister-in-
law Madame Démére, who is well acquainted with every facet
of glass-house life."

He rose to his feet, the interview at an end. He was a small
man, with great presence and dignity, but he had to look up at
my mother, who overtopped him by a good four inches.

"Am I permitted to speak?" she enquired.

Monsieur Brossard bowed. "Naturally, Madame Busson," he
replied.

"I'm a bailiff's daughter, as you know," she said. "I have grown
up with some experience of the law. I used to help my father
sort his papers and make out his assessments, before cases were
brought to trial."

Monsieur Brossard bowed again. "I have no doubt you were
very helpful to him," he remarked.

"I was," answered my mother, "and I want to be helpful to

my husband, too. You have promised him a directorship before long, either here or in a glass-house of his own. When this happens, and he is obliged to be absent from time to time I want to be able to direct the glass-house myself. I cannot do that without first knowing how all the work is done. This morning I took my first lesson in sorting the quartz."

Monsieur Brossard stared at her. So did my father. She did not give them time to answer, but continued her speech.

"Mathurin, as you know, is a designer," she went on. "His head is full of his inventions. Even now he is not thinking about me, but about some new design. When he has a glass-house of his own he will be too busy to occupy himself with day-to-day business. I intend to do that for him."

Monsieur Brossard was nonplussed. None of his master glass-makers, until now, had taken unto themselves so formidable a wife.

"Madame Busson," he said, "all this is very praiseworthy, but you forget your first duty, which is that of rearing a family."

"I have not forgotten," she replied. "A large family will be only part of my work. Thank God I am strong. Child-bearing will not worry me. I will stop working with the women if you consider that it makes Mathurin lose face, but, if I consent to this, perhaps you will do something for me in return. I should like to know how to keep the glass-house records, and how to deal with the merchant buyers. This seems to me the most important business of all."

My mother achieved her purpose. Whether it was her looks that did it, or her tenacity of will, she never disclosed, and I don't think my father knew either; but within the month she had surrounded herself with books and ledgers, and Monsieur Brossard himself gave orders to the store-keeper to instruct her in all matters relating to finance. Perhaps he thought it the best way of keeping her within doors, and from distracting the attention of the workmen and their wives. It did not prevent her, though, from rising at midnight, with the rest of the women, when my father was on night-shift, and crossing to the furnace-house to brew coffee. This was part of the tradition she believed in following, and I doubt if she missed a night-shift during the whole of her married life. Whether there was any small jealousy or not on the part of the other craftsmen's wives because of my mother's superior intelligence, and the favour she had found with Monsieur Brossard, I cannot say, but I hardly think so. None of them, except my aunt Démeré, could read or write, and they certainly did not know how to keep figures in a ledger.

However it may have been with the women, it was during the first year at la Brûlonnerie, in the forest of Fréteval, that she came by the nickname which stayed with her to the end of her days and by which she was known, not only there and in later houses, but throughout the whole of the glass-trade, wherever my father did business.

It was his particular ambition, in these early days as a young man, to design for the Paris market, and for the American continent too, scientific instruments to be used in chemistry and astronomy—for it was the start of an age when new ideas were spreading fast. Because he was ahead of his time he succeeded in inventing, during this period at la Brûlonnerie, certain pieces of an entirely new form. These instruments are now made in bulk and used by doctors and chemists all over France, while my father's name is forgotten, but a hundred years ago the "instruments de chimie" designed at la Brûlonnerie were sought after by all the apothecaries in Paris.

The demand spread to the perfumery trade. The great ladies at Court wished for bottles and flasks of unusual designs to place on their dressing-tables—the more extravagant the better, for this was the moment when the Pompadour had such sway over the King, and all luxury goods were very much in fashion. Monsieur Brossard, bombarded on all sides by tradesmen and merchants eager to make their fortune, implored my father to forget for a moment his scientific instruments, and design a flask to please the highest in the land.

It began as a jest on my father's part. He told my mother to stand up before him while he drew the outline of her figure. First the head, then the square shoulders—so singular in a woman—then the slim hips, the long straight body. He compared his drawing with the last apothecary's bottle he had designed; they were almost identical. "You know what it is," he said to my mother. "I thought I was working to a mathematical formula, when all the while I've been drawing my inspiration from you."

He put on his blouse and went over to the furnace-house to see about his moulds. No one to this day will know whether it was the apothecary's bottle he shaped into a new form or my mother's body—he said it was the latter—but the flask he designed for the perfumeries of Paris delighted the merchants, and the buyers too. They filled the flask with eau-de-toilette, calling it the perfume of "la Reyne d'hongrie" after Elizabeth of Hungary, who had remained beautiful until she was past seventy, and my father laughed so much that he went and told everybody in the glass-house. My mother was very much annoyed. Nevertheless, she became la Reyne d'hongrie from that moment, and was affectionately known as this throughout the glass-trade until the Revolution, when she became la citoyenne Busson, and the title was prudently dropped.

Even then it was revived, from time to time, by my youngest brother Michel, when he wished to be particularly offensive. He would tell his workmen, within earshot of my mother, that all Paris knew that the odour emanating from the corpses of those ladies whose heads had but recently rolled into the basket was none other than that of a famous eau-de-toilette, distilled by the mistress of the glass-house some forty years before, and bottled by her own fair hands for the use of the beauties of Versailles.

TWO

ONE OF MONSIEUR BROSSARD'S associates was the marquis de
Cherbon, whose family had, in the previous century, constructed
a small glass-house in the grounds of their château of Chérigny,
only a few miles from my father's native village of Chenu and
my mother's home at St. Christophe. This little foundry was at
present in a poor state, through indifferent supervision, and the
marquis de Cherbon, who had lately married and succeeded to
his estate at the same time, was determined to put his glass-
house to rights and make a profit from it. He consulted Monsieur Brossard, who at once recommended my father as director
and lessee, the idea being that my father would thus have his
first chance to prove himself a good organiser and business man,
as well as a fine craftsman.

The marquis de Cherbon was well satisfied. He already knew
my father, and my mother's uncle Georget of St. Paterne, and
felt sure that the administration of his glass-house would be in
capable hands.

My mother Magdaleine and my father moved to Chérigny
in the spring of 1749, and it was here in September that my
brother Robert was born, and three years later my brother Pierre.

The setting was very different from la Brûlonnerie. Here at
Chérigny the glass-house was on a nobleman's private estate,
and consisted of a small furnace-house, with work buildings
attached, and workmen's cabins alongside, only a few hundred
yards distant from the château itself. There was barely a quarter
of the men employed here compared with la Brûlonnerie, and it
was truly a family affair, with the marquis de Cherbon taking a
personal interest in all that went on, though he never interfered
with the work.

My uncle Déméré had remained at la Brûlonnerie, but my

father's brother Michel Busson had moved to Chérigny with my parents, and about this time another sister, Anne, married Jacques Viau, the melting master at Chérigny. All the members of this small community were closely related, but the differences in status were still strictly kept, and my father and mother lived apart from the others in the farmhouse known as le Maurier, about five minutes' walk from the glass-house. This gave them not only privacy, which had been lacking at la Brûlonnerie, but the necessary degree of importance and privilege which was so strictly adhered to in the glass-trade.

It meant more hard work for my mother, though. Besides keeping the records and writing to the merchants—for she had taken upon herself this part of the business—she had to manage the whole of the farm, see that the cattle were milked and put to pasture, the chickens reared, the pigs killed, and the few acres of ground about the farmstead tilled. None of this dismayed her. She was capable of writing three pages disputing the amount paid for a consignment of goods to Paris—and this at ten o'clock at night after a long day's work in the house and about the farm —of walking across to the glass-house and brewing coffee for my father and those on night-shift, returning and snatching a few hours of sleep, and then rising at five to see that the cows were milked.

The fact that she was carrying my brother Robert, and later nursing him, made no difference to her activities. Here, at le Maurier, she was free to organise her own day as she pleased. There were no watchful eyes about her, no one to criticise or accuse her of breaking with tradition; and if any of my father's relatives should venture to do so, she was the wife of the director, and they never did so twice.

One of the pleasantest things about life at the glass-house of Chérigny was the relationship between my parents and the marquis and marquise de Cherbon. Unlike many aristocrats at that time they were seldom absent from their property for long periods, never went to Court, and were respected and loved by their tenants and the peasantry. The marquise, in particular, made a great favourite of my mother Magdaleine—for they were about the same age, the de Cherbons having been married two years before my parents—and when my mother could spare the time from the farm she would go across to the château, taking my brother with her, and there in the salon the pair of them, my mother and the marquise, would read together, or play and sing, with my brother Robert crawling about the floor between them or taking his first unsteady steps.

It has always seemed to me significant that Robert's first memories, whenever he spoke of them, should not be of the farmhouse le Maurier, or of the lowing of cattle, the scratching of hens and other homely sounds, or even of the roar of the furnace chimney and the bustle of the glass-house; but always of an immense salon, so he described it, filled with mirrors and satin-covered chairs, with a harpsichord standing in one corner, and a fine lady, not my mother, picking him up in her arms and kissing him, then feeding him with little sugared cakes.

"You cannot imagine," he used to tell me in after years, "how vivid is that memory still. The sensation of perfect delight it would be to sit upon that lady's lap, to touch her gown, to smell her perfume, and then for her to set me down upon the floor and to hear her applaud me as I walked from one end of that seemingly immense salon to the other. The long windows gave on to a terrace, and from that terrace paths stretched into the infinite distance. I felt that it was all mine—château, park, harpsichord, and the fine lady too."

If my mother had known what small seed of longing she was sowing in my brother's being, to develop into a folie de grandeur that nearly broke my father's heart, and certainly was partly responsible for his death, she would not have taken Robert so often to the château at Chérigny, to be fed and fondled by the marquise. She would have put him to play amongst the hens and pigs in the muddied farm-yard of le Maurier.

My mother was to blame, but how could she foresee that her indulgence then would help to destroy this first-born son of hers whom she so fiercely loved? And what more natural than to accept the grace and hospitality of so gentle a lady as the marquise de Cherbon?

It was not solely for the pleasure of her society that my mother prized the friendship of the marquise, but also because it gave her the opportunity, when occasion favoured, to speak about my father and his ambitions; how he hoped in time to become just such another as Monsieur Brossard—who was, of course, Robert's godfather—and direct a glass-house, or glass-houses, which should be among the finest in the land.

"We know this will take time," my mother told the marquise, "but already, since Mathurin has been director here at Chérigny, we have doubled our consignments to Paris and have taken on more workmen, and the foundry itself has had a favourable mention in the *Almanach des Marchands*."

This was no boast. It was all true. The little glass-house at Chérigny had now established itself as one of the foremost "small houses", as they were known, in the trade, specialising in glass for the table, goblets and wine decanters.

The marquis de Cherbon and Monsieur Brossard united in developing further glass-houses, not only la Brûlonnerie, where my uncle Démérè was now director in partnership with my father—who alternated between there and Chérigny—but also at la Pierre, Coudrecieux, situated in the midst of the forests of la Pierre and Vibraye, an immense property belonging to a widow, Madame le Gras de Luart. Here, for a time, the marquis de Cherbon installed as director my uncle Michel Busson, who had married a niece of my uncle Démérè, but uncle Michel, though a fine engraver of crystal, was no use as an administrator, and the foundry at la Pierre began to fall away and lose money.

Some time between the birth of my brother Pierre in 1752 and my brother Michel in '56 the marquise de Cherbon died in childbirth, to my mother's great distress. The marquis married a second time—for which she never forgave him, though she never failed in civility towards him—choosing his wife from a neighbouring parish to Coudrecieux. His new father-in-law's land adjoined Madame le Gras de Luart's extensive property at la Pierre, and the marquis had, therefore, no wish to see the glass-house there run at a loss. After many months of discussion between all parties, my father dared a very great venture. He, my uncle Démérè, and a Monsieur Eloy le Riche, a Paris merchant, entered into partnership, taking on the lease of la Pierre from

the marquis de Cherbon and dealing direct with Madame le
Gras de Luart, who fortunately for my parents, with their growing family, did not inhabit her late husband's property.

The lease, which was to enter into force on All Saints' Day,
1760, gave the partners the full rights for nine years to develop
the glass-house on the domain and everything belonging to it,
with the use of timber for the furnace, and to retain the château
for their own use. For this they were to pay yearly the sum of
880 livres, and in addition to supply Madame le Gras de Luart
with eight dozen crystal glasses for her dining-table. The fact
that my uncle Démèré would continue to live at la Brûlonnerie,
and Monsieur Eloy le Riche in Paris, meant that my parents,
on their own, became tenants of the immense château of la
Pierre. Here was a change from the farmhouse le Maurier, and
from the master's lodging at la Brûlonnerie!

I believe the shade of the first marquise de Cherbon must
have been with my mother when she took possession of la Pierre
and surveyed the great staircase and the enormous rooms opening out from one to the other, over which she would now have
complete jurisdiction. She chose for herself and my father the
big bedroom with its view of the park and the forest beyond,
and she knew that her children would grow up here, free to roam
wherever they pleased, having the right to do so, just as the
children of previous seigneurs had done through the centuries.
They would have an added freedom, too. For there were no
cooks and scullions here, no powdered footmen and lackeys, but
only my mother herself to keep order, and those few wives of the
glass-house workmen whom she cared to employ. Half of the
château remained dust-sheeted and shuttered, but not always
silent; for here my brothers romped and shouted, chasing one
another in and out of the great rooms stacked with furniture,
halloing along the corridors, finding their way to the attics under the massive roof.

To Robert, now ten years old, la Pierre was an enhancement
of his dream. Not only did he live in a château that was larger
and grander than Chérigny, but our parents possessed it—or so
it seemed to him. He would manage somehow or other to obtain
the key of the grande salle from my mother's key-ring, and creep

into the room alone. Lifting a corner of a dust-sheet, he would seat himself on one of the brocaded chairs and make believe that the shrouded, silent room was full of guests, and he the host.

Pierre and Michel had no such fancies. The forest lay outside their windows, and this was all they asked for, Pierre especially. Unlike the pleasant woodlands and paths of Chérigny, the forest here was deep and even dangerous, stretching further than the eye could see from the turret windows of the château; it was the haunt of wild boars, perhaps of robbers. Pierre was always in trouble. Pierre climbed highest and fell furthest. Pierre tumbled into streams and soaked his clothes. He was the collector of all wild things, bats, birds, voles, foxes, and would try to tame each one of them in turn, hiding them in the disused rooms of the château, to my mother's fury.

Here, at la Pierre, she was mistress of the glass-house and châtelaine as well. She was responsible, not only for the well-being of the workmen and their wives—and there must have been well over a hundred of them, not counting the charcoal-burners in the forest—but for any damage done in the precincts of the château. The presence of her three lively sons did not make this any easier for her, although Robert, thanks to the recommendation of Monsieur Brossard and the marquis de Cherbon, was being instructed in French and Latin grammar by the curé at Coudrecieux, who had also taught the son of Madame le Gras de Luart.

My mother lost two babies in infancy, a girl and a boy, before I was born in November of '63, followed by my sister Edmé three years later. Our family was now complete, and a very united one at that, with the two youngest members of it, the girls, alternately teased and petted by the older brothers.

If there was any difference of opinion between children and parents, the cause was generally my brother Michel's stammer. Edmé and I grew up with it—we never heard him speak otherwise, and we thought nothing of it—but my mother told us that it came about after the birth of the two babies Françoise and Prosper, who had followed closely upon each other and died as infants, when Michel himself was between four and five years old.

Whether it bewildered him to see these unfortunates come into the world, be nursed by my mother, and as suddenly depart, causing her great grief, nobody ever discovered. Children do not speak of these things. Perhaps he thought that he too would disappear, and so lose all he knew. In any event, he began to stammer badly about this time, soon after my parents came to la Pierre, and there was nothing they could do to cure him. Michel was exceptionally bright and intelligent, apart from this defect, and it exasperated my parents, especially my father, to see the boy struggle with his words, fighting, as it were, for breath, almost as though in this very effort he imitated the convulsions of the poor babies who had died.

"He does it on purpose," my father would say sternly. "He can pronounce his words perfectly well if he chooses to do so." He would send Michel from the room with a book, from which he must learn a page and then repeat it aloud afterwards, but it never did any good. Michel would turn sullen and rebellious, and sometimes he would run off for hours at a time and seek out the charcoal-burners in the forest. They did not mind how much he stammered, for it amused them to teach him their own rough speech and see what he made of it.

Naturally, Michel was punished for this. My father was a great disciplinarian, and then my mother would intervene, and ask forgiveness for him, and he would be allowed to go with my father to the glass-house and watch the men at work, for this was what he liked to do most of all. Edmé and I were so much younger than our brothers that our lives were quite different from theirs. To us, the little girls, our father seemed a most gentle, tender parent, taking the pair of us upon his knees, bringing us presents after his visits to Paris, laughing with us, singing and playing with us, and in every way treating us as though we were his one relaxation from daily cares.

It was very different for the boys. They must all stand up when he entered the room, wait to sit until he seated himself, never speak at table unless spoken to. When their turn came to be apprenticed at the glass-house they were obliged to obey the rules more rigidly, and were given more menial work to do, sweeping the furnace-house floors, and so on, than the apprentice sons of my father's workmen.

My brother Robert, despite his fine education at the hands of the good curé at Coudrecieux, did not object to this harsh treatment. He wished to be a master glass-maker like his father, or, better still, like his godfather Monsieur Brossard, who had so many friends amongst the aristocracy; and to achieve this end he knew he must start at the bottom.

Michel too, although he rebelled against his father in other ways, never minded hard work, indeed, the rougher and dirtier the work the better it was for him. He liked to mix with the workmen and share their worst duties, and he was never in so good a humour as when he came back from the furnace-house, his blouse scorched and bespattered, for it meant that he had taken his shift beside his comrades, and had fared as well or ill as they.

It was Pierre who gave my father the biggest problem—good-tempered, a perfect sans-souci, impossible to train to anything. He was apprenticed, of course, to the glass-house, but was forever slipping away and playing truant—gathering wild strawberries in the forest, or merely wandering at will, and then returning when fancy pleased him. Beating him did no good at all. He accepted punishment or praise with equanimity.

"He is an eccentric," my father would say, dismissing his second son with a shrug of the shoulders. "He will never make anything of himself. Since he seems to prefer life in the open he had best go off to the American colonies and settle there."

This was when Pierre was about seventeen years old, and my father, whose business dealings now ranged far and wide, arranged for Pierre to be shipped off to a rich planter in Martinique. I was about six years old at the time, and I well remember the tears and consternation at home—for the three brothers were devoted to one another—and my mother's tight-lipped silence as she packed a trunk for Pierre, wondering in her heart if she would ever see her son again. Even my father appeared remorseful now that the actual moment of departure had arrived, and himself escorted Pierre to Nantes, where my brother was to embark, and shipped a large consignment of glass of inferior quality abroad with him, which, he told Pierre, he could sell to the colonists and make his fortune.

It seemed very dull at the château without Pierre. His cheerful ways and original antics had enlivened the atmosphere, which was sometimes rather solemn for Edmé and myself, two small children left on our own to play, with our brothers at work at the glass-house next door and our mother continually preoccupied, either with my father's business or with the management of the château itself. We were soon to forget him, though, in the months that followed, for two events stand out in my memory as markers to that time.

The first was when my brother Robert became a master glassmaker, after his three years' apprenticeship. The second was the visit of the King to the glass-house of la Pierre. Both events took place during the year of 1769.

The first happened on a Sunday afternoon in June, with every craftsman and workman assembled in his holiday clothes by two o'clock to await the arrival of the musicians. The previous day my mother, and the other masters' wives, had prepared the long trestle tables in the furnace-house—it was between heats, as we termed it, the fires having been allowed to go out—and the tables were now laden with food for all the workers at the glass-house, and for the guests as well.

Numbers of people were invited. All our relatives, of course, and those merchants and tradesmen with whom my father did business, but besides these were the mayor of Coudrecieux, the bailiff, the curé, and the keepers and foresters on the estate, with every woman and child in the district.

A procession was formed, headed by the musicians, and then the two senior masters—in this case my uncle Michel and another engraver—led the master-to-be, my brother Robert, between them, with all the members of the glass-house following behind in strict order of precedence. First the masters, next the journeymen and carriers, then the stokers, apprentices, and so on, and finally the women and children. They processed from the glass-house, through the great park gates, and so to the steps of the château itself, where my father and mother, with the curé, the mayor and other officials, waited to receive them.

A short ceremony followed. The new master was sworn in and blessed by the priest, and then there were speeches. After this the whole procession turned round and marched back to the glass-house. I remember glancing up at my mother and seeing the tears come into her eyes as she watched my brother Robert take his oath.

Both my father and mother had powdered their hair for the occasion—perhaps they felt they were representing the absent family of le Gras de Luart—and my mother wore a brocade gown and my father satin breeches.

"He'll make a fine man," I heard the curé murmur to my father as they waited for the procession to stop in front of them. "I have every confidence in his ability, and I hope you have the same."

My father did not reply immediately. He too was moved by the sight of his eldest son taking the same oath as he had done some twenty-five years before.

"He'll do well enough," he said at last, "providing he keeps his head."

These words were lost on me. I had eyes only for Robert, who, to his six-year-old sister, was the outstanding figure in the whole procession. Tall, slim, fair-haired (my mother had stopped him from powdering it at the last moment), he did not appear to me to be in danger of losing anything. He carried himself erect, and walked as proudly to the steps of the château as though he were to be made a marquis, and not merely a master glass-maker.

A great burst of cheering followed the swearing-in. Robert bowed to the assembled company, the guests and the whole crowd of craftsmen and their families gathered there, and I noticed that he threw a quick glance up at my mother Magdaleine, impetuous, proud, as though to say, "This is what you expected of me, isn't it? This is what both of us wanted?" It seemed to me that she bowed in return, half to my brother, half to herself, and as she towered above me, magnificent in her brocade gown, her whole aspect strangely changed with the powder in her hair, I felt, child as I was, that she was more than my mother; she was some sort of deity, more powerful than the gentle statue of the Blessed Virgin standing in the church at Coudrecieux, the equal of God himself.

The second event gave me a very different impression, and this was, I think, because my parents were relegated to a minor rôle. My father came in one evening and announced in solemn tones, "We are to be much honoured. The King is hunting in the forest of Vibraye next week, and intends paying a visit to the glass-house of la Pierre."

Everyone was at once in consternation. The King . . . What would he say, what would he do, how was he to be fed, to be entertained? My mother at once began preparing the great rooms that were never used, and every woman on the estate and in the glass-house precincts was summoned to scrub, to polish, to sweep. And then, within a few days of the King's visit, Madame le Gras de Luart and her son arrived to do the honours themselves.

"Naturally," she said to my mother—I was there at the time and heard every word—"it is only right that my son and myself should be in residence on this great occasion. No doubt you and your family will find quarters in the glass-house."

"Naturally," replied my mother, who, to tell the truth, had been secretly looking forward to acting châtelaine. "I hope you will find the rooms prepared as they should be. We did not have much warning."

"Oh, as to that, don't concern yourself," replied Madame le Gras de Luart. "The servants will see to it."

Then from carriage, coach and every sort of vehicle tumbled a great crowd of footmen, lackeys, cooks, scullions, all marching through the château as though the place belonged to them, turning the kitchen upside down, stripping the beds of covers and spreading others they had brought with them, speaking rudely to my mother as if she were a lower-paid servant who had been dismissed. We, the family, were turned out of doors and sent packing, with only time enough to thrust our own belongings into one room and turn the key in the lock, and then make our way across to the glass-house to beg shelter from my uncle Michel and his wife.

"It was only to be expected," said my father quietly. "Madame le Gras de Luart is perfectly within her rights."

"Her r-r-rights," stammered my brother Michel, who would then have been about fourteen years old. "What r-r-rights has an old r-r-raddled woman like that to t-t-turn us out of our home?"

"Hold your tongue," commanded my father sharply, "and remember that the château of la Pierre is held on lease only. It never can be, and never will be, ours, any more than the glass-house itself."

Poor Michel looked dumbfounded. He must have believed, as I did, that la Pierre was ours forever. He turned very white, as he always did when he was angry and unable to express himself, and went off to the furnace-house to try and explain the situation to his friends the stokers.

The only member of the family who looked forward to the King's visit with all his heart was my eldest brother Robert. He was to be on show for the occasion, and act as glass-blower beside the other masters, for the King had expressed a wish, so my father said, to see every part of the work at the foundry, from the moment when the liquid first formed in the blow-pipe to the engraving of a finished glass by my father and my uncle Michel.

The great day dawned. We were all of us astir early, myself and my sister Edmé prinked out in our best white frocks. Then, to my great disappointment, my mother did not put on her beautiful brocade gown, but wore her ordinary dark Sunday dress, with the addition of a lace collar. I was about to protest, but she silenced me. "Let those who wish to be peacocks do as they please," she said. "I feel more dignified as I am."

I did not understand why she should put on a brocade gown for my brother and wear nothing but her Sunday dress for the King. My father must have approved, though, for he nodded his head when he saw her, and said, "It's better so." For my part, I thought otherwise. Then, almost before we were aware of it, the party from the château was upon us. Madame le Gras de Luart had driven to the entrance gates of the park in her coach, and her son was on horseback, and there were a lot of other noblemen on horseback too, and several ladies, all in hunting-costume, and, to my critical eye, rather disordered too. There were grooms and keepers all around, and barking dogs; it was not at all my idea of a royal party.

"The King," I whispered to my mother, "where is the King?"

"Hush!" she murmured. "That is he there, dismounting now, talking to Madame le Gras de Luart."

I was almost in tears with disappointment, for the elderly gentleman to whom Madame le Gras de Luart made a great sweeping curtsey looked just like anybody else, in hunting coat and breeches, with his wig not even curled—perhaps, I consoled myself, because he had been hunting all morning he kept his best one in a box. Then, as he looked about him, and the great crowd of craftsmen and workmen's wives gathered to applaud him, he waved his hand in a half-salute and said wearily to his hostess, "My party is famished, we breakfasted early. Where do we eat?"

So instead of the glass-house being visited first, the programme had to be changed. Orders were quickly given and the work re-arranged in the glass-house at great inconvenience, and the royal party went off to the château to dine a full three hours before they were due to do so. We were told afterwards that Madame le Gras de Luart was so flustered that she had to be given restoratives, and I thought it served her right for having been discourteous to my mother. Then, later in the day, when all the workmen at the glass-house had been kept waiting for hours, the royal party returned, their stomachs well-lined when ours were empty. They were laughing and talking and in great humour, the ladies exclaiming at everything they saw but quickly turning aside to examine something else, giving the impression that they understood nothing.

My mother was presented to the King, who said something over his shoulder to one of the gentlemen attending him—I think it was a reference to her height, for she certainly dwarfed the pair of them—and then they passed on, and we followed, and they stood and watched my brother Robert use his blow-pipe. He managed it with infinite grace, turning it this way and that, manipulating the long rod with his hands, just as though no one was looking at him, while I knew very well he could see that the King was standing a short distance away, and all the ladies admiring him.

"What a beauty," one of them said, and even at six years old I knew that they were not referring to the blow-pipe but to my brother Robert. Then a dreadful thing happened. My brother Michel, who had been standing in the background amidst a crowd of apprentices, leant forward to get a better view of the royal party, and he slipped and measured his length before the very feet of the King himself. Scarlet with shame he picked himself up, and the King, good-naturedly, patted him on the shoulder.

"Better not do that when you become a glass-blower," he said. "How long have you worked in the glass-house?"

The inevitable happened. Poor Michel tried to speak, but instead one of his worst attempts at speech followed.

He gasped and spluttered, his head jerking at every sound just as it always did when he was nervous, and everyone in the royal party burst out laughing.

"There is a lad who must save his breath for his blow-pipe," said the King, moving on amidst great merriment, and I saw one of the older apprentices, a comrade of Michel's, pull my brother back into line and hide him from view.

After this, it was all spoilt for me. Even the sight of my uncle Michel engraving the glass, which generally was so great a treat, could not make amends for my brother's shame, and when my father presented the King with a goblet taken from the finished batch they had worked upon for the occasion, with the royal initials and the fleur-de-lys upon it, I almost wished it would shiver to fragments at his feet.

It was over. The royal party left the glass-house and re-mounted outside the château gates close by, and we watched them disappear into the forest in the direction of Semur. Weary and dispirited, I trailed after my mother to my uncle's house. Edmé was already asleep upon her shoulder. We were soon joined by my father, my uncle and my brothers, the grown men looking much relieved that the great ordeal was over.

"It went well," my father said, with satisfaction. "The King was most gracious. He seemed very pleased with all he saw."

"I never thought to engrave a goblet for the King himself," said my uncle, a shy man, who thought only of his work. "This is a day to remember all my life."

"Very true," rejoined my father, turning to his sons. "We have been greatly honoured today, and we must never forget it." He took one of the goblets in his hand and examined it. "We'll never do finer work than this, Michel," he said to my uncle. "We should be well content. If you can ever equal it, Robert, you will have good reason to be satisfied. I suggest we preserve this goblet as a family symbol, and if it does not bring us fame and fortune it shall serve as a reminder of high craftsmanship through succeeding generations. When you marry, Robert, you may pass it on to your sons."

Robert examined the goblet in his turn. He seemed much impressed. "To anyone who was ignorant," he observed, "the royal insignia might be taken for a family device, and our own at that. I suppose we can never aspire to such an honour." He sighed, and gave the goblet back into my father's hands.

"We have no need of insignias," replied my father. "What we Bussons create with our brains and with our hands is proof of our honour. Here, Michel, don't you want to touch the goblet for luck?" He made as though to hand the precious glass to my youngest brother, but Michel shrank back from him, shaking his head violently.

"It's b-b-bad luck it would bring me," he stammered, "b-b-bad luck, not good. I d-d-d-don't want to touch it."

He turned suddenly and ran out of the room. I immediately began to cry and would have followed him, but my mother prevented me.

"Let him alone," she said quietly, "you will only irritate him further." She then told my father and my uncle of the incident in the glass-house, which they had not seen.

"A pity," observed my father. "Nevertheless, he must learn self-control."

He turned to my uncle and began discussing other matters, but I heard Robert whisper to my mother, "Michel is an idiot. He should have cut some caper and made the King laugh with him, instead of against him. By acting so he would have delighted everyone, including himself, and been the crowning success of the royal visit."

My mother was not impressed. "Not all of us," she said, "have your capacity for turning a situation to his own advantage."

She must have noticed his striking pose with the blow-pipe, and heard the gasps of admiration from the ladies of the Court party. In any event, despite poor Michel's misfortune the goblet did bring us luck. I was convinced of that the very next day.

Madame le Gras de Luart departed from the château with her retinue of servants, and the mud from her carriage wheels had barely settled in when we saw a very different equipage approaching the iron gates from the direction of Coudrecieux. It was a pedlar's cart, strung about with pots and pans, the kind of cart that would roam the countryside, plying between la Ferté-Bernard and Le Mans, and seated beside the driver, or rather standing and waving his hand joyously, was a familiar figure in a multicoloured jacket and a crimson waistcoat, with—unbelievably—a squawking parrot on either shoulder. It was my brother Pierre. My father, who was with us, stood rooted to the ground.

"Where in the world have you come from?" he called sternly, as my brother jumped from the pedlar's cart and ran towards us.

"From Martinique," said Pierre. "It was much too warm, I could not endure it. I have decided, after all, I would rather work in the glass-house." He bent to embrace us, and, happy as we were to see him, we all stepped back a pace, for fear of the squawking parrots.

"I take it," said my mother, "that you have not made your fortune with the packages of glass your father gave you?"

Pierre smiled. "I sold none of it," he said. "I gave it all away."

The pedlar handed down his trunk, which Pierre, despite my father's remonstrances, insisted on opening upon the spot. It contained nothing from the Martinique of any value; only quantities of gaudy coloured waistcoats, woven in the native bazaars, which he had brought as presents for each member of his family.

THREE

By the time I was twelve or thirteen years old my father Mathurin Busson had control of four glass-houses. He had obtained an extension of his lease of la Pierre and was still associated with la Brûlonnerie and Chérigny, and now he added the glass-house of le Chesne-Bidault, between Montmirail and le Plessis-Dorin. Here, as at la Pierre, the owner, Monsieur Pesant de Bois-Guilbert, simply leased the foundry to my father, having no say in the management, living himself in his château at Montmirail.

The glass-house of le Chesne-Bidault, like la Pierre, was set in mid-forest, though it was a smaller concern, with the master's house and the farm standing close to the single furnace-house, and the long row of workmen's dwellings opposite.

The grandeur of la Pierre, with the vast château in its fine park, was very different from the rough, somewhat rustic appearance of le Chesne-Bidault; but my mother loved it from the first, and at once set about making the master's house fit and habitable for Robert, the idea being that he should act as manager for my father, and so gain experience for the future.

Le Chesne-Bidault was not more than an hour's ride from la Pierre, and it was one of my great delights to go over there with my mother, for two or three days at a time, to see how Robert was progressing.

He had by now grown into a strikingly handsome young man, with great self-assurance and an excellent manner. In fact, my father used to say that his manners were over-polished, and if he was not careful he would be taken for a flunkey. This annoyed Robert exceedingly.

"My father is quite out of touch with the manners of today," he would say to me, after there had been some words on the

subject. "Just because he has spent his life dealing with merchants and traders he assumes that I must do the same, and never
move out of the glass milieu. What he does not understand is
that by mixing in a more refined society I shall obtain many
more orders for glass than he ever does."

When he had been working at la Pierre, and my father was
absent, Robert would go as often as he dared to Le Mans, for
during the past years the social life of the town had become very
gay; there were concerts and balls and plays, and many aristocrats who usually spent all their time at Versailles would now
think it fashionable to open up houses and châteaux in the country, and vie with one another as to who would hold the wittiest
salon. Freemasonry was all the rage, and whether it was now or
later that Robert became a Freemason I am not sure, but certainly, from his talk, he had obtained a foothold in this smart
Manceaux society and elsewhere, and once away from the immediate jurisdiction of my father, and on his own at le Chesne-
Bidault, it was easier for him to slip off and meet his friends.
My mother, very naturally, was quite unaware of this. Robert
was never absent when we arrived for a visit, and she would at
once become absorbed in all the work of the glass-house, from
keeping the books to managing the farm and the house, and
seeing that the workmen and their wives lacked for nothing.
Also, Robert was by now a fine craftsman on his own account,
and she was proud of the wares that he dispatched weekly to
Paris.

Nothing pleased me more than to be Robert's confidante, to
hear of his amours and his escapades. In return for listening to
him, he would give me lessons in history and grammar, for since
Edmé and I were girls, and certain to marry within the industry,
my father did not think it necessary to teach us anything but
the rudiments of education.

"He is quite wrong," Robert would argue. "Every young
woman should know how to comport herself, and how to mix
in society."

"Surely it depends upon the society?" I would reply, despite
my anxiety to learn. "Take aunt Anne at Chérigny. Neither she,

nor my uncle Viau, can sign their names properly, and they do very well as they are."

"No doubt," said Robert, "and they will never move from Chérigny to the end of their days. You wait until I have a glass-house of my own, in Paris, and you come to visit me there. I can't introduce my sister to society unless she does me credit."

A glass-house in Paris . . . What ambition! I wondered what my parents would think of it if they knew.

Meanwhile Robert continued as manager of le Chesne-Bidault without running into trouble, and presently Pierre, who had become a master in his turn, joined him there—chiefly, I think, so that Robert could slip off into what he called "society" when he had the mind, but naturally neither my father nor my mother had any idea of this.

Pierre had his head filled with new ideas also, but of a rather different sort. He had returned from Martinique with great stories of the hardships the natives endured there, and he had begun to read a great deal, forever quoting Rousseau and saying, "Man is born free, but is everywhere in chains," much to my father's irritation.

"If you must read philosophy," he would say, "read someone of merit, not a scoundrel who allowed his illegitimate children to be brought up in an orphanage."

Pierre would not be dissuaded. Every state, he declared, should be conducted according to the theories of Jean-Jacques, for the good of all, without distinction of persons. Boys should be educated "naturally", living in the open air, receiving no tuition until they were past fifteen.

"A pity," my father would reply, "that you did not stay in Martinique and turn native. The life would have suited you better than becoming the indifferent craftsman in the glass-trade which you are at present."

The sarcasm was lost on Pierre. He was forever bubbling over with some new enthusiasm, some new cause, and infecting Michel with his ideas, so that my father, who had been so pro-gressive himself as a young man with his chemical and scientific inventions, could not understand what had come over his sons.

My mother took it more calmly. "They are young," she said.

"The young always have some new fad or other. It will pass."

One day my brother Robert rode over to la Pierre with the excuse of business between the two foundries, but in reality to swear me to secrecy over a new project, which nobody must know but myself and Pierre.

"I've joined the corps d'élite of the Arquebusiers," he told me, in a state of great excitement. "Only as a temporary officer, of course, but it means doing my turn of service in Paris for three months in the year. Some of my friends at Le Mans persuaded me, and I've received the necessary recommendation. The point is, somehow or other my father must be kept from visiting le Chesne-Bidault during my absence."

I shook my head. "It can never be done," I said. "He is bound to find out."

"No," said Robert. "Pierre is also sworn to secrecy, and the workmen too. If my father should ride over to le Chesne-Bidault, then he will be told I have gone to Le Mans on some necessity. He never stays more than a day."

During the next few weeks I did everything possible to make myself indispensable to my father. I would accompany him to the foundry in the morning, and be waiting for him when he returned, and I feigned to take a great interest all of a sudden in the day's work. He was both flattered and surprised, and told me I was growing into a sensible girl, and that one of these days I should make a fine wife for a master of a glass-house.

My plans were so successful, and he enjoyed my company at la Pierre so much, that he never once rode over to le Chesne-Bidault. But towards the end of the period of my brother's absence he looked across at me, during the evening meal, and said; "How would you like to pay your first visit to Paris?"

I thought immediately that all had been discovered, and this was a stratagem to make me speak out. I glanced quickly at my mother, but she smiled at me encouragingly.

"Yes, why not?" she nodded to my father. "Sophie is quite old enough to be your companion. Besides, I shall be all the easier if she goes with you." The little pretence that my father might come to no good alone in the capital was a standing joke between my parents.

"Nothing in the world would please me better," I told them, gaining confidence. At once Edmé clamoured to come too, but here my mother was firm. "Your turn will come later," she said to my sister, "but if you behave yourself we will drive over to see Robert at le Chesne-Bidault while your father and Sophie are away."

This was the last thing I wanted, but there was nothing to be done about it, and I soon forgot my anxiety two days later when we were seated side by side in the diligence on our way to the capital. Paris . . . My first visit . . . And I an ignorant country girl not yet fourteen, who had only seen one city in her life so far, Le Mans. We were twelve hours or more upon the road, having left very early in the morning, and it must have been six or seven in the evening as we approached the capital, and I sat with my face pressed to the window, half sick with excitement and exhaustion.

It was June, I remember, and there was a warm haze over the city and a dusty radiance everywhere, with the trees in full leaf, and people thronging the streets, and line upon line of carriages all returning to Versailles from the races. King Louis XVI and his young Queen Marie Antoinette had only been crowned a year, but already, my father said, there had been changes at Court, the old formality was going, the Queen was setting the fashion for balls and opera-going, and the King's brother, the comte d'Artois, and his cousin the duc de Chartres vied with one another in horse-racing, a sport very popular in England. Perhaps, I thought, staring eagerly from the diligence, I too would see some duke or duchess coming away from the races; perhaps those young gallants picking their way across the crowded Place Louis XV in front of the Palais des Tuileries were the King's brothers? I pointed them out to my father, but he only laughed.

"Lackeys," he said, "or coiffeurs. They all ape their masters. But you don't catch a prince of the blood royal on his feet."

The diligence deposited us at its terminus in the rue Boulay. Here all was jostling and confusion, with no one I could possibly call a gallant, or even a coiffeur. The streets were narrow and evil-smelling, with a broad stream running down the centre to carry the sewage, and beggars holding out their hands for alms. I remember my sudden feeling of fright when my father's back was turned to see to our luggage, and in a moment a woman had thrust her way between us, with two little barefooted children beside her, clamouring for money. When I drew back she shook her fist at me, and cursed. This was not the Paris I had expected, where all was gaiety, laughter, driving to the Opera, and bright lights.

It was my father's custom to put up at the Hotel du Cheval Rouge in the rue St. Denis, close to the Church of St. Leu and the great central market of les Halles, and this was where he took me now, and where we stayed during our three days' visit.

I confess I found myself disenchanted. We hardly moved from this quarter, so crowded, so ill-smelling, among the poorest of the people, and when we did walk out it was only to call at the various warehouses where my father did his business. I thought our charcoal-burners at home in the forest of la Pierre were rough, but they were gentle and courteous compared with the people in the streets of Paris, who jostled us without apology, staring rudely all the while. Child as I was, I dared not venture out alone, but was obliged to stay beside my father the whole time, or remain in the bedroom at the Cheval Rouge.

The last evening of our visit my father took me to the Porte St. Martin to see coaches and carriages arriving for the Opera, and here was a change indeed from the poor quarter by our hotel. Glittering ladies, their bare bosoms gleaming with jewels, stepped down from their carriages escorted by gallants as gorgeously dressed as they were themselves. All was colour and brilliance and high affected voices—it was as though they spoke a French totally unlike our own—and the very way the ladies moved, and held their skirts, and the gentlemen swaggered by their side, calling out, "Make way, there, make way for madame la marquise", thrusting the crowds aside before the steps of the Opera, seemed to me like make-believe. A wave of perfume came from these fine folk, a strange exotic scent like flowers no longer fresh, whose petals curl, and this stale richness somehow mingled with the drab dirt of those beside us, pressing forward even as we did, in a dumb desire to see the Queen.

Her coach arrived at last, drawn by four magnificent horses, and the footmen sprang from behind to open the doors, while attendants brandishing staves appeared from nowhere to push back the staring crowds.

The King's brother, the comte d'Artois, descended first, for the King himself was said to dislike opera, and never went. A plump young man, with a pink and white complexion, his satin coat covered with stars and decorations, he was immediately followed by a young lady all in rose, with a jewel glistening in her powdered hair and a haughty, disdainful expression on her face. We heard afterwards that she was the comtesse de Polignac, the intimate friend of the Queen. Then, for a brief moment, I saw the young Queen herself, the last to descend. Dressed all in white, diamonds about her throat and in her hair, her pale blue eyes sweeping past us in complete indifference as she gave her hand to the comte d'Artois and disappeared from view, she looked as exquisite, and as fragile, as those porcelain figures my father had pointed out to me that morning, reposing side by side in one of the warehouses of a merchant friend.

"There we are," said my father. "Now are you content?"

Content or not, I could not say. It was a glimpse into another world. Did these folk really eat, I wondered, and undress, and perform the same functions as we did ourselves? It was hardly credible.

We walked the streets the rest of the evening, to "cool off", as my father expressed himself, and it was when we had stopped in the rue St. Honoré a moment, to chat to one of his business acquaintances, that I saw a familiar figure approaching us, clad in the splendid uniform of an officer in the corps d'Arquebusiers. It was my brother Robert.

He saw us instantly, paused for a moment, then pirouetted swiftly like a ballet-dancer, leaping the stream that ran down the centre of the rue St. Honoré, and disappeared into the gardens of the Palais des Tuileries. My father, who happened to turn his head at this moment, stared after the retreating figure.

"Did I not know my eldest son to be at the glass-house of le Chesne-Bidault," he observed drily to his companion, "I would think that I had recognised him in the person of that young officer whom you can see vanishing into the distance there."

"All young men," remarked my father's acquaintance, "look much the same in uniform."

"Possibly," replied my father, "and have an equal facility for getting themselves out of a scrape."

No more was said. We turned and walked back to our hotel in the rue St. Denis, and the following day returned home to the château at la Pierre. My father never again alluded to the incident, but when I asked my mother if she had visited le Chesne-Bidault during our absence she looked me straight in the eye and said, "I am impressed by the manner in which Robert manages the glass-house and succeeds in amusing himself at the same time."

Playing at soldiers was one thing; dispatching consignments of glassware to Chartres without entering them in the foundry books was another. Anyone who attempted to fool my mother where the merchandise was concerned would be sorry for it.

We were spending our customary two days at le Chesne-Bidault for my mother to check on the orders, and all went smoothly until my mother suddenly announced her intention of counting the empty crates which had returned from Paris the previous week.

"That is quite unnecessary," said my brother Robert, who this time was not on leave of absence. "The crates are piled one on top of the other in the store until our next batch is ready for the road. Besides, we know the figure is two hundred."

"It should be two hundred," replied my mother. "That is what I want to find out."

My brother continued his protestations. "I cannot vouch for the order in the store," he continued, glancing at me with warning in his eye. "Blaise has been sick, and the crates were stacked anyhow, as they came in. I can promise you everything will be satisfactory in time for the next batch."

My mother disregarded him. "I shall need two strong labourers," she said, "to shift the crates so that I can count them. Perhaps you will see about it now. And I shall want you to come with me."

She found fifty crates missing, and as ill-luck had it the journeyman-carrier called at the glass-house that afternoon. On being questioned by my mother he explained to her, in all innocence, that the missing crates were at the moment in Chartres with a consignment of very special table-glass for the regiment of the Dragons de Monsieur, which was just then stationed in that city.

My mother thanked the journeyman for his information, and then asked my brother Robert to accompany her back to the master's house.

"And now," she said, "I should like your explanation as to why this consignment of 'special table-glass' has not been entered in the books?"

It might have helped my eldest brother then had he been cursed with a defect of speech like my youngest brother Michel.

"You must realise," he said glibly, "that in dealing with noblemen like the colonel of the regiment, the comte de la Châtre —who, as everyone knows, is an intimate friend of Monsieur, the King's brother—one does not expect payment on the spot. To have the honour of his custom is almost sufficient payment in itself."

My mother stabbed at the open ledger with her quill.

"Very probably," she said, "but your father and I have not had the doubtful pleasure to date of doing business with him. All I know of the comte de la Châtre is that his château at Malicorne is famous for every extravagance and intrigue, and he is said to have ruined himself and every tradesman in the district, none of whom can get a sou out of him."

"Quite untrue," said my brother, with a disdainful shrug. "I am surprised you should listen to spiteful gossip."

"I don't call it spiteful gossip when honest tradesmen, whom your father knows, are obliged to beg for assistance or go hungry," replied my mother, "because your nobleman friend builds a private theatre on his domain."

"It is very necessary to encourage the arts," protested my brother.

"It is more imperative to pay one's debts," replied my mother. "What was the value of the consignment of glass dispatched to this regiment?"

My brother hesitated. "I am not sure," he began.

My mother insisted.

"Some fifteen hundred livres," he admitted.

I was glad not to be in my brother's shoes. My mother's blue eyes turned as frozen as a northern lake.

"Then I shall myself write to the comte de la Châtre," she said, "and if I do not obtain satisfaction from him I had better address myself to Monsieur, the King's brother. Surely one or the other of them will have the courtesy to reply and honour the debt."

I could tell by Robert's face that this extreme measure would not do at all.

"You can spare yourself the pains," he said. "To be brief—the money has already been spent."

Here was trouble indeed. I began to tremble for my brother. How in the world could he have disposed of fifteen hundred livres? My mother remained calm. She glanced about her at the plain furnishings of the master's house, which she and my father had supplied.

"As far as I am aware," she said, "there has been no expenditure here or in any of the buildings on these premises."

"You are perfectly right," replied Robert. "The money was not spent at le Chesne-Bidault."

"Then where?"

"I refuse to answer."

My mother closed the ledger, and rising to her feet walked towards the door. "You will account for every sou within three weeks," she said. "If I have not an explanation by that time I shall tell your father that we are closing down the glass-house here at le Chesne-Bidault because of fraud, and I shall have your name erased from the list of master glass-makers within the trade."

She left the room. My brother forced a laugh, and, seating himself in the chair she had just relinquished, lounged back with his feet upon the table.

"She would never dare do such a thing," he said. "It would be my ruin."

"Don't be too sure," I warned him. "The money will have to be found, that's certain. How *did* you spend it?"

He shook his head. "I shan't tell you," he said, beginning to smile despite his serious situation. "The point is that the money has gone, beyond recovery."

The truth came out in an unlikely way. About a week later my uncle and aunt Démèré paid us a visit at la Pierre from la Brûlonnerie, and as usual there was much talk of local affairs, besides gossip from Paris, Chartres, Vendôme and other big cities.

"I am told there was great excitement in Chartres with the masked ball," began my aunt Démèré. "All the young good-for-nothings in the town were present, with or without their husbands."

I became all attention at the mention of Chartres, and glanced at my brother Robert, who was also present.

"Is that so?" asked my father. "We heard nothing of any ball. But we are a long way from such frivolities out here in the country."

My aunt, who disapproved of gaiety on principle, made a moue of disdain.

"All Chartres was discussing it when we were there two weeks ago," she continued. "It appears there was some sort of wager between the officers of the Dragons de Monsieur and the young blades in the corps d'Arquebusiers as to which regiment could best entertain the ladies of the district."

My uncle Démèré winked at my father. "The ladies of Chartres are known for their enjoyment of hospitality," he said. My father bowed in mock understanding.

"It appears they kept it up to all hours in the morning," went on my aunt, "drinking, dancing, and chasing each other round about the cathedral in a disgraceful manner. They say the officers of the Arquebusiers squandered a fortune providing for the affair."

"I am not surprised," said my father, "but as these gentlemen have the fashion set for them by a young Court at Versailles it is only to be expected. Let us hope they can afford it."

Robert had his eyes fixed upon the ceiling, suggesting he was either plunged in thought or had noticed a patch of worn plaster.

"And the Dragons de Monsieur," enquired my mother, "what part did they play in the business?"

"We were told they had lost their wager," replied my uncle. "The dinner they gave was no match for the masked ball. In any event, the Dragons are now quartered elsewhere and the Arquebusiers, who have a short term of service, are presumably resting on their laurels."

It was to my mother's credit that not a word of this escapade ever reached my father's ears, but she left me, young as I was, in charge of the château at la Pierre, while she returned with my brother Robert to the glass-house at le Chesne-Bidault, and remained with him there until he had himself replaced, by his own craftsmanship, the table-glass he had dispatched to the Dragons de Monsieur.

It was now the spring of the year 1777. The long lease of the château and glass-house of la Pierre, which had been our home for so long, had come to an end. The son of Madame le Gras de Luart, who had succeeded to the property, wished to make other arrangements, and with sad hearts we bade good-bye to the beautiful home where both Edmé and I had been born, and where our three brothers had grown from small boys to young men.

It was impossible for Edmé and myself, and certainly for Pierre and Michel, not to look upon le Gras de Luart as an interloper who, just because he was the seigneur and owner of la Pierre, had the right to turn over his property to a new tenant, or live in it himself for a few months in the year. As to the glass-house itself, which my father had developed from a small family affair to one of the foremost houses in the country, this must now be given up into other hands, and perhaps allowed once more to fall into decay or be exploited by outsiders. Our parents were more philosophical than we were. A master glass-maker must accustom himself to moving on. In old days they had always been wanderers, going from one forest to another, settling for a few years only. We had to consider ourselves fortunate to have been brought up at la Pierre, and to have had such happiness there through our childhood years. Luckily the lease of le Chesne-

Bidault had many years to run, la Brûlonnerie too, and the family could divide itself up between the two.

My father, mother, Edmé and I removed ourselves to le Chesne-Bidault, and Robert and Pierre went to la Brûlonnerie. Michel, who was twenty-one this year, had elected to go out of the family altogether for a time to gain experience, and was working as master glass-maker near Bourges, at le Berry. My three brothers, to distinguish themselves in the trade one from the other, had added suffixes to their names: Robert signed himself Busson l'Aîné, Pierre Busson du Charme, and Michel Busson-Challoir. These marks of distinction were, needless to say, Robert's idea. Le Charme and le Challoir were small farm properties owned by our parents, forming part of their original marriage portion.

The use of these names struck my mother as extravagant. "Your father and his brother," she said to me, "never thought it necessary to distinguish themselves. They were the Busson brothers, and that was good enough for them. However, now that it pleases Robert to call himself Busson l'Aîné perhaps he will realise his responsibilities at last and settle down. If he can't pick a wife to keep him in order, I must find one for him."

I thought she was joking, for Robert at twenty-seven was surely old enough to choose for himself. Nor did I at first see the connection between my mother's more frequent visits to Paris with my father on business, and her sudden expressed wish to meet the families of some of his trade acquaintances, with the decision on her part that my brother must marry.

It was only when the three of them began to put up at the Cheval Rouge, ostensibly to discuss matters relating to both glass-houses, and my mother mentioned casually on her return that Monsieur Fiat, a well-to-do merchant, had an only daughter, that I began to suspect the motive for her visit.

"What is the daughter like?" I asked.

"Very pretty," replied my mother, which was strong praise for her, "and seemed very much taken with Robert and he with her. At least, they had plenty to say to each other. I heard him ask permission to call next time he is in Paris, which will be next week."

This was match-making with a vengeance. I felt jealous, for up to the present I had been Robert's sole confidante.

"He will soon become tired of her," I ventured.

"Perhaps," shrugged my mother. "She is the very opposite of Robert, apart from her good humour. Dark, petite, large brown eyes, and a quantity of ringlets. Your father was much impressed."

"Robert will never marry a tradesman's daughter," I pursued, "not even if she is the prettiest girl in the whole of Paris. He would lose face among his fine friends."

My mother smiled. "What if she brought him a dot of ten thousand livres," she returned, "and we guaranteed a similar sum, and your father made over to them the lease of la Brûlonnerie?"

This time I had no answer. I went off to my own room to sulk. But such promises, with the addition of pretty, twenty-year-old Catherine Adèle into the bargain, proved too much for my brother Robert to resist.

The agreements were drawn up between the parents of bride and groom, and on the 21st day of July, 1777, the marriage took place at the church of St. Sauveur, Paris, between Robert Mathurin Busson and Catherine Adèle Fiat.

FOUR

THE FIRST SHOCK CAME about three months after the wedding.
My uncle Démére rode over to le Chesne-Bidault to tell my
father that Robert had leased la Brûlonnerie to a master glass-
maker by the name of Caumont, and had himself rented the
magnificent glass-house of Rougemont, which, with its superb
château alongside, belonged to the marquis de la Touche, in the
parish of St. Jean Froidmentel.

My father was at first stunned by the news, and refused to believe it.

"It is true," insisted my uncle. "I have seen the documents,
signed and sealed. The marquis, like so many others of his kind,
is an absentee landlord, caring nothing about his property as
long as it brings him rent. You know what the place is like.
They've been losing money there for years."

"It must be stopped," my father said. "Robert will ruin himself. He will lose everything he possesses, and his reputation
into the bargain."

We set forth the very next day, my father, my mother, my
uncle Démére and myself—I was determined to be of the company, and my parents were too concerned with what had happened to consider that I made quite an unnecessary fourth. We
stayed an hour or two at la Brûlonnerie for my father to speak
to the new lessee, Monsieur Caumont, and see the signed documents for himself, and then we drove on through the forest to
Rougemont, which stood in the valley across the high road between Châteaudun and Vendôme.

"He is mad," my father kept repeating, "mad . . . mad . . ."

"We are to blame," said my mother. "He cannot forget la
Pierre. He imagines he can do at twenty-seven what you only

achieved after years of hard work. We are to blame. We have spoilt him."

Rougemont was truly a stupendous place. The glass-house itself consisted of four separate buildings fronting an enormous courtyard. The right-hand building was the lodging of the master glass-makers, and beside it stood the great furnace-house with two chimneys, and beyond this the depots and storehouses, the workrooms for the engravers, and opposite again the workmen's dwellings. Through the courtyard were massive iron gates, and the château itself, splendid, imposing, set amidst formal gardens. My father had hoped to surprise my brother, but as always in our glass-world someone had whispered news of our approach and Robert came forward to meet us as soon as we drove into the courtyard, gay and smiling, brimming with self-confidence as usual.

"Welcome to Rougemont," he called. "You could not have come at a better moment. We started a melt this morning and both furnaces are in use, as you can see from the chimneys, with every workman on the place employed. Come and see for yourselves."

He was not himself wearing a working blouse as my father always did during a shift, but sported a blue velvet coat of extravagant cut, more suited to a young nobleman parading the terraces of Versailles than to a master glass-maker about to enter his furnace-house. I thought myself that he looked remarkably well in it, but was abashed for him because of my father's expression.

"Cathie will receive my mother and Sophie in the château," Robert continued. "We keep some of the rooms there for our personal use." He clapped his hands and shouted, like an Eastern potentate summoning a blackamoor, and a servant appeared from nowhere, bowed deeply, and flung open the iron gates leading to the château.

My mother's face was a study as we followed the servant to the entrance door of the château, through ante-rooms to a great salon with stiff-backed chairs ranged against the wall, long mirrors reflecting us as we walked. There awaiting us—she must have perceived our arrival from the window—was Robert's bride,

Cathie, Mademoiselle Fiat the merchant's daughter, dressed in a flimsy muslin gown with pink and white bows upon it, as delicious as a piece of confectionery from her own wedding-cake.

"What a pleasant surprise," she fluttered, running to embrace us, and then, remembering the presence of the servant, stood stiffly, and requested him to bring us some refreshment, after which she relaxed and asked us to sit down, and the three of us sat staring at each other.

"You look very pretty," said my mother at last, opening the conversation. "And how do you like being the wife of a master glass-maker here at Rougemont?"

"Well enough," replied Cathie, "but I find it rather fatiguing."

"No doubt," said my mother, "and a great responsibility. How many workmen are employed here, and how many of them are married with families?"

Cathie opened large eyes. "I have no idea," she said. "I have never spoken to any of them."

I thought this would silence my mother, but she quickly recovered.

"In that case," she continued, "what do you do with your time?"

Cathie hesitated. "I give orders to the servants," she said, "and I watch them polish the floors. The rooms are very spacious, as you can see."

"I can indeed," replied my mother. "No wonder you are fatigued."

"Then there is the entertaining," pursued Cathie. "Sometimes ten or twelve to dinner, and all at a moment's notice. It means stocking the larders with food that may be wasted. It is a very different matter from living in the rue des Petits-Carreaux in Paris, and going to the market if we had unexpected company."

Poor Cathie. It was true. She *was* fatigued. It was not so easy after all for a merchant's daughter to adopt the ways of a châtelaine.

"Whom do you entertain?" asked my mother. "It has never been the custom of masters and their wives to eat in each other's lodgings."

Once again Cathie opened large eyes. "Oh, we don't entertain amongst the people here," she explained, "but those friends and acquaintances of Robert's from Paris, who either come to visit us for that purpose, or are travelling between the capital and Blois. It was the same at la Brûlonnerie. One of Robert's chief reasons for moving to Rougemont was so that we could use the rooms in the château for entertaining."

"I see," said my mother.

I felt sorry for Cathie. Although I did not doubt her love for my brother, I sensed that she would be more at her ease back in the rue des Petits-Carreaux. Presently she asked us if we would care to see the rooms that had been put at their disposal, and we wandered through them, each one larger than any we had had at la Pierre. Cathie, trotting ahead of us, pointed out the two great chandeliers in the dining-hall, which, she told us, held thirty candles each, and must be replenished every time they dined there.

"It is a very fine sight when they are lighted," said Cathie proudly. "Robert sits at one end of the table and I at the other, English-fashion, with the guests on either side of us, and he gives me the signal when it is time to withdraw to the salon."

She closed the shutter so that the sunlight should not harm the long strip of carpet that ran down one side of the room.

"She is like a child playing at houses," whispered my mother. "What I ask myself is this—where will it all end?"

It ended precisely eleven months afterwards. The upkeep of the glass-house and the château of Rougemont mounted to a figure far in excess of my brother's reckoning, and the situation was made worse by certain miscalculations in the amount of goods sold to the Paris trading-houses. The greater part of Cathie's "dot" had thus been swallowed up in less than a year, with Robert's portion likewise, and the one merciful thing about the whole affair was that the lease of Rougemont had been for a twelvemonth only.

My father, despite his bitter disappointment at Robert's folly, and the throwing away of so much money, implored my brother to return to le Chesne-Bidault and work beside him as manager. There, with my father on the spot, he could come to no harm.

Robert refused. "It is not that I am ungrateful for the suggestion," he explained to my parents when he came home to discuss the matter, bringing with him a subdued and rather wistful Cathie, who had had a hard time of it explaining matters to an irate Monsieur and Madame Fiat in the rue des Petits-Carreaux, "but I already have prospects in Paris—I can't say more than that at the moment—which promise to turn out well. A certain Monsieur Cannette, one of the bankers to the Court of Versailles, is thinking of setting up a glass-house in the quartier St. Antoine, in the rue des Boulets, at my recommendation, and of course if all works out well he will appoint me as director."

My father and mother looked at one another and then back to my brother's eager, smiling face, which showed no trace of anxiety or any other mark after his late disaster.

"You have just lost a small fortune," said my father. "How can you guarantee that it won't happen again?"

"Easily," Robert replied. "This will be Monsieur Cannette's venture, not mine. I shall be paid for my services."

"And if the venture fails?"

"Monsieur Cannette, not I, will be the poorer."

I was not more than fifteen at the time, but even a child of that age could see that there was some sense lacking in my brother—call it moral, call it what you will, but whatever it was it betrayed itself in his very manner of speaking, his carelessness where the property or the feelings of others were concerned, and an inability to understand any viewpoint but his own.

My mother made a last attempt to dissuade him from this new course. "Give up the idea," she pleaded. "Come home, or, if you will, go back to la Brûlonnerie and work under your own tenant. Here in the country everyone knows one another, we are all established. In Paris new houses are continually being set up that come to nothing."

Robert turned to her impatiently. "That's just it," he said. "In the country you are set in your ways, the life here is—well, frankly provincial. Nothing will ever advance. Whereas in Paris . . ."

"In Paris," my mother finished for him, "a man can be ruined in less than a month, with or without friends."

"Heaven be thanked I have friends," returned Robert, "men of influence—Monsieur Cannette is a case in point, but there are others—men even closer to Court circles who have only to say the right word in the right quarter and I am made for life."

"Or finished," said my mother.

"As you will. But I would rather play for high stakes than for none at all."

"Let him go," said my father. "Argument is useless."

The glass-house was set up in the rue des Boulets, Robert was made director of it, and in six months' time Monsieur Cannette, the Court banker, had lost so much money that he sold the enterprise over my brother's head, and Robert was asking Cathie's father Monsieur Fiat for a substantial loan to tide him over "temporary" difficulties.

Then came a long silence. Robert did not write to us at le Chesne-Bidault, nor did we visit Paris, for all of us at home were in a state of agitation over my father's health. He had fallen from his horse riding back one day from Châteaudun, and was in bed six weeks or more, with my mother and Edmé and I taking it in turn to nurse him. The news came at last, not by word of mouth or by letter, but in a trade journal that my father took monthly, which one of us bore up to his bedroom when he was but partially recovered.

The journal was dated November, 1779, and the item ran as follows:

"Monsieur de Quévremont-Delamotte, a banker in Paris, has asked permission of the Minister of the Interior to manufacture glass in the English method at the glass-house of Villeneuve-St. Georges, outside Paris, formerly maintained by the Bohemian glass-manufacturer Joseph Koenig. Monsieur de Quévremont-Delamotte has already spent the sum of 24,000 livres upon this establishment, while it was under the direction of Monsieur Koenig, whose talent and intelligence proved, however, to be smaller than Monsieur de Quévremont-Delamotte had anticipated. He reserves to himself the usual privileges and letters patent, and intends to install as director of this enterprise Monsieur Busson l'Aîné, who has wide connections in the region. Monsieur Busson was brought up in the glass-house of la Pierre by his father Monsieur Mathurin Busson, who has written papers for the Académie on flint glass. Thus Monsieur Quévremont-Delamotte has every expectation that work of the highest possible standard will be forthcoming from the glass-house of Villeneuve-St. Georges, thanks to the care and skill of his young director."

Edmé and I did not read the piece in the journal until later. The first we knew of it was when the furious clanging of the bell in the passage below sent us both hurrying up to my father's bedside. He was lying half across the bed, the front of his nightshirt stained with blood, and blood on the sheet as well.

"Call your mother," he gasped, and Edmé flew downstairs, while I tried to support him on the pillow. It was the second time he had suffered such a haemorrhage; the first was immediately after he had fallen from his horse. My mother came instantly, the surgeon was sent for, and although he pronounced my father to be in no immediate danger he warned my mother that any undue shock or excitement might prove fatal.

Presently, when my father was easier, he pointed to the journal which had fallen on the floor during all this commotion, and we guessed the reason for his sudden attack.

"As soon as I can safely leave him," my mother told me later, "I shall go myself to Paris and see if anything can be done to prevent further mischief. If Robert has agreed to go to Villeneuve as manager only, no great harm may have been done. If, on the other hand, he has committed himself financially, then he is heading for a disaster worse than the one he sustained at Rougemont."

We could but wait and see. My father's health appeared to improve, and my mother left him in my care and proceeded to Paris. When she returned home a week later we learnt at once from her face that the worst had happened. Robert had not only become director of the glass-house at Villeneuve-St. Georges, but had agreed to purchase the property from Monsieur de Quévremont-Delamotte for the sum of 18,000 livres, payable within six months of the date of signature.

"He has until May of next year to find the money," said my mother, and I had never seen her before with tears in her eyes. "He will never do it. Thousands have already been sunk in this particular foundry, and it would need many more thousands spent on it before it could begin to show a profit. It needs a new furnace and new sheds, and the workmen's lodgings are worse than pig-sties. Most of the money spent so far has gone in putting up temporary buildings for the English craftsmen brought over by the last owner, Koenig, who, it now seems, did nothing but drink all the time."

"But why has Robert attempted it?" I asked. "Did he give any excuse at all?"

"The usual one," replied my mother. "He is supported, so he said, by 'influential' friends. A certain marquis de Vichy is interested in the project, and according to your brother may ultimately buy the glass-works from him."

"In that case," put in Edmé, "why did Robert bother with the property in the first place?"

"Because," returned my mother fiercely, "what he has done is known in trade circles as speculation. Your brother is a gambler. There is the crux of the matter."

Then she softened. She put out her arms to us both and we tried to console her. "I am to blame," she said. "All his highhanded folly is due to me. We are both too proud."

Now Edmé was near to tears. "You are not proud," she protested. "How can you accuse yourself? Robert's behaviour has nothing to do with you."

"Oh, yes, it has," replied my mother. "I taught him to aim high, and he knows it. It's too late to expect him to change now." She paused, and looked at each of us in turn.

"Do you know what grieved me most," she said, "more than my anxiety for his future? He never let me know, during all these past months of silence, that Cathie was expecting a baby. They had a little girl, born on the 1st of September. My first grandchild."

Robert a father . . . I could not imagine him in the rôle, any more than I could see Cathie as a nurse. She would be better pleased with a doll.

"What have they called her?" asked Edmé.

My mother's face changed very slightly. "Elizabeth Henriette," she replied, "after Madame Fiat, naturally."

Then she went upstairs to break the news to my father.

During the next few months we heard rumours, but no more. The marquis de Vichy had lost interest in the glass-house at Villeneuve-St. Georges . . . My brother had approached another banker . . . Monsieur de Quévremont-Delamotte was said to be considering an association with his former partner, Joseph Koenig, in a foundry at Sèvres . . .

My father was still not well enough to travel, and he sent Pierre up to Villeneuve-St. Georges early in February to bring back news.

Pierre at twenty-seven, no longer the carefree youth he had been at seventeen, was yet hopeful enough that Robert would succeed in his new undertaking.

"If he does not succeed," he told my father, "he can have all my savings, for I don't need them"—proof that his heart had not changed, despite his maturer years. Alas, it needed more than Pierre's savings to protect my oldest brother from the shame of bankruptcy.

Pierre returned from Villeneuve-St. Georges at the end of the month with a lock of the baby's hair for my mother, a clock of exquisite workmanship whose crystal surround had been designed at the glass-house there by Robert himself for my father—and a copy of a deposition signed before the judges of the Royal Court at the Châtelet in Paris, admitting Robert's insolvency.

My father, ill as he was, accompanied by my mother and myself, and leaving Pierre in charge of Edmé and le Chesne-Bidault, set forth a fortnight later for Paris. I looked out of the windows of the diligence with very different feelings from those upon my first visit nearly four years before. Then, with my father hale and hearty, and I myself full of expectation and excitement, the journey, though exhausting, had been all pleasure; now, in bitter weather, my father ill, my mother anxious, I had nothing to look forward to but my brother's public disgrace.

Villeneuve-St. Georges lay in the suburbs of Paris to the south-east, and we proceeded directly there, after resting one night at the hotel du Cheval Rouge in the rue St. Denis.

This time, unlike the day of our unannounced arrival at Rougemont, Robert was not standing in the courtyard to welcome us, and here was no imposing structure or grandiose château alongside, but a straggling collection of buildings in a poor state of repair, with two furnace-houses separated from one another by a wide ditch full of broken masonry and rejected glass. There was no sign of life. No smoke came from the chimneys. The place had already been abandoned.

My father tapped on the window of our hired vehicle and hailed a passing labourer.

"Has work ceased entirely at the foundry?" he asked.

The fellow shrugged his shoulders. "You can see for yourself it has," he replied. "I was paid off a week ago, like the rest, and we were told we were lucky to get what we did. A hundred and fifty of us suddenly without work, and families to keep. Not a word of warning. Yet there was stuff going out of here to Rouen and other cities in the north, crates of it, every day—someone's been paid for it, that's what we say, but where's the money gone?"

My father was much distressed, but there was nothing he could do. "Can you find other employment?" he enquired.

The workman shrugged again. "What do you expect? There's nothing here for any of us, with the foundry closed. We'll have to take to the roads."

He was staring at my mother all the while, and suddenly he said, "You were here before, weren't you? You're the director's mother?"

"I am," replied my mother.

"Well, you won't find him in the master's house, I can tell you that. We broke the windows for him, and he legged out of it, taking his wife and child."

My father was already reaching for coins to give the workman, and the fellow accepted them with an ill grace, not to be wondered at under the circumstances.

"Return to the rue St. Denis," my father told the driver, and we turned about, away from the desolation of my poor brother's foundry, where he had left behind him not only a failed venture but the ill-will of one hundred and fifty hungry workmen.

"What do we do now?" asked my mother.

"What we might have done in the first place," said my father. "Enquire of Cathie's father in the rue des Petits-Carreaux. She and the child will be there, if Robert is not."

He was mistaken. The Fiats knew nothing of what had happened, and had not seen Robert or Cathie for at least two months. Coolness on the part of the Fiats—doubtless because of the loan made to their son-in-law, and pride and loyalty on the part of their daughter—had caused this temporary estrangement.

When we arrived back at the hotel du Cheval Rouge we found a message from Robert awaiting us. It was addressed to my mother.

"Word has reached me that you are in Paris," it said. "No need to worry my father, but I am at present confined in the hotel du St. Esprit, in the rue Montorgueil, pending the hearing of my case. I am engaged in drawing up a list of my debts and assets, and should like your opinion. I am confident that the assets will amount to more than the debts, particularly as la Brûlonnerie is still mine, and there is also a portion of Cathie's 'dot' due to me from her parents. The marquis de Vichy let me down, as doubtless you have already heard, but I am not concerned about the future. English flint glass is all the rage, especially in Court circles, and I have it on good authority that Messieurs Lambert and Boyer are to obtain permission to set up a glass-house for the purpose of developing flint glass in the park of St. Cloud, under the direct patronage of the Queen. If I can get out of this present scrape without too much difficulty, I have every hope of being employed there as first engraver, as I am the only Frenchman in the country to understand anything of the process. Your affectionate son, Robert."

Not a word about Cathie and the child, nor any expression of sorrow for what had happened.

My mother passed the letter in silence to my father—it was useless to attempt to hide the truth from him—and together they went to see my brother in his hotel. They found him well and in excellent spirits, totally unmoved by his insolvency.

"He had the effrontery to tell us," my father—who appeared to me to have aged ten years during his hour with his son—told me afterwards, "that it was good experience to fall into such misfortune. He has given power of attorney to some associate at Villeneuve, as he is forbidden to sign any bills himself."

My father showed me the statement, signed by the judges, of the preliminary hearing on the very day we had travelled to Paris.

"In the year 1780, on March 15th, in the Chambre de Conseil, before us, judges of the Court, appointed by the King, in Paris, appeared le sieur Tréspaigné, resident in Paris and at the glass foundry of Villeneuve-St. Georges, having power of Attorney for sieur Robert Busson the owner of the glass-works at Villeneuve-St. Georges, who was ordered to appear before us and has asked us to appoint whomever we shall judge right to carry out the examination of the accounts of the above named Busson, declared insolvent from the statements deposed at the Record office, conforming to the Ordinance of 1673 and the Edict of the King, dated November 13th, 1739. For this matter we have called the sieur Tréspaigné named above, giving him power to call all the creditors of the said Busson to appear in person by special order, in this Court, before us, Judges of the Council, and to show and establish their titles of creditors, in order to have them examined and verified as the case may demand.

"This is the official verbatim report of the Court which was made. Signed. Guyot."

I handed the document back to my father, who was preparing to go out once more and seek further advice from the best lawyers in Paris, but my mother dissuaded him.

"You will kill yourself," she told him, "and that would help neither Robert nor anyone else. The first step is to consider what he calls his assets, and I have the papers here with me."

As she sat herself down in the hotel bedroom, she might have been home at le Chesne-Bidault reckoning up the weekly expenditure in her ledger. Something had to be salvaged from the wreck of her son's affairs, and no one was better suited to the task than his mother.

"Where is poor Cathie and the baby in all this?" I asked.

"Hiding in lodgings," she replied, "in Villeneuve-St. Georges."

"Then the sooner somebody brings them here to Paris the

better," I said, having more sympathy at this moment for his wife and child than for my brother.

We went to Villeneuve the following day, and found Cathie and the little Elizabeth Henriette lodging with one of the journeyman-carriers and his wife, a couple named Boudin, who had taken no part in the window-breaking at the master's house, but had been seized with pity for the master's family. Cathie herself had been too upset, and too proud, to go home to her parents.

She looked wretched, her pretty face spoilt with weeping, her hair tangled and unkempt, a very altered Cathie from the young bride who had shown us round the château at Rougemont. To make matters worse the baby was ill, too ill, she declared, to be moved. My mother dared not leave my father alone at the Cheval Rouge, so it was decided, with the consent of the good couple Boudin, that I should remain in the lodgings at Villeneuve-St. Georges to help Cathie.

A most miserable few weeks followed. Cathie, already distraught over Robert's disgrace, was in no way capable of looking after her baby, whose sickness, I felt sure, had come about through wrong feeding and neglect. I was only sixteen, and hardly wiser than my sister-in-law. We had to depend upon Madame Boudin for advice, and although she did everything possible for the baby the poor little thing died on the 18th of April. I think I was even more upset than Cathie. It was so needless a loss. The baby lay in the small coffin like a waxen doll, having known seven months of life, and would have been living still, I felt certain, if Robert had never gone to Villeneuve-St. Georges.

My mother came for us the day after the baby died, and we took poor Cathie home to her parents in the rue des Petits-Carreaux, for, although Robert was now staying at the Cheval Rouge with my parents, his affairs were still unsettled and the final reckoning would not be until the end of May.

Robert's list of creditors was formidable, even greater than my father had feared. Quite apart from the 18,000 livres owed to Monsieur Quévremont-Delamotte for the glass-house at Villeneuve-St. Georges, he had debts of nearly 50,000 livres to merchants and dealers all over Paris. The total amounted to something like 70,000 livres, and to meet this appalling sum there was only one answer, and that was to sell the single worthwhile asset he possessed—namely, the glass-house at la Brûlonnerie, given to him in trust at his wedding, valued by my father at 80,000 livres.

It was a bitter blow to my parents. Here was the glass-house where my father had first served as apprentice under Monsieur Brossard, and where he had taken my mother as a bride, which he had later developed with my uncle Démeré as one of the foremost foundries in the country, now to be sold to strangers to pay my brother's debts.

As to the smaller creditors, the wine-merchants, the clothiers, the house-furnishers—even the livery-man who had supplied a carriage for Robert to drive to Rouen and back on some extravagant purchase of material never used—all these debts were paid by my mother out of her own private income, derived from small farm-rents in her native village of St. Christophe.

Even then, when he appeared before the judges for the last time at the end of May, and was given clearance, I do not believe my brother understood the magnitude of what he had done.

"It's really a matter of knowing the right people," he confided to me when we were packing up to return home to le Chesne-Bidault. "I have been unlucky to date, but it will be very different in the future. You wait and see. I won't attempt to direct a foundry, the responsibility is too wearing. But as first engraver at a high salary—and they'll have to pay me well, or I won't accept the position—there is no telling where I might not end up, perhaps at le Petit Trianon itself! I am sorry my father has been so put out about it all, but then, as I have so often said, his outlook is provincial."

He smiled at me, as confident, as gay and as self-possessed as he had always been. Thirty years old and a brilliant craftsman, he had no more sense of responsibility than a child of ten.

"You must know," I said to him with all the weight of my sixteen years, and with the sight of his poor dead baby fresh in my memory, "that you have nearly broken Cathie's heart, and my father's too."

"Nonsense," he replied. "Cathie is already looking forward to living at St. Cloud, and another baby will console her. She will have a son next time. As to my father, once he is back at le Chesne-Bidault and away from Paris, which he has always detested, he will soon be himself again."

My brother was mistaken. The very next day, when we were due to take the diligence and travel home, my father was seized with another haemorrhage. My mother got him to bed at once and sent for the surgeon. There was little he could do. Too weak to travel home, yet conscious enough to know that he was dying, my father lingered on in that hotel bedroom of the Cheval Rouge for another seven days. My mother never left his side, or when she did it was only to snatch some sleep in my adjoining room, while I took her place. Those faded red hangings to the bed, the cracks on the plastered walls, the chipped ewer and basin in the corner of the room, these things became planted in my memory as I watched my father's progress towards death.

A stifling heat had descended upon Paris too, adding to his suffering, but the window giving on to the noisy, narrow rue St. Denis below did not open more than a few inches only, bringing a turmoil of sound and a fetid air that only turned the room more sour.

How he longed for home—not only the dear familiarity of his surroundings at le Chesne-Bidault, but for his own terrain, the forests and the fields where he had been born and bred. Robert might call his attitude provincial, but our father, and our mother with him, had their roots deep in the soil; and from this same soil which had nurtured them both, the lush Touraine, the very core of France, he had built up his glass-houses, creating with his hands and with his life's breath symbols of beauty that would outlast his time. Now his life was ebbing from him, vanishing like the air in a blow-pipe laid aside, and the last night we were together, while my mother was sleeping, he looked at me and said, "Take care of your brothers. Keep the family one."

He died on the 8th of June, 1780, aged fifty-nine, and was buried close by in the church of St. Leu in the rue St. Denis.

We were too worn out with weeping to notice it at the time,

but later it was a source of pride to all of us that every merchant, trader and workman in the glass-trade with whom he had ever done business came to St. Leu that day as a mark of respect to his memory.

FIVE

MY FATHER'S PERSONAL estate amounted to some 167,000 livres gross, and it took my mother and Monsieur Beaussier, the notary of Montmirail, until the end of July to sort out his papers, complete the inventory and the list of debts and assets, and finalise the net figure of 145,804 livres. Half of this sum was my mother's, and the other half was divided equally amongst us, the five children. Robert and Pierre, having attained their majority, received their portion at once, while Michel, Edmé and I, as minors living at home, had our one-fifth in trust, our mother acting trustee. The lease of le Chesne-Bidault, held jointly by our parents, would continue now in my mother's name alone, and she decided to manage the foundry herself as "maîtresse verrière", a title held by no other woman in the trade. She decided to keep for her eventual retirement the small properties in St. Christophe which she had inherited from her father Pierre Labbé; meanwhile she would reign over the community at le Chesne-Bidault.

I well remember how we all assembled, in the August of 1780, in the master's room at home, and discussed the future. My mother sat at the head of the table, the widow's cap topping her grey-gold hair somehow adding to her dignity; and the mock title, la Reyne d'hongrie, seemed better suited to her now at fifty-five than ever before.

Robert stood at her right hand, or paced the room, continually restless, forever touching some ornament which he thought must be his by right of inheritance; while to the left sat Pierre, deep in his own dreams, which I felt sure had little to do with laws or legacies.

Michel, at the end of the table, had grown the most like our father in appearance. Small, dark, thickset, he was now twenty-four years old, and a master glass-maker at Aubigny in le Berry. We had not seen him for many months, and I do not know whether it was absence from home that had matured him, or the sudden realisation of my father's death, but he seemed to have lost his old reserve, and was the first of us to volunteer an opinion upon the future.

"S-s-speaking for myself," he began, with far less hesitation than usual, "I have no more to l-learn at Aubigny. I am now w-willing to work here, if my mother will have me."

I watched him with some curiosity. Here was indeed a new Michel, who, instead of sitting with a sullen expression on his face and eyes firmly fixed upon the floor, looked straight at my mother as though to challenge her.

"Very well, my son," she replied, "if you feel that way I am equally willing to employ you. Remember that I am mistress of le Chesne-Bidault, and while I remain so I expect my orders to be obeyed and carried out."

"That s-s-suits me," he answered, "providing the orders are s-sensible."

He would never have spoken thus a year ago, and although I was surprised at his daring I was secretly filled with admiration. Robert ceased his incessant prowling to throw a glance in Michel's direction, and nodded approvingly.

"I have never given an order yet," my mother remarked, "which was not of immediate benefit to the glass-house under my control. The only error in judgement was to advise your father to give la Brûlonnerie to Robert as his marriage portion."

Michel was silenced. The sale of la Brûlonnerie to meet Robert's debts had been a blow to the interests of all of us.

"I see no necessity," said Robert, when the silence had become too long for comfort, "to revive the old business of my marriage portion. It's over and done with. And my debts are paid. As you all know, and my mother as well, my immediate future has great promise. I become first engraver in crystal at this new establishment in St. Cloud within a few months. Should I wish to have a small financial interest in the place it will now be possible."

Here was a dig at my mother. As a beneficiary under my father's will he was now independent of her and could use his money as he pleased. The will had been drawn up long before my father's illness, and before Robert had started his career of extravagance. My mother wisely ignored his remark and turned to Pierre.

"Well, dreamer?" she said. "We have all known since you came home ten years ago from Martinique that you followed your father's trade through want of ability at anything else. As it has turned out, you have done very well. But don't imagine I shall force you to remain a master glass-maker now that you have your share of the inheritance. You can go and live à la Jean-Jacques if you care to—become a hermit in the forest and exist on hazel-nuts and goat's milk."

Pierre awoke from his dream, yawned, stretched, and gave her a long, slow smile.

"You are perfectly right," he said. "I have no desire to stay in the glass-trade. I thought seriously some months back of going out to North America and fighting for the colonies in their War of Independence against England. It's a tremendous cause. But I have decided to remain in France. I can do more good amongst my own people."

We all stared. This was indeed a statement from dear, lazy Pierre, the "eccentric", as my father used to call him.

"So?" My mother nodded encouragement. "What's in your mind?"

Pierre leant forward in his chair with a determined air.

"I shall buy a notary's practice in Le Mans," he said, "and offer my services to any client who cannot afford lawyer's fees. There are hundreds of poor fellows who cannot read or write and need legal advice, and I shall make it my business to help them."

Pierre a notary! Had he said a lion-tamer I should have been less astonished.

"Very philanthropic," replied my mother, "but I warn you, you won't make a fortune out of it."

"I have no desire to make a fortune," returned Pierre. "Whoever enriches himself does so at the expense of some poor beggar or other. Let those who wish to be wealthy reconcile themselves to their conscience first."

I noticed that he did not look at Robert as he spoke, and I wondered suddenly whether his brother's disasters, first at Rougemont and then at Villeneuve-St. Georges, had affected Pierre more than the rest of us had realised, so that now, in this strange fashion of his own, he had decided to make amends for it.

It was Michel, despite his stammer, who found his tongue first.

"My c-congratulations, Pierre," he said. "As I am never likely to m-make a fortune either, I shall p-probably be among your early clients. In any event, if no one wants your advice, you can always d-d-draw up marriage contracts for Sophie and Aimée."

He could never manage the Ed in Edmé, and Aimée she had become through long habit. My young sister, indulged by all of us, and my father in particular, had remained remarkably quiet throughout these proceedings, but now she spoke up in her own defence.

"Pierre can draw up my marriage contract if he likes," she announced, "but I make the stipulation that I may choose my own husband. He will be fifty years old and as rich as Croesus."

This, said with the determined authority of fourteen years, helped to relax the tension—I asked her afterwards, and she told me that she did it on purpose, for we were all becoming too serious—and so it was that the future of my three brothers was discussed and arranged without ill-feeling among any of us.

One final point remained to be settled. Robert walked over to the glass cabinet standing in one corner of the room, opened the doors, and took out the precious goblet that had been made at la Pierre on the famous occasion of the late King's visit.

"This," he announced, "is mine by right of heritage."

For a moment nobody spoke; we all looked at my mother.

"Do you think you deserve it?" she asked.

"Possibly not," Robert answered, "but my father said it should be mine to hand down to my children, and I have no reason to believe that he would have gone back on his word. It will look very well in my new house at St. Cloud . . . By the way, Cathie expects another baby in the spring."

This was enough for my mother. "Take it," she said, "but remember your father's words when he promised it to you. It was to serve as a reminder of high craftsmanship, and was not intended to bring either fame or fortune."

"Perhaps not," said Robert, "but it rather depends on the hands that hold it."

When Robert left us to return to Paris he had the goblet wrapped up with the rest of his possessions, and the following April, when his son Jacques was born, he and the many fine friends at St. Cloud who were invited to the christening toasted the child in champagne drunk from the goblet.

Meanwhile the rest of us settled down to life at le Chesne-Bidault without my father—with the exception, of course, of Pierre our eccentric, who, true to his decision, bought a notary's practice in Le Mans and gave himself up to helping those less fortunate than himself. I thought myself that he should have had the goblet rather than Robert, for although he would no longer make glass he was a craftsman in his own way, and deliberately chose to live up to the high standard set by my father. Certainly he never lacked clients, and the poorer they were the better pleased was Pierre; he always had a string of unfortunates waiting on his doorstep. I had it in mind to go to Le Mans and keep house for him—it was practically settled between my mother and myself—and then, without a word to either of us, he went and got himself betrothed to a merchant's daughter, a Mlle. Dumesnil of Bonnétable, and was married within the month.

"So exactly like Pierre," observed my mother. "He extricates the merchant from a difficult deal and gets landed with the daughter."

The fact that Marie Dumesnil was older than Pierre, and brought him nothing very much in the way of a "dot", prejudiced her in my mother's eyes. However, she was a good creature and an excellent cook, and if she had not been suited to my brother he would never have taken her.

"Let us hope," said my mother, "that Michel will not allow himself to be caught so easily."

"Don't f-f-fret yourself," replied her youngest son. "I have enough to do at le Chesne-Bidault k-keeping out of your way without s-saddling myself with a wife."

The truth was that Michel and my mother had settled down remarkably well together, and now my father was no longer there to find fault with him, or become exasperated with his stammer, Michel was proving himself an excellent master—under my mother's direction, needless to say. Two or three of the craftsmen who had worked with Michel at Aubigny in le Berry had followed him to le Chesne-Bidault, which showed the influence he must have had upon them. Others had been either workmen or apprentices at la Pierre, and had known him from boyhood.

We were indeed a community at le Chesne-Bidault, with my mother the ruling spirit, and Michel more of a comrade to the men than manager. He was a natural leader, as my father had been before him, but his ways were very different. When my father had entered the furnace-house at the start of a melt, the noisy clatter and rough joking that went with a crowd of men living at close quarters would instantly cease; each man went to his appointed task in silence, without further ado. It was not that they feared the master, but they held him in deep respect. Michel expected neither silence nor respect. His theory was that the greater the clatter the better the response to work, especially if the loudest singing—for all glass-workers are natural singers —and the broadest jokes were started by himself.

He always knew when my mother was likely to make her rounds, which she did every day as matter of principle; then he would give the signal for order, and the men would respond. I think she suspected what went on in her absence, but the output from the glass-house remained steady, so she had no cause for complaint.

The chemical and scientific instruments that had been perfected by my father at la Brûlonnerie continued to be made at le Chesne-Bidault—we would send them locally to Saumur and to Tours, and naturally to Paris too. The fine table-glass that my uncle Michel had designed at la Pierre was not made by us at the smaller foundry. For one thing we had not the craftsmen, although we employed over eighty men, and for another the instruments were less costly to produce. Here at le Chesne-Bidault my mother had the farm to attend to, besides the orchard and garden, and well over forty families in her care, some of whom lived down the hill at le Plessis-Dorin and others through the forest near Montmirail, though the majority were housed in lodgings around the glass-house itself.

Edmé and I were brought up to care for the families just as our mother did. This meant visiting some of them every day and seeing to their needs—for none of the wives could read or write, and perhaps needed letters sent to distant relatives which we would write for them. Often it would be necessary to drive to la Ferté-Bernard or even to Le Mans on some errand for the families, for their lodgings were bare enough; they had little in the way of comforts, and wages were low.

We were continually asked to be godparents, which meant that more than usual attention had to be paid to our godchildren. Edmé and I found this something of an added burden, but our mother insisted. She must have had thirty godchildren at least, and she never forgot the birthday of one of them.

We were never idle at le Chesne-Bidault. If we were not visiting the families we were employed by my mother about the house, sewing, mending, making preserves; or gardening and fruit-picking, depending on the season of the year. My mother would never allow anyone to be idle, and in winter, when there was snow on the ground and we could not get out, she would set us to stitching blankets for the women and children.

I expected no other life, and was never dissatisfied. All the same, I looked upon it as a great treat when I was allowed to visit Robert and Cathie in Paris perhaps two or three times a year.

So far there had been no repetition of his former folly. His position as first engraver in crystal to the glass-house in the park of St. Cloud, near the pont de Sèvres, had brought him some renown, and in 1784 the foundry had for title "Manufacture

des Cristaux et Emaux de la Reine". My brother and Cathie
had lodgings close to the glass-house, and although they only
had two or three rooms of a very different size from those at
Rougemont Robert had furnished them in the latest style, and
Cathie herself was prinked out like a lady of the Court. She
was as pretty and as affectionate as ever, always delighted to
see me, and the baby Jacques was a fine little fellow.

As to Robert himself, I never could help contrasting his appearance, and his manner too, with those of Pierre and Michel.
If I stayed overnight at Le Mans, as I sometimes did, Pierre
would invariably return from his office late, having been de-
tained by one of his unfortunate clients. His hair would be un-
brushed and his neckerchief anyhow, and there would be a
patch on his coat as likely as not, and he would snatch something
to eat, hardly aware of what he tasted, while he recounted to
me some tale of poverty that had been unfolded to him, which
he was determined to redress.

Michel, too, cared little for his appearance. My mother was
forever at him to shave close, and to trim his nails, and to cut
his hair, for he would go about looking as rough as the charcoal-
burners.

But Robert . . . For one thing, his hair was always powdered,
which instantly gave him distinction. His jackets and breeches
were from the best tailors. His stockings were silk, never worsted,
and his shoes either pointed or square, according to the current
fashion. He would return to Cathie and me in the evening as
immaculate as when he had sallied forth in the morning—or the
other way round, depending upon the shift—and his conversation, instead of being about his working day, which I was accustomed to from both Pierre and Michel, would be fresh and
amusing, frequently scandalous, more often than not malicious,
and generally bearing upon some lively topic of Court circles.

These were the days when gossip was becoming rife about
the Queen. Her extravagance, and love of balls and theatre-
going, were well known; and although the birth of the Dauphin
had caused general rejoicing, and made a fine occasion for fes-
tivities and firework displays throughout the capital, there was
much sniggering and chatter at the same time, with whispers

that the child had been sired by anybody but the King himself.

"They say . . ." Objectionable phrase, a hundred times repeated by my brother, who, with the Queen as patron of the glass-house at St. Cloud, ought to have known better.

"They say" the Queen has half-a-dozen lovers, the King's brothers amongst them, and doesn't even know herself who is the father of her son . . .

"They say" that her latest ball-gown cost two thousand livres, and the dressmaking-girls who made it were so worn out with getting it put together in time that half of them died in the process . . .

"They say" that when the King comes home exhausted from hunting and goes straight to bed, the Queen disappears into Paris with her brother-in-law le comte d'Artois and her friends the de Polignacs and the princesse de Lamballe, and that they wander in the worst quarters disguised as prostitutes . . .

Who started the rumours nobody knew. It certainly amused my brother to spread them, and he always insisted that he got them at first hand.

When I was staying with Robert and Cathie in the spring of 1784, I was the unwitting cause of an incident that was to have a marked effect upon my brother's future. I was due to leave Paris on the 28th of April, and on the day before, the 27th, the author Beaumarchais was to present the first performance of a new play *Le Mariage de Figaro* at the theatre. Robert was determined to see the play—all Paris would be there, and it was said to be profoundly shocking, full of allusions to happenings at Versailles though disguised in a Spanish setting—and nothing would content him but that I must be present too.

"It will be an education, Sophie," he insisted. "You are far too provincial, and Beaumarchais is all the rage. If you see this piece you may spend the rest of the year discussing it at home."

This last was quite unlikely. Michel would mock, my mother would raise her eyebrows, and as to Pierre, he would only tell me that here was further proof of the decadence of society.

However, as it was my last day I allowed myself to be persuaded. We left Cathie in St. Cloud in charge of young Jacques and set forth ourselves in a hired carriage, myself in a gown made up by the dressmaker in Montmirail, but Robert a perfect dandy.

The crowds were immense outside the theatre, and I was all for driving straight back again to St. Cloud, but Robert would have none of it.

"Take my arm," he said. "We'll get ourselves inside at least, if you promise not to faint. Afterwards, leave all to me."

We pushed, we struggled, we finally gained entry. Needless to say, not a seat to be found.

"Stay here, and do not move," commanded my brother, placing me beside a pillar. "I will contrive something. There is sure to be someone I know," and with this he disappeared into the crowd.

I would have given anything to be in Cathie's shoes, minding young Jacques. The heat was intolerable, and so was the stench of paint and powder from the chattering women about me, all of them in grande tenue, dressed up in frills and furbelows.

I watched the orchestra come in and take their places. Soon the overture would begin, and still there was no sign of my brother. Then, over the heads of the crowd, I saw him beckon me, and stammering almost as badly as my brother Michel I made my excuses, and edged my way towards him.

"Couldn't be better," he murmured in my ear. "You shall have the best seat in the theatre."

"Where . . . what?" I began, and to my horror he led me towards a box close to the stage, where a magnificently dressed nobleman, wearing the grand cordon bleu, was seated entirely alone.

"The duc de Chartres," whispered Robert, "Grand Master of the Supreme Orient and of all Freemasonry in France. I belong to the same Lodge."

He knocked on the door before I could stop him, made a secret masonic sign of recognition, so he told me afterwards, and in a few hurried words explained the situation to the King's cousin.

"If you could possibly give my sister a seat," my brother said, pushing me forward, and before I knew what was happening the duc de Chartres was offering me his hand, and smiling, and pointing to the chair beside him.

The orchestra started the overture. The curtain rose. The play began. I saw nothing, heard nothing, too acutely conscious of my brother's audacity and my own agony of embarrassment to be aware of anything that happened on the stage. Never before, or since, have I endured hours of such misery. I could not join in either the laughter or the applause; and when the entr'actes came—there were four of them—and the box filled with friends of the duc de Chartres, all of them splendidly dressed, eager to discuss the play, I sat motionless, my face scarlet, never daring once to lift my head.

The duke himself must have been conscious of my confusion, for he wisely left me to myself, and did not again address me; it was only when the play was over, and Robert advanced from the back of the box to fetch me, that I caught his eye, managed to dip a curtsey, and retreated with my brother into the crowds below.

"Well?" said Robert, his eyes shining with pleasure and excitement. "Wasn't that the most delightful evening you have ever spent in your life?"

"On the contrary," I replied, bursting into tears, "the most hateful."

I remember him standing there in the foyer, staring at me in utter bewilderment, while the hordes of painted, powdered and bejewelled ladies filed out past us to their waiting carriages.

"I just don't understand you," Robert repeated again and again, as we rattled back to St. Cloud in our hired conveyance. "To have the chance of a seat beside the future duc d'Orléans, who happens to be the most influential and popular man in the whole of France at this present time, and when one little word in his ear might make your brother for life—and all you can do is to blub like a baby."

No, Robert did not understand. Handsome, gay, debonair, perfectly self-possessed, he had yet not grasped the fact that his young sister, with her smattering of education and her provincial dress, belonged to a world that he had long left behind him, a world which, despite its apparent backwardness and rustic simplicity, had greater depth than his.

"I would rather," I said to my brother, "work a whole shift before the furnace in le Chesne-Bidault than spend another such evening."

The adventure had its sequel. The duc de Chartres, who was to succeed his father as duc d'Orléans in the following year, lived at the Palais-Royal, and in face of much opposition he pulled down a number of properties overlooking his gardens and designed an entirely new lay-out. His palace was now surrounded with arcades, where the people of Paris could wander at will, and beneath these arcades were cafés, boutiques, restaurants, billiard-rooms, "salles de spectacles", and every sort of device to catch the public eye. Above these ground-floor premises were gambling-rooms and clubs.

To wander in the Palais-Royal, to look in the boutique windows, to mount the stairs or even to penetrate to the back-quarters to see the peculiar temptations more than occasionally lurking there, had become the most popular pastime in Paris. My brother took me there one Sunday, and, although I pretended to be amused, I was never more shocked in my life. It did not altogether surprise me therefore, knowing Robert's audacity, that having once dared the presence of the future duc d'Orléans he should venture to do so again. The soirée at the theatre, and renewed thanks for the great honour bestowed upon his little sister from the provinces, furnished the excuse for a visit to the Palais-Royal. He took care to leave behind him some two dozen crystal glasses for the personal use of the prince, which were accepted with a further exchange of masonic signs and symbols.

Some three months after the presentation of *Le Mariage de Figaro*—which was later banned by the King because of its shocking allusions to Court society, all of which had passed over my head—my brother Robert, while continuing to act as first engraver in crystal at the glass-house of St. Cloud, also became the proprietor of a boutique, No. 255, Palais-Royal.

Here he displayed not only objets d'art engraved by himself at St. Cloud, but certain other curiosities of oriental design, rather more costly, for the purchase of which the prospective customer needed a special introduction, and was then obliged to step into a curtained inner room.

"I suppose," remarked my mother in all innocence, when she heard about the Eastern bric-à-brac, "that Freemasons like to exchange objects of a ritual nature."

I did not disabuse her.

SIX

WHEN THE LEASE of le Chesne-Bidault became due for renewal in the autumn of 1784, my mother decided that the time
had come for Michel to take full responsibility. For one thing,
we had a new landlord. The whole property of Montmirail and
its dependencies, including the glass-house, had passed out of
the hands of the Bois-Guilberts into those of a Monsieur de
Mangin, a rich young speculator who threatened to spoil the
forests by selling timber at exorbitant prices and making all sorts
of changes. He held some high position at Court, calling himself
Grand Audiencier de France, and had been instrumental in
buying St. Cloud for the Queen.

My mother disliked speculators on principle—she had seen
too much of it with her eldest son, and the ruin it could bring—
and she preferred to retire from the management of the glass-
house before she saw the whole forest destroyed before her eyes.
As it turned out, the new owner of Montmirail let the forest and
the foundry alone and ruined himself over another property in
Bordeaux, but my mother was not to know this when she made
over the lease of le Chesne-Bidault to my brother Michel.

Michel at once went into partnership with a lively young
friend of his called François Duval, who, although hailing originally from Evreux in Normandy, had been managing the iron-
works near Vibraye for the past few years. The pair had struck
up a great friendship, Michel, who was the older by three years,
always the more forceful of the two, and his partner the aider
and abetter of all his schemes.

My mother raised no objection to the partnership. Indeed,
young Duval was a favourite of hers, making a point of asking
her opinion on every sort of topic from iron-work to market
prices, all done with tact and an air of modesty. That he had

been primed by my brother did not strike my mother until the deed of partnership had been signed, but it would have made no difference had it done so.

"I like young Duval," she continued to say. "He respects superior knowledge, and has pleasant manners to his elders and betters. We shall all get along together very well."

The fact that she intended to stay on for a while at le Chesne-Bidault, despite having handed over the lease, had not occurred either to my brother or to his friend, and they were hard put to it to get rid of her.

"They are starting to f-fell the f-forest," Michel would say. "Soon almost all the area b-between here and Montmirail will be d-devastated."

It was not true, of course. Not an axe had been taken to a single tree, beyond what was usual in the ordinary course of felling.

"That doesn't concern us," replied my mother calmly. "Under the terms of our lease we have a long-term arrangement for the supply of timber for fuel."

"I was th-thinking," continued my brother, "of the natural b-beauty of the surroundings. You had b-better move to St. Christophe before it is all s-spoilt."

My mother would smile and make no comment, knowing perfectly well what was in his mind. Then young Duval would have his turn, going about the business in a different way.

"I wonder, madame," he would begin, "that you are not more anxious about your properties in the Touraine. I am told the frosts have been exceptionally severe this winter, and many of the vines destroyed."

"I have relatives," my mother would answer, "who take care of my vines for me."

"No doubt, madame," young Duval would shake his head, "but it is not the same as being on the spot oneself. You know how it is if one leaves one's possessions to others."

My mother would regard him steadily, and thank him for his concern, but I could tell from the twitch at the corner of her mouth that he had not deceived her. She was careful never to interfere in any way with the management of the foundry, but she continued to care for the welfare of the families, besides supervising the household for her son and his friend.

Edmé spent most of her time these days with Pierre and his wife in Le Mans, for she was much more intellectual than I was, and Pierre used to instruct her in the evenings in history and geography and grammar, with more than a smattering of the philosophy of Jean-Jacques.

Thus I remained the daughter at home, acting as general aide to my mother, and confidante at the same time to my brother Michel and his friend.

"You know w-what you must do," Michel said one evening when the three of us were alone—it was between melts, so that there was no night shift for either of them, and my mother had gone early to bed—"you must pretend to f-f-fall in love with F-François here, and he with you, and then my mother will be in such a f-fright she will take you off to St. Christophe instantly."

The idea was brilliant, no doubt, but personally I had no desire to leave le Chesne-Bidault and disappear with my mother to the Touraine.

"Thank you," I replied. "I am quite incapable of acting a part."

Michel seemed disappointed. "You w-wouldn't have to d-do anything," he urged, "just sit about s-sighing a great deal and not eating m-much, and when François entered the room you would look d-distressed."

It was really too much. First Robert using me to advance his affairs in Paris, and now Michel trying to push me into a pretended infatuation for his friend.

"I'll have no part in it," I said, in great indignation. "You should be ashamed of yourself for thinking of such a deception."

"Don't tease your sister," put in young Duval. "We will excuse her if it is such an ordeal. But you cannot prevent my paying attention to you, can you, mademoiselle Sophie? Seeming red and uncomfortable in your presence one moment, and desirous of sitting close to you the next. It may well have the right effect upon your mother."

How this reprehensible conduct affected my mother mattered

very little, as it turned out; what mattered was the change it brought about in both François Duval and myself.

The game began with all sorts of private jokes and winks, nods between Michel and his friend, and various stratagems to leave us alone together, later to be surprised by my mother. But instead of being outraged at the discovery of her daughter sitting either in silence or in conversation with a young man, she appeared quite unmoved, even conniving, and would say, on entering the room, "Don't let me disturb you. I have only come for some writing paper, and will write my letters upstairs."

This resulted in François and myself taking advantage of our opportunities to get to know one another better. He proved not so entirely under Michel's influence as I had imagined, and was very willing to exchange that influence for mine. Nor did I turn out to be the homely daughter-of-the-house and general go-between that he had at first envisaged, but instead a young woman with plenty to say for herself, and a capacity for affection into the bargain. In short, we *did* fall in love, and there was no play-acting about it. We went hand-in-hand to my mother and asked for her blessing on our betrothal. She was delighted.

"I saw it coming," she declared. "I said nothing, but I saw it coming. Now I know that le Chesne-Bidault will be in safe hands."

François and I looked at one another. Could it be that, unknown to us, my mother had been busy planning this from the start?

"You shall be married as soon as Sophie attains her majority," said my mother, "which will not be until the autumn of '88. She will then come into her portion of the inheritance, and I will add to it from my own settlement. Meanwhile, you will continue to grow in mutual affection and understanding. It never hurts young people to wait."

I thought this unfair. My mother had been married herself at twenty-two. We were both about to protest, but she cut us short.

"You have forgotten Michel, haven't you?" she asked. "It will take him some time to adjust to this new state of affairs. If you take my advice you will keep your betrothal secret, and let him get used to the idea by degrees."

So Michel remained in perfect ignorance of the fact that François and I had become attached to each other, and did not discover the truth until much later.

Meantime, my brother Robert was in trouble again, and serious trouble, too. It dated back to the sale of la Brûlonnerie. He had, it now appeared, entirely without my father's or my mother's knowledge, mortgaged that property and all its contents to a merchant in the rue St. Denis in exchange for a jeweller's shop called Le Lustre Royal. At the time of his bankruptcy, when he had sold la Brûlonnerie to pay his debts, he had ignored, or conveniently forgotten, this mortgage. Now, the arrears of rent for the shop in the rue St. Denis having mounted, the merchant, a Monsieur Rouillon, wished to foreclose on the mortgage of la Brûlonnerie, and discovered that the property had already been sold in 1780. He at once sued my brother for fraud. The first we heard of the affair was a desperate letter from Cathie to tell us that Robert was imprisoned in La Force. This was in July, 1785.

Once again my mother and I made the long journey to Paris, with Pierre to support us, and the whole wretched business of litigation had to begin all over again—and this time with Robert, a proven fraud, living side by side with common criminals.

Pierre and I refused to allow my mother to visit her son in prison. She remained in the house with Cathie and little Jacques, but we went ourselves; and I felt as if I were back again in the theatre foyer . . . My brother was still the perfect dandy, dressed as though for a reception, with a clean shirt and neckerchief brought to him every day by one of his servers from the boutique in the Palais-Royal, along with wine and provisions, which he shared out with his fellow-prisoners—a mixed bunch of debtors, rogues and petty thieves.

These gentlemen, some dozen of them, were confined in a space about half the size of the master's room at le Chesne-Bidault, with a grille for air high up in the dank walls and straw pallets for beds.

"I do apologise," said Robert, advancing with his usual smile and waving a hand at his surroundings. "Rather close quarters, but charming fellows, every one of them!" He then proceeded to introduce us to his companions as if he were host in some salon, and they his guests.

I bowed, and said nothing; but Pierre, instead of remaining on his dignity, immediately shook hands with each rascal, enquiring if he could do anything to aid them, as well as my brother. They all fell to talking and discussing their cases, while I remained standing by the door, a target for the eyes of those who could not get close enough to Pierre, until one of them, bolder than his companions, approached me close and dared to seize my hand.

"Robert!" I cried—as loud as I dared, for I had no wish to be the centre of attention—and my brother, aware for the first time of my distress, moved blandly to my rescue.

"We are not renowned for courtesy in La Force," he said, "but don't let it worry you. So long as you left your jewellry at home . . ."

"You know very well I don't possess any," I told him, more angry now than frightened. "The point is—how do you intend to get out of this calamity?"

"I shall leave it to Pierre," he replied. "Pierre has an answer to everything. I have friends too, in the right quarters, who will do everything possible . . ."

I had heard all this before. I had never yet met any of his influential friends—with the exception of his highness the duc d'Orléans, who was very unlikely to come to his assistance in La Force.

"I will tell you one thing," I said. "My mother will not raise the money to help you out of this new scrape, nor can you expect anything from my portion of the inheritance."

Robert patted my shoulder. "I wouldn't dream of asking either of you," he replied. "Something will turn up. It always does."

Pierre's eloquence could not save his brother, or any special pleading before the judges. It was Cathie who proved Robert's saviour. She went herself and served behind the counter in the boutique of No. 255, Palais-Royal, for three months, leaving

Jacques in the care of her parents. By October she had put enough money aside to stand surety for Robert, to come to an agreement with his creditor Monsieur Rouillon, and to obtain her husband's release.

"I knew Cathie had it in her to rise to a crisis," declared my mother when we heard the news—for by this time we were back at le Chesne-Bidault. "If I had not been sure of her character I would never have chosen her for Robert. Your father would have been proud of her."

The months of anxiety had taken their toll of my mother, with the journeys backwards and forwards to Paris which had continued during the summer. She had never cared for the capital; and now, she told us, she had no desire to set foot in it again.

"I have one desire left," she said, "and that is to see both you and Edmé settled. Then I shall retire to St. Christophe and end my days alone amongst my vines."

It was said without rancour or regret. Her working life was over, and she knew it. Little by little she would go more often to the Touraine, taking Edmé and me with her, preparing her small property l'Antinière, an inheritance from her father Pierre Labbé, in readiness for the future.

"Lonely?" she would say to us, scoffing, when we argued gently that her farmstead was isolated, some little way from the village itself. "How can anyone be lonely who has as many interests as I have? Cows, chickens, pigs, my few acres to till, an orchard, and vines on the hillside. Anyone who cannot occupy herself with such things and be content had best give up living altogether."

There was one further blow to her pride before she could turn her back on le Chesne-Bidault and leave the glass-house in our care. This time it was not Robert who was at fault, but Michel.

François had thought it best to tell him of our betrothal, on one of the occasions when my mother and I were absent in St. Christophe. He took it well, better than François had expected, saying that the joke had been on him, and served him right.

"There's only one s-solution now," he told me, when I returned, "and that's for Aimée to live with us here, and make a quartet of it. She always t-took my part when we were children."

It was as though the prospective marriage between François and myself had reminded him of the old forgotten days when my father was alive and he the odd man out, rejected by his parents.

"It won't make any difference, Michel," I assured him. "François loves you dearly, and so do I. Everything will go on exactly as it has always done, with you as master here, and he your partner."

"Easy s-s-said," replied my brother bitterly, "you and he like t-turtle doves above, and I alone down here."

I was upset, and went to François, but he made light of it.

"It's nothing," he said. "He'll soon get over it."

I approached Edmé on the subject of living with us at le Chesne-Bidault and taking on my mother's work of managing the books—for she had a good head for figures—but she would have none of it.

"I have other plans," she told me, "and since you have brought up the subject of my future you may as well know what they are."

She then informed me, well-nigh bursting with pride and importance, that a Monsieur Pomard, a man considerably older than herself, who had the lucrative profession of fermier général to the monks at the abbey of St. Vincent in Le Mans (a fermier général being, in those days, a receiver of dues and taxes, on which he pocketed a large percentage), had been courting her, with Pierre's knowledge though hardly his approval, detesting, as he did, every fermier général on principle.

"And Monsieur Pomard is only waiting for your betrothal to be formally announced," said Edmé, "to speak to my mother on our behalf."

So . . . she had held to her vow of taking a husband of middle-age who, if not as rich as Croesus, was not far off it.

"You are certain," I asked, doubtfully, "that you will be doing right, and this is not just an attempt to copy me?"

She flared up at once, much put out at my suggestion.

"Naturally I am certain," she returned. "Monsieur Pomard is a man of great education, and it will be much more interesting living with him in Le Mans than with you three here, or with my mother in St. Christophe."

Well, that was for her to decide. It was not my business. And not long afterwards both betrothals were officially recognised, with my mother's full approval. Furthermore, she agreed that Edmé should not wait until she attained her majority, so that the two of us could have a double wedding, in the summer of '88.

"Far simpler," she declared, "to make one ceremony of it, and be dressed alike. In that way there will be no ill-feeling afterwards."

No doubt she was right, though both of us felt a certain deprivation . . .

There was much to do during the months preceding the wedding, our trousseaux to prepare, lists of guests to be drawn up, much going to and from le Chesne-Bidault, Le Mans and St. Christophe—for my mother had insisted that the double wedding should take place in her native village.

She was a firm believer in etiquette on these occasions; therefore both future bridegrooms were invited there frequently for consultation. I must confess that I did not greatly admire Edmé's choice—he was too rubicund and portly for my liking, as though he collected the wine for the abbey of St. Vincent in addition to the tithes and taxes—but he seemed good-humoured enough, and very devoted to her.

It was inevitable, in the circumstances, that my brother Michel was left on his own at le Chesne-Bidault more often than was good for him. He had few friends other than those amongst his fellow-craftsmen at the glass-house, for his stammer made him an awkward guest in strange company. He only felt at his ease in the narrow circle of the foundry, or among the charcoal-burners in the forest, or yet again amidst the strange collection of tinkers, pedlars, wandering gypsies and vagabonds who would roam the countryside in search of seasonal work.

I noticed a certain preoccupation on his part during the autumn of '87, particularly in November, when the three of us—François, Michel and myself—acted as godparents to the child of one of our workmen. He was one moment jocular and rowdy, unusual for him, and the next moment silent and seemingly ill-at-ease.

"What is the matter with Michel?" I asked François.

My future husband, in his turn, looked discomfited.

"Michel will settle down," he said, "when you and I are in the house to look after him."

I was far from reassured, and asked the same question of good Madame Verdelet, who had cooked for us for many years.

"Monsieur Michel is always out," she said abruptly. "That is to say, of an evening when he is not working on shift. He visits the charcoal-burners in the forest, the Pelagie brothers, and others. He had their good-for-nothing sister working here until I sent her packing."

I knew the Pelagies, a rough, wild couple, and the sister too, a bold, handsome girl, older than Michel.

"Things will be better," added Madame Verdelet, "when you are here for good, and take madame's place."

I sincerely hoped so. Meanwhile, it was useless to worry my mother. We gave a party at le Chesne-Bidault at the end of April, 1788, to all the workmen and their families who would not be able to travel to St. Christophe for the wedding, for only the senior craftsmen had been invited to the ceremony; with Monsieur Pomard's guests as well as ours, the numbers would have been too great.

Supper was set in the furnace-house for over a hundred of them, and there was singing to follow, as was the custom, and toasts, and speeches, with my mother presiding at what would be her last occasion to do so—for at any future event this would be my duty.

All went well. The cheers for François, and for Michel too, showed that our glass-house was a happy one, and the community well content. It was only when it was over, and everyone had gone home, that my mother produced a note she had received from the curé of le Plessis-Dorin, M. Cosnier, excusing himself from attending the supper. "In the circumstances," ran the note, "and with no disrespect to you, madame, I find myself unable to accept hospitality from your son."

My mother read this aloud, and then, turning to Michel, demanded an explanation.

"I should like to know," she asked, "in what way you have

offended the curé, who is a very good friend of mine, and of all of us?"

I received a warning glance from François, and kept silent. Michel had turned pale, as he used to do in the old days when questioned by my father.

"You are w-w-welcome to his f-friendship," he said sullenly. "He's no f-friend of mine. He m-meddles in things that are n-not his concern."

"Such as what?" asked my mother.

"You had b-better go to the p-presbytery and find out," replied Michel, and with that he flung from the room.

My mother turned to François. "Have you anything to add?" she asked.

François looked uncomfortable. "I know there has been some trouble," he murmured. "More than that I cannot say."

"Very well," said my mother.

These were the words she always used in the old days when we had misbehaved as children and deserved punishment. No more was said that night, but in the morning my mother told me to accompany her to le Plessis-Dorin. The curé, Monsieur Cosnier, was in the presbytery awaiting us. As always in our community, word of our coming had preceded us.

"What is all this about Michel?" asked my mother, coming at once to the point.

For reply the curé opened his register, which he had ready for inspection, and pointed to one of the entries.

"You have only to read this, madame," he replied, "to understand."

The entry stood as follows: "On the 16th of April, 1788, Elizabeth Pelagie, born of an illegitimate relationship between Elizabeth Pelagie, servant, and Michel Busson-Challoir, her employer, was baptised by us. Godfather, Duclos, workman. Godmother, the daughter of Durocher, workman. Signed, Cosnier, curé."

My mother stood rigid. For a moment she was speechless. Then she turned to the curé. "Thank you," she said, "there is no need to discuss this further. Where are the mother and child?"

The curé hesitated before replying. "The child is dead," he

then said. "Fortunately, perhaps, for its own sake. I understand the mother is no longer with her brothers the Pelagies, but has gone to relatives in another district."

We bade the curé good-day and walked back up the hill to le Chesne-Bidault. My mother said nothing until we were nearly home, then she paused for breath, midway up the hill, and I saw that she was deeply shocked.

"Why is it," she asked, "that two of your brothers should deliberately go against every principle I hold dear, and so destroy themselves in the process?"

I could not answer her. There seemed no reason for it. We had all of us been brought up in the same fashion.

"I do not believe," I ventured at last, "that anything they do wrong is done deliberately. Robert, Michel and Pierre, too, are rebels. It's as though they want to have done with tradition and authority, and all the things you and my father respected. Had you yourself been less forceful a person it might have been otherwise."

"Perhaps . . ." said my mother, "perhaps . . ."

Michel was on shift when we returned, but she had no compunction in sending for him forthwith, and speaking plainly.

"You have abused your position as master here, and disgraced your name," she told him. "That entry on the parish register of le Plessis-Dorin is there for all time. I don't know which has disgusted me more—your behaviour, or Robert's bankruptcy."

My brother did not defend himself. Nor did he accuse the Pelagies and their unfortunate sister. One man only had earned his hatred, the curé, Monsieur Cosnier.

"He refused the child b-burial," Michel said savagely, "and t-took it upon himself to s-send the g-girl from the district. It's his f-finish as far as I'm c-concerned, and that g-goes for every pr-priest in the county."

He went back on shift without another word, nor did he join us that night for the evening meal. The following day my mother and I returned to St. Christophe, and afterwards the preparation for the double wedding took up all our time. The disgrace had cast a shadow, though, upon rejoicing; it was as though the bloom had been brushed off anticipation.

It seemed strange, a few months later, to settle down at le Chesne-Bidault as wife of the joint-master, and take my mother's place in the community. I remember how she came to collect the last of her possessions, promising to be back every so often to see that all was well.

We stood at the entrance-gates of the glass-house, and watched her climb into one of the foundry vehicles that was to take her back to the Touraine. Cheerful, smiling, she kissed the three of us in turn, giving last instructions to François and Michel about a batch of glass destined for Lyon which, as it was to go to a trading-house well-known to her and my father, had particularly concerned her.

The workmen who were not on shift were all lined up in the road to see her go, along with their wives and children. Some of them had tears in their eyes. She leant out of the window and waved her hand. Then the driver whipped up his horse and she was gone, with the sound of the carriage wheels rumbling down-hill to le Plessis-Dorin.

"It's the end of an era," said Michel, and glancing up at him I saw that he looked lost, like an abandoned child. I touched his arm, and the three of us moved back inside the gates of le Chesne-Bidault, to begin our life together.

It was not only the finish of the rule of the Reyne d'hongrie, who had held sway over our community of glass-houses for over forty years, but also—within a twelvemonth, could we but know it—the end of the ancien régime in France, which had lasted for five centuries.

PART TWO

La Grande Peur

SEVEN

THE WINTER OF 1789 was the hardest within living memory. No one, not even the old people of the district, had ever known anything like it. The cold weather set in early, and, coming on top of a bad harvest, led to great distress among the tenant farmers and the peasants. We were hard hit at the foundry too, for conditions on the road became impossible, what with frost and ice, and then snow; and we were unable to deliver our goods to Paris and the other big cities. This meant that we were left with unsold merchandise on our hands, and little prospect of getting rid of it in the spring, for in the meantime the traders in Paris would be buying elsewhere—if, that is, they ordered at all. There was a general drop in demand for luxury commodities at this time, owing to the unrest throughout the country. I had heard my brothers in the past—especially Pierre—discussing with my mother the mounting frustration in the glass and other trades, with inland customs duties and various taxes all adding to the costs of production, but it was not until I became the wife of a master glass-maker that I began to realise the difficulties under which we worked.

We paid the proprietor of le Chesne-Bidault, Monsieur de Mangin of Montmirail, an annual lease of 1200 livres, which was not heavy, but we were responsible for the state of the buildings and for all repairs. We also had to pay manorial dues and tithes on top of this, and had the right to take only a certain portion of forest-timber for our furnace. We were fined if our animals grazed beyond the foundry limits; and if any of the workmen were found pilfering wood in those parts of the forest reserved for hunting we were obliged to pay an indemnity of 24 livres for each of them.

Wages had increased since my father's time because of the

cost of living. The top craftsmen, the engravers and blowers, received about 60 livres a month, the less skilled men 20 to 30 livres, and the boys 15 to 20 livres, or less. Even so, life was hard for them, for they had to pay a head tax and a salt tax; but what came heaviest upon all our workmen and their families was the price of bread, which had reached as much as 11 sous for a 4 lb. loaf during recent months. Bread was their main fare—they could not afford meat—and a man earning at the rate of one livre or 20 sous a day, with a hungry family to feed, paid half his wages on bread alone.

I realised now how much my mother had done during her time for the wives and children in the country, and what a heart-breaking business it could be to try and prevent near starvation amongst them, while striving to keep the manufacturing costs as low as possible.

It was impossible to stop the men from taking wood from the forest that hard winter, or from poaching the deer. Indeed, we had no desire to do so, for the state of the roads, and the dif-ficulty of getting into la Ferté-Bernard or Le Mans, made living equally difficult for us.

There was much bitterness throughout all France because of the high prices, but at least in the country we were spared the strikes and disturbances that were continually breaking out in Paris and in the big cities. Nevertheless, the general feeling of apprehension reached us even in the forest, where rumours were magnified because of our very isolation.

Pierre, Michel and my François had all become Freemasons during the past year, joining different Lodges at Le Mans—the Saint-Julien de l'Etroite Union, le Moira, and St. Hubert re-spectively. Here, before the hard winter made travel difficult, my two glass-masters would foregather with the progressive Manceaux thinkers of the day, many of them lawyers and pro-fessional men like my brother Pierre, or merchants and master-craftsmen like themselves. There was a fair sprinkling, too, of the more enlightened members of the aristocracy and the clergy, but bourgeois or middle-class interests predominated.

I knew little about municipal affairs, and less of how the coun-try was run as a whole—which was apparently the topic of conversation at all these gatherings—but I could see for myself that taxes and restrictions made trading increasingly difficult for all of us, that the high price of bread fell most heavily upon the poorer workmen, and that those who had the greatest amount of money—the nobility and the clergy—were excused from all forms of tax.

Meanwhile France, like my brother Robert some few years previously, was, according to the general opinion, on the verge of bankruptcy.

"I've been saying this for years," my brother Pierre would remark, when he came to visit us. "What we need is a written Constitution as they have in America, with equal rights for all, and no privileged classes. Our laws and legal system are out of date, along with our economy; and the King can do nothing about it. Feudalism has him in thrall as it has the whole country."

I was reminded of the days when he used to read Rousseau and so annoy my father. Now he was a greater enthusiast than ever, and burning to put Jean-Jacques's philosophy into practice.

"How," I asked, "would having a written Constitution make any of us the better off?"

"Because," answered Pierre, "by abolishing the feudal system the power of the privileged would be broken, and the money they take from all our pockets would go towards giving the country a sound economy. Prices would then come down, and your question would be answered."

This seemed to me all in the air, like so much of Pierre's talk. The system might one day change, but human nature remained the same, and there were always people who profited at the expense of others.

Just now we had a common hatred of the grain hoarders, those merchants and land-owners who withheld large stocks of grain and then released them upon the market when prices reached their peak. Sometimes bands of hungry peasants and unemployed workmen would raid the granaries or even seize the grain from the carts on the way to the markets, and we had every sympathy with them.

"V-violence is the only thing that w-works," Michel used to

say. "S-string up a few g-grain merchants and l-land-owners, and the price of bread would s-soon fall."

Our business was almost at a standstill, and we were obliged to lay off workmen, some of whom had been with us for years. To save them from actual starvation we gave them unemployment pay of 12 sous a day, but there was no relaxation in the rents, taxes and dues which we had to pay.

Robert wrote from Paris, where they were having continual strikes and risings, and it seemed business was equally bad for him. The glass-house at St. Cloud had changed hands and been closed down shortly after his imprisonment, and he now depended entirely on what he could sell in the boutique in the Palais-Royal, which he supplied with goods made by himself, and a few pupils from a small laboratory he had set up in the rue Traversière, in the quartier St. Antoine.

In Paris he was close to the centre of political thought, and as a Freemason, and living in the Palais-Royal, he was forever quoting my one-time host, the duc d'Orléans, formerly duc de Chartres.

"The man's generosity is beyond all praise," wrote my brother. "During the worst of this winter, with the Seine solidly frozen for weeks, he has given away more than a thousand livres' worth of bread to the poor of Paris every day. Every woman in labour in our part of the Palais-Royal has been cared for at his expense. He has rented empty buildings in the St. Germain district and set up food kitchens for the homeless, where the poor wretches are served and fed by his own servants in livery. The duc d'Orléans is, without a doubt, the most loved person in the whole of Paris; which is very much resented at Court, where he is detested—they say the Queen won't speak to him. Next to the duc d'Orléans, Necker, the Minister of Finance, is the man of the hour, and it seems he has given two million livres out of his own funds to the Treasury. If the country can hold together until the States General are summoned in May, we may see great changes then, especially as Necker has succeeded in doubling the representation of the Third Estate, which will then outnumber in voting strength the aristocracy and the clergy. Meanwhile, here are several pamphlets which you might ask Pierre to distribute in Le Mans, and Michel and François in la Ferté-Bernard and Mondoubleau. They are being sent out from the duc d'Orléans' headquarters here at the Palais-Royal, and give all the latest political information."

So Robert too was following the fashion of the day and becoming involved in current topics. Ministerial intrigues had taken the place of Court scandal, and the question "What is the Third Estate?" was now a more burning one than "Who is the Queen's latest lover?"

Like many others of my generation, I had never heard of the States General, and it was Pierre again who had to explain to me that they were deputies representing the entire nation, divided into three separate bodies—the aristocracy, the clergy, and the Third Estate, the last comprising all the other classes in the kingdom. These bodies were to assemble in Paris to discuss the future of the country for the first time since 1614.

"Don't you understand," said Pierre, "that it is people like ourselves whom the Third Estate will represent? Deputies from towns and districts throughout the whole of France will go to Paris and speak for us. This has not happened for over a hundred and seventy years."

He was in a great state of excitement, and so apparently was everyone else in Le Mans, especially the lawyers and intellectuals among his friends.

"Did any good come from their meeting in 1614?" I asked.

"No," he admitted, "none of the representatives could agree. But this time it will be different. This time the Third Estate, thanks to Necker, will outnumber the others."

He, Michel and François read the pamphlets that Robert had sent with lively interest, and so, I gathered, did Edmé behind her husband's back—as a fermier général collecting taxes for the monks at St. Vincent, Monsieur Pomard's profession was one of those most attacked. The pamphlets also suggested that lists of grievances should be drawn up in every parish and handed to the deputies when they were elected. In this way the whole mass of the people would be represented, and their views made known when the States General met in Versailles.

The idea of a new constitution conveyed nothing to our workmen at le Chesne-Bidault. All they wanted was an end to the hated salt and head taxes, a promise of steady employment, and a drop in the price of bread. I tried to do as my mother had done, and visit the families and listen to their troubles; but the days were over when jugs of soup and wine and a few warm blankets from the master's house were accepted as a welcome luxury in times of sickness. These women did not have enough bread to feed their children; I was met with poverty, sickness and hunger in every dwelling. All I could do was to tell them repeatedly, day after day, that the winter would soon be over, trade would improve, prices would ease, and when the deputies got together with the King something would be done for all of us.

Conditions came hardest upon the old people, and the very young. There was hardly a dwelling in our community that remained untouched by death that winter. Lung disease, scourge of the glass-trade in all seasons, trebled its victims now amongst our older workmen, while sheer privation took its toll of young children and babies.

I think my most vivid memory of that winter was when Durocher, one of our finest workmen, opened his lodging door to me with his dead baby in his arms, and told me the ground was too hard for burial—he was going to take the little corpse to the forest and conceal it beneath a stack of frozen timber.

"And another thing, Madame Sophie," he said to me, his rugged face set in lines of despair. "I have always been an honest man, as you know, but today some of us from le Chesne-Bidault are going to seize the grain-carts on their way between Authon and Châteaudun, and if the drivers show fight we shall break their heads for them."

Durocher . . . whom my mother would have trusted with all the resources of the glass-house any day of the week.

"Please," I said to Michel, "do something to stop them. They will be recognised at once, and then reported. Durocher won't help his wife and children if he is flung into prison."

"They w-won't be reported," replied Michel. "The d-drivers won't dare to do so. We've earned a name for t-toughness these days at le C-Chesne-Bidault. If D-Durocher seizes the g-grain-carts, he does it with my b-blessing."

I looked at my husband François, who glanced away from me, and I saw that he had assumed his old rôle of follow-my-leader to my brother.

"It isn't that I don't sympathise with what Durocher wants to do," I told them, "but it's breaking the law. How can that help any of us?"

"These l-laws were designed to be b-broken," returned Michel. "Do you know what a b-bishop was reported as saying last week? That there would be enough b-bread for everyone if the p-peas-ants threw their children in the r-rivers. And that it d-didn't hurt anyone to live for a t-time on roots and grass."

"It's true," echoed François, seeing my look of disbelief. "It was the bishop of Rouen or Rennes, I forget which. These churchmen are the worst hoarders of grain. Everyone knows they keep sacks of it in their cellars."

"Everyone knows . . ." This was on the level of "they say" and Court gossip. It was regrettable that Michel and François should spread rumours in their turn.

As to the grain-waggons, Durocher and his companions did what they had intended to do. Nor were they betrayed to the authorities.

In the middle of April, with the winter at last behind us, I received a sudden plea from Cathie to go to Paris. She was ex-pecting another baby at the end of the month, and wanted me to be with her. Her parents, it seemed, had both been ill during the winter, and did not feel equal to taking charge of young Jacques, who was now a sturdy lad approaching his eighth birthday. As to Robert, besides the boutique in the Palais-Royal, and his laboratory in the rue Traversière, he had become much involved in the entourage of the duc d'Orléans, and was forever at politi-cal meetings. I was four months pregnant myself, and had little desire to go to Paris; nevertheless there was something about Cathie's note that disturbed me, and I persuaded François to let me go.

My brother Robert met me at the terminus of the diligence in the rue Boulay, and making light of Cathie's condition he at once passed on to the one topic of the day—the meeting of the

States General within a few weeks—and how a national crisis was approaching, and all Paris was in a political ferment.

"No doubt it is," I agreed, "but how about Cathie and your son?"

He was far too impatient to discuss such mundane matters as his wife's near confinement or his boy's birthday.

"You know what it is," he said, hailing a fiacre and putting my traps upon it. "If the duc d'Orléans was at the head of affairs there would be an end to the crisis." He appealed to the driver for confirmation. "You see?" he added. "Everyone agrees . . . I tell you, Sophie, I have my finger on the country's pulse, living at the Palais-Royal. We have the rooms over the boutique now, you know. There is nothing I don't hear."

And repeat, I thought to myself. And exaggerate a thousand-fold.

"We are all patriots at the Palais-Royal," he continued, "and I get the news at first-hand from the Club de Valois round the corner. Not that I am a member myself, but I have many acquaintances who are."

He began to reel off a string of names of the highly-placed individuals entrusted with the duc d'Orléans' private and public affairs. Laclos—author of *Les Liaisons Dangereuses*, which my mother never allowed me to read—was apparently the prince's right-hand man, and directed all.

"There are hundreds of smaller fry," confided Robert, "closely bound up with the duke's interests. Laclos has only to say the word and . . ."

"And what?" I asked.

My brother smiled. "I am talking too much as usual," he said, folding his arms and cocking his hat sideways. "Suppose you tell me what they are saying in Le Mans instead."

I preferred to keep my own counsel. There was unrest enough in our part of the country already, without stirring up Robert's interest.

I found Cathie tired and strained, but pitifully glad to see me. Almost as soon as Robert had delivered me at the door he was off again, on what he termed light-heartedly "matters of State".

"I wish it were false," whispered Cathie, but could say no more just then, for my lively nephew Jacques burst in upon us—fair-haired, blue-eyed, my brother in miniature—and I had to exclaim at the playthings he had been given for his eighth birthday.

Later that evening Cathie told me her fears.

"Robert is forever with these agents and agitators of the duc d'Orléans," she said. "Their whole purpose is to spread rumours and make trouble. Robert accepts money from them, I know this for a fact."

"Surely," I argued, "the duc d'Orléans does not need to stir up trouble. He is too much loved by the people. And when the States General meet everything will be settled, so Pierre says."

Cathie sighed. "I don't understand the half of it," she admitted. "I believe, as you say, that the duc d'Orléans himself has no wish to make trouble. It's his entourage that is at fault. These past months, since Monsieur de Laclos came to the Palais-Royal, the atmosphere of the whole place has changed. The gardens and arcades, where everyone came to amuse themselves, are now full of whisperers, and groups of men talking in corners. I am certain most of them are spies."

Poor Cathie. Her condition made her fanciful. How could there be spies in the streets of Paris? The country was not at war. I tried to distract her by talking of the coming baby, and of Jacques' pleasure in having a young brother or sister, but it did little good.

"If only," she confessed, "we could be out of Paris, and living with you at le Chesne-Bidault. Your winter was hard, I realise that, but you do not live in constant terror of riots as we do."

I began to understand something of her fear during the succeeding week. Paris *had* changed since my last visit some four years previously. The faces of the people in the streets or in the shops were either sullen or withdrawn or tense like Cathie's; or yet again excited and somehow expectant like my brother's. And Cathie was right, there were whisperers everywhere. One came upon them in the arcades, or at street corners, or in small groups in the gardens of the Palais-Royal.

Once, I saw the duc d'Orléans himself, in his coach, leaving for the races at Vincennes with his mistress, Madame du Buffon, at his side. He had grown much fatter since our famous encounter at the theatre, and I was disappointed, as his coach turned out of the palace gates and he waved a pudgy hand at the cheering crowd, who were crying "Vive le duc d'Orléans, vive le père du peuple!" I had expected our leader, if he was to be our leader, to look more alert, more alive to the crowds about him, not lounging back on his seat, laughing at some remark made by his mistress.

Robert would say I was provincial . . . I determined to say no word in dispraise of his idol.

It so happened that my brother would have ignored any remark made by me that evening, for he returned to the boutique from his laboratory in the rue Traversière full of a speech made at the Electoral Assembly of his particular parish of St. Marguerite. A Monsieur Réveillon, a wealthy wallpaper manufacturer, had held forth about the high cost of production, and its relation to wages—he lamented the days, it seemed, when his workpeople had managed on 15 sous a day. Now, he had said, the higher wages interfered with production.

"It's very true," I told my brother. "We find the same at le Chesne-Bidault, but unless we increase wages our workmen will starve."

"Quite so," replied Robert, "but when these things are said in public they can sound unfortunate. Réveillon had best watch out for his windows."

He seemed highly amused at the thought of a fellow-merchant having the same trouble that he had experienced himself a few years back, and he went out again later that night to one of his mysterious gatherings—whether to one of the Clubs or to the Lodge of the Grand Orient we could not say. The next morning, when I went to market for Cathie, the talk was all of how some of the rich manufacturers in the quartier St. Antoine were going to cut their workmen's wages down to 10 sous a day, and one enormous fishwife, thrusting my purchase into my hand, declared loudly that, "It's people like them who are robbing honest folk, and they deserve to be hanged".

Regretting the days when wages were lower seemed a very different thing from cutting them down, and I wondered which was the true version of the story. I told Robert what I had heard, and he nodded approvingly. "It's all over Paris by this time," he said, "each version more garbled than the last. Someone told me Henriot, the powder manufacturer, expressed the same opinion as Réveillon. I wouldn't be in either of those fellows' shoes."

Cathie glanced across at me and sighed. "But Robert," she asked, "didn't you tell us that Monsieur Réveillon had merely lamented the old days, and said nothing about cutting down his workmen's wages?"

"Those were his words," shrugged my brother, "but of course anyone is free to put what emphasis he likes upon them."

Sunday was usually a busy day in the boutique, for the Parisians came to stroll in the arcades and in the gardens of the Palais-Royal, but it seemed to both Cathie and myself, on the Sunday of the 26th of April, that the crowds were more than usually thick, milling to and fro in front of the palace and down the rue St. Honoré towards the Tuileries. Robert's fine display of glass and porcelain lured no purchasers, and that evening he put up his shutters early. The following day, Monday, was a workers' rest-day, when Cathie and Robert usually took Jacques for an outing to another part of Paris, to see his Fiat grandparents, perhaps, or to walk in the Bois. Today, however, my brother told us at breakfast that we were to remain within doors, to keep the boutique shuttered, and on no account whatsoever to venture out into the streets.

Cathie turned pale and asked him the reason.

"There may be disturbances," he answered lightly, "and it is wiser to take precautions. I shall go to the laboratory and reassure myself that all is well there."

We implored him to stay with us rather than run the risk of coming to some harm in the crowds, but he would not listen, and insisted that nothing would happen to him. I could see, and so could Cathie, that he was tense with excitement; he had hardly swallowed his coffee before he was off, leaving the shuttered boutique below in charge of the apprentice boy Raoul.

The femme de ménage, who usually helped Cathie with the house, had not come, which was another sign that something unusual was afoot. We went to the upper rooms above the boutique, and I tried to distract Jacques, who was protesting at being kept indoors on a holiday.

Presently Cathie, who had been in her bedroom, beckoned to me.

"I've been sorting through Robert's clothes," she whispered. "Look what I have found."

She showed me a great heap of small change of deniers, 12 of which went to the sou; on one side of them was the head of the duc d'Orléans, with the words "Mgr le duc d'Orléans, citoyen", and on the reverse "The hope of France".

"These are what Laclos and the rest of them wish to spread amongst the people," Cathie said. "Now I know why Robert's coat pockets were bulging this morning. Who is to benefit by this?"

We stared down at the money, and then Jacques called to us from the adjoining room. "There are crowds running," he said. "Can I open the window?"

We too heard the sound of running feet and opened the windows, but the stone-work and arches of the arcades blocked our view; all we knew was that the sound came from the place du Palais-Royal and the rue St. Honoré. Besides the running feet there was a murmur, growing ever louder, swelling, like a river torrent, and it was something I had never heard before, the roar of a crowd in anger.

Before we could prevent him Jacques had rushed downstairs to tell Raoul, and the apprentice had drawn back the bolts of the door and gone to the place du Palais-Royal to find out what was happening. He was soon back, breathless and excited, saying someone in the crowd had told him the workmen were out in strength in the quartier St. Antoine; they were going to attack the property of some manufacturer who had threatened to cut wages.

"They will burn everything on sight," exclaimed the apprentice.

It was then that Cathie fainted, and when we had carried her upstairs and to her bed I perceived that worse was to follow; it was likely that her labour would start this very day, within a few hours, perhaps. I sent Raoul for the surgeon who was to attend her, and while we waited the roar of the crowd increased outside, all making their way towards St. Antoine. When Raoul returned, hours later, he informed us that the surgeon had been summoned with others to the district where the rioters were gathering, and at my wits' end—for Cathie's pains had started— I sent the lad out once more, to summon anyone from the streets who might have a knowledge of delivery in childbirth.

Poor Jacques was as scared as I was, and I put him to boiling water and tearing up old linen while I held Cathie's hand and tried to comfort her.

Ages passed, or so it seemed—in reality some forty minutes— and when Raoul next returned he had with him, to my horror, the stout fishwife from the market. She must have seen the expression on my face, for she laughed with rough good-nature, and introduced herself as "la femme Margot".

"There's not a surgeon anywhere in the quarter," she told us, "nor likely to be this side of midnight. They say the riot has spread from the rue de Montreuil down to the royal glass-foundry in the rue de Reuilly. They're carrying dummies made to look like Réveillon and Henriot the manufacturers, and serve them right—they ought to burn the men themselves, not the dummies. What's the trouble? A child on the way? I've delivered dozens."

She pulled the sheets aside to examine Cathie, who looked at me in anguish, but what were we to do? We were forced to accept the woman's help, for despite my own condition I was almost as ignorant as young Jacques. How I longed for my mother, or for any of our own workpeople from le Chesne-Bidault . . .

I now asked Raoul to go to the laboratory in the rue Traversière to fetch my brother, that is, if he could force his way through the crowds, and he dashed off, more excited to see what was afoot than filled with any concern for us. It was not until he had gone that our midwife announced cheerfully, "He'll never get there, he'll be swept off his feet."

I kept the windows open in the top rooms, and despite our distance from the troublous quarters we could hear the far-off roar of the crowds, and now and again the clatter of horses as the troops rode to disperse the rioters.

The day wore on, poor Cathie's sufferings increased, and there

was still no sign of my brother. It was falling dusk when the
market-woman called me into the bedroom and asked me to assist
her. I bade Jacques brew coffee in the kitchen—the poor child
was distraught from hearing his mother's cries—and between us
the "femme Margot" and I brought Cathie's baby into the world,
still-born, poor infant, the cord about its neck.

"A pity," muttered the midwife, "but the surgeon himself
wouldn't have saved it. I've seen too many so. Feet first, they
strangle themselves."

We made Cathie as comfortable as we could. I think she was
too worn out to weep for her dead baby. I made much of Jacques,
who, with a child's curiosity, kept wanting to peep at the dead
infant, which we had placed in its basket and covered. And then
we became aware suddenly that it was now quite dark, and the
sound of the rioting had ceased.

"There's no more I can do," said the midwife. "I'd best get
home myself and see if my good man has come back with a
broken head. I'll look in tomorrow. Let her sleep. It's nature's
best cure."

I thanked her, and pressed some money into her hand, which
she refused to take. "No call for that," she said, "we're all equal
in times of trouble. It's a pity about the baby. Still, she's young.
There'll be others . . ."

I had never thought I could be sorry to see her go; but as I
locked the door of the boutique below I felt strangely chilled.

Robert did not return that night. Jacques was soon asleep, and
Cathie too, but I sat by the open window, listening for footsteps.

Early the next morning, Tuesday, the rioting began again.
I must have snatched a few hours of sleep, when I was wakened
once more by the tramping of feet, and shouting, and presently
someone thundering on the door. I thought it might be Raoul,
but it was a stranger.

"Open up . . . open up," he shouted. "Every working man is
needed on the streets today. We're to carry the riot across the
bridges to the left bank. Open up, open up . . ."

I shut the window, and heard him thundering next door, and
so on, into the rue St. Honoré. He was soon followed by others,
yelling and shouting, and as the day lengthened we could hear

the crowds first in one quarter, then in another, with increasing sound of shooting, and the riding to and fro of the cavalry.

There was no sign of our midwife today. Either she had joined the crowds or was bolted within doors like ourselves, for no one seemed to be abroad who had not some part in the disturbances. Jacques, craning out of his own small window high in the roof, said he had seen men with bandaged heads carrying others who were bleeding freely—whether this was his imagination or not I could not say.

We had been two days now without fresh food, and our bread was finished, but I dared not leave the house to go to the market for fear of the riots. Cathie awoke and seemed hungry, which I thought a good sign. I made her some soup, but she was instantly sick when she had swallowed it, and complained of pain something similar to the labour pains of yesterday. The pain increased as the day wore on, and she seemed much weaker. I did not know what to do, for I saw that she was losing a lot of blood, and this did not seem to be right. I could only tear up more linen to staunch the flow.

Jacques, now that his mother no longer moaned as she had done the day before, was content to lean from the window, shouting to me now and again that the sound of the rioters was increasing or decreasing, as the case might be, and he would cry out, "I can hear the troops—I can hear the jangle of cavalry, and the horses. I wish I could see them". As each musket shot echoed in the distance, "Crack . . ." he kept shouting, in high delight, ". . . crack . . . crack . . . crack . . ."

Cathie was now deathly pale. It was once more between seven and eight in the evening, and she had lain still without moving since three in the afternoon. Jacques became tired of his game of "Crack . . . crack . . ." and demanded his supper. I made some more soup, but we had no bread to dab into it, and he continued to complain of hunger. Then, for he was only eight years old and had been penned indoors since Sunday, he decided to run up and down the stairs between the boutique and the upper rooms where we were living, and this sound seemed to me now more deafening than the distant rioting and firing that came from St. Antoine.

There was an acrid smell upon the air of burning straw—houses must be ablaze somewhere, or else it was the powder in the soldiers' muskets—and all the while Jacques kept running up and down the stairs, jumping from one step to another, and it grew dusk once more in Cathie's room, and I knelt by her bed holding her limp hand in mine.

Once again we heard the footsteps of the stragglers returning to our quarter—those who had gone forth to watch the riots—and at last there came a rattle on the door. Jacques gave a great shout of excitement, "It's my father come home!" and ran down the stairs to let him in.

I rose from Cathie's bedside and lit the candles, and I heard Robert laughing and talking with the boy below. I went and stood at the head of the stairs with a candle in my hands, and looked down upon my brother.

"Did Raoul not bring you word yesterday?" I asked.

He glanced up the stairs, smiling, and began to climb towards me, with Jacques at his heels.

"Word?" he said. "Of course he did not bring me word! There have been 3,000 men or more between here and the rue Traversière for the past thirty-six hours. I did well to get back here tonight. Well, they've destroyed Réveillon's property, and Henriot's too, and done heaven knows how much damage besides—when a Paris crowd gets roused there are no half-measures. I watched most of it from my windows in the laboratory, and a fine sight it was too, with the crowd shouting, 'Vive le Tiers Etat!', 'Vive Necker!'—though what the Third Estate or the minister have to do with the riots I cannot say! Anyway, poor fellows, dozens of them paid for this with their lives when the military fired on them. At least twenty dead and more than fifty wounded, from what I saw, and that was only in the rue Traversière."

He had now reached the top of the stairs and stood beside me.

"Where's Cathie?" he asked. "Why the darkness?"

We went into the bedroom together. I took the candle to the bedside, and I said to him, "We've been alone here since last night. I have not known what to do."

I let the light shine down on Cathie's face, and it was waxen white. Robert bent over and took her hand, and then he said, "O! Mon Dieu . . . Mon Dieu . . . Mon Dieu . . ." three times, just like that, and turned to me. "She's dead, Sophie, can't you see?"

Outside there was still the sound of tramping feet as the last of the straggling crowd made their way home. A group of them were laughing and singing:

> "Vive Louis Seize
> Vive ce roi vaillant,
> Monsieur Necker,
> Notre bon duc d'Orléans!"

Jacques came running into the room and climbed the window-sill, calling "Crack . . . crack . . ." after the marching men. Then the sound of the singing died away down the rue St. Honoré.

EIGHT

MY FIRST INSTINCT was to take Jacques away from the unrest of Paris and home with me to le Chesne-Bidault, but Robert, after the first shock of Cathie's death, said he could not bear to part with the boy, and that the pair of them would lodge for the time with Monsieur and Madame Fiat, Cathie's parents, who now lived in the rue Petits Piliers in les Halles, within easy distance of the boutique at the Palais-Royal. The Fiats, having complained originally that they were too old to care for their grandchild during Cathie's confinement, were now bowed down by remorse, and as anxious to have Jacques with them now as they had been reluctant before. Nevertheless, it was with a heavy heart that I bade good-bye to the little fellow, and to my brother too, who still hardly realised the loss that had come upon him.

"I shall work hard," he told me, when he saw me to the diligence. "There is no other cure for grief." But I could not help wondering whether it was some ploy in the affairs of the duc d'Orléans that concerned him, rather than the creation of glass and porcelain in his laboratory.

As I journeyed south-west from the capital, the talk in the diligence was all of the Réveillon riots, and how curiously they had arisen. Not one of the manufacturer's own men had joined the riot, apparently—they were all workmen from rival foundries, along with men from other trades, locksmiths, joiners, and dockers, while two had been arrested from the royal glass factory in the rue de Reuilly, only a short distance from my brother's laboratory in the rue Traversière.

I kept silent, but was all ears for information, especially when one fellow-traveller, well-dressed and with an air of authority, said he had had it from a cousin employed as an official in the

Châtelet that many of those arrested were carrying coins with the effigy of the duc d'Orléans upon them.

"One does not know what to believe," echoed the traveller opposite me. "My brother-in-law tells me that members of the clergy, disguised as ordinary citizens, were bribing onlookers to join the riots."

This, I thought grimly, should be recounted to Michel . . .

The diligence put me down at la Ferté-Bernard, where I had an uncomfortable wait for a half-hour or so at the Petit Chapeau Rouge, as my conveyance had been ahead of time. This small hostelry was the meeting-place of all the vagabonds in our part of the country: hawkers, tinkers, pedlars and mountebanks of all description, who used to earn a precarious living by knocking on farmhouse doors and selling worthless articles, trinkets, almanachs, and so on.

I waited in the small room set aside for passengers on the diligence, but I could catch some of the talk behind, where the drinks were served, and it seemed that Paris had not been alone in having riots. There had been insurrections at Nogent too, and at Bellême. I caught a glimpse of one fellow who appeared to be blind—until he raised his black patch and I perceived that he could see as well as anyone else, but they would disguise themselves thus to win sympathy when begging. He kept hammering the floor with his stick and shouting, "They should seize all the grain-carts and hang the drivers; in that way we wouldn't starve."

I could not bear to think of good Durocher, and others of our workmen, being misled by men like these.

Presently François and Michel arrived to fetch me, and, like all stay-at-homes when a traveller returns, they were more interested in giving me their news than in hearing mine. Cathie's death, the Paris riots, these, after quick expressions of sympathy, were soon brushed aside, and I had to hear how many seasonal farm-labourers in outlying districts had been told there was no work for them, and were now going about in bands terrorising the neighbourhood. Farm animals were being mutilated in revenge, and early crops uprooted, and the wandering marauders were being joined by others from further west, from Brittany and the coast, as destitute as themselves.

"These men are brigands," declared François, "who think nothing of coming by night and rousing the entire household to obtain money. We shall soon have to establish a militia in every parish."

"Unless we j-join the brigands," said Michel. "Most of our fellows would d-do so, if I gave the word."

So I was back again to privation and distress and the poor state of trade; perhaps it was as well I had not brought young Jacques with me after all. Yet as I leant out of my window that night, and breathed the good sweet air, fragrant with blossom from the orchard below, I was thankful to be home again, under my own roof, and away from the fearful murmur of that Paris crowd, the memory of which would haunt me night after night during the months to come.

My brother Robert, when he wrote, said little of his own feelings, or of his son's; once more it was the political pulse in the capital that preoccupied him. He had managed by some means or other to be on the fringe of the crowd when the States General assembled at Versailles on May the 5th, and so heard the first reports from eye-witnesses within. What troubled him most was that the deputies of the Third Estate were all dressed soberly in black, and, according to him, made a sorry showing beside the high dignitaries of the Church and the lavish costumes of the aristocracy.

"What is more, they were all penned up in an enclosure by themselves like a lot of cattle," he wrote, "while the aristocracy and the clergy surrounded the King. It was a deliberate affront to the bourgeoisie. The duc d'Orléans received a tumultuous welcome, and the King and Necker had a big ovation too, but the Queen was almost ignored, and they say she looked very pale and never smiled once. As to the speeches, they were disappointing. The Archbishop of Aix, speaking for the clergy, made a good impression, and even produced a wretched piece of black bread to show what appalling stuff the poorest people had to eat. But he was quite eclipsed by one of the deputies of the Third Estate, a young lawyer called Robespierre—I wonder if Pierre has heard of him?—who suggested that the Archbishop would do better if he told his fellow-clergy to join forces with the patriots who were friends to the people, and that if they wanted to help they might set an example by giving up some of their own luxurious way of living, and returning to the simple ways of the founder of their faith.

"I can imagine how Pierre would have applauded this speech! Depend upon it, we shall hear more of this fellow."

Meanwhile, we had the furnace going again, but not more than three days during the week, and some of our younger workmen took themselves off to look for employment elsewhere until trade should improve. I hated to see them drift away, for there was little likelihood of their finding anything beyond casual work on the land, hay-making and so on, and they would only add to the numbers of vagrants wandering the countryside.

The agonies of the winter were over, thank heaven, and our small community was not so sorely tried, but every day came news of more unrest and disturbance from all parts of the country, and it seemed to me that the meeting of the States General in Versailles had so far achieved nothing. Pierre, as usual, was full of optimism when he came to see us at the end of June. He brought with him his good-natured wife, and his two boys whom he was bringing up à la Jean-Jacques. They did not know their alphabet, ate with their fingers, and were as wild as hawks, but lovable enough.

I remember we were taking advantage of the weather that day, and carrying the hay to the barns beside the master's house.

"Agreed, there is deadlock at the moment," said Pierre, whistling to his boys to cease tumbling down the shocks of hay which had been so carefully stacked, "but the Third Estate have at least formed themselves into a National Assembly, a show of force has failed to disband them, and the King will be obliged to agree to a new Constitution. None of the deputies will return until this is achieved. You have heard the oath they swore on the 23rd? 'Never to separate until such time as the Constitution be firmly established.' What I would have given to have been there! This is the voice of the true France."

He went on whistling to his boys, and they continued to ignore him.

"The King is ill-advised, more's the pity," said François. "If it were he alone, the Assembly would have no trouble. It's the Court party who do the damage, and the Queen especially."

"B-b-bitch," exploded Michel.

How many other families, I wondered, were discussing this same subject, and echoing the same gossip, throughout the country this same day.

"Call her what you will," I said to Michel. "Do not forget she lost her little boy barely three weeks ago."

It was true. I, like the rest of the women at the glass-house, had been shocked to hear of the Dauphin's death on the 2nd of June, a child only a few months younger than my nephew Jacques.

"If you think," I went on, "that a mother cares about politics at such a moment . . ."

"Then why doesn't she s-stop interfering," said Michel, "and let this c-country govern itself?"

I could not match his arguments, nor Pierre's either, when he began to side with Michel. It seemed to me presumption on our part to think we knew anything of what went on in high places. Here was Pierre laying down the law about what the King should say to the Assembly, or what the Assembly should say to the King, and yet he could not order his own unruly boys to come down from off the hay-shocks. My mother would have done so and boxed the ears of the pair of them.

Another letter came from Robert in the first week in July. There had been great excitement at the Palais-Royal. Supporters of the duc d'Orléans (who, incidentally, had taken his seat as an ordinary citizen of the Third Estate) had encouraged the crowd to free eleven guardsmen from the Abbaye prison—the guardsmen had been imprisoned in the first place for refusing to fire on demonstrators on the 23rd of June—and in many cafés and restaurants the French Guards were fraternizing with the unruly crowds, telling them, if trouble came, that they would never fire on fellow Frenchmen.

"They say," continued Robert, "that foreign troops have already entered the country to support the Court party, should they be needed, and many of the bridges are already guarded. The latest rumour is that the King's brother, the comte d'Artois, and the Queen have had a secret tunnel built under the Bastille which is to admit hundreds of troops and ammunition, and at a given word—if the National Assembly don't behave themselves—the troops will set light to a mine powerful enough to destroy them and almost all of Paris."

If this was true, though I could hardly credit it, then there was only one thing to do, and that was for Robert to leave the capital at once, and bring Jacques with him, and the Fiats too, if they were willing to travel.

"W-what did I tell you?" said Michel grimly, after I had read the letter aloud to him and François. "That d-damned Court party and the aristocracy will do anything to b-break up the National Assembly. Why don't the people of P-Paris get out into the streets and f-fight? If it were happening in Le Mans, I'd soon be on the s-streets with the whole of le Chesne-Bidault b-behind me."

I wrote at once to Robert, imploring him to leave Paris, though I had very little hope of his agreeing to do so. If he was still in the pay of Laclos or others of the duc d'Orléans' entourage, it would seem as if their supreme moment might be about to strike.

The hideous story of the Queen's plot to blow up the National Assembly, if not the whole of Paris, had reached Le Mans—Pierre was full of it when Michel and François went into town the following week. It appeared that one of the deputies had confirmed the tale in a letter to an Elector, the Electors being men of authority in every district who had voted for the deputies of the Third Estate. "Paris is surrounded by troops," Pierre told his brother and my husband, and for once his equanimity seemed shaken. "The wife of a deputy arrived back yesterday who had heard on the best authority that the Prince de Condé has only to give the word and 40,000 troops will occupy the capital, with orders to fire on anyone who supports the Assembly. If this happens there will be a massacre."

The story in its turn was contradicted by Edmé, whose husband, Monsieur Pomard, in his capacity as contractor to the Abbey of St. Vincent, had attended a dinner at the Oratoire given by the officers of the Dragons de Chartres to welcome back their colonel, the vicomte de Valence. According to the vicomte, morale in the capital had never been higher, and the duc d'Orléans and Necker were still the men of the hour.

"Of course," Edmé told Michel, "the vicomte de Valence is one of the duc d'Orléans' supporters. He is married to the daughter of the duke's ex-mistress, Madame de Genlis, and is the lover of the duke's stepmother. You can't be more involved in a family situation than that!"

Edmé had some of Robert's talent for searching out gossip, and when Michel repeated the tale I felt relieved that we lived in the country and not in Le Mans.

"I don't give a f-fig for the gossip," said Michel. "The point is that I trust n-none of the aristocracy, whether they support the d-duc d'Orléans or not. As to that ass P-Pomard, he'd best keep his mouth shut, along with the damned m-monks at St. Vincent."

My husband and brother returned home to le Chesne-Bidault with these various tales, and a parting shot from Pierre that if trouble broke out in Paris the patriots and Electors in Le Mans would form a committee and take over the municipality, with orders to every able-bodied citizen to enrol at the hotel de ville and form a people's militia.

"And there will be no trouble," he added significantly, "from the Dragons de Chartres."

Which, I thought to myself, bore out Edmé's gossip after all.

As it happened, we were more concerned at le Chesne-Bidault with the ripening corn in our farm acres than with the preparations for possible disturbances in Le Mans. The bands of vagrants roaming the countryside were trespassing on the farms by night and cutting the wheat and barley. Whether they intended to eat it or hoard it nobody knew—but we all feared for our crops, for should there be a disaster to this year's harvest then, without question, next winter we should starve.

Michel and François posted men as sentries every night to guard the fields, but even so we would go to bed uneasy, for the vagrants were said to be armed. They were also raiding timber stacks in the forests, to sell as fuel, no doubt, against the colder weather to come, and this was an equal threat to our livelihood; if our stocks of timber were purloined, we should not be able to keep the furnace fire alight. Already in the forest of Bonnétable this had happened. Pierre's wife came from Bonné-table; we had the story direct from her.

"There's n-nothing for it," said Michel, "but to have patrols of men, d-day and night, keeping watch b-between here and Montmirail."

He and François would take it in turn to go out on night patrol, and during those first ten days in July I would lie awake, alone and anxious if my husband had gone; but if he were by my side then I would worry about Michel, standing sentinel out there somewhere in the forest, watching and waiting for the brigands who did not come.

It must have been the Monday or Tuesday, the 13th or 14th of July, I forget which, when François brought the news from Mondoubleau that the Court party had persuaded the King to dismiss Necker from his post as Controller of Finance, and the minister had gone into exile. Paris was in a state of siege, customs barriers outside the city were being burnt down or overthrown, and the customs officers forced to fly for their lives—the people everywhere were out of control and raiding the ammunition de-pots for arms.

"The worst of it is," said François, "that the whole of the underworld of Paris has been let loose upon the countryside. Prisoners, beggars, thieves, murderers—all the unemployed of the capital—they are making south, leaving honest citizens to fight it out with the Court party and the aristocracy."

François had driven in from Mondoubleau in one of the foundry waggons, and both he and his horses were sweating with heat and exhaustion. In a moment he was surrounded by a group of workmen, with Michel amongst them.

"What is it? What has happened? Who told you of it?"

He repeated his tale, and almost immediately Michel started giving directions to the men to split into groups—all work at the foundry was to cease until further orders—and these groups were to go to le Plessis-Dorin, Montmirail, St. Avit, le Gault, and west to Vibraye, to inform the people in these communes what was happening in Paris, and to prepare against brigands. Another group would stay at le Chesne-Bidault in charge of the foundry. Either he or François would go to la Ferté-Bernard to seek further news when the change-coach arrived from Paris.

It was my business, naturally, to counsel the families, calling upon all of them in turn, warning them not to stir from the foundry precincts, nor to let the children wander out of earshot. As I repeated my warnings, and saw their anxiety, I myself felt seized with their apprehension; doubt and uncertainty were in the air, we none of us knew what might happen next, and the thought of the brigands penetrating so far south, burning and pillaging as they went, filled all of us with terror.

No more news came to us that night, other than what we had already heard through François from Mondoubleau. Two days passed without direct contact with Paris, save that there had been fighting in the streets and many killed—some said the Bastille had been blown up by gunpowder, others that the English Prime Minister Pitt had sent hundreds of troops into France to support the aristocracy and chase the brigands into the French country-side to disrupt communications.

On Saturday, the 18th of July, it was the turn of François to go into la Ferté-Bernard to obtain news from those who might be travelling by the diligence plying from Paris to Le Mans, descending at Bellême and changing coaches to la Ferté. The thought of staying alone at the master's house, guarded by a small group of workmen, with François away and Michel on patrol in the forest, was more than I could bear.

"I'm coming with you," I told my husband. "I'd rather face the dangers on the road than wait here, hour after hour, without even the roar of the furnace fire to keep me company."

He took one of the small covered carrioles and I climbed up on the seat beside him like a market-woman. If we were stopped by vagrants they would find nothing in the cart but ourselves, and the worst they could do would be to overturn it and force us to walk home.

We found la Ferté-Bernard in an uproar. No one was working, everyone was in the streets. The bells of Notre-Dame-des-Marais were sounding the tocsin. It was the first time in my life to hear church bells peal an alarm instead of a call to prayer, and the incessant sound was far more agitating and conducive to fear than a bugle call or a roll of drums.

We went to the Petit Chapeau Rouge to put up the carriole. Although there were no vagrants there, the crowds were thick in the street outside, and François agreed with me that many of them were not local townsfolk, but strangers.

Suddenly there was a movement amongst the crowd, which divided, and we saw the change-coach approaching through the town from Bellême. We ran towards it, ourselves part of the crowd, seized with the same passionate hunger for news, and then as the driver reined in his horses, and the coach shuddered to a standstill, the first passengers broke from within, to be immediately surrounded by a mob of questioners.

A slim figure caught my attention as he paused an instant before descending, giving his hand to a child.

"It's Robert," I cried, catching at François, "it's Robert and Jacques."

We pushed forward towards the coach, and at last succeeded in reaching the passengers beside it. There was my brother, calm, smiling, answering a dozen questions at once, while little Jacques sprang into my arms.

Robert nodded to us. "I'll be with you directly," he called. "First I have a letter here from the mayor of Dreux that I must deliver in person to the mayor of la Ferté-Bernard."

The crowd drew back, eyeing François and myself with a new respect because of our connection with this seemingly important traveller, and we followed in Robert's train, Jacques clutching my hand, while my brother and a group of men in authority walked to the hotel de ville.

We could get no sense out of Jacques. There had been fighting in Paris for two days, he said, there were men wounded and killed everywhere, and we had to listen to the news from other passengers, who were now telling the tale to the surrounding crowd.

The Bastille had been stormed and taken by the people of Paris. The Governor had been killed. The King's brother, the comte d'Artois, had fled, also the King's cousin, the Prince de Condé, and the de Polignacs, the friends of the Queen. The

National Assembly was in control of the capital, with a citizen militia to protect it under the command of General La Fayette, hero of the American wars.

François turned to me, stupefied.

"We've beaten them," he said. "It can't be possible. We've beaten them."

People around us began shouting and cheering, waving their arms and laughing, and from nowhere, it seemed, the driver of the coach, a great, red-faced fellow, began distributing amongst the crowd cockades of rose and blue, which he had brought with him from the diligence at Bellême. "Come on," he was shouting, "help yourselves. These are the colours of the duc d'Orléans, who with the help of the people of Paris has beaten the aristocracy," and everyone pushed forward to snatch the colours. The enthusiasm took hold of us. François, being tall, reached over the heads of several and secured a cockade, which he gave me, laughing, and I did not know whether to laugh or to cry as someone shouted "Vive le Tiers Etat . . . Vive l'Assemblée . . . Vive le duc d'Orléans . . . Vive le Roi."

Then we saw Robert come out of the hotel de ville—he was still surrounded by Electors and other officials—but they none of them responded to the crowd. They were talking anxiously amongst themselves, and a murmur began to spread from one to the other of us waiting in the place beyond. "The danger isn't over yet . . . the fighting continues . . ."

Then the mayor of la Ferté came forward and held up his hand for silence, and we could just catch his words above the murmur of the crowd: "The National Assembly are in control of Paris, but an army of brigands, 6,000 strong, is said to have fled from the capital, fully armed. Every man must make himself available for a citizen's militia. Women and children and the infirm and elderly are to remain within doors."

Now joy had turned to panic, and the people strove this way and that to free themselves from the crowd, to offer their services, to go home, to get away—no one knew which—and the tocsin kept ringing from Notre-Dame-des-Marais so that the mayor's voice was drowned by the sound.

Robert pushed through from the hotel de ville towards us, and we made our way to the carriole at the Petit Chapeau Rouge. There were others trying to do the same thing, and much confusion, with the horses restless and stamping, and Robert kept calling out to everyone, "Warn the outlying parishes and communes to sound the alarm from the churches. Forewarned is forearmed. Vive la nation . . . Vive le duc d'Orléans." His words seemed to increase the confusion rather than allay it, and I heard people asking, "What has happened? Is the duc d'Orléans to be king?"

At last we were safely aboard the carriole, with François urging the horse forward and out of the town, and so down the road to Montmirail and the forest beyond.

By now it was dusk, and the road home seemed dark and forbidding. Poor Jacques, still clutching fast to my hand, kept saying, "What if the brigands come, what shall we do, will they kill us?"

Robert bade his boy be silent—I had never heard him so sharp with the child before—and then he told us how the Bastille had been stormed four days earlier. Some nine hundred persons had taken the fortress, and forced the Governor to surrender. "The people cut off his head with a butcher's knife later," whispered my brother. And yes, it was true, there had been a plot by the aristocracy to overthrow the National Assembly, but it had failed, and the comte d'Artois and all his friends and the Prince de Condé had fled to the frontier, "taking with them, so I hear," said Robert, "all the gold in the kingdom."

"But the brigands?" I asked, as fearful as Jacques. "What is the truth about the brigands."

"No one knows," replied my brother with strange satisfaction. "In Dreux they say that 6,000 were on their way from the other side of Paris, and had joined up with Pitt's mercenaries. That is why I spread the news in every town at which we stopped from Dreux to Bellême. The driver of the diligence has instructions to report it as he continues his journey to Le Mans."

I thought of Pierre and his wife and children, who might be at Bonnétable, through which the diligence would pass. Pierre would at once leave for Le Mans himself, to offer his services to the municipality, or rather to the committee which had vowed to take it over. Yet surely it was in the forest of Bonnétable that we had first heard of brigands?

"Robert . . ." I asked, taking my brother's arm, "what do you see for the future? Where will this all end?"

My brother laughed. "Don't talk about the end," he said. "This is only the beginning. This isn't just another Réveillon riot, you know. What has happened in Paris will happen throughout the country. This is revolution."

Revolution. I thought of my mother at St. Christophe. She was alone in her small farm-property, except for her servants and the cowman and his family near by. Who would look after my mother?

Robert shrugged aside my fears. "Don't concern yourself," he said. "They are all patriots in the Touraine. My mother will be the first to wear the blue and rose cockade."

"But the brigands?" I persisted.

"Ah yes," replied my brother, "I had forgotten the brigands . . ."

By now Jacques had fallen asleep on my shoulder, and I sat stiff and straight to support him during the remaining drive to le Chesne-Bidault. We had passed Montmirail, and were through the forest and nearly home, when a group of men sprang up from the side of the road and surrounded us.

Thank God—it was Michel and his patrol. For a moment we paused for Robert to seize his hand and give him the news; then, as we were about to proceed and turn down the road to the foundry, Michel said, "The brigands have been seen. One of the women was gathering sticks in a clearing, and she heard a movement and saw a dozen men, their faces blacked, crouching in the undergrowth. She ran back to the foundry to give warning. I sent word to the commune to give the alarm."

Even as he spoke, across the warm night air came the thin high summons from the church bell at le Plessis-Dorin.

NINE

I BELIEVE NONE OF us slept that night except Jacques and Robert.
Jacques dropped into the bed I had prepared for him with all
the exhaustion of a child who had been more than ten hours
on the road, and his father—after showing us the pistol concealed
under his coat—observed that, as one who had watched the
storming of the Bastille, it would take more than a dozen black-
faced brigands to prevent him from sleeping. For myself, I
dragged my way upstairs and undressed and got into bed, but
the sleep for which I yearned would not come to me. I could
hear François moving about below, giving orders to another patrol of workmen to relieve Michel and his band in the forest, and
this going to and fro in the foundry yard disturbed the farm
animals nearby. The cows lowed, the horses were restless in
their stalls—for since the disturbances began we had not dared
let any of the cattle graze by night.

Michel must have warned them at Montmirail and at Mel-
leray, for the bells from these churches sounded the tocsin as
well as from le Plessis. I could hear the peal coming from beyond
the forest, the deeper note of Montmirail on the hill sounding
more urgent and more ominous than the little reedy warning
from our own parish.

I kept thinking of the brigands, thousands of them, so Robert
said, from the prisons and the back streets of Paris, hungry,
armed, and desperate, let loose on our countryside, some of them
even now crouching in the forest where Michel and his band
had been patrolling, biding their time to seize our crops, slaughter our beasts.

Presently François came upstairs and lay down by my side,
but he did not undress, and he too laid a pistol on the chair
beside him.

Perhaps I slept—I have no idea how long. I know I awoke heavy-eyed and weary. Nor did my condition make fatigue any easier to bear, for I was by now seven months gone with my first child.

I found Jacques awake and downstairs and demanding his breakfast from Madame Verdelet in the kitchen, and my two brothers, with my husband, in conference in the master's room. They fell silent at my entrance, and ironically I enquired whether I had disturbed a Freemasons' gathering.

"You don't know, Madame Duval," said my brother Robert with a smile, "how near you are to the truth. We should have posted a watch on the door as we do usually in our Lodges. No harm done, though. Our discussion is finished."

He got up from his chair and began parading the room in his usual restless fashion. I glanced at the others. My husband François looked thoughtful. Michel, on the contrary, was tense and excited, with his eyes on his eldest brother.

"Well, come on, let's g-get on with it," he said impatiently, "no point in s-sitting here. The s-sooner everything is organised the b-better for everyone."

Robert held up his hand. "Keep calm, keep calm," he replied. "I leave you and François to work out the business of your own patrols between you. As to myself and Jacques, all I ask is the loan of the carriole, which I will return to you here within a few days."

"Agreed," said Michel. "I'll s-see about it s-straight away." He seized the excuse to be off and out of the room, while I saw François watching me doubtfully.

"What has been decided?" I asked suspiciously. "You don't mean to take the child off again before he has recovered from his journey and his fright?"

"Jacques is as tough as I am," Robert said, "and none the worse for yesterday. It is my intention to take him today to my mother at St. Christophe . . ." St. Christophe, a journey of some 15 leagues or more, and heaven knew how many thousand brigands at loose about the countryside.

"Are you mad?" I protested. "When we none of us know the state of the roads between here and the Touraine?"

"The risk will be mine," said Robert, "and I foresee no difficulties. In any event, we shall be ahead of the brigands, and part of my purpose in travelling south will be to alert the countryside."

I thought so. The safety of his boy meant little at the present time. His mission was to sow disunity, and whether the object was to satisfy his own warped humour or to obey the orders given by the duc d'Orléans' entourage did not matter to me. I cared only for my nephew of eight years old.

"If," I said to my brother, "you intend passing coins with your patron's head upon them as an encouragement to violence, as you did before the Réveillon riots, that is your affair. But for mercy's sake don't drag your son into the business."

My brother raised his eyebrows. "The Réveillon riots?" he repeated. "What in the world has a workmen's rising, easily quelled, to do with the revolution of the whole nation?"

"I don't know," I answered, "but do not tell me the two are disconnected, and that your friends have no interest in fermenting trouble."

Once again I saw my husband look uncomfortable—I was reminded of the time before our marriage when he hoped to shield Michel from disgrace—but Robert laughed, in his inimitable fashion, and patted my cheek.

"My sweet Sophie," he said, "don't confuse the duc d'Orléans, whose only desire is to serve the people, with princes like the comte d'Artois and the comte de Provence, the King's brothers, whose one interest is to hold fast to privilege and damn the bourgeoisie. They are the men who seek to spread disorder through France, not the duc d'Orléans."

"In that case," I said, "you must be accepting pay from their agents too."

Had I thrown a brick at his head he could not have looked more startled. He stared at me for a moment, but quickly recovered his composure and shrugged his shoulders.

"My little sister is overwrought," he said lightly, then turning to my husband he added, "If you knew your business properly she would be hanging about your neck instead of arguing with her brother."

This put me on my mettle. François would never desert me in my hour of need as Robert had deserted Cathie.

"I stayed by your wife in a dangerous hour," I told my brother, "and I will stay by your son. If you insist on taking Jacques to St. Christophe today, then you can have me with you for the journey."

At this François came forward, protesting that I was in no fit state for a long day on bad roads. There was no need for panic, he said; the report about brigands being seen in the district the night before had been a false alarm. I should respect his wishes if I stayed at le Chesne-Bidault.

"And you," I asked him, "what are your plans for today?"

He hesitated. "The parishes in the district must be alerted," he said, after a moment. "Trouble may come tomorrow, or the day after. As Robert says, forewarned is forearmed."

"In other words," I said, "you and Michel have both agreed to play Robert's game. Instead of blowing glass, you will blow rumour across the countryside. In the circumstances, I should prefer to be with my mother at St. Christophe."

So . . . Robert must be pleased with himself. He had succeeded in causing trouble between husband and wife, besides sowing dissension between Paris and la Ferté-Bernard.

"Your first tiff?" he enquired. "No matter, a few days absent from one another in these early months works wonders. I shall be pleased to have you as nurse to Jacques, Sophie, providing you keep your mouth shut on the journey and leave me to do the talking."

We left as soon as I had gathered a few things together, summoned Jacques from playing in the furnace yard, and given directions to Madame Verdelet to see to things in my few days of absence.

She was much concerned at my going. "Is it because of the danger?" she asked. "Are the brigands near us after all?"

I consoled her as well as I could, but as we drove away from the glass-house I saw many of the families watching me from their dwellings hard by, and I had an uneasy feeling that they believed I was deserting them.

As we passed through le Plessis-Dorin we saw the curé, Monsieur Cosnier, standing outside the church with a group of his parishioners. Robert drew rein to have a few moments' conversation with him.

"Is it true the brigands are within a few miles of us here?" asked the curé anxiously.

"No one knows," replied my brother. "It is essential to take every precaution. These vagabonds will stop at nothing. It might be safest to have all the women and children within the church, and then sound the tocsin without ceasing should you be attacked."

As we turned on to the Mondoubleau road I looked round behind our carriole and saw the curé giving directions to the excited group around him.

For myself, I could think of nothing more likely to cause panic and consternation amongst a crowd of women than to be shut up within a church without their menfolk, and to have the incessant clanging of that same church's bell sounding its warning from the belfry above their heads.

At Mondoubleau we fell in with one of our journeymen-carriers, who told us that word had come the night before via Cloyes and Châteaudun, from the diligence on the Paris route through Chartres to Blois, that brigands had been heard of in thousands, and it was all a plot of the aristocracy to break the power of the Third Estate. The tocsin was ringing here, just as it had been in our small parish of le Plessis-Dorin, and people were standing about in the streets in anxious groups, not knowing what to do.

"Is all safe at le Chesne-Bidault?" asked the journeyman, surprised, no doubt, to see me in the carriole beside my brother and nephew.

Before I could reassure him, Robert shook his head doubtfully and answered, "Brigands were seen in the forest there last night. We have put a strong guard round the foundry itself, for these villains are said to be burning everything on sight."

He spoke with such sincerity that I was instantly afraid: had my husband's words earlier that the reports were false been said to soothe me? Perhaps the foundry was in truth surrounded, and François had allowed me to go with Robert and Jacques to ensure my greater safety.

"You told me . . ." I began fearfully, but Robert whipped up the horse and we were once more on our way, leaving the honest journeyman staring after us in great perplexity.

"What is the truth?" I asked, in renewed agony of doubt—for had I, after all, done wrong in leaving my husband to his possible fate at le Chesne-Bidault? Were hordes of brigands even now setting fire to my home and everything I held dear?

"The truth?" repeated Robert. "Nobody ever knows the truth in this world."

He jerked the reins, whistling a tune between his teeth, and I was reminded of that time long ago when he had dispatched the consignment of glass to Chartres without my mother's knowledge, giving a masked ball on the proceeds. Was he playing upon my fear today, and the fear of hundreds like me, just as he had once played upon my mother's ignorance—and all to inflate his sense of power?

I glanced at him as he sat beside me, the reins in his hands, his eyes on the road, with the boy Jacques behind his back, and I realised a fact I had forgotten because of his eternally youthful appearance—that my eldest brother was now nearly forty years old. None of his trials and troubles had done anything for him except to make him, if it were possible, more of an adventurer than ever before: one who gambled, not only with his own and with other people's money, but with human failings as well.

"Take care," my father used to say, when first instructing Robert in the art of blowing glass. "Control is of supreme importance. One false movement and the expanding glass will be shattered." I remember the dawning excitement in my brother's eyes—could he, dared he, go beyond the limits proscribed? It was as though he longed for the explosion that would wreck his own first effort and his father's temper into the bargain. There comes this supreme moment to the glass-blower, when he can either breathe life and form into the growing bubble slowly taking shape before his eyes, or shatter it into a thousand fragments. The decision is the blower's, and the judgement too;

the throwing of the judgement in the balance made the excitement—for my brother.

"At St. Calais," said Robert suddenly, his voice breaking in upon my thoughts, "we may be first with the news. In any event, it would be wise to call in at the hotel de ville."

I was sure then that I was right. Whether he was in the pay of the duc d'Orléans' entourage, of the King's brothers, even of the National Assembly itself, was not of primary importance to my brother. What had driven him from Paris to le Plessis-Dorin and on to the road today was that same desire for self-intoxication which had made him buy the glass-house of Rougemont twelve years before. He was drunk with a power that he did not possess.

We found St. Calais quiet. All seemed as usual. Yes, said a passer-by, there had been talk of disturbances in Paris, but nobody had heard of brigands. My brother left the reins in my hands and was absent for some twenty minutes at the hotel de ville.

Throughout the whole of that long, hot summer's day, as our road took us through one parish after another, with nearly all the inhabitants out working in the fields, there was no sign of agitation—only the dust we brought with us on our own wheels; yet whomsoever we passed, whether it was an aged man slumbering under the shade of a tree, or a woman standing at her door, Robert would hail them with the news that brigands were on their way south from Paris threatening the peace of the countryside.

At la Chartre, where we rested to bait our horse and to eat ourselves, we were met with an answering wave of rumour—Bretons in their thousands were marching inland from the coast. Here was a match for our own brigands, and I do not know who looked the more discomfited, Robert or myself. The brigands I had already doubted for some hours . . . but Bretons? Had we not already heard earlier in the year that in the west they were refusing to pay the salt tax, and many granaries had been pillaged and burnt? The tocsin was ringing in la Chartre, and there was all the confusion and commotion that we had witnessed the day before at la Ferté-Bernard.

"How did you hear the news here in la Chartre?" my brother

asked at the inn, as we sat down to our first mouthful since leaving le Chesne-Bidault early that morning. The innkeeper, who hardly knew whether to serve us or barricade his house from the approaching Bretons, informed us that the change-coach from Le Mans had reported it soon after seven o'clock that morning.

"They had the news from the Paris diligence late last night," said the innkeeper. "Brigands are travelling south from the capital, Bretons are marching from the coast. Between the two we shall be annihilated."

The driver of that diligence, I thought, had done his work well. We had now come full circle. The original rumour, breathed upon the air at Dreux, had gathered momentum.

"Now," I said to my brother, "are you satisfied?" And I told the distraught innkeeper that we had come that day from beyond Mondoubleau and had seen no brigands on the road.

"Perhaps not, madame," answered the man. "Brigands or Bretons, they are all the same, and will show small mercy to folk like us. But it is not only strangers who are uttering threats, but our own peasants too. The same change-coach that brought the news this morning brought information also that the carriage of two deputies of the aristocracy had been flung into the river at Savigné-l'Evêque, and the deputies themselves would have lost their lives had not someone in the neighbourhood offered them asylum."

Savigné-l'Evêque was the final stopping-place, after Bonnétable, for the Paris diligence before Le Mans.

"What were the names of the deputies?" asked my brother.

"The comte de Montesson and the marquis de Vassé," replied the innkeeper.

Both names were familiar to me by hearsay. They were deputies who had become unpopular in Le Mans because of their hostility to the Third Estate. Here, then, was an assault that could not be blamed on either brigands, Bretons, or the fertile imagination of the driver of the Paris diligence.

"Strange," murmured Robert. "The marquis de Vassé is a member of the Lodge of Parfait Estime. I should have thought . . ."

He left his sentence unfinished. Whether he meant to imply

that Freemasons should come unscathed through times of trouble I did not know, but it occurred to me that both rumours and revolutions might be among those things which rebound very frequently upon the heads of those who start them.

Le Chartre, with its sounding tocsin and agitated crowds, was no place in which to linger, and we were soon on the road again, past Marçon and through Dissay, and the lush rolling countryside of my mother's Touraine opened out on either side of us, the ripe corn golden in the light of the setting sun. Here were no black-faced brigands or swarthy Bretons, but the bent bodies of the harvesters scything their wheat and barley—for they were earlier with the harvest here than we were in the forest.

We drove out of the village of St. Christophe to my mother's small farm property l'Antinière, lying in a hollow, surrounded by its orchard and few acres; and although it was by now late in the evening my mother and her helpers were still out in the fields. I recognised her tall figure on the skyline. My brother hallooed, and we saw her turn and gaze down the field to the carriole, then slowly she began to walk down the field towards us, her hand above her head in recognition.

"I did not know," exclaimed young Jacques, surprised, "that my grandmother worked in the fields like a peasant."

In a moment she was with us, and I had climbed down from the carriole and was in her arms crying—whether from fatigue or joy or relief I did not know. In her arms was security, all that was stable of our old world, which had been so disrupted; against her heart was refuge from my own fears of the present, my own doubts of the future.

"That's enough, now, that's enough," she said, holding me close, and then releasing me with a pat on the shoulder as if I were a child younger than Jacques. "If you have come all the way from le Chesne-Bidault you are hungry, thirsty, and tired. We will see what Berthe can produce for us in the house. Jacques, you have grown. Robert, you look more irresponsible than ever. What are you doing here, and what is it all about?"

Yes, she had heard of the disturbances in Paris. She had heard that the first two Orders were making trouble for the Third Estate.

"What can you expect from people like that?" she asked. "They have had things their own way too long, and find it unpleasant to be challenged by others."

No, she knew nothing of the storming of the Bastille on the 14th of July, nor had she been warned against brigands.

"If any black-faced vagrants show their faces in this neighbourhood, they will get more than they bargained for," she said.

She looked at the fork leaning against her barn, and I believe she would have faced an army with this weapon, turning it from her door armed with the fork only, and her own determination.

By the time we had finished our explanations, she and Berthe between them had laid the table in the kitchen and spread a meal before our eyes—a great side of home-cured pork, and cheese, and bread baked in the oven, and even a bottle of home-brewed wine to wash it all down.

"So . . ." said my mother, sitting in her customary place at the head of the table, making me fancy we were under her supervision once again at the glass-house. "The National Assembly have the situation in hand and the King has promised a new Constitution. Why, then, so much commotion? Everybody should be well pleased."

"You forget the first two Orders," replied Robert, "the aristocracy and the clergy. They will not accept this without a struggle."

"Let them struggle," said my mother. "Meantime we can gather in the harvest. Wipe your mouth, Jacques, after drinking."

Robert told her about the plots of the aristocracy, the six thousand brigands ravaging the countryside. My mother remained unmoved.

"We have come through the hardest winter in living memory," she said. "Naturally there are vagrants wandering about demanding work. I employed three myself last week, and fed them too. They appeared grateful. If the Paris prisons have been opened, as you say, then people like you have all the more reason to remain in the capital now they have gone. The place should be more tranquil."

Whatever were the rumours my brother had brought with him

those many miles from Paris to la Ferté-Bernard and beyond, they had no effect upon the imperturbability of l'Antinière.

Robert had succeeded once in breaking down my mother's reserve, when he was imprisoned for fraud in La Force. He would not do so again, not even with the news of a revolution.

"As to you, Sophie," she said, fixing her eyes upon me in her usual direct fashion, "you have no business to be here at all with your baby due in eight weeks' time."

"I had hoped," I murmured, greatly daring, "that I might stay here with you and have the baby at l'Antinière."

"Out of the question," replied my mother. "Your place is with your husband at le Chesne-Bidault—besides, who would look after the families in your absence? I have never heard of such a thing. I will keep Jacques, if Robert wishes—the air is better here than in Paris, and I can feed him well, despite the hardships of the past months."

As always, she was in command of the situation and setting us to rights; even Robert was hard put to it to defend his action in leaving Paris. That he had done so for the greater security of his son did not impress my mother.

"I wonder you did not think of the security of your boutique," she remarked, "if the Palais-Royal is now the centre of activity you describe. I should fear for my stock. Have you left anyone in charge?"

She accepted with raised eyebrows his reply that the boutique was being looked after by friends.

"I am glad to hear it," she said. "It is in times of trouble that we depend upon our friends. A few years ago they were lacking when you most needed them. Perhaps this revolution will change all that."

"Since my patron the duc d'Orléans will probably mediate between the King and the people of Paris, and become lieutenant-general of the kingdom, I sincerely hope so," replied my brother.

They faced each other across the table, the pair of them, like a couple of fighting cocks, and I have little doubt they would have been at it until midnight had not a new sound, familiar now to me but new to my mother, caused her to lift her head and listen.

"Hark!" she said. "Who in the world would be ringing the church bell at this time of the evening?"

The tocsin was sounding across the fields from St. Christophe. Jacques, tired by now, and overwrought, burst into tears and ran to my side. "It's the brigands," he said, "the brigands have followed us from Paris."

Even Robert looked astonished. We had seen no one to speak to when we had driven through the village earlier. My mother rose to her feet and called out to the cowman in the yard outside.

"See that the animals are within and all secure," she said. "And you had better bolt your own door too before going to bed."

She turned herself, and bolted the door of the house behind her.

"Brigands or not," she said, "there is no sense in being unprepared. The curé would never have given orders for the church bell to ring an alarm had he not received a warning of some sort. Word must have come through Château-du-Loir from Le Mans."

I was wrong to have expected peace even at l'Antinière. The driver of that diligence had done his work too well. Rumour and revolution had caught up with us once more.

TEN

WE REMAINED AT St. Christophe with my mother on Monday and Tuesday, and on Wednesday the 22nd of July, no brigands having been seen in our immediate neighbourhood, my brother decided to delay our return no further; but, instead of retracing our route through la Chartre and St. Calais, to go west by way of Le Mans, and there obtain the latest news from Paris.

"If the Electors in Le Mans have formed a committee to take over the municipality, Pierre will somehow be connected with it, we can be sure of that," said Robert, "and they will be in touch with the capital. I suggest we waste no further time here but leave at once."

I was reluctant to do so, but I felt I had no choice. My mother plainly thought it my duty to go back to le Chesne-Bidault, and I would rather face a thousand brigands than her disapproval. I had no qualms for young Jacques, who was already my mother's shadow, and was so eager to be out in the fields helping with the harvest that he could barely spare the few minutes necessary to bid his father good-bye.

Whether, as Pierre used to say, we are watched over by the Great Architect of the Universe, or, as my mother taught me, by the Blessed Virgin and all the Saints, I shall always think it providential and merciful that whoever plans our destiny hides our future from us. None of us knew that the little boy of eight years old would be twenty-two before he saw his father again, and how bitter the encounter would be. As for my mother, this was the last time she was to hold her son in her arms.

"You have lost your Cathie," she said to him. "Hold fast to what is left."

"Nothing is left," my brother replied. "That is why I brought you my son."

He was not smiling now, and he looked his forty years. Could his air of detachment be a façade after all? None of us knew how much of his youth had gone into the grave with Cathie.

"I will take great care of him," said my mother. "I wish I could believe you will take equal care of yourself."

We mounted the carriole and drove up the hill from l'Antinière on to the road. Looking back, we saw grandmother and grandson standing there hand-in-hand waving to us, and it was as though they represented all that was steadfast and enduring in past and future, while our own generation—Robert's and mine —lacked stability, and was at the mercy of events which might prove too strong for all of us.

"We are only a short distance from Chérigny, where I was born," said Robert, pointing left with his whip. "The marquis de Cherbon left no heir. I forgot to ask my mother who owns it now."

"Our cousins, the Renvoisés, still maintain the foundry after a fashion," I told him. "We can go and call on them, if you like."

Robert shook his head. "No," he said, "what's past is past. But the thought of that château and all it stands for will be with me until I die."

He whipped the horse to a smarter pace, and even now, I thought, I do not know whether my brother speaks from envy or nostalgia, whether the château of Chérigny was something he wished to possess, or to destroy.

We came to the market-town of Château-du-Loir, and immediately we were in the midst of rumour and counter-rumour. There were crowds standing beneath the mairie, and people were shouting, "Vive la nation . . . vive le Tiers Etat" in a bewildered fashion, as though the very words themselves served as a charm to ward off danger.

It was market-day, and there must have been some trouble, for stalls were overturned and chickens scattering in all directions, with several women weeping and one, bolder than her companions, shaking her fist at a group of men running towards the mairie.

Our carriole, strange to the town, became the centre of attention, and we were at once surrounded and asked our business, while one fellow seized hold of the horse's bridle, jerking it and forcing the poor animal backwards, shouting to us as he did so, "Are you for the Third Estate?"

"Certainly," answered my brother, "I'm cousin to a deputy. Let my horse alone." And he pointed to the rose and blue cockade that he had brought with him in the diligence from Paris, and had remembered to fix on the roof of the carriole.

"Put it in your hat, then, where everyone can see it," cried the man, and if Robert had not done so forthwith I believe they would have dragged him from his seat, though whether any of them knew the meaning of the word Third Estate, or what the colours stood for, was another matter. We were then asked why we travelled and whither we were bound—Robert had an answer for every question—but when he told them Le Mans another fellow in the crowd advised us to turn around and go back again to St. Christophe.

"Le Mans is surrounded on all sides by brigands," he told us. "They are ten thousand strong in the forest of Bonnétable. Every parish between here and the city has been alerted."

"We'll take the risk all the same," said Robert. "I am due to attend a meeting of Electors there this evening."

The word Electors had a great effect. The crowd fell back, and we were allowed to proceed. Someone called after us on no account to give a lift to any wandering friar who might be travelling on our road, as brigands disguised in monks' garb had been seen in all parts of the country. The old fear came upon me once again, and when we were away from the town and on the road to Le Mans I thought to see dark-robed friars behind each tree, or waiting in ambush beyond the rise of every hill.

"Why should the brigands dress as monks or friars? What would be the sense of it?" I asked my brother.

"Every sense in the world," he answered calmly. "A man so disguised could gain an entry into any house he cared, beg his bread, say his prayers, and then murder the inhabitants."

Perhaps, like poor Cathie three months before, my pregnancy made me more nervous and imaginative than I otherwise would be, but I longed with all my heart to be back again with my mother and Jacques. The nearer we came to Le Mans through the long day, the more evident it was that the inhabitants of every parish were in the grip of fear. Villages were either dead and silent, with closed doors, and faces staring down at us like ghosts from upper windows, or, as in Château-du-Loir, in a state of ferment, with the tocsin ringing and the people at once surrounding us to ask for news.

Twice, three times during the journey we perceived groups of men ahead of us on the road who at first sight appeared to be, must be, the dreaded brigands; and Robert, as a precaution, drew the carriole into the side under cover of the trees in the hope that we should escape notice. Each time we were observed and the groups came tearing down the road to question us, and they would prove to be bands of armed villagers, patrolling between parishes, much as Michel and François would be doing from le Chesne-Bidault. Each group had heard some fresh rumour—châteaux were being burnt to the ground and their owners forced to fly for their lives, the town of la Ferté-Bernard was in flames. The brigands were marching that day upon Le Mans, the comte d'Artois had not left the country after all but was advancing with twenty thousand English soldiers to lay waste the whole of France.

When late that afternoon we approached the outskirts of Le Mans, I was prepared to find the city razed to the ground, or the streets running blood—anything but the unnatural calm pervading, and our sudden unceremonious forced descent from the carriole.

We were stopped at the entrance to the city by sentries of the Dragons de Chartres and ourselves and the carriole searched, and we were only allowed to proceed into the centre of the town after Robert had given Pierre's name as surety. We were then ordered to go to the hotel de ville and report our arrival to the officials there.

"Organisation at last," murmured Robert in my ear. "But what else would one expect from their colonel, the comte de Valence, a personal friend of the duc d'Orléans?"

I did not care who was their colonel. The sight of men in uniform gave me confidence. Surely with this regiment in charge of the city's safety the brigands would not dare to advance further?

It was not so calm in the centre of the town. There were crowds everywhere in the streets, and an air of excitement. Most people were wearing a cockade of red, white and blue, and the rose and blue of Robert's emblem seemed out of place.

"Fashion has passed you by," I said to him. "The duc d'Orléans does not appear to be lieutenant-general of the kingdom after all."

For a moment my brother seemed disconcerted, but he quickly recovered.

"General La Fayette was giving cockades of red, white and blue to the citizen militia of Paris the day I left," he said. "No doubt these colours will be adopted by the whole country with the duc d'Orléans' approval."

The order that had impressed us at the gates of the city was lacking at the hotel de ville. Armed citizens, wearing the tri-colour cockade, were doing their best to keep back the crowds, which took very little notice of them. There were the inevitable cries of, "Vive la nation . . . vive le Roi . . .", but not a single, "Vive le duc d'Orléans."

My brother, prudently, perhaps, removed the outmoded colours from his hat.

There were other vehicles drawn up at one corner of the place, and we left the carriole in charge of an old fellow who had roped off an enclosure with the words "Reservé aux Electors du Tiers Etat" written on a placard beside it. Robert's air of authority, and his distribution of largesse, left the man in little doubt that my brother was at least a deputy.

We fought our way through the crowd to the interior of the hotel de ville. Here were more armed citizens of the new militia, full of pride and self-importance, who directed us to a closed door behind which we waited for forty minutes or more, along with a small group of people as bewildered as ourselves. Then the door was opened, and we filed past a long table behind which were seated officials of various sorts—whether they were members of the new committee, and whether one of them was the mayor himself, I could not say—but all wore the cockade of red, white

and blue. Our names and addresses and the particulars of our
business in Le Mans were noted down and immediately filed by
a harassed individual who seemed far less concerned with the
fact that Robert hailed from Paris (and might conceivably be a
brigand in disguise) than with the revelation that we had no
idea to which company of the Citizens' Militia our brother
Pierre belonged.

"But I have explained to you already," said Robert patiently.
"We have been three days in the Touraine. We know nothing
of the Citizens' Militia here in Le Mans."

Our interlocutor looked at us suspiciously. "At least you know
in what quarter of the city your brother lives?"

We gave the addresses of Pierre's house and of his chambers,
and this perplexed the man more than ever, for it seemed that
recruits to the Citizens' Militia were drawn from both business
addresses and places of residence, and Pierre might thus be in
two places at once. Finally we were allowed to depart, having
been issued with passes to show that we were brother and sister
to Pierre Busson du Charme, member of the lodge of St. Julien
de l'Etroite Union, which, when Robert remembered it, had an
instant effect upon our official.

"Influence is all," whispered Robert in my ear, "even when a
city is swept by revolution."

While we were surrounded by the militia and by officials we
had been spared rumour, but once outside the hotel de ville we
were caught up in it again. Brigands, thousands strong, were
known to be in the forest of Bonnétable. There were also bands
of marauders from the forest of Montmirail terrorising the countryside from la Ferté-Bernard to Le Mans. Hearing this, I was
for returning home as soon as possible, despite the danger, but
Robert steered me through the crowd and back to the carriole,
making light of this latest piece of news.

"First, you and I and the horse cannot go further this night,"
he said, "and secondly, Michel, François and the whole foundry
are very well able to take care of themselves."

When we arrived at Pierre's house near the church of St.
Pavin we found it full to its rooftop, not only with his boys, who
were sporting miniature cockades and shouting "Vive la nation"

at the top of their voices, but with clients out of their luck who had come to my lawyer brother for support—an elderly merchant retired from business, a widow and her daughter, and a young fellow who, unable to earn his living in any other way, was paid by Pierre to be companion to his sons. Pierre's youngest stood naked in his cot, which was draped in red, white and blue.

My brother himself was out on guard with his section of the Citizens' Militia, but his wife Marie soon had me upstairs and into the boys' room—the boys, I was thankful to note, dismissed to the attic—and I fell at once into an exhausted sleep, only to be awakened the next morning by the hated tocsin ringing from the church nearby.

The tocsin . . . were we ever to be rid of it? Must its summons continually haunt us by day and night, only to foster greater fear? I dragged myself from bed and went to the window; I could see people running in the street below. I went to the door and called my sister-in-law. I had no answer, save a wail from the youngest child in his cot. I dressed slowly and went downstairs. There was no one in the house but the widow and her daughter, left to mind the baby; everyone else had gone out into the streets.

"The brigands have come without a doubt," said the widow, rocking herself to and fro, and the cot as well, "but Monsieur Busson du Charme will repulse them. He is the only person in Le Mans with any integrity."

Since she had lost her all in a lawsuit which Pierre had defended, and as recompense he had offered the hospitality of his home for as long as she cared to remain there, it was small wonder the widow thought so well of him.

I went to brew myself some coffee, but the boys must have overturned the pan, for everything was scattered, nor could I find any bread. If my brother expected dinner on his return from guard there was precious little to feed him, here in his own kitchen.

People were still shouting in the street outside, and the tocsin was sounding. If this is revolution, I thought, we were better without one—then I remembered the winter, and the families at the foundry, and anything, even fear, was preferable to what we had endured.

It was midday before Marie and the boys returned, and all the excitement was because the officer in charge of the artillery had been seen mounting the guns on the walls of the city, and rumour had gone around that as he was a member of the aristocracy the guns would be turned upon the people.

"Every cart entering the city is now being searched for hidden weapons," exclaimed my sister-in-law. "The peasants from the countryside are having to turn out all their produce, and they have been rioting in the Place des Halles, which has added to the confusion."

"No matter," replied the widow, "your husband will see to everything."

Evidently she was as great an optimist as my brother Pierre himself, who, my sister-in-law informed me, could know nothing of what was going on in the town since his orders had been to guard the cathedral crypt. There was no sign of Robert, but it did not surprise me when one of the boys said that it had been his uncle's intention to speak with the officials at the hotel de ville. My eldest brother, true to type, believed in keeping his finger on the city's pulse . . .

My sister-in-law set to work to produce a meal for all of us from the produce upset in the market-place, and, as my brother Pierre insisted on every member of his household eating their vegetables raw and refraining from meat, this did not take long to do under the circumstances.

We then remained within doors waiting for our menfolk—for I was determined not to set foot outside if the peasants were still rioting—and, while the boys played leapfrog with the youth who was meant to tutor them, I nursed the youngest, my sister-in-law slept, and the widow told me the whole history of her lawsuit.

It was five or six o'clock before my brothers returned, and when they did they arrived together, Pierre resplendent with musket and tricolour cockade, and Robert also wearing the national colours. Both looked grave.

"What news?" "What has happened?"

The same words sprang to all our lips, even to the widow's.

"Two citizens of Le Mans butchered near Ballon," said Robert—Ballon was a commune some five leagues from the city. "The brigands cannot be blamed for it," he added. "These men were murdered by ruffians from a neighbouring parish. Couriers have just ridden into Le Mans with the news."

Pierre came forward to kiss me, for it was my first sight of him since our arrival in his house the night before, and he confirmed Robert's story.

"It was a silversmith by the name of Cureau, the wealthiest man in Le Mans," he told us, "detested by everyone and suspected of being a grain hoarder. However, that doesn't excuse his murder. He had been in hiding in the château of Nouans north of Mamers these past two days, and it was broken into early this morning by a band of excited peasants, who forced him and his son-in-law, one of the Montessons, a brother of the deputy who lost his carriage the other night, to return with them to Ballon. There they battered the wretched Cureau to death with an axe, shot Montesson, and paraded through the parish with the severed heads on pikes. There's no hearsay about this. One of the couriers saw it for himself."

My sister-in-law, usually so equable and calm, had turned very pale. Ballon was only a short distance from her own home at Bonnétable, where her father was a grain merchant.

"I know what you are thinking," said Pierre, putting his arm round her. "Your father has not been accused of hoarding . . . yet. And he is known to be a good patriot. In any event, once this news has spread, we must hope that every parish in the district will form its own militia to keep law and order. The priests are the trouble. Not a single curé can be trusted to keep his head in an emergency, but must run blabbing from parish to parish alarming the people."

I went and sat by my sister-in-law and took her hand. Although I knew nothing of the murdered men, the news of their butchery by local peasants from a nearby parish, and not by brigands, made their death all the more horrible. I thought of our workmen at the foundry, Durocher and others, who had gone out that night in the winter to attack the grain-carts. Could

Durocher, blinded by resentment and hatred, be capable of committing murder too?

"You say they were peasants who did this terrible thing," I said to Pierre. "Were they out of work and starving—what did they hope to gain by it?"

"A momentary satisfaction," answered Pierre, "after months, years, centuries of oppression. No use shaking your head, Sophie. It's true. The point is that bloodshed of this sort is useless, and must be stopped, and the culprits punished. Otherwise we have anarchy."

He went to the kitchen to find the meal of fruit and raw vegetables that his wife had prepared for him, but his boys had been at it already and left him nothing. I thought of my father, and what would have happened if his sons had dared to interfere with the dinner kept hot for him when he came off shift. Pierre, however, did not seem to care.

"The boys are growing," he said, "and I am not. Besides, by going hungry I can learn something of what those poor devils went through before suffering brought them to the point of murder."

"The poor devils you are sorry for," observed Robert, "were neither hungry nor desperate, as it happened. I had it straight from an official at the hotel de ville who had spoken to one of the couriers. Two of the murderers were domestic servants—one of them servant to a colleague of yours, the notary at René, and exceedingly well-fed. Their excuse was that they were egged on to do it by vagabonds from the forest."

We were still talking of the murder when we went to bed that night, and in the morning the boys, who had been roaming the town though forbidden by their mother to do so, reported that people everywhere were discussing little else. The guard outside the hotel de ville had been doubled, not through fear of bandits, who were now said to be dispersing, but because the peasants outside the town were threatening all folk decently dressed and accusing them of belonging to the aristocracy.

Pierre's boys, brought up by their father to go barefoot, told me gleefully that they had amused themselves running through the streets shouting "A mort . . . à mort . . ." at the sight of every carriage, and had narrowly escaped arrest at the hands of the Citizens' Militia.

Pierre himself, and Robert also, were somewhere in the city, Pierre on guard, supposedly, and Robert, for all I knew, making further enquiries at the hotel de ville. I summoned up my courage and ventured forth, with the boys as escort, to pay a call on Edmé during the afternoon, but the crowds today, Friday the 24th, were even worse than on Wednesday when we had arrived, and despite the presence everywhere of the armed militia there seemed more disorder too. The national cockade, donned more for protection than for any other reason by the older generation of Manceaux (I was thankful for mine stuck prominently on my hat), appeared to be a symbol of defiance when worn by the young. Youths in groups of twenty or more paraded the streets carrying staves entwined with the tricolour, and at the sight of more timid wayfarers, the elderly, or women like myself, would dash towards us waving their banners and shouting, "Are you for the Third Estate? Are you for the nation?", at the same time yelling and shrieking like creatures possessed.

When we came to the Abbey of St. Vincent, beside which Edmé and her husband had their lodging, I was alarmed to see an even bigger crowd surrounding the walls and building. Some of the bolder spirits had swarmed upon the walls, and they were waving sticks and staves, encouraged by the crowd, and calling "Down with the grain hoarders! Down with those who starve the people!"

A few of the Citizens' Militia, posted by the Abbey doors, stood like ineffectual dummies unable to control their own muskets.

"You know what is going to happen," said Emile, Pierre's eldest boy. "The crowd will overwhelm the Militia, and break into the Abbey."

I had the same thought, and turned to make my way out of it all as soon as possible. The boys, being small and agile, ducked their heads and squeezed their way under arms and legs and so out to the fringe of the crowd behind us, but I was caught up in a surge towards the Abbey and then carried forward, helpless and impotent, part of the human tide.

The supreme fear of every pregnant woman of being over-whelmed and crushed was now mine in full measure. I was packed tight, jammed against my fellows. Some of them, like my-self, had joined the crowd as onlookers, but most were aggressive, hostile towards the inmates of the Abbey, and in all probability, did they know his lodging, towards Edmé's husband, Monsieur Pomard, the contractor and tax-collector to the monks.

We swayed backwards and forwards outside the Abbey walls, and I knew that if I fainted, which I was near to doing, there would be no hope for me; I should be overborne and trampled underfoot.

"We'll have him out of it," they were shouting ahead of me. "We'll have him out and serve him as they served his fellows at Ballon," and I did not know whether it was the Abbot they cried for or my brother-in-law, for the words "grain hoarder" and "hunger-merchant" were yelled again and again. I remembered, too, that the unfortunates who had been butchered at Ballon were not aristocrats but bourgeois, incurring the enmity of the people because of their wealth, and the murderers themselves were not starving peasants but ordinary men like these now with me in the crowd, who, for a moment, had turned to devils.

I could feel hatred, like a tide, rise up from a hundred throats about me, and those who had been peaceable before were now infected. A woman and her husband who five minutes earlier had been walking casually towards the Abbey, even as I had done with my nephews, were now shouting in anger, their arms raised above their heads, their faces distorted. "Grain hoarder," they yelled. "Fetch him out to us . . . grain hoarder."

Then, just as a new surge from the crowd behind us drove us towards the Abbey, a cry went up, "The Dragons . . . the Drag-ons are here . . ." and in the distance I could hear the clatter of hoofs coming in our direction and the high-pitched call from the officer in command. They were among us in an instant, scatter-ing us to right and left, and the great burly form of the man be-side me served, through no action of his own, as a barrier between me and the approaching horses. Somehow he thrust me sideways out of harm, but I could smell the warm horseflesh and see the raised sabre of the Dragon menacing the crowd, and down on her face under the horse's hoofs fell the woman who had been yelling just ahead of me. I shall never forget her scream, nor the shrill whinny of the horse as it reared, and stumbled upon her.

The people fell apart on either side, the Dragons in the midst of them, and I had blood on my dress—the woman's blood. I began to walk stiffly, hardly knowing what I did, towards the door of Edmé's lodging beside the Abbey. I knocked upon it and no one came. I went on knocking, and crying and calling, and a window opened on the floor above, and a man's face, white with terror, stared down upon me without recognition. It was my brother-in-law, Monsieur Pomard, and he straightway shut the window once again and left me knocking on the door.

The shouting of the crowd, and the cries of the Dragons, and the singing in my ears all turned to one, and I sank down upon Edmé's doorstep in sudden darkness, nor did I feel the hands that touched me afterwards, and lifted me, and carried me inside. When I opened my eyes I was lying on a narrow bed in the small salon that I recognised to be my sister's, and Edmé herself was kneeling beside me. The unusual thing about her was that she was almost as dusty and torn as I was myself, with face begrimed and hair loose about her, but stranger still was the great band of tricolour ribbon she was wearing round her shoulders. Intuition told me what had happened. She too had been amongst the crowd, but not as a spectator. I closed my eyes.

"Yes, it's true," said Edmé, as if she had read my thoughts, "I was there. I was one of them. You don't understand the impulse. You are not a patriot."

I understood nothing except that I was a woman near her time, carrying a baby that might be born dead even as Cathie's had been, and that I had narrowly escaped death myself through being caught up in a screaming mob which had no knowledge why it screamed.

"Your husband, Edmé," I said, "were they shouting for him?"

She laughed in scorn. "He thought they were," she answered. "That was why he stayed hidden there upstairs, and would not admit you. Thank heaven I found you, and forced him to come down and help me carry you inside. But this is his finish. I've done with him."

"What do you mean, you've done with him?"

She rose from her knees and stood at the end of the bed, her arms folded, and I thought how suddenly she had grown from a young girl into a woman, and a woman who believed it right to judge her husband, some twenty-five years older than herself.

"I've had proof these many months that he made his fortune from the percentage he took from the tithes and taxes," she said. "A year ago I might not have cared, but I do now. The whole world has changed in the last three months. I'm not going to go about being pointed at as the wife of a fermier général. That is why I joined the crowd outside. I was returning home and got caught up in it, and part of it, and I'm glad that I did. I belong with the people out there. Not here, in his grace-and-favour lodging."

She looked about her in disgust, and I wondered how much of her revulsion was due in truth to a surge of patriotism, and how much was resentment at having married an old man.

"Suppose the crowd had broken down the door and forced an entry?" I asked her. "What would you have done then?"

She evaded the question just as Robert would have done.

"The crowd, and I amongst them, wanted to break into the Abbey, not into the house," she answered. "Didn't you hear us shout for Besnard?"

"Besnard?" I repeated.

"The curé from Nouans, the parish near Ballon, where those grain hoarders were hiding yesterday," she said. "You heard how they were killed, I suppose, and a good riddance too. The curé, who defrauded the people just as they did, fled here to his friends the monks as soon as he had learnt what happened to Cureau and Montesson. Well, the Dragons saved his life today, but we'll get him in the end."

A year ago Edmé, my frivolous if intellectual little sister, had been a bride like me, her head full of her own trousseau and the figure she would cut in bourgeois society. Now she was a revolutionary, more violent even than Pierre, talking of leaving her husband because she disapproved of his profession, and desiring the death of some parish priest she had never even met.

Suddenly her face clouded, and she looked at me suspiciously.

"I have not asked you yet what *you* are doing in Le Mans?" she enquired.

I told her briefly of Robert's arrival with Jacques the Saturday before and of our journey to St. Christophe, and how we were now with Pierre, awaiting our chance to return to le Chesne-Bidault. Edmé's face cleared.

"Since the 14th of July nobody has been able to tell for certain who is a patriot and who a spy," she said. "Even members of the same family lie to one another. I'm glad to hear Robert is one of us; knowing what little I do of his life in Paris, I should have feared the contrary. That's one good thing about your François and Michel. No one is likely to accuse either of them of being traitors to the nation after yesterday."

I rested on the bed, aware now of my intense exhaustion, and barely listening to her talk. Presently there came a knock at the door. It was Robert and Pierre, warned by the frightened boys of the fate that might have befallen me. Edmé's husband remained upstairs, and, although I heard his name several times in the murmured conversation between the three of them, neither of my brothers went up to talk to him.

They had a fiacre waiting outside the house, and when I felt well enough to move they helped me to it, for I preferred to be under Pierre's roof, despite the uproar and disorder, rather than Edmé's, in its present atmosphere of resentment and mistrust.

My brothers refrained from asking questions. They were too alarmed, I imagine, as to what might have happened in that crowd to fatigue me further, and as soon as we were safely inside the house I went to bed.

Lying awake, I went over in my mind the hideous events of the afternoon, and how nearly I had missed death. I longed for my home, and for my husband. I wondered if François and Michel were at le Chesne-Bidault or on patrol, and like a flash Edmé's words came back to me: "No one is likely to accuse either of them of being traitors to the nation after yesterday."

Yesterday, the 23rd of July, had been the day on which

Cureau the silversmith and his son-in-law Montesson had been butchered at Ballon; and those accused of the crime, according to the report current in the hotel de ville, had been egged on by vagabonds from the forest. Which forest? It was then that I remembered the rumour, one of many heard on the evening of our arrival on Wednesday, that the brigands were dispersing, but bands of marauders from the forest of Montmirail were terrorising the countryside from la Ferté-Bernard to Le Mans.

ELEVEN

ROBERT TOOK ME home to le Chesne-Bidault on Sunday the 26th of July. We went by way of Coudrecieux and our old home of la Pierre, and then through the forest of Vibraye, but this time, though we stopped to talk to people on the way, no one had sighted brigands. They had dispersed, so we were told, they had scattered south to Tours, or westward to la Flèche and Angers, burning and pillaging as they went; yet no one could say for certain whose land had been laid waste, which property destroyed—all was hearsay, rumour, as it had been all along.

When we arrived at le Chesne-Bidault everything was quiet. The place had a deserted look, as though in our absence work had been abandoned. No smoke came from the furnace chimney, the sheds and store-rooms were locked, and the master's house itself was shuttered, with no sign of life within. We went round to the back, through the orchard, and hammered on the door there, and presently we heard the shutters open in the kitchen and Madame Verdelet, her face pale as a ghost, peered out at us from the chinks. She gave a gasp at sight of us, then came to the door and opened it, and immediately threw herself upon me, bursting into tears.

"They said you would not be back," she wept, taking my hand and holding it fast. "They said you would remain with madame at St. Christophe until the trouble was over, many weeks perhaps, until the baby was born. Praise be to the Blessed Virgin and all the Saints that you are safe."

I went inside and looked about me. Save for her own kitchen the house had an empty feeling, stale and close, and by the look of the big living-room—the master's room—no one had occupied the chairs since we left.

"Who told you," I asked, "that I should not be back?"

"Monsieur Michel and Monsieur François," she answered. "The day you left they told me to keep the house barred and shuttered, for fear of brigands—luckily I had food enough, and could manage—and a few of the men were left to guard the foundry, but the women were given the same orders as myself, to stay within doors, or at most not to stir beyond the foundry gates."

I glanced at Robert. He betrayed nothing in his face, but went about the room throwing open the shutters, letting light and air into the room.

"It's over now," he said. "The brigands have gone south. We shan't be troubled again."

I was far from reassured. Not that I any longer feared the brigands, but something worse, which I could not explain to Madame Verdelet.

"Where are Monsieur Michel and Monsieur François now?" I asked.

"I don't know, Mam'zelle Sophie," she said. "They, and most of the men with them, have been on patrol in the forest the whole week. The guards here told me there had been much fighting at la Ferté-Bernard and further west at Bonnétable, and perhaps our men have been mixed up in it. Nobody knows."

She was near to tears again, and I led her back into the kitchen to console her, and to start her in the preparation of a meal for us. Then with a heavy heart, remembering where duty lay and what my mother would have done, I went out across the foundry yard to the cottage to see the families.

One or two of them had witnessed our arrival, and now they came crowding out of their lodgings to greet me, most of them as bewildered and as fearful as Madame Verdelet had been. All I could do was to repeat Robert's statement; the brigands had dispersed, the worst was over, and we had met with no trouble on the road from Le Mans.

"If the danger is over, why don't our men return?" asked one of them. And this became the general cry. "Where are our men? What are they doing?" I could not answer them. I could only say they were still on patrol in the forest, or giving assistance, perhaps, to the Citizens' Militia in la Ferté-Bernard, if there had indeed been fighting there.

Madame Delalande, wife of one of our top craftsmen, stood watching me with folded arms.

"Is it true," she asked, "there have been two traitors killed by the people in Ballon?"

"I don't know about traitors," I answered carefully. "Two respectable citizens of Le Mans were murdered on Thursday. I can't tell you more than that."

"Grain hoarders," she retorted, "members of the aristocracy, and serve them right. These are the men who have been starving us all winter. They deserve to be torn to pieces, the whole lot of them."

This won approval from the rest of the women, and there was much murmuring and nodding of heads, and another of them called out that her husband had told her, before he went off on patrol, that there was a great plot amongst the aristocracy in the country to murder all the poor people. The rumour had started in Paris, and now it had spread to our district, and Monsieur Busson-Challoir and Monsieur Duval had gone off from the foundry to fight the aristocrats because of it.

"That's right," said Madame Delalande, "my André told me the same. And the King is on our side, and the duc d'Orléans, and they have promised that everything shall belong to the people in future, and nothing to the aristocrats. We can take their châteaux from them if we wish."

This last sounded to me as unlikely as the arrival of six thousand brigands in our homes, or a general massacre of all the poor people in France. "We shall learn the truth of what is happening in Paris before long," I said. "Meanwhile, whether the men are with us or not, our first thought should be for the harvest. The foundry acres are ready to cut, and we might make a start with it tomorrow. The more we gather in, the less likely we are to starve next winter."

This met with general approval, and I was able to get back to the master's house without further talk of fighting aristocrats or seizing châteaux, which, though it might have won approval from Edmé, sounded to me as impracticable and useless as if we

set forth there and then to Versailles demanding bread from
the Queen herself.

I found Robert talking with the guard, which had shown up
at last from within the furnace-house, where, I imagine, they
had all been asleep. There were not more than a dozen of them,
yawning and sheepish: Mouchard and Beriet the stokers, Duclos, one of the engravers who had been sick for some months
anyway, Cazar, assistant to the flux-burner, and the rest ordinary
workmen and apprentices.

The fire had been out since Michel gave the order, and no
work had been done at the foundry. They had no idea where
the masters had gone with the rest of the workmen. To la Ferté-
Bernard or Authon. Whether to fight the brigands or the aristocrats they could not say. It was all the same anyway. Robert and
I went into the house and sat down to the supper Madame
Verdelet had prepared for us.

"Perhaps," I said to my brother, "you have some idea what
has happened to François and Michel?"

Robert was too busy eating to answer at once. When he did
so he wore the quizzical, half-mocking expression I knew so
well.

"There is no reason to believe that anything has happened to
them," he replied. "If they followed instructions they will have
been on patrol in the forest, and kept away from the towns."

"Instructions? Whose instructions?"

He had made a slip, and realised it. He shrugged his shoulders
and went on eating.

"Advice was the word I should have used," he said after a
moment or two. "It was all decided upon before you and I left
for St. Christophe. Any brigands advancing south from Paris
could more easily be turned and scattered from the forests, where
they would lose themselves, than upon the roads."

"If there were in truth any brigands to scatter," I answered.

He poured himself some wine and looked at me over the rim
of his glass. "You heard the rumours like the rest of us," he said.
"Brigands were seen in Dreux, in Bellême, in Chartres. The
least anyone could do was to alert the people of the countryside."

I pushed my plate aside, sickened suddenly by food and all I had been through, with a vivid memory, for no good reason, of that screaming woman who had fallen beneath the horse outside the Abbey of St. Vincent. "You brought the rumour in the diligence from Paris," I said, "and no one else."

He wiped his mouth and stared at me. "The diligence I travelled in with Jacques was one of several," he said. "There must have been a dozen or more taking other routes out of the capital on the Saturday morning when we left. When we came away from the terminus in the rue du Boulay there was talk of little else but brigands, and what we might meet with on the road."

"I believe you," I said. "And were there in those other diligences agents like yourself, paid either by Laclos for the duc d'Orléans, or by some other source, for the very purpose of spreading rumour, and so causing fear and panic through the country?"

My brother smiled. He took up the knife and fork he had laid upon his plate. "My little sister," he said gently, "your travels have exhausted you, and you don't know what you are saying. I suggest you go to bed and sleep it off."

"Not until you tell me the truth," I answered, "and by whose instructions François and Michel took the workmen into the forest."

He did not answer. I watched him finish what he had on his plate, then we sat, the two of us, in silence, with no sound save the ticking of the old clock on the dresser, which took me back, as it always did, to childhood days at la Pierre, with my father at one end of the table, my mother at the other, my three brothers one side and Edmé and myself on the other, waiting for my father to give permission to speak.

"If I admitted to you, which I don't," he said at last, "that I had been paid to do just what you suggest—spread rumour to disrupt the countryside—you would never, for one moment, understand the reason for it. No woman would."

"Go on," I told him.

He got up and began to pace up and down the room, and it was as though something struggled within him for release that had been contained too long, since boyhood, perhaps, and had never yet found freedom.

"All my life," he said, "I have wanted to get out of here. Oh, not le Chesne-Bidault, not this particular glass-house—after all, I did as I pleased here for a time, when I ran the place for my father—but from the setting, from the confined space of the foundry, from any foundry. For one moment, in Rougemont, I thought I had succeeded—do you remember how you, and my father and mother, came to see us there? It was a proud day, nothing seemed beyond my grasp then; but the venture failed, as you know, and there have been other failures since. You will say, my father would have said, the fault is mine alone; but I'm not reconciled. Society failed me before I ever failed myself. Quévremont Delamotte at Villeneuve-St. Georges, Caumont, and others—the marquis de Vichy who promised me thirty thousand livres and withdrew his promise—those are the men who made success impossible, or have done so, until now."

He paused in his stride, and stood facing me across the table.

"Now the moment to revenge myself has come," he said. "No, revenge is too dramatic a word. Shall we say, meet life on equal terms at last? What has happened these past months, since May, and more especially these past two weeks, has overthrown society. I can't tell you, nobody can tell you, what the future will bring, which way the wind will blow. But for an opportunist—and there are hundreds, thousands, like me—this is the hour. I don't mind, none of us minds, what disruption may follow. If there is anything in this moment for us, then that is all that matters."

Once again, as he had done before, during the drive to St. Christophe, he looked his forty years, yet something else besides; someone who was staking all on a final throw, with a total disregard for possible disaster. If he lost, he would take care that those about him lost as well.

"Did Cathie's dying bring you down to this?" I asked him.

"Leave Cathie out of it," he said. "Those memories are dead."

Suddenly he looked lonely standing there, and vulnerable. My heart ached for him, and I was about to go to him, and put my arms about him, when he burst out laughing, resuming his old mask of gaiety.

"How serious we have become!" he exclaimed. "Instead of rejoicing that the world gets more exciting every day, which indeed it does, as the next few months will show. Go to bed, Sophie."

It was a warning against emotion, and I understood. I kissed him and went upstairs to bed, and the next day we were both of us out early in the fields with the men and the families, Robert in his shirt-sleeves like the rest, gleaning and stacking the wheat as though he had done nothing else his whole life long, laughing and joking, his usual airs and graces thrown aside. I found it hard to suit my mood to his, for there was still no sign of François or Michel, and the long day passed without a sight of a stranger, or any fresh rumour from beyond the forest.

I went early to bed that night, and Robert too, exhausted with his labours in the fields. I awoke in the small hours, between three and four, when a false dawn throws a pallid light into a room. Some sound must have stirred me, though what it was I could not tell, but instinct whispered, "They are back."

I got out of bed and went to Pierre's old room, which looked out over the foundry yard by the furnace-house, and they were all there, some thirty or forty of them, moving about like ghosts in that grey light, yet murmuring low, as if hushed on purpose, still mindful that they were a forest ambush on patrol. Now and again one laughed, above the rest, as boys would laugh who had played some hoax or other. They had the back door of the furnace-house open and were passing in and out, bearing sacks on their shoulders.

I heard Robert's footstep along the passage outside Pierre's room, and his tread on the stairs—so he had been awakened, too —and in a few minutes he had unbarred the door below and gone out into the yard. Then I turned and went back to my room, thinking, in foolish fashion, that François would be up to join me within a moment or two, full of concern for me, and I planned to be somewhat cool to make him sorry; but I waited for nearly a half-hour, and he did not come.

Then anxiety got the better of my pride, and I put a wrapper on and went to the head of the stairs to listen. I could hear voices coming from the master's room, Michel's raised loud, as always when he was excited, and Robert's laugh. I went downstairs and opened the door.

The first thing I saw was François lying on the floor with pillows beneath him. Robert and Michel were sitting astride two chairs, Michel with a bandage about his head. I ran at once to my husband and knelt beside him to see where he was wounded. His eyes were closed and he was breathing heavily, but I could see no blood, no bandage.

"What's wrong, where is he hurt?" I asked my brothers.

They showed no concern, to my great astonishment and anger, and Robert made a grimace at Michel, half-laughing as he did so.

"N-nothing's wrong," said Michel, "he's d-drunk, that's all."

I looked down again at my husband, whom I had never seen the worse for drink in the few years I had known him, and I saw then that they were right—I could smell it on his breath. François was stupefied.

"Let him lie," said Robert. "No harm done. He'll sleep it off."

Then I saw the table, which they had dragged to one side of the room, and it was piled high with every sort of object from food to furniture. A great side of bacon lay on top of a satin stool, sacks of flour were wrapped about by brocaded curtains, a quantity of silver lay stacked beside bars of salt and jars of preserves.

They waited for me to speak. I could see their eyes upon me. I knew if I waited long enough Michel would break the silence.

"Well?" he said. "Aren't you going to s-say something?"

I went over to the table and touched the brocade curtains. They reminded me of those that used to hang in the grande salle at la Pierre.

"Why should I?" I replied. "You didn't find these in the forest. That's all there is to it. If you choose to close the foundry and find your living this way, it's your affair, not mine. But you might leave my husband behind next time you go fighting brigands."

I turned to go back upstairs, when Michel spoke again.

"Don't f-fool yourself, Sophie," he said. "François didn't need p-persuading, I assure you. And what you s-see on the table is nothing. We've got the f-furnace-house stacked high. I'll tell you one thing. Neither F-François nor I are prepared to see the men endure another w-winter like the last. That's final."

"You won't have to," I answered him. "If what Robert says is right, the whole world has changed. Paradise is round the corner. Meanwhile, I'd be obliged if the pair of you would carry François up to bed. Not to my room, but Pierre's."

I went away without looking back at them, and when I had shut the door of my room I heard them lumbering my husband up the stairs. He was protesting and mouthing nonsense in the way a drunk man will, and my brothers were hushing him to silence, laughing at the same time.

I lay back on my bed and watched the dawn come clear, and then after the first hush, and the stirring of birds under the window, heard the usual clatter and sound from the farm beyond the master's house, the cows lowing before milking, the dogs barking, and all that went to make the start of another summer's day.

It was a strange feeling, lying there in my mother's room, in that same room she had shared with my father, which I had made my own since my marriage, believing that François and I would, though in a different fashion, continue in their tradition. Now, overnight—or was it in truth much longer, the events of the past week linking back to Cathie's death and the riots in Paris, with the long winter overshadowing it all?—now, most unmistakably, I knew that a great gulf lay between our time and all that had gone before.

My brothers, my husband, even Edmé, my little sister, belonged to this moment, had waited for it, even, welcoming change as something they could themselves shape and possess, just as they moulded glass to a new form. What they had been taught as children did not matter any more. These things were past and done with; only the future counted, a future which must be different in every way from what we had known. Why, then, did I lag behind? Why must I be reluctant? I thought of the winter, and how the families and ourselves had suffered, and I knew what Michel meant when he said it must never happen again; yet, even so, everything within me baulked at what he had done.

I did not fool myself. The things that lay on the table below in the master's room were stolen property, looted in all probability from that château at Nouans where the wretched silversmith Cureau and his son-in-law had hidden before being dragged forth to Ballon to die. What I did not know, what I might never know, was whether my husband and my brother had been amongst those who butchered them.

I fell asleep at last, all feeling numb within me, and when I awoke it was to find François by my side, begging forgiveness, so greatly shamed for being drunk that he was blubbering like a child, and there was nothing for it but to hold him in my arms, and comfort him.

I was not going to question him, but he came out with it, eager, I think, to be rid of secrecy. I had guessed right; they had been to Nouans. The patrol had marched far beyond the limit set for them, rumours of a plot by the aristocracy drawing them on. Panic was great in the whole district south of Mamers, down to Ballon and Bonnétable, no one knowing what was rumour, what was true—someone told them there were brigands dressed as friars, that same old story we had heard upon the road.

"It was this drove Michel mad," said François, "a tale of friars armed, finding their way into the villages, frightening the people. We heard that the curé Besnard of Nouans was a grain hoarder, and that he was absent in Paris getting arms and ammunition to bring back to the château to use against his parishioners. So we went there, to the château. A crowd had already broken into it, seizing the silversmith Cureau and his son-in-law as hostages. They took them off to Ballon. We did not follow them."

"You know what happened to them afterwards?" I asked.

He was silent a moment. "Yes," he said at last, "yes, we heard."

Then, raising himself up and leaning over me, he said, "The murder was none of our doing, Sophie. The people were mad. They had to have a victim. No single one of them was to blame, it was like a fever sweeping them."

The same fever that had swept the crowd outside the Abbey of St. Vincent, so that a woman was trampled to death. The same that had gripped my sister Edmé, so that, caught up in it, she forgot her husband and her home.

"François," I said, "if this goes on, murder, looting, taking life and property, it's an end to law and order, a return to barbarism. This is not building the new society Pierre talks about."

"It's one way of achieving it," he answered. "At least, so Michel says. Before you can build anything, you must first destroy —or, at least, sweep clean the ground. Those men who were . . . who died, Sophie, at Ballon, they were plotting against the people. They would not have hesitated to shoot them down had they possessed guns at the château. They deserved to die, as an example to the rest of their kind. Michel explained it all, the men were asking him."

Michel said . . . Michel explained . . . It was as it had always been. My husband followed his friend, followed his leader.

"So you took what you wanted from the château and came home?" I asked.

"You can put it that way," he replied. "Michel said that whoever had gone cold and hungry through the winter might make amends for it now. The men were nothing loath, you can imagine. We made camp in the forest for four nights, to let things quieten. We had plenty of food and wine with us, as you saw for yourself. That's when I . . ."

"Took what you did to quieten your conscience," I said to him.

After that we lay still for a while without speaking. We both had travelled far in time, if not in distance, during the week we had been away from one another. If this was indeed the new society, it would not be easy to adjust to it.

"Don't be too hard on me," he said presently. "I don't know what happened. We lit a fire there in the forest, and ate and drank, Michel and I beside the men. It was a strange feeling— nothing mattered but ourselves, we had no thought of yesterday or tomorrow. Michel kept saying, 'It's finished . . . it's finished . . . the old ways have gone forever. The country belongs to us.' It's as I said before, a sort of fever swept us . . ."

Then he fell asleep, lying there in the crook of my arm, and later, when he awoke once more, and we dressed and went downstairs, we found the master's room swept and tidied, the table in the middle of the floor again, and the only sign of change was that for our dinner that day we had fine silver set out, with monograms upon the forks, and spoons, and the canister for sugar.

"I wonder," I said to Madame Verdelet, to try her, "what my mother would say to this if she could see it."

We were examining the cupboards in the kitchen, where the rest of the silver was now neatly stored. Madame Verdelet picked up a great candlestick and breathed upon it, polished it awhile, then set it down again.

"She would do as I do," she replied, "accept such blessings, and ask no questions. It's as Monsieur Michel says, folk who own such treasures, and starve the poor who work for them, deserve to lose everything they have."

It was a comforting philosophy, but I was not sure why the benefit should be ours. I only knew that as the days passed I became used to the sight of that monogrammed silver upon the dinner table, and a week later it was I myself who helped Madame Verdelet to cut up the brocaded curtains to fit the smaller windows of the master's room.

There was no more talk of brigands. The Great Fear that had swept the whole of France and ourselves after the Bastille fell petered out into oblivion. Born on rumour's breath, spread by all our fears, the panic went as swiftly as it came, but the impression it left upon our lives remained indelible.

Something within each one of us had been awakened that we had not known was there; some dream, desire or doubt, flickered into life by that same rumour, took root, and flourished. We were none of us the same afterwards. Robert, Michel, François, Edmé, myself, were changed imperceptibly. The rumour, true or false, had brought into the open hopes and dreads which, hitherto concealed, would now be part of our ordinary living selves.

The only one of us to rejoice wholeheartedly and stay uncorrupted by events was Pierre. It was he who came to tell us, in the second week in August, of the great decisions taken in

Paris on the night of the 4th by the National Assembly. They had heard the news in Le Mans two days before, and he had taken the first chance to ride into the country and break it to us. The vicomte de Noailles, brother-in-law of General La Fayette, and one of the deputies of the aristocracy who held progressive views, had put forward a suggestion to the whole Assembly—that all the feudal rights should be abolished, that men should be declared equal whatever their birth or position. Titles were to be no more and men free to worship God how they pleased, office was to be open to all, privileges to go forever.

The Assembly had risen to their feet as one man to cheer the deputy's suggestion. Many were in tears. One after the other, those deputies of the aristocracy who shared the same views as de Noailles swore that the rights they had held for centuries were theirs no longer. A kind of magic, Pierre said, must have come upon the Assembly gathered there in Versailles. The aristocracy, the clergy, the Third Estate—all three were suddenly united.

"It's the end of all injustice and tyranny," said Pierre. "It's the beginning of a new France."

I remember that as he told us the news, standing there in the master's room, he suddenly burst into tears—Pierre, whom I never saw cry as a boy, except once, when a kitten died—and in a moment we were all of us crying and laughing and embracing one another. Madame Verdelet came in from the kitchen, and the niece who helped her. Michel rushed out into the foundry yard to ring the bell and summon all the workmen to tell them that he and François, Pierre and Robert, and all of them were brothers.

"The old laws are d-dead," he shouted. "All men are equal. Everyone is made new and b-born again."

There had been nothing like it, surely, since Pentecost. The happiness and desire for good that swept us all was like the hand of God upon each one of us. Robert, his eyes shining with excitement, told everyone that the duc d'Orléans must be behind it all—the vicomte de Noailles would never have thought of it by himself.

"Besides," he added in my ear, "de Noailles has no possessions to give up anyway. He's in debt to his eyebrows. If debts are to be abolished as well as privileges, we have reached the millennium."

He was already making plans to return to Le Mans with Pierre, and take the diligence there next day for Paris.

The foundry bell kept ringing; no tocsin this time, thank God, but a peal for joy. The men and their wives, and the children, began flooding into the house, shyly at first, then more boldly, as we welcomed them and shook their hands. There was no feast prepared, but somehow we found wine for all of them; and the children, losing their awkwardness, started calling and shouting, and chasing each other about the foundry yard.

"Today everything is p-permitted," said Michel. "The laws of adults are abolished along with f-feudal right."

I saw François look at him and smile, and for the first time I watched it without jealousy. The hand of God must have been upon me too.

I have no recollection of the weeks that followed. All I remember is that the harvest was safely gathered in, the foundry furnace was started once again, and Edmé came to be with me when my son was born on September the 26th.

He was a lovely boy, the first fruit, so Edmé said, of the revolution. Because he heralded good news, I called him Gabriel. He lived two weeks. . . . By then our mood of Pentecost had passed.

PART THREE

Les Enragés

TWELVE

My own grief has no part in this story. Many women lose their first child. My mother, in the days before I was born, lost two within as many years. I had seen it happen twice to Cathie, and with the last she herself went as well. Men call us the weaker sex. Perhaps it's true. Yet to carry life within us as we do, to feel it bud and flower and come from us fully formed as a living creature, separate though part of ourselves, and watch it fade and die—this asks for strength and spiritual endurance.

Men stand aloof, helpless at such times, their very gestures awkward and ill at ease, as though from the beginning—which indeed is true—their part in the whole business has been secondary.

As to the two masters of the glass-house, I leant most upon my brother Michel. He was roughly tender, practical as well, bearing away the cradle from my room so that I should not be reminded of my son. He told me too—I had once heard the story from my mother, long ago—of his first fears, when the infant brother and sister had died, that he might have contributed towards their death by plucking off their coverings for fun.

François made himself too humble for my comfort. He went about abashed, as though our child's loss had been his doing; and, to show this, whispered, or trod on tip-toe through the rooms. When he spoke to me, half cringing in doing so, it nearly drove me mad. He would see the irritation in my face, or hear it in my voice, and naturally, though I could not help it at the time, this contributed to his abject look, making me disfavour him the more. I had no pity, and did not let him near me for six months or longer, and then perhaps—who knows?—it was more from lassitude than inclination. They say it takes a woman her full time again to recover from the birth of a first child, if she should lose it.

Meantime, the Declaration of the Rights of Man made all men equal, if it did not make them brothers, and within a week of its passing into law there were riots in Le Mans, and disturbances in Paris too, with the price of bread as high as it had been before, and unemployment rife. Bakers were blamed in every city for charging too dearly for their 4 lb. loaf, and they in turn put the blame upon the grain merchants; all men were at fault save those who levelled the accusations.

The Manceaux were still divided as to whether the murderers of the silversmith and his son-in-law should be punished or let free, and there were insurrections about this as well, with people going out into the streets armed with knives and stones to use against the Citizens' Militia—now called the National Guard—and shouting, "Let the men of Ballon free"! I never heard if Edmé was amongst them.

The Abbey of St. Vincent had been taken over by the Dragons de Chartres, and as to Monsieur Pomard, Edmé's husband, his title of tax-collector to the monks was abolished, together with many other professions and privileges. He left the city, and where he disappeared to I do not know, for Edmé never followed him. The officers of the Dragons were quartered in her home, and she went to live with Pierre.

The municipality showed itself firm with the butchers of Ballon, and one ring-leader was sentenced to death and another condemned to the galleys. The third, I believe, escaped. So the anarchy Pierre feared was stifled. The few times I went to Le Mans there was little to show for our fine new equality, except that the market-people were more pert, and those who had the material for it draped their stalls with tricolour.

In Paris they had survived another Bastille day, this time without bloodshed. A mob of people, half of them women—fishwives, Robert our informant called them, and I thought of Madame Margot who had helped me with Cathie that fatal day—had marched to Versailles on the 5th of October and camped there in the courtyard for the night, shouting for the royal family. They were thousands strong, prepared to do damage, too, and it was only the intervention of La Fayette and the National Guard that turned the day from near disaster to a triumph.

The King and Queen, with the two children and the King's sister, Madame Elizabeth, were persuaded, indeed forced, to leave Versailles and take up their residence at the Palace of the Tuileries in Paris, and the procession from the one place to the other was, so Robert wrote us, the most fantastic sight imaginable. The royal coach, escorted by La Fayette and a number of his National Guard recruited from the Paris sections, set out with a motley crowd of citizens some six or seven thousand strong, carrying crowbars, muskets, bludgeons, brooms, all shouting and singing at the tops of their voices, "Long live the Baker, and the Baker's brats".

"They were six hours on the road," wrote Robert, "and I watched the circus at the tail end of the journey, turning into the Place Louis XV. It was like a menagerie of ancient Rome, and the only things that were lacking were the lions. There were women, half-naked some of them, sitting astride guns as though they rode elephants, and they had torn branches from the trees on the way and decorated the guns with foliage. Crones from the faubourgs, fishwives from the Halles, street-girls with the paint still on their faces, and even respectable shopkeepers' wives prinked out in their holiday best with hats on—they might have been the mænads fêting Dionysus! No loss of life, except one unfortunate incident before the cohort left Versailles. One of the King's bodyguard, like an idiot, fired at a lad of the National Guard and killed him. The result of it, that same member of the bodyguard and his companion were torn to pieces. Their heads, on pikes, led the van as the procession marched for Paris."

Michel, to whom the letter was addressed, read it aloud. He and François thought it all good fun, but they had never seen, as I had, the faces of Parisians before a riot, nor smelt the stale air in the streets with the damage done.

I snatched the letter from my brother, for between his laughter and his stammer he made little sense. Robert went on to say that now the King was in Paris amongst his people things would settle down, bread would be more plentiful, and honest merchants like himself could sleep at night without fear of broken windows.

"I'm a member of the National Guard, of course," he said, "that is, for this section of the Palais-Royal. My duties are few. We simply patrol the street, fully armed, the cockade upon our hats as a badge of office. When scum approaches—and they swarm from every alley-way these days, as bold as cockroaches— we thrust our loaded muskets in their bellies, and they vanish. The women find us irresistible. One glance and they're hanging on us, strung about with ribboned tricolour. I'd be in high good humour but for the fact that trade is dead."

No word in all this of Laclos, or the duc d'Orléans. La Fayette was the man of the hour, or so it seemed. Then—and it was not Robert who wrote it, but Pierre, who had seen the news in a journal at Le Mans, and had it confirmed—we learnt that the duc d'Orléans, Laclos, his aide-de-camp Clarke, and his mistress Madame de Buffon had left Paris for Boulogne on the 14th of October en route for England. The excuse was a foreign mission.

"But," he added, "the comte de Valence, colonel of the Dragons de Chartres here in Le Mans, and a friend of the duc d'Orléans, has put it about that La Fayette and certain members of the Assembly believe the duc to have been behind the march on Versailles, indeed encouraged the whole disturbance, and that it would be 'diplomatic' for all concerned if the prince should disappear for a while. So the people's favourite has taken himself to London, and they say is enchanted to do so; the racing in England is so much better than in France!"

I remembered the carriage turning out of the Palais-Royal on its way to Vincennes, the two lovers lolling on the cushions, the wave of the languid hand. Had Robert staked his all on the wrong horse after all?

November passed, and we had no word from him. Michel and François were busy with the foundry work, which luckily was picking up, though slowly, for until all the new laws were passed nobody knew how they would affect our merchandise. Then, at the beginning of December, a letter came from Robert addressed to me.

"I'm in great trouble again," he wrote, "on the brink of the same disaster that overtook me in 1780, and in '85."

He must be referring, of course, to his bankruptcy. Perhaps to imprisonment too.

"I received a great shock, as you may well imagine," he continued, "when the duc d'Orléans and Laclos left Paris without a word of warning to those, like myself, who had faithfully served him during the past months. I forget who it was that said, 'Put not your faith in princes'. There may be, of course, some explanation, which no one has yet heard. Being an optimist, I live in hopes. Meanwhile, for my financial affairs, there is only one course to take. I can't tell you of it in a letter, or of another matter concerning my future. I want you to come to Paris. Please don't refuse me."

I kept the contents of this note to myself for twenty-four hours. It had been written to me, and made no mention of Pierre or Michel. My mother was too far away, otherwise I should have consulted her. Pierre was the most obvious counsellor, and he knew the law, but I was aware that he was much concerned at that time with matters of the municipality in Le Mans, and could ill afford to be absent. Besides, the very fact that he was a lawyer might make my eldest brother wary. Had he needed Pierre he would have sent for him. I turned the matter over in my mind, and in the end I took the letter to Michel.

"You must g-go, of course," he said, without any hesitation. "I'll m-make it all right with François."

"No need for that," I told him.

It was two months since Gabriel had died, and my husband was still out of favour with me. I knew it would pass, but for the moment I could hardly look at him. A few days without the guilty knowledge that I hurt him might be good for both of us. Then, with the memory of that last visit to Paris still vivid and unhappy, I said to Michel, "Come with me."

Apart from his apprentice years in le Berry, Michel had never left our glass-house country, or seen a larger city than Le Mans. In old days, I would never have suggested it; he looked, and was, a product of the foundry, black as a charcoal-burner and at times almost as uncouth. But now, with all men equal, since the Revolution had abolished distinction between persons, could not my youngest brother, if he had the mind to do so, elbow a Parisian off the pavement? Perhaps he had the same thought. He smiled at me, as he might have done years past when promoted to work on shift beside his elders.

"V-very well," he said. "I'd l-like to come."

We set forth for Paris within a day or two. The only concession Michel made to taste and fashion was to have his hair trimmed by the barber in Montmirail, and to buy a pair of shoes; as for the rest, his Sunday coat and breeches would have to serve.

"Had I known f-five months back I was to act as your escort," he told me slyly, "I'd have p-prised open the closets at the château de Nouans and d-dressed up like a peacock."

The first thing I noticed when the diligence drove into the capital was that there were fewer carriages in the streets, and the thoroughfares were bare of all but trading vehicles. Many of the bright cafés and small shops that I remembered had boards across the windows, with signs "To Sell" or "To Let" upon them, and although there were many people walking about there were fewer loiterers; most of them seemed intent upon their business, and were plainly dressed, as we were ourselves. True, it had been April when I last came to Paris, and the month was now December, bleak and wet, yet something had vanished from the scene, hard to define. The carriages and the folk who rode in them, gorgeously if sometimes absurdly attired, had made a kind of magic, and given a fairy-tale glitter to the capital. Now it seemed just like any other city, and Michel, peering through the windows of the diligence at the murky gloom about us, observed that no doubt the buildings were very fine, but it was not all that different from Le Mans.

There were no fiacres waiting in the rue du Boulay to take up passengers from the diligence, and the man who set our luggage down said the drivers did not find it paid them now to wait for travellers. Most of them had put themselves at the disposal of the deputies.

"That's where the money is these days," said the fellow, winking. "Hire yourself as a driver or courier to a member of the

Assembly, and your worries are over. Nearly all the deputies are from the provinces, and as easy to fleece as unweaned lambs."

Michel shouldered our bags, and presently we found ourselves at the Cheval Rouge in the rue St. Denis. I did not wish to thrust ourselves upon Robert unprepared, and this was the only place I knew.

The patron was the son of the old people of my father's time, but he had some recollection of our name, and made us welcome. A deputy and his wife had the best room, the one my parents always had—the new patron made much of this, for they were evidently his most important clients—and later we passed them on the stairs, a plain-featured, stout little man swollen with self-importance like a pouter-pigeon, with a dim-faced wife who cooked most of their dinner in their rooms, because she did not trust the hotel chef. The deputy had been a notary somewhere in the Vosges, and until he was elected to the Assembly had never seen Paris in his life.

We were served with a meal of soup and beef, hardly as well-cooked as we should have had at home, and the patron, who came over to chat with us, told us there was no holding a servant since the day the Bastille fell. They lived in hourly expectation of being made masters, and would hardly settle in one place for more than a week.

"As long as the deputies remain in Paris I shall keep the hotel open," he said, "but when they disperse . . ." he shrugged his shoulders . . . "it may not pay me to remain. I might do better to buy a small place in the provinces. No one wants to come to Paris any more. Life is too dear, the times are too unsettled."

When we had finished, Michel took one look at the rain falling on the dark empty street and shook his head.

"The b-bright lights of the Palais-Royal can wait," he said. "If this is the capital, give me the f-furnace fire at le Chesne-Bidault."

I was up early next morning, and looking into his room saw he was still asleep, so I let him lie there, and scribbled him a note giving him directions how to find the Palais-Royal. Then I went off alone, for somehow I felt it best to see Robert by myself, and let him know that Michel had accompanied me.

Morning in the Paris streets was always busy, with people marketing and going to work. There was little difference here, the usual jostling and rudeness I remembered. A new factor was the presence of the National Guard patrolling the streets, walking in couples, giving a martial air to the scene about them. At least they were a protection against thieves, if nothing else.

The Palais-Royal, when I came to it, wore the usual forlorn appearance of any unlived-in château, and being so large a palace perhaps it showed the more. The windows were all shuttered, the big gates closed. Only the side gates were open to admit people to the gardens and arcades. Members of the National Guard did sentry duty, but they let me pass without question, and it seemed to me they served small purpose standing there.

It was early in the morning, and anyway too late in the season for garden loiterers; but whether it was the absence of the duc d'Orléans and his household in London, or simply, as my brother had warned me, that trade was bad, somehow the appearance of the Palais-Royal had changed. The arcades themselves had a drab winter look, the paving was full of puddles. It reminded me of a fairground after the fair has gone. Many of the boutiques were boarded up, with the tell-tale sign "For Sale" upon them, and those that were still in business displayed goods in their windows that must have been there for months. Some flair for the times, or spirit of imitation, had seized upon all the traders; faded tricolour ribbon draped every window, and prominent amongst the bric-à-brac on show were models of the Bastille, made in everything from wax to chocolate.

I arrived at No. 255 and saw with a pang of disillusion, though I had expected it, the notice "For Sale" hanging on the door. The windows, though unshuttered, were bare of goods.

How different from eight months past, when, despite the riots, the windows had been backed by velvet, and some half-dozen of Robert's most saleable "objets d'art" set in full view of the prospective buyer! "Never crowd a window," he used to say. "It puts the buyer off. One good piece on show suggests twenty more within. Dressing your window is an art like anything else.

The rarer the bait, the more eager the customer." Now there was nothing to draw anyone. Not even a solitary cockade.

I rang the bell with small hope that it would be answered, for the rooms above looked as blank as those beneath. Presently I heard footsteps from inside, and someone unbolted the door and opened it.

"I'm sorry. The boutique is closed. Is there anything I can do for you?"

The voice was soft and low, the manner guarded. I was staring at a young woman of about Edmé's age, or younger, whose undoubted beauty but startled eyes suggested that a member of her own sex, dressed for a morning call, was the last person in the world she had expected to see.

"Monsieur Busson?" I enquired.

She shook her head. "He is not here," she answered. "He is living temporarily above his laboratory in the rue Traversiére. He may be here later in the morning if you care to call back. What name shall I say?"

I was about to tell her I was Monsieur Busson's sister, when caution held me back.

"I received a letter from him some days ago," I said, "asking, if I should be in Paris, to look in on him upon a business matter. I only arrived last night, and came straight from the hotel."

She was still suspicious, and watched me, with her hand on the door. The curious thing was that she reminded me, in some indefinable way, of Cathie. Taller, slimmer, she had the same enormous eyes, though set in a sallow skin; and her hair fell about her shoulders as Cathie's had done when she was first married to my brother.

"Forgive my rudeness," I asked, "but what exactly is your own business here? Are you Monsieur Busson's concierge?"

"No," she said, "I'm his wife."

She must have noticed the change in my expression. I could feel it myself. My heart began thumping, and the colour rushed into my face.

"I beg your pardon," I said, "he never told me he had married again."

"Again?" She raised her eyebrows, and smiled for the first time. "I'm afraid you have made a mistake," she told me. "Monsieur Busson has never been married before. You are perhaps confusing him with his brother, who is proprietor of a great château between Le Mans and Angers. He is a widower, I know."

Here was complete confusion. I felt giddy from shock. She must have sensed it, for she pulled a chair forward, and I sank into it.

"Perhaps you are right," I said to her. "There is sometimes confusion between brothers."

Now, looking up at her from the chair, I found her smile engaging. Less frankly warm than Cathie's, it was somehow youthful, artless.

"Have you been married long?" I asked her.

"About six weeks," she answered. "To tell you the truth, it is still a secret. I understand his family might make difficulties."

"His family?"

"Yes, this brother, the owner of the château, in particular. My husband is his heir, and was expected to marry someone of his own position. It happens that I am an orphan, without fortune. That is something the aristocracy can't forgive, even in these days."

I began to see it all. Robert had reverted to his old game of make-believe. Here was another practical joke, such as joining the Arquebusiers, and giving a masked ball to the ladies of Chartres. It would test all his ingenuity, though, to keep up with this deception.

"Where did you meet?" I asked her, curiosity now boundless.

"At the orphanage at Sèvres," she said. "There was a big glass manufactury there, as you probably know, which is now closed down. My husband unfortunately lost money in it at one time. Somehow he met the director of the orphanage over business— this was soon after the fall of the Bastille—and they made an arrangement about me. I had worked, you understand, for the director and his wife since growing up. Anyway, I came here to the boutique, and in a few weeks we were married."

She glanced down at her wedding-ring, and a second one

besides, a fine ruby, which must have cost my brother a small fortune, unless he stole it.

"It doesn't daunt you," I asked, "to have a husband nearly twenty years older than yourself?"

"On the contrary," she told me, "it makes for experience." This time her smile was more engaging still. I regretted Cathie, but I could hardly blame my brother.

"I wonder," I said, "that he cares to leave you alone at nights."

She seemed surprised. "With the windows shuttered and the door barred?" she queried.

"All the same . . ." I gestured, leaving my phrase unfinished.

"We see each other during the day," she murmured. "Business may be pressing, and his affairs in the hands of lawyers, but Robert can always find time for an hour or two with his wife."

It seemed to me that she had little to learn for one reared in an orphanage, however credulous she might be as to my brother's background.

"I'm sure he can," I answered, aware, with sudden humour, that my voice must be sounding as acid as my mother's would have done in the same circumstances. Then, after the light feeling of amusement, came a sudden shadow. Glancing up the stairs I was reminded, all too swiftly, of my last visit, of helping poor dear Cathie up to her room and to her bed, which she would never leave again save for her coffin. Here was her successor, complacent, dewy-eyed, knowing nothing of the predecessor who had trodden those same stairs before her not eight months since. My brother might be able to forget, but I could not.

"I must go," I said, rising from the chair, sick suddenly with distaste, and despising myself for it—God knows, I thought, if this helps Robert's loneliness then he is welcome. She asked what name she should give when her husband came, and I told her Duval, Madame Duval. We bade each other au revoir, and she shut the door of the boutique behind me.

It was raining again, and in the palace gardens the old leaves of autumn lay scattered that had been in bud when last I came. I hurried away, not wishing to linger in a place so haunted by poor Cathie's ghost and the young living Jacques, bowling his hoop before me. The shuttered windows of the Palais-Royal, and the yawning sentries of the National Guard, proclaimed another world from the one I had known in spring.

I retraced my steps, disheartened, to the Cheval Rouge, and found Michel on the doorstep, about to set forth in search of me. Instinct, I don't know why, made me hold the secret. I told him I had been to the boutique and found it shuttered, with no one there. He accepted this as natural. If Robert was near to bankruptcy once more, his boutique would be the first to go.

"C-come on, let's walk the streets," urged Michel, with all the impatience of a newcomer to the capital. "We can f-find Robert later."

To chase the glooms away I let myself be led by him, it hardly mattered where, over much of the same ground that I had already covered. Michel knew none of it. Finally we came to the Tuileries, where the King and Queen now lived. We stared at the great palace, or what we could see of it beyond the court, and watched the Swiss guard marching to and fro, and wondered, as many a provincial must have done before us, whether the King and Queen watched us from the windows.

"Imagine it," said Michel, "all those rooms to house f-four people. F-five, if you count the King's sister. What do you suppose they d-do all day?"

"Much as we do," I suggested. "Perhaps the King plays cards with his sister after dinner, and the Queen reads to the children."

"What?" said Michel. "With all the c-courtiers looking on?"

Who could say? The place looked grey, forbidding, on this December day. I remembered the Queen stepping from her coach to go to the Opera that evening more than ten years ago, a porcelain figurine that a breath could shatter, with the comte d'Artois giving her his arm, and the pageboys in attendance. Now he was an émigré, one might almost say a fugitive, and the Queen was hated, by all accounts, and forever plotting the downfall of the Assembly from behind those windows in the Tuileries. Whether this was true or not, one thing seemed certain; the days of opera-going and masked balls were over.

"It's dead," said Michel suddenly, "like looking at a s-sepulchre. Let's l-leave them there to rot."

We walked back by the quays, where at least, so Michel said, however stinking it might be, there was some sign of life and labour, with flat-bottomed timber barges warped against the river banks, and husky fellows shouting to one another. I need not have feared for my brother's provincial looks. There were few people in this part of Paris to put him to shame. Beggars were everywhere, and he would have had no money left to settle our account at the Cheval Rouge if I had let him give to all of them.

"If it was these folk who b-broke the Bastille down, you can hardly b-blame them," observed Michel. "If I'd been here I'd have razed the T-Tuileries to the g-ground as well."

He had a wish to see where the Bastille had stood, and we found our way there finally, and looked at the heap of rubble and blocks of stone that once had been a fortress. There were gangs of men with picks working on the site.

"That was the d-day!" said Michel. "What I would have g-given to have been amongst those who stormed it."

I am not so sure. The Réveillon riots, and the shouting before the Abbey of St. Vincent, had taught me all I wished to know of insurrection.

By this time it was long past noon, and both of us were hungry, and exhausted too. Like all strangers to the capital, we had walked too far, with little sense of direction. The Cheval Rouge could be east, or west, or just beside us, for all we knew. We found a small café nearby, not much of a place, and none too clean, but we dined there and ate well, and the lad who served us told Michel that we were in the Faubourg St. Antoine. I remembered then that it was somewhere here that Robert had his laboratory.

When we had finished eating I asked for the rue Traversiére, and the lad pointed with his finger. It was barely five minutes distant. Michel and I discussed what we should do, and we decided to go to the laboratory—I knew the number—and see if our brother was there. I warned Michel to wait outside. I wanted to talk to Robert first alone.

The rue Traversiére seemed endless, all warehouses and stores, and I was glad of Michel's company. It was full, too, of labourers who stared, and carters backing their great drays, cursing their horses.

"I can't m-make it out," said Michel suddenly. "You'd think Robert would have been content to stay at la B-Brûlonnerie. He's like Esau—selling his b-birthright for a mess of pottage. Not even that. Can you t-tell me what he's gained in life by this?"

He pointed at the grey-black buildings, the filthy street with the sewage running down it, the savage carter whipping his pair of horses.

"Nothing," I answered, "except the right to call himself Parisian. It may not mean much to us, but it does to him."

We came at last to No. 144. A dank, tall house, adjoining a little court. I made a sign to Michel to stay outside, and crossed the court and read a list of names scrawled upon an inner door. I at length descried the faded lettering "Busson", and an arrow pointing to the basement. I groped my way down the stairs, coming to a passage-way where crates were stacked, and beyond it to a large bare room, with a centre furnace—this must be the laboratory—unlighted, of course, and débris and dust upon the floor, the litter of weeks unswept.

Voices, and the sound of hammering, came from a small room nearby, the door half-open. I picked my way across the litter of the laboratory and there, in the small room, I saw my brother seated at a table covered with paper, all in great disorder, while a workman knelt on the floor hammering nails into a crate. Robert lifted his head as I entered, and for a second his expression had all the surprise and panic of an animal trapped. He instantly recovered, and sprang to his feet.

"Sophie!" he exclaimed. "Why, in the name of God, didn't you let me know you were in Paris?"

He took me in his arms and kissed me, telling the man to leave his work and go.

"How long have you been here, and how did you find this place? I apologise for the mess. I'm selling out, as you probably realise."

He gestured with a half-laugh, and shrugged his shoulders, watching me closely at the same time, and I had the impression that it was not the disorder for which he apologised, but the poor quarters themselves. The word "my laboratory", when he had used it in the past, had conjured to my mind a fine big place, well fitted-up and orderly; not this dim cellar, with a window-grating high in the wall to the street above.

"I came yesterday," I told him. "I'm putting up at the Cheval Rouge. This morning I called at the boutique in the Palais-Royal."

He drew a long breath, stared at me a moment, then burst into a laugh.

"Well?" he said. "So now you know my secret—one of them, that is. What did you think of her?"

"She's very pretty," I replied, "and also very young."

He smiled. "Twenty-two," he said. "Straight from that orphanage at Sèvres. She knows nothing of life, she can't even sign her name. But I found out all about her parentage from the people who had the orphanage, and it's nothing to be ashamed of. She was born in Doudan, her father a merchant in a small way, and the mother was a niece of the famous Jean Bart, the privateer. She has good blood in her."

Now it was my turn to smile. Did he really think I cared about her parentage? If he liked her well enough to marry her, this was all that mattered.

"You know more about her family than she does of yours," I remarked. "I never knew you had a brother who was proprietor of a château between Le Mans and Angers."

For a moment he was disconcerted. Then he laughed once more, and, dusting the one chair, made me sit down upon it.

"Ah well," he said, "she is so innocent, and it makes for excitement. I think she enjoys my love-making the more, believing me a seigneur hounded by misfortune. A glass-blower on the verge of bankruptcy is no great catch. Why break a young girl's dream?"

I looked about me at the tumbled papers and the disorder of the room.

"It's true, then?" I asked. "You've come to it again?"

He nodded. "I've given power of attorney to a friend of mine, a lawyer of the old Parliament, Monsieur Mouchoux de Bellemont," Robert answered. "He will deal with all my creditors, see to the sale of this place and the boutique too, and if he can salvage anything—which I doubt—place it to Pierre's credit in Le Mans. In any event, he will write to Pierre after I have gone, telling him all the circumstances, which are too involved to tell you now."

I stared at him. He was making a pretence of clearing the papers.

"Gone?" I asked. "Gone where?"

"To London," he said, after a moment's pause. "I'm emigrating. Clearing out of the country. There's nothing here for me any more. And they want engravers in crystal over there. I have work waiting for me with one of the foremost London glass-manufacturers."

I was dumbfounded. I had thought he might go out of Paris, to Normandy, perhaps, where there were several glass-houses, or even come back again to our neighbourhood, where he was respected and known. But not to leave the country, not to emigrate like some scared member of the aristocracy who could not face up to the implication of the new régime . . .

"Don't do it, Robert," I said. "I beg of you, don't do it."

"Why not?" His voice was sharp. He gestured angrily, scattering some of the papers on the table on to the floor. "What is there to keep me here?" he cried. "Nothing but debts, more debts, and a certainty of prison. In England I can begin life anew, with nobody asking questions, and a young wife to give me courage. It's all settled, and no one will make me change my mind."

I saw that nothing I could say would persuade him.

"Robert," I said gently, "Michel is with me. He's waiting in the street above."

"Michel?" Once again the trapped animal look came into his eyes. "Did he go with you to the Palais-Royal?" he asked.

"No, I went alone; nor did I tell him you had remarried."

"That wouldn't worry me, he would understand. But this, my going away . . ." He paused, staring straight in front of him. "Pierre would argue by the hour, yet have the consideration to see both sides of the question. Not Michel. He's a fanatic."

I felt depression come upon me. I had done wrong to bring Michel. Had I known of Robert's intention to emigrate I never would have done so. For my eldest brother had chosen the right word. Michel would never understand. He was indeed a fanatic.

"He'll have to know," I said. "I'd better fetch him."

He crossed over to the window-grating and shouted. "Michel?" he called. "Come along down, you rascal. Michel?"

I saw my brother's feet pass the grating above our heads and pause a moment. Then came his answering shout, and the feet moved away. Robert crossed into the laboratory, and in a few moments I heard them greet one another, and the sound of their laughter, and they came back to the little room together, arm-in-arm.

"Well, you've run me to earth like a baited badger," Robert was saying, "and there's nothing left of my equipment, as you can see. The place is cleared. But I've done good work here in my time."

I saw by Michel's puzzled look that he was as surprised as I had been to find Robert, his admired eldest brother, in a basement lair.

"I'm sure of it," he said politely. "No p-place looks its best when it's bare, and the fires are out."

Robert, to evade the issue, suddenly bent and picked up a package from the floor.

"Here is salvage anyway," he said, unwrapping the object and placing it on the table triumphantly. "The famous glass."

It was the goblet, engraved with the fleur-de-lys, that had been blown at la Pierre for Louis XV nearly twenty years before.

"I've copied it before and will do so again," said Robert. "A glass with this device will sell for double its value where I'm going."

"Where are you going?" asked Michel.

I had the hot feeling of unease that comes before disaster. Robert glanced at me, with mock-embarrassment, and said, "Tell him what you found today at the boutique."

"Robert has married again," I said. "I wanted to have his permission before I told you."

A warm smile came over Michel's face, and he went and clapped his brother on the shoulder.

"I'm so very g-glad," he said, "the best thing you can do. S-Sophie was an idiot not to tell me. Who is she?"

Robert began his explanation of the orphanage, and Michel nodded his approval.

"She sounds a b-beauty," he said, "without any airs and g-graces. I expected you to remarry, but feared some haughty young woman with aristocratic p-prejudices. Well, if you've sold this, and your boutique too, where do you p-plan to live?"

"That's just it," said Robert. "I'm obliged to leave Paris. As I've already explained to Sophie, my creditors are after me, and I refuse to face another period in La Force."

He paused, and I saw he was thinking out how best to deliver his blow.

"I am all in f-favour of your leaving Paris," said Michel. "How you have stood the city all these years is b-beyond me. Come to us, mon vieux. If not to le Chesne-Bidault, at least within d-distance of it. Why, you might make some arrangement with the present t-tenant of la Pierre. Everything's changing hands. With so many f-frightened land-owners running from the country like rats, the opportunities are boundless. We'll f-find something for you, never fear. Forget your debts."

"It's no good," said Robert abruptly, "it's too late."

"Nonsense," replied Michel, "it's n-never too late. Trade has been bad these last months, I know, but it's p-picking up every day. There's a great future ahead for all of us."

"No," said Robert, "France is finished."

Michel stared at him. He looked as though he had not heard aright.

"That's my opinion, anyway," said Robert, "so I'm clearing out, emigrating. I'm taking my young wife to London. They need engravers in crystal there, and, as I've just told Sophie, I have work waiting for me. It's been arranged by friends."

The silence hurt. I felt sick, looking at Michel's face. He had gone white, and his eyebrows, meeting in a straight line above the bridge of his nose as my father's had done, were pencil dark in contrast.

"By f-friends," he said at last, "you mean, by t-traitors."

Robert smiled, and took a step towards his brother.

"Come now," he said, "don't jump to conclusions. It just so happens that I have no great faith in what the present Assembly are going to do for trade or for anything else. These past few months in Paris have taught me much. It's all very well to be a patriot, but a man must see to his own future. And as things are at present, there's none for me here in France. That's why I'm quitting."

When Robert had gone bankrupt, the year my father died, Michel had been absent in le Berry. The family shame had somehow passed him by, leaving him untouched. If he considered it at all, I believe he understood Robert to have been unfortunate. At the time of the second trouble, in '85, Michel was too much concerned with the running of le Chesne-Bidault, and his growing friendship with François, to worry overmuch about his eldest brother. Robert had always been extravagant, his fine friends had let him down. But this was different.

"Have you written to t-tell Pierre?" he asked.

"No," said Robert, "I shall do so before I leave. In any event the lawyer who has power of attorney for my affairs will write a full explanation to him."

"What about Jacques?" I asked.

"I've arranged for that as well. Pierre will act as guardian. I've suggested that Jacques should remain with my mother. I take it she will provide for him. It will be up to him to make his own way in life."

He might have been speaking about some crate to be dispatched. Not the future of his son. The unconcern in his voice was nothing new to me. This was the Robert with whom I had journeyed to St. Christophe, the man who had lost Cathie, the man who lived from day to day. It was a being unknown to his youngest brother. I could tell, by Michel's eyes, that the illusion of a lifetime had been destroyed. Whatever tales Robert had told him when he was with us at le Chesne-Bidault after the Bastille fell, of patriotism, and of a new world dawning, were now shown up as fables. Robert himself had not believed a word of them.

Perhaps losing my first child had made me hard. Nothing Robert could say or do would ever again surprise me. If he chose to leave us this way, although my heart yearned after him it was his choice, not ours.

I had not realised Michel would take it the way he did. His faith was shattered. He put his hand up to loosen his cravat. I thought for a moment that he was going to choke; his face had turned from white to dullish grey.

"That's f-final, then," he said.

"That's final," Robert repeated.

Michel turned to me. "I'm g-going back to the Cheval Rouge," he said. "Come with me if you are ready to d-do so. I shall take the d-diligence in the morning. If you want to s-stay here, that's for you to decide."

Robert said nothing. He had turned pale too. I looked from one to the other. I loved them both.

"You can't part in this way," I said. "In the old days it was the three of you against my father when things went wrong. We have none of us ever quarrelled. Please, Michel."

Michel did not answer. He turned on his heel and began to walk away through the laboratory. I threw a helpless look at Robert, and went after him.

"Michel," I cried, "we may never see him again. Surely you will wish him luck, if nothing else?"

"Luck?" echoed Michel, over his shoulder. "He's g-got all the luck he needs in that glass he'll t-take with him. I thank God my f-father did not live to see this day."

I looked back again at Robert, who was staring after us, a strange, lost figure amidst the disorder of his papers in that bleak basement room.

"I'll come to you in the morning," I said. "I'll come to the Palais-Royal to say good-bye."

He gave a shrug, half amusement, half despair. "You'd be wiser to take the diligence and go home," he said.

I hesitated, then went quickly to him and put my arms round him. "If things go wrong in England," I told him, "I'll be waiting for you. Always, Robert."

He kissed me, a smile that meant nothing flickering for a moment on his face.

"You're the only one," he said, "the only one in the family to understand. I shan't forget."

Hand-in-hand we crossed the débris of the laboratory, and followed Michel up the stairs. The workman had disappeared. Michel was waiting for me in the little court.

"Look after le Chesne-Bidault," Robert said to him. "You're as fine a craftsman as my father, you know that. I'll take the glass with me to London, but I'll leave the family honour in your hands."

I felt that one gesture from Michel then might have made Robert stay. One smile, one clasp of the hand, and they could have fallen into argument, delayed decision, and somehow saved the day. Had it been Pierre standing there in the court, there would have been no bitterness. Illusions might be destroyed, compassion would remain. Michel had been cast in a different mould. Whoever hurt his pride hurt all. Forgiveness was not a word in his vocabulary. He stared across that small dank court at Robert, and there was so much anguish in his face that I could have wept.

"Don't t-talk to me of honour," he said. "You've never had any, I s-see it now. You're nothing but a traitor and a f-fraud. If this country fails in the future, it will be b-because of men like you. Like y-you." The old endearment, the "thou" between brothers, faltered on his tongue, and he turned, almost ran from the court and into the street, saying it still, stammering all the while, "Like y-you, like y-you".

The years vanished. He was a child again, wounded beyond his comprehension. I did not look back at Robert. I ran into the street after Michel, and walked beside him up the rue Traversière until, by the mercy of heaven, we found a wandering fiacre, hailed it, and drove to the Cheval Rouge. Michel went straight to his room and locked the door.

Next morning we took the diligence together, saying nothing of Robert or of what had passed. It was only at the end of the day, with our journey nearly done, that Michel turned to me and said, "You can tell François what happened. I never want to speak of it again."

The brightness of the new world had faded for him too.

THIRTEEN

Robert's emigration was a profound shock to the family. His marriage was accepted as natural, if somewhat hasty, but to abandon his country just at the moment when every man of intelligence and education was needed to prove the worth of the new régime was something only contemplated by cowards, aristocrats—and adventurers, like my brother.

Pierre, stricken at first almost as much as Michel, found fewer grounds for condemnation when the lawyer's papers arrived from Paris. There was little doubt that every sou obtained from the sale of the boutique in the Palais-Royal, and the laboratory in the rue Traversière, must go to pay Robert's creditors, and even so they would not be paid in full. Once again he had lived beyond his means, promising goods that he had never delivered, entering into negotiations with merchants the terms of which he could not fulfil. Had he not fled the country, months in prison would surely have been his fate.

"We could all have joined together to pay his debts," said Pierre. "If only he had consulted me, this tragedy would have been avoided. Now he has lost his name for ever. No one will believe us if we say he has gone to London for a few months to perfect his knowledge of English glass. An émigré is an émigré. They are all traitors to the nation."

Edmé, like Michel, refused to mention Robert's name again. "I have no eldest brother," she said. "As far as I am concerned he is dead."

Now that she had left her husband she passed her days helping Pierre in his work as notary, writing letters for him as a clerk would do, and seeing his clients for him too, when he was busy with the affairs of the municipality. She was as good as a man at the work, Pierre said, and finished it in half the time.

My mother did not concern herself much with the political implications of Robert's act. It was the fact that he had abandoned his son that grieved her most. Naturally she would keep Jacques, and bring him up in St. Christophe, until such time as Robert might return; for she refused to believe he would not return within the year.

"Robert failed in Paris," she wrote to us. "Why should he succeed any better in a strange country? He will come home, once the novelty has worn off and he finds that his charm cannot fool the English people."

I had two letters from him soon after his arrival in London. All was couleur de rose. He and his young wife had found lodgings without difficulty, and he was already working as engraver to a large firm and, so he said, "made much of by his employers". He was picking up English fast. There was a coterie of Frenchmen and their wives settled in London in the same district as themselves—Pancras, he called it—so they were never at a loss for company.

"The duc d'Orléans has a house in Chapel Street," he wrote, "where Madame de Buffon keeps house for him. He spends most of his time at the races, but I am told on good authority that he is likely to be offered the crown of the Low Countries. If this should come about, it might very well make a difference to my plans."

It did not come about. The next we heard of the duc d'Orléans was when we read in the Le Mans journal that he had returned to Paris and presented himself to the Assembly to take the oath to the Constitution. This was in July of 1790, and for the whole of the month I expected to hear that Robert, faithful to the entourage, had returned to Paris too. I hoped in vain. A letter came at last, but brief, giving little news except that his wife, Marie-Françoise, was expecting her first child. As to the duc d'Orléans, there was no mention of his name.

Meanwhile, we ourselves had survived our first nine months under the new régime, and, although the paradise they promised us had not yet come about, business was brisk. We had no cause to complain.

There was no repetition of the previous winter's severity, nor of last year's famine, though prices were still high and people grumbled. What kept us all alert and interested were the decrees forthcoming from the Assembly, month by month, substituting new laws for the whole nation.

The old privileges abolished, there was not a man now in the kingdom who could not better his position and rise to high office if he had the wit and initiative to do so. The legal system was reformed, much to my brother Pierre's satisfaction, and a judge could no longer pronounce guilt—a civil trial must be held before a citizen jury. In the army, a common soldier could become an officer—and because of this many of the existing officers emigrated, and were no great loss.

The greatest shock to those who still held to the old ways was the reform of the clergy, but to men like my brother Michel it was the supreme achievement of that year of 1790. The religious orders were suppressed in February. That was only a beginning.

"No more f-fat friars and b-big-bellied monks," cried Michel gleefully, when we heard the news. "They'll have to work for their l-living in the future like the rest of us."

On the 14th of May a decree was passed giving all the church lands and property to the nation. Michel, who commanded the National Guard of le Plessis-Dorin—made up, it must be admitted, almost entirely of his own workmen from the foundry—had the supreme satisfaction of going to the presbytery and handing a copy of the decree in person to his old enemy the curé Cosnier.

"I could hardly c-contain myself," he told us afterwards, "from putting all the v-village cows and pigs into his strip of f-field, to prove that the land belonged to le P-Plessis-Dorin, and not to the Church."

Worse was to follow, though, for poor Monsieur Cosnier. Later in the year, in November, the Assembly declared that every priest must take an oath to serve the Civil Constitution of the Clergy, now part of the State—the Pope's authority was no more—and if a priest refused, then he would be replaced in office and forbidden to give the sacraments.

The curé Cosnier would not take the oath, and the curé Cosnier went. . . .

"I've waited t-two years for this," said Michel. "When the Assembly m-makes up its mind how and when to s-sell church lands, I shall be the f-first to buy them."

The Assembly above all needed money, to bolster the tumbling finances of the nation, and they issued bonds called assignats, representing church lands, to those patriots who wished to acquire them in return for ready cash. The more assignats a man held, the greater a patriot he appeared to be in the eyes of his fellow-countrymen, and later, when the actual land began to be distributed, he could either exchange the assignats for the land itself or for its equivalent in coinage.

It was a mark of civic pride to be known as an "acquirer of national property", and in our district of Mondoubleau, Loiret-Cher (for all the départements of France had been re-grouped and renamed under the new system), my brother Michel and my husband François headed the list of those patriots bearing the title.

It was in the February of '91 that Michel redeemed his assignats, buying up a bishop's château and the land belonging to it somewhere between Mondoubleau and Vendôme, which cost him some 13,000 livres—and all because of his hatred for the Church.

He had no intention of living there himself. He put a man in to farm the land, and he would go over there and walk about the acres, and stare at the place feeling, I suppose, that in some way he had revenged himself upon the curé Cosnier, and—in some curious fashion—upon his eldest brother too. Robert had squandered money he did not possess, defrauding his associates. Michel, in the name of the people, would somehow make good the loss.

I do not pretend to explain how his mind worked, but I do know that little by little, as Michel became an "acquirer of national property", so there developed in him, at the same time, a love of power for its own sake. I remember—and this was before he bought the land, and so must have been in the November of 1790—that I was visiting the Delalande family one afternoon, for their little girl was sick. I was about to leave, when

Madame Delalande said to me, "So our men are off with the National Guard this evening to Authon."

It was the first I had heard of it, but I had no wish to appear ignorant before her, and answered, "I believe so".

She smiled, and added, "If they return fully loaded as they did a year ago, during the time of the forest patrols, we shall all benefit. They say the château de Charbonnières is a fine place, stacked to the roof with fine furniture. I've told my André to bring me back some bedding."

"The duty of the National Guard is to protect property, not to seize it," I answered coolly.

She laughed. "Our men interpret duty in their own fashion," she replied, "and anyway, everything belongs to the people these days. Monsieur Busson-Challoir says so himself."

I went back to the master's house, and as the three of us sat down to dinner I enquired about the expedition. François said nothing. As usual, he flashed a look at Michel.

"Yes, you heard right," said my brother shortly, "b-but it's not the château we're going after, it's the owner."

"The owner?" I repeated. "Isn't he Monsieur de Chamoy, who commands a garrison at Nancy, away on the frontier?"

"The same," answered Michel, "but a t-traitor, by all accounts. Anyway, I've had word he's in hiding at his château of Charbonnières, and the G-Guard under my command are going to get him."

It was not my business to interfere. If Monsieur de Chamoy was a traitor, it was the duty of the National Guard to apprehend him. I knew the château, only a short way away, within easy marching distance, this side of Authon, and I knew Monsieur de Chamoy too; he had bought glass from us in the old days, a pleasant, courteous man, rather a favourite with my mother. I thought it unlikely he would be a traitor. He was a serving officer, and he had not tried to emigrate.

"Don't forget your manners when you arrest him," I said. "The last time he came here was after our father died, and he called to offer sympathy."

"He won't get any s-sympathy from me if he t-tries to evade

arrest," answered Michel. "A cord round his wrists, and a kick on the s-seat of his breeches."

They set out as soon as it was dark, about seventy of them, fully armed, and when they did not return the following day I feared the worst—another butchery like Ballon, and this time our men the murderers. There was no question of brigands now, nor of grain hoarders, and the countryside was quiet.

I summoned Marcel Gautier, one of the younger workmen who, because of a sore foot, had not accompanied the others, and bade him drive me to Authon. I had acted godmother to his baby two months before, and he was willing to please me.

It was a raw, damp day, and we took the small carriole, in which Robert and I had driven to St. Christophe. When we arrived near the château of Charbonnières we found a junction of roads there barricaded, and some of our men on guard. No one was allowed through without permission, but they recognised me at once and let us pass. The National Guard were standing about in front of the château, André Delalande apparently in command, and one of the first things I saw, amongst the pile of loot in the carriage-way, was a great pile of bedding. He had remembered his wife's request.

He came up to the carriole, somewhat surprised, I think, to see me, but saluted and told me that the bird had flown—some spy had informed Monsieur de Chamoy of his danger, and he had fled before the National Guard arrived. Because of this, my brother and my husband had gone on to Authon to question the people there.

I bade Marcel turn the carriole round and continue to Authon, and as we wheeled in front of the château others of the Guard emerged, some half-dozen of them, bearing chairs and tables, and clothing too. Marcel took a sly look at me, but I said nothing.

The road entering Authon was cordonned off, but the sentries recognised the carriole once more and let us through. We drew up before the hotel de ville, where a small crowd had gathered in consternation. When I enquired the reason, I was told that the commandant of the National Guard had commanded a house-to-house search for Monsieur de Chamoy.

"He is not here," a woman cried from the crowd, "none of us have seen him in Authon. But it makes no difference. The Guard insist on turning every house upside down."

Indeed, I could see some of them at it as I watched. There was Durocher, who should have known better, pushing some shopkeeper before him with his musket, demanding admittance to the grocery beyond, with two small children running in front and crying.

I descended from the carriole and went up the steps into the hotel de ville. And there were François and Michel, seated at a table with two of the workmen on sentry-go behind their chairs, and standing to attention before them, grey with fear, a little man whom I took to be the mayor. No one noticed me as I stood by the door, for all eyes were directed at Michel.

"You understand I have my d-duty to do," he was saying. "If de Chamoy is f-found hiding in any house in Authon, you will be made responsible. Meanwhile, we shall remain here for at least f-forty-eight hours, to allow time for a thorough search to be made. We d-demand free quarters for ourselves and our men for that p-period. Is that clear?"

"Quite clear, mon commandant," said the mayor, bowing and trembling, and he turned to another frightened official at his side to give his orders.

Michel murmured something to François at his side, and I saw my husband laugh, and sign some paper with his usual masonic flourish.

I could tell by their faces that they were in high good humour. To scare the mayor, to quarter themselves upon the little town, was like a boyhood prank all over again; Michel might have been playing Indians with Pierre in the forest long ago.

It was not a game, though, for the mayor. Nor for the townsfolk whose homes were broken into, and who were forced to feed our men.

Then François lifted his eyes and saw me. He turned bright scarlet and nudged Michel.

"W-what are you doing here?" asked my brother.

"I only wondered if you would be home for dinner," I replied. Somebody tittered, one of the young workmen, I think, who had lately been recruited to the National Guard. Michel banged his hand on the table.

"S-silence," he shouted.

There was an instant hush. The mayor turned whiter than before. My husband kept his eyes fixed on the paper before him.

"Then you can go b-back at once to le Chesne-Bidault," said Michel. "The National Guard is here to s-serve the nation, and when the nation's b-business is settled, the Guard will return. Vaillot, Mouchard, escort Madame D-Duval outside."

The two guards walked on either side of me to the door, and I had the doubtful satisfaction of knowing that, if my intrusion had caused my brother and my husband to lose face, it had done little else besides; except, perhaps, to make them harsher with the mayor.

Marcel and I took the road back to the foundry, and as we left Authon I saw yet another detachment of the National Guard come out and scatter in the fields on either side of the road, hullooing to one another, probing the ditches with their muskets, for all the world like boar-hounds after prey.

"They'll get him if he's there," said Marcel with satisfaction, "and there won't be much left of him afterwards, not with our lads."

He clicked his tongue at the horse to go faster. This, I thought, was the man who had stood bare-headed at the font of le Plessis-Dorin not two months since, tears in his eyes, when his baby girl was christened.

"You hope they catch him, then?" I asked.

"Catch him and cook him, m'dame," he answered. "The sooner the country is rid of all his kind the better."

They never did find Monsieur de Chamoy. Indeed, he found his way back to Nancy, I believe, and on proving not to be a traitor was reinstated in the garrison there, though we did not hear this until later.

What degraded me in my own eyes was that, in driving back to Plessis, I thought I espied a humped figure in a ditch, and instead of keeping silent about it called out instantly to Marcel, in great excitement.

"There he is, crouching by the thorn bush yonder. After

him . . ." I cried, almost seizing the reins out of my driver's hands to run the fugitive down. It was nothing but the stump of a long-dead tree, and my instinctive feeling of disappointment shocked me to silence.

This was only one of several expeditions on the part of the masters of le Chesne-Bidault and their workmen in the guise of the National Guard, and for his zeal and patriotism my brother Michel was made adjutant-general of the district of Mondoubleau. Sickened at first, I soon became resigned, accepting as natural these forays into the countryside, even feeling a thrill of pride when the women told me that "Messieurs Duval and Busson-Challoir were the most feared men between la Ferté-Bernard and Châteaudun". Michel was still the leader, but François increased in stature too, with a new air of authority about him which was more pleasing to me, his wife, than his old air of submission used to be.

He looked well, too, in his uniform of the National Guard, being tall and broad, and I liked to think he had only to march with a company of men to one of the communes in our district, for all the inhabitants to be on their toes at sight of him.

My François, who, when I married him, was no more than a master glass-maker at a small foundry, now had the power to walk into a château and arrest the proprietor of it, should he be suspect—that same proprietor who, a few years back, would have shown him the door.

There was one occasion when the pair of them, my brother and my husband, with just a handful of the National Guard, arrested half the commune of St. Avit, seized two former members of the aristocracy, the brothers Belligny, and a third, Monsieur de Neveu, disarmed them, and packed them off under escort to Mondoubleau, on suspicion of being traitors to the nation. The municipality at Mondoubleau kept all three under arrest, for they dared not countermand the orders of the adjutant-general. A few days afterwards, visiting two or three of the families at le Chesne-Bidault, I saw they all had fine new knives and forks on display, some of them silver, with monograms upon them, and I thought no more of it than if they had been purchased in the market-place.

Custom, it is said, makes all things acceptable. Gradually I came to look upon any fair-sized property as something the owner had no right to possess, if he had been a member of the aristocracy under the old régime. Like Michel and François, I began to suspect these people of harbouring revenge, perhaps of storing arms, which one day they might decide to use upon us. The new laws, after all, had hit the aristocracy hard; it would not be surprising if they banded together in secret and worked for the overthrow of the new régime.

What Pierre thought of the forays I never heard. They were not discussed when we visited Le Mans, for he had so much news of his own to tell. He had become an ardent member of the Club des Minimes, a branch of the Jacobins Club in Paris, famous for its progressive views, started by those deputies of the Assembly who were forever agitating for further reforms to the Constitution. The sessions at the Club des Minimes were often stormy, and there was one towards the end of January of '91 when Pierre rose to his feet and made an impassioned speech against some three hundred priests and as many ex-nobles in Le Mans who, he swore, were moving heaven and earth to destroy the revolution.

I heard it all from Edmé when she came to stay for a few days at le Chesne-Bidault.

"Pierre had it from me in the first place," she told me. "The wife of one of his clients, a Madame Foulard, came to me and said that when she went to Confession the priest ordered her to use her influence to prevent her husband from being a member of the Club des Minimes. If she did not so do, the priest said, he would refuse her Absolution."

I could hardly believe a priest would go thus far, but Edmé assured me that this was not the only case; she had heard the story repeated by other women.

"There's an ugly spirit of reaction in Le Mans," she said, "and I blame the officers of the Dragons de Chartres. There is a brigadier quartered in my old house at the Abbey of St. Vincent, and he told me that the officers have forbidden the men to fraternise with the National Guard. Pierre agrees with me. He says the Club des Minimes wants to get rid of the regiment altogether. They've served their original purpose, and too many of the officers have relations who are émigrés and have joined the Prince de Condé in Coblenz."

The Prince de Condé, the King's cousin, and the comte d'Artois were both in Prussia attempting to raise an army of volunteers from amongst the émigrés who had followed them into exile, and with the help of the Prussian prince, the duke of Brunswick, hoped in time to invade France and overthrow the new régime.

I had heard nothing from Robert for many months, and my fear was that he might have left England and gone, as so many had done, to Coblenz. Living, as he must be doing, amongst little groups of reactionaries who would not rest until the aristocracy and the clergy had been reinstated, he would inevitably become tainted with their ideas, and learn nothing of what had been achieved here at home for the good of the country.

Whenever I saw Pierre he would look at me first, before embracing me, and raise his eyebrows in a question, and I would shake my head. No more would be said unless we found ourselves alone. It was a stigma, a mark of shame, to have a relative who was an émigré.

Edmé was right, though, when she said that there were forces of reaction in Le Mans. This was very easily seen at the theatre—we were told that exactly the same thing happened in Paris—when allusions to liberty and equality in a play would be loudly applauded by all the patriots in the audience, but if the subject should turn upon loyalty to a throne or to princes there would be counter-cheers and applause from those who felt that our own King and Queen were facing difficulties in Paris.

I happened to be staying with Pierre early in February of '91—just about the time Michel bought his piece of church property beyond Mondoubleau, so neither he nor François could accompany me to Le Mans. I arrived on the Monday, and on the next day Pierre and Edmé returned home to dine, full of an uproar there had been at the salle de Comédie the night before. The band of the Dragons de Chartres, engaged as orchestra, had refused to play the popular song "Ça Ira", although requested to do so by a crowd of spectators in the cheap seats.

"The municipality are furious," announced Pierre, "and have already complained to the officer commanding the parade of the Dragons this morning. If you want to see some fun, Sophie, come to the theatre with Edmé and me on Thursday, when they are giving *Semiramis*, followed by a ballet. The band of the Dragons are to play, and if we don't have 'Ça Ira' I'll get up on the stage and sing it myself."

The song "Ça Ira" was the rage of Paris, and now everyone in the country was either whistling it or humming it, though it had been written as a carillon, and should have been played on bells. Heaven knows it was infectious. I had it from morning till night at the foundry with the apprentice boys in the yard, and even from Madame Verdelet in the kitchen, though a good deal out of tune. I suppose it was the words that pleased the boys, and it must have been the words too that offended the conservative band of the Dragons de Chartres. If I remember rightly, the opening verse began thus:

> "Ah! Ça ira! Ça ira! Ça ira!
> Les aristocrates à la lanterne,
> Ah! Ça ira! Ça ira! Ça ira!
> Les aristocrates on les pendra!"

At first this song had been sung lightly, as a sort of jest—the Parisians had always been famous for their mockery—but as the weeks passed, and feeling grew against the émigrés and those at home who might be thinking of following their example, the words of this nonsense song began to hold more meaning. Michel had adopted it as his marching song for the National Guard at le Plessis-Dorin, and when he had his men formed up outside the foundry and they started out on some foray, legitimate or otherwise, I must confess that the words and the tune with it, shouted by some sixty fellows stamping their feet, would have made me bolt my door and hide had I been suspected of non-patriotism.

As it was . . . "Ah! Ça ira! Ça ira! Ça ira!" rattled round my head, as it did everyone else's. It became a kind of catch-phrase amongst us at le Chesne-Bidault and in Pierre's circle at Le Mans—whenever we heard of a new piece of legislation likely to offend the forces of reaction, or if at home one or the other of us had some plan which we were determined to put into practice, we said "Ça ira!" and there was no further argument.

On the night of Thursday the 10th of February Pierre, Edmé and I set forth for the salle de Comédie—Pierre's wife had remained with the children, and had tried to persuade me to do the same, for I was four months pregnant again and she feared a crush. It was lucky that Pierre had had the foresight to buy tickets, for the crowd was so great outside the building that we could barely force our way inside.

We had the best seats, stalls, near the orchestra, and the whole house was packed. The play—Voltaire's *Semiramis*—was well acted and passed off without incident, and it was in the entr'acte that Edmé nudged me, and murmured, "Watch out—they're going to begin."

Edmé, for a young woman of the provinces, was always ahead of fashion. Tonight, scorning the elaborate coiffure of the day, with hair piled on top of the head like a hay-stack decorated with ribbons, she wore a little jaunty Phrygian cap in velvet, set on the one side, for all the world like an errand lad in the street. How she thought of it I do not know, but it was certainly a forerunner of the "bonnet rouge" worn by the Paris crowds in later months.

We looked about us in the stalls and tried to guess which amongst the audience were reactionaries. Edmé insisted she could spot them at a glance. Pierre, who had risen from his seat to talk to friends, came back and whispered that the National Guard were gathered in force by the only entrance to the street.

Suddenly a stamping of feet began in the cheap seats behind us, and members of the National Guard, in uniform, standing by the gangways, called out: "Monsieur le chef d'orchestre! If you please, the people want to hear 'Ça Ira'."

The conductor took no notice. He lifted his baton, and the band of the Dragons began to play a brisk military march of no political implication.

The stamping of feet grew louder, with the slow clapping of hands, and voices started the inevitable rhythm of, "Ça ira! Ça ira! Ça ira!"

It had a menacing sound, sung thus, in a low chant to the stamping of feet, and against the discordant background of the military march. People stood up in the audience, shouting instructions at cross-purposes, some calling for "Ça Ira", others to let the Dragons continue their programme.

Finally members of the National Guard approached the rostrum, and the conductor was obliged to order his band to cease playing.

"These interruptions are a scandal to the city," he cried. "Let those who have no wish to listen to music leave the building."

There were cheers and counter-cheers, boos and stamping of feet.

The officer commanding the National Guard, a friend of Pierre's, called out, " 'Ça Ira' is a national tune. Every patriot in the house wants to hear it."

The conductor turned red and looked down into the audience. "There are also those present who do not," he answered. "The words of 'Ça Ira!' constitute an offence to all loyal subjects of the King."

Hoots and howls greeted his retort, Edmé beside me joining in, much to the embarrassment of her neighbors on the other side, and people from every section of the audience began to call out and wave their programmes in the air.

Then those officers of the Dragons who were amongst us in the stalls, and some of them in the boxes too, sprang to their feet and drew their swords, and one of them, a captain, calling at the top of his voice, ordered any of the regiment present to fall in under the officers' box close to the stage, and see that no harm came to the musicians.

The National Guard were ranged opposite, fully armed. A shiver of apprehension could be felt amongst the audience, for if the two sides fell to fighting what would happen to all of us seated there, unable to get out, with the exit barred?

It was my ill-luck, I thought, to be caught in crowds when I was pregnant, and yet this time, for some reason unknown to myself, I was without fear.

Like Edmé, I hated the sight of the supercilious Dragon officers, whom I would see strolling about the streets of Le Mans as if the place belonged to them. I glanced up at Pierre, who had donned his uniform of the National Guard for the occasion, and thought how well it became him. He was not yet forty, but his light hair had turned nearly white, which gave him greater distinction than before, and his blue eyes, so like my mother's, were blazing now in indignation.

"Let those amongst the audience who don't wish to hear 'Ça Ira!' stand up, and let us see them," he called out. "In that way we shall quickly discover who are the enemies of the people."

Shouts of approval greeted this suggestion, and I felt a glow of pride. Pierre, our impractical Pierre, was not going to be bullied by the Dragons.

A few half-hearted figures stumbled to their feet, only to be pulled down hastily by their companions, afraid no doubt of the epithet "aristocrat". Shouts and arguments filled the air, with the Dragons, sabres in hand, preparing to drive in amongst us all and cut us down.

The mayor of Le Mans, dressed in his municipal scarf, marched down the gangway to the stage, in company with another official, and in a firm voice he bade the officer commanding the Dragons to put up his sword and order his men to do likewise.

"Tell your musicians," he said, "to play 'Ça Ira!'"

"I am sorry," replied the officer—a Major de Rouillon, so someone whispered beside Edmé—"but the song 'Ça Ira!' is not in the repertoire of the band of the Dragons de Chartres."

Immediately a chorus of, "Ça n'ira pas" came from every officer present, and from many of the audience too, while those opposed to the Dragons continued with the stamping of their feet and their own rendering of the song without the music.

Finally, there was a compromise. Major de Rouillon agreed to allow his band to play the song if they could follow it up with the famous air "Richard, O mon roy; l'univers t'abandonne". This was known to be a great favourite during the days when the King and Queen held court at Versailles, and the implications were obvious. For the sake of peace, and in order to proceed with the ballet, which was the rest of the evening's entertainment, the mayor of Le Mans conceded.

I thought the singing of "Ça Ira!" would lift the roof. I even joined in myself, wondering inconsequentially what my mother would have said if she could see me. "Richard, O mon roy" sounded like a whisper in comparison, the only singers being the Dragons de Chartres themselves and one or two women in the stalls who wished to make a show of themselves.

We left before the ballet began—it would have been an anti-climax after the scene we had witnessed—and walked home from the salle de Comédie, the three of us, arms linked, Pierre between us sisters, singing—

"Ah! Ça ira! Ça ira! Ça ira!
Les aristocrates à la lanterne,
Ah! Ça ira! Ça ira! Ça ira!
Les aristocrates on les pendra!"

The next day there was a great demonstration in the city, the crowds demanding the expulsion of the Dragons de Chartres, and Pierre and Edmé began a house-to-house petition to obtain signatures for the same purpose. Le Mans was divided on the subject. Many citizens, in the municipality too, held the opinion that the Dragons had given good service to the city, and had guarded it through perilous times; the rest, Pierre, Edmé and all their circle, were insistent that a counter-revolutionary spirit was rife amongst the officers, and that the National Guard was sufficient to keep the peace.

For the moment the problem was shelved, but during my week's visit we had one more excitement, and this was election of the new bishop to the episcopal seat—Monseigneur Prudhomme de la Boussinière—who was obliged to swear his oath to the Constitution.

We went out into the streets to watch the procession, and cheer the bishop on his way to the cathedral to attend the Constitution Mass. He was escorted by a detachment of the National Guard—Pierre amongst them—and by the Dragons de Chartres as well, and this time there was no mistaking the roll of the drums, and whistle of the fife, as the band struck up "Ça Ira!"

At the end of the cortège marched a long line of ordinary citizens, armed with pistols for fear of trouble, and women carrying rods, threatening those amongst us who might hold old-fashioned views about the clergy.

As for the Dragons de Chartres, matters came to a crisis three months later in mid-May, when I was once more on a visit to Pierre, this time accompanied by both François and Michel. The ceremony of planting a May tree had taken place in the place des Jacobins a few days before our arrival, and, as a symbol of the times, it had been draped with the tricolour. The tree was sawn to pieces during the night, and the Dragons were at once suspected of this act of vandalism, the more so as a bunch of them, that same evening, had insulted an officer of the National Guard.

This time the whole populace of the city was roused. It might have been '89 all over again. Tremendous crowds assembled in the place des Jacobins shouting, "Vengeance! Vengeance! The Dragons must go." People began flocking into Le Mans from the countryside beyond, for as always the news had spread, and suddenly, as though from nowhere, came hordes of peasants armed with pikes and forks and axes, threatening to burn the city to the ground unless the inhabitants themselves took action and forced the municipality to dismiss the Dragons.

This time I stayed within doors, remembering the horrors of that riot before the Abbey of St. Vincent nearly two years before, but leaning from the window of Pierre's house, with his excited boys beside me, I could hear the roar of the crowds. Nor did it make for ease of mind to know that Pierre, Michel, and Edmé, too, were there amongst them, shouting for vengeance in the place des Jacobins.

The National Guard, without orders from the municipality, had raised barricades in the streets, and mounted guns. If the officers commanding the Dragons had given but one hasty order to advance, the guns would have been fired against their men, and a bloody massacre would have followed.

The officers of the Dragons, all credit to them, kept their men in check. Meanwhile, the flustered officials of the municipality went from one headquarters to another, seeking advice from superior authority.

At eight o'clock in the evening the crowds were as thick and as menacing as ever, backed by the National Guard, and one and all shouted, despite the efforts of the officials to make them disperse, "No half-measures. The Dragons go tonight!"

Once more they took up the old cry "Ça ira!" The whole city must have rung with the song that night, and still the officials hesitated, fearing that if the regiment left the city the ordinary citizens must be at the mercy of all the riff-raff from outside.

Some time between eleven and midnight the decision must have been taken, although how and where I never heard; but at one in the morning, with the crowds still waiting in the streets, the Dragons de Chartres left the city. I had gone to bed, anxious for the safety of François and my brothers who were still in the streets. The shouting died away, and all was quiet. Then, just after the church nearby had struck one, I heard the sound of cavalry. There was something ominous, almost eerie, about that steady clip-clop in the darkness of the night, the jingle of the trappings and the harness, loud at first, then fading, then dying right away. Whether it would bring good or evil to the city, who could tell? Two years ago I should have trembled for my life at their departure. Now, lying awake, waiting for François and the others to return, I could only smile at the thought that a regiment of soldiers had been defeated by a citizens' militia without a shot being fired.

The departure of the Dragons de Chartres from Le Mans was a signal of victory for the Club des Minimes and others like it, and from that day forward their influence was paramount in the affairs of the city. Those officials of the municipality and others who had favoured the retention of the regiment lost office, and the National Guard itself was purged of anyone who might have sympathy with the old régime.

To mark the change the very names of the streets were altered, heraldic signs were pulled down, and at the same time the sale of church property began.

I saw the start of this before I left for home. Michel, hearing that workmen had begun demolishing one of the smaller churches in the city, and that the contents were on offer for anyone who cared to purchase them, suggested that we should step by out of curiosity.

It was a strange sight, and I did not care much for it. It seemed sacrilege to trade objects we had always looked on with respect. The actual demolition had barely started, but the church was stripped of its altar and screen and pulpit, which were being sold in lots to city tradesmen. At first bidding was slow, the people hesitant, no doubt, for the same reason as myself, staring with goggling eyes at such destruction. Then they became bolder, half-laughing with a certain awkwardness, and one big fellow, a butcher by trade, stepped forward with a roll of assignats and bought the altar-railings as a frontage to his shop. There was no more hesitation after this. Statues, crucifixes, pictures, all were for sale and briskly purchased. I saw two women staggering under the load of a fine picture of the Ascension, and a little lad, clutching a crucifix, whirled it around his head for a weapon, as children will. I turned away and went out into the street, dismayed. I had a sudden vision of Edmé and myself as children in the chapel of la Pierre, and the good curé blessing us after our first Communion.

Presently I heard laughter behind me. It was Michel, François and Edmé, all bearing trophies from the sale. Michel had a vestment, a chasuble, flung over his shoulder like a cape.

"I've needed a new working blouse for some time past," he called. "Now I can set the tone at le Chesne-Bidault. Here, catch this."

He threw me an altar-cloth, which he intended, I suppose, for the master's table. As I held it with a burning face, the crowd around me watching curiously, I saw that François and Edmé had each one of them a chalice, and, with mock solemnity, gestured towards me as though to drink my health.

FOURTEEN

THE NEWS OF THE flight of the royal family from Paris in '91 reached Le Mans on the afternoon of June the 22nd. The shock was considerable. Panic seized the municipality, and leading citizens, believed to be in sympathy with the old régime, were at once arrested and held for questioning. Our old enemy rumour spread through the countryside once more. The King and Queen, so it was said, were on their way to the frontier to join forces with the Prince de Condé, and once in Prussia would summon vast armies to their side to invade France, and then reinstate the old way of life.

The flight, so Michel said, would be a signal for a mass exodus. All the faint-hearts and the disgruntled, who up till now had shown a façade of patriotism, would try a similar escape and so help to swell the growing crowd of émigrés. We talked of nothing else for two whole days. I remember how the women gathered round to have their say, and one and all were sure the King had gone reluctantly; it was all the Queen's doing, the King would never have thought of it but for her.

Then came the good news. The royal family had been arrested at Varennes near the frontier, and were on their way back to Paris under escort.

"That's their f-finish," said Michel. "No one will have any respect for them any more. The King's f-forfeited all honour. He ought to abdicate."

We believed for a time that this would happen. The duc d'Orléans' name was mentioned as possible Regent for the little Dauphin, and there was even talk of a Republic. Then somehow the scare died down, the Court resumed its life at the Tuileries, though heavily guarded, and later, in September, the King took his oath to the Constitution.

Feeling towards the royal family was never the same again. As Michel said, the King had forfeited respect. He was just a tool in the hands of the Queen and the Court party, whom the whole nation knew to be in secret correspondence with the princes and the émigrés abroad. Security tightened. A close watch was kept on those members of the aristocracy who remained in the country, and on the clergy who would not take the oath to the Constitution. Feeling ran so high in Le Mans that certain women, who refused to go to Mass when it was celebrated by the state priests, were publicly whipped in the place des Halles and forced to attend. This seemed to me excessive, but it did not do to express an opinion, and anyway my own life had more interest for me that summer.

My second baby, Sophie Magdaleine, was born on the 8th of July, and my mother and Jacques came up from St. Christophe for the event. It was a joy to have my mother with me once again, supervising the master's house as if she had never left it. Wisely, she kept her own counsel on the changes, though I know she noticed everything, from the brocade curtains to the monograms on the silver. Nor did she speak of the work in progress at the foundry, where the engraving upon the glass was designed to please a different clientèle from the one she had known. Gone were the fleur-de-lys, and the lettering interlaced. These emblems were out of fashion, even decadent. We now had torches upon our glass, representing liberty, with hands clasped in friendship, and the words "égalité" and "fraternité" scrawled at the base. I cannot say they were an improvement on the past, but they fetched a good price in Paris and Lyon, which was our main concern.

Sitting up in her old room, watching me nurse my baby, listening to the happy laughter of Jacques, now a sturdy boy of ten, playing with the Durocher children in the orchard, my mother smiled at me and said, "The world may alter, but there's a sight won't change."

I looked down at the baby at my breast, and stopped her feeding or she would have choked herself.

"One never knows," I answered. "The Assembly might pass a law condemning this as self-indulgence."

"It would not surprise me," said my mother, "what any of those people did. They're half of them only lawyers and little jumped-up clerks."

It was as well Pierre could not hear her, or Michel either. Anyone who spoke one word in criticism of the Assembly was a traitor in their eyes.

"Surely you are not against the revolution?" I asked her, greatly daring.

"I'm against nothing that benefits honest people," she answered. "If a man wishes to get on in life, he should be encouraged to do so. I don't see what that has to do with revolution. Your father became a rich man through his own efforts. He began at the bottom, like any apprentice boy."

"My father had talent," I argued. "Talented men will always make their way. The new laws are designed to help those who have nothing."

"Don't you believe it," replied my mother. "The peasants are no better off than they were in the past. It is the middle men who are climbing to the top today. Shopkeepers and the like. I would not grudge it them if they kept their manners."

Watching the baby feed, listening to the boys climbing the trees outside, the spirit of revolution seemed a world away.

"That child has had enough," said my mother suddenly. "She's feeding now from greed, like any adult. Put her in her cradle."

"She's a revolutionary," I answered. "Revolutionaries always demand more, and are never satisfied."

"That is my point," said my mother, taking Sophie Magdaleine from me and patting her back for wind. "She does not know what is good for her, any more than all the so-called patriots in the country. Someone should have the nerve, and the power, to say 'Enough'. But they're like a lot of sheep without a shepherd."

It was good to hear her talk. Good to listen to her practical strong sense. Revolutions might come and go, whispers and rumours blow about the countryside, society, as we had known it, tumble upside down; my mother remained herself, never reactionary, never pig-headed, only most blessedly sane. She stood by the cradle, gently rocking it, as she had done for all of us in days gone by, and said, "I wonder if your brother has a little one like this?"

She meant Robert, and I saw by the expression on her face how much she yearned for him.

"I expect he has, by now," I answered. "The last time he wrote they expected a child."

"I've heard nothing," she answered, "nothing for ten months. Jacques no longer asks after his father. It's a strange thought; if there is a brother or a sister for him there in London, it will be English-born. Some little cockney, knowing nothing of his own country."

She stooped and made the sign of the cross over my baby, then murmured something about dinner for the men when they came off shift, and went downstairs. The room was full of shadows when she had gone, and I felt suddenly bereft. All we had lived through during the past two years seemed valueless. I was dispirited, lost, for no good reason.

When she went away again, back to St. Christophe, taking Jacques with her, it was as though peace and sanity departed too. François and Michel stood about the foundry yard in lifeless fashion, and for all three of us it seemed that our whole day had grown dim. During her brief visit my mother had managed, without anyone realising it, to establish her old authority. My menfolk came to the table groomed and clean, Madame Verdelet scrubbed the kitchen once a day, the workmen whipped off their caps and stood to attention when she spoke to them—and all of this by instinct, not through fear. There was not a soul in the foundry who did not have a regard for her.

"It's a q-queer thing," said Michel after she had gone, "but my mother achieves more with one l-look than we do with all our c-curses and cajolery. It's a pity they don't have women d-deputies. She'd be elected every t-time."

I don't know how it was, but during the four weeks of her stay with us my brother did not once call out the National Guard on an expedition, though he had them parade for her benefit before the church at le Plessis-Dorin.

In September, after the elections were held, and the new deputies to the Legislative Assembly, as it was called, took their seats in Paris, we were able to talk with some authority on public matters—or pretended to do so, to impress Pierre and Edmé in Le Mans—because my husband's eldest brother, Jacques Duval of Mondoubleau, was elected one of the deputies for our département of Loir-et-Cher. Like all progressives, he was a member of the Club des Jacobins, and when he returned home from Paris François and Michel would either go to Mondoubleau to see him and hear the news, or he would spare the time to visit us at le Chesne-Bidault. He it was who told us of the divisions within the new Assembly, some favouring moderate measures, others, including himself, a more forward policy; and there was a continual jockeying for position amongst the leaders of each group.

There was still deep mistrust of the King, more so of the Queen, known to be corresponding with her brother the Emperor of Austria and urging him to make war upon France. It was felt by the progressive deputies, all of whom were members either of the Club des Jacobins or the Club des Cordeliers, that a far stricter watch should be kept on the aristocrats remaining in the country, and on the clergy who refused to take the oath. These people, my brother-in-law inferred, were a menace to security, provoking unrest and dissatisfaction in many parts of the country. As long as they remained at liberty they would hold up the work of the revolution, and stifle progress.

Jacques Duval became a close friend of Marat, editor of *L'Ami du Peuple,* one of the most widely read and popular newspapers in Paris, and he used to send this down to us every week, so that we could keep abreast of all that was said and done in the capital. I was not sure what to make of it myself; it was an inflammatory sheet, whipping its readers to violence, and urging them to take action against the "enemies of the people" if legislation should be slow. Michel and François read every word of it, and passed it on to the workmen too—a mistaken gesture. They had enough to do in the foundry as it was, keeping production going and fulfilling our orders, without roaming the countryside in quest of erring nobles and refractory priests.

For myself, I let them talk, and shut my ears to argument. My baby took up all my time. Those nine months that I was

blest with her are bright now with her memory alone. Nothing
else counted.

She caught a cold in spring that went to her chest, and although I nursed her day and night for almost a week, and sent
for a doctor from Le Mans, we could not save her. She died on
April the 22nd, 1792, two days after Prussia and Austria declared war on France; I remember we heard the news the same
day we buried Sophie Magdaleine. I was quite numb with grief,
and so were François and Michel and the people at the foundry,
for the baby had been a radiant child, delighting all of us.

Like other persons suddenly bereaved, I heard of war with
bitter satisfaction. Now I should not be the only one to suffer.
Thousands would mourn. Let men fight and cut themselves to
pieces. The quicker invasion came and we were all decimated,
the sooner personal sorrow would be wiped out.

I think I hardly cared that spring what happened to the country, but, later, helpless misery at my baby's death turned to hatred of the enemy. Hatred of the Prussians and the Austrians
who dared to interfere in France's affairs and make war upon us
because they rejected our régime, but above all hatred of those
émigrés who were now bearing arms against their country.

Any sympathy I might have had for them in the beginning
had now vanished. They were traitors, every one of them. My
brother Robert, who had not written to me for a year, might
even now be amongst the number enrolled in the armies of the
duke of Brunswick. The very thought of it made me sick. Now,
when Michel and François set forth with the National Guard
on a tour of inspection, I cheered them on, and had as great a
satisfaction as any woman at the foundry when they returned
from seizing property for the nation's benefit.

All the lands belonging to émigrés suffered the same treatment as those held by the Church, and it was about this time
that we ourselves, François and I, bought the small property
at Gué de Launay outside Vibraye, with an eye to the future
and our middle age.

Everywhere châteaux were standing empty, their owners having fled. The le Gras de Luarts had gone from la Pierre, the de
Cherbons from Chérigny. Our landlord, Philip de Mangin,

had been evicted from the château of Montmirail, but his father-in-law, Jean de la Haye de Launay, did not come under suspicion, and was allowed to remain in residence.

Day after day we would hear of more rats running, most of them to join the army of the Prince de Condé under the duke of Brunswick, and as their names were listed on the sheet of émigrés, and their property was sequestered, we had the dubious satisfaction of knowing that should they ever return they would find their homes given to others, if not burnt down and pillaged, and every sou they possessed the property of the nation.

The Legislative Assembly was not hard enough on the traitors. François' brother, Jacques Duval, and many others who thought like him pressed for stronger measures; every suspect in the country to be rounded up and questioned, and if necessary kept in custody unless they could prove their innocence. The country was in mortal danger, with two armies invading it from the east; nor was this the only threat, for in Brittany and to the south-west in the Vendée there was known to be strong royalist feeling and much sympathy for the émigrés.

The war, of course, played havoc with the economy, and our own glass-trade was amongst the first to suffer. Many of the younger men obeyed the call to arms and joined the army, and we were left with the older workmen, and our furnace alight scarcely three days in the week.

Horses and vehicles were requisitioned for the troops, grain prices rose once more, and this time some deputies in the Assembly demanded the death penalty for hoarders, but the measure was not passed. The more the pity, I remember thinking, and looked back, without revulsion, to the killing of the silver-merchant and his son-in-law at Ballon. I had grown wiser in three years, or less compassionate. Being wife to an officer of the National Guard, and sister-in-law to a deputy, gave one a bias in favour of authority—if authority was on our side.

Jacques Duval's friend Marat, the journalist, was right when he denounced the timid members of the Assembly in his paper *L'Ami du Peuple*, and advocated the seizure of power by a strong group of proved patriots who would not hesitate to use stern measures to unite the country and put down opposition. There was one deputy in whom we all had confidence, the little lawyer Robespierre, who back in '89 had spoken with such fervour at Versailles. If anyone had the force and ability to control the situation, which rapidly worsened through the summer, here was the man to do it, said my brother-in-law.

Robespierre . . . known as "the Incorruptible" amongst his friends, for nothing and no one could deflect him from what he believed to be right and just. Others might look with leniency upon those who failed to prosecute the war, or remain friendly with the émigrés in case the tide turned and the enemy were successful, but not Robespierre. Again and again he warned the ministers who controlled policy in the Assembly that the King's position had become untenable; his obstinacy in refusing to sign decrees necessary for the safety of the country meant that he was playing for time, hoping that the forces of the duke of Brunswick would defeat the army of the French people. If the King would not co-operate with government, the King must be deposed. Government must be strong, or the nation would perish.

These were the arguments we heard during the feverish summer of '92, either through reading *L'Ami du Peuple* or direct from François' brother Jacques Duval. But the news that roused us most, and indeed every man and woman in the country, was when, on the 1st of August, the invading general, the duke of Brunswick, issued a manifesto threatening to deliver Paris to "military execution and total destruction" if "the slightest violence" was committed against the royal family. The royal family were not even in our thoughts. We were all too concerned with the imminent invasion and the danger to our homes to be concerned with them. The manifesto, intended to frighten us into submission, did just the opposite, and, far from making us feel tender towards the King and Queen, turned us, almost overnight, into republicans.

When, on the 10th of August, the Paris crowds rose en masse and marched on the Tuileries, destroyed the Swiss guards, and forced the royal family to take shelter behind the manège where the Assembly sat, our small community at le Chesne-Bidault had every sympathy with the people. Now, we felt, let the duke of Brunswick do his worst. We were ready for him. One triumph resulted from this fracas, and this was that the weak men within the Assembly were broken. The local government of Paris, the municipality, or Commune as it was called, now had control, and in September a new Assembly, to be known as the National Convention, would be elected by universal suffrage, which Robespierre had been demanding all along.

"At last," said my brother Pierre, "we shall have a strong government."

In fact, one of the first decrees passed, the day after the storming of the Tuileries, was an order giving every municipality throughout the country the right to arrest suspects on sight.

I think if Michel could have had his way every prison would have been at bursting-point. As it was he, and the National Guard, could now round up every non-juring priest for deportation, though in Paris the commune used harsher measures and imprisoned them.

The royal family were confined in the Temple, where the pernicious influence of the Queen could do no further damage, and letters to her nephew the emperor of Austria no longer find their way across the frontier.

Marat, in *L'Ami du Peuple*, declared that the only way to save the Revolution for the people was to slaughter the aristocrats en masse; yet if this happened the innocent might suffer with the guilty. Somehow, we no longer seemed to preach the brotherhood of man.

Meanwhile, both François and Michel were preoccupied with the primary elections to take place in the last week in August. Our département of Loir-et-Cher was divided into thirty-three cantons, and each canton comprised several parishes or communes. Every man over twenty-five was allowed to vote for an Elector or Electors in his canton, and these Electors in their turn voted for the deputies who would represent the people of the département in the Assembly.

Both my husband and my brother were to stand as Electors for the canton of Gault, and both were determined to see that no one who might have the slightest reactionary tendency should offer themselves as candidates beside them. They were supported in this by Jacques Duval, my husband's brother, who

wrote to François from Paris urging the importance of a majority of progressives in the next Assembly—the National Convention. This, he said, could only come about if the Electors
themselves were progressives, and could thus make sure that the
right deputies were returned to power. He was not offering himself for re-election, for his health was bad. This was a great blow
to François and Michel, for they felt that so close a relative,
holding a position in Paris of such importance, was not only a
help to our own small business but a security should things go
wrong.

"We must be f-firm on one thing," declared Michel, a week or
so before the primary elections were to be held, "and that is to
see that no p-priest or ex-m-member of the aristocracy is allowed
to vote."

"What about priests who have already sworn the oath to the
Constitution?" asked François.

"They can s-swear as hard as they like," replied my brother,
"we'll k-keep them out. In any event, we'll march the National
Guard around every parish first, and make sure the n-nominees
for election have taken the oath."

It was on the Sunday preceding the elections, I remember,
that he had the National Guard of le Plessis-Dorin, and others
from a neighbouring parish, on parade in the foundry yard. They
went off in strength, some eighty strong, under the command
of André Delalande—whom Michel had promoted to commandant—to force any prospective Elector of doubtful patriotism to
take the oath.

There was not a parish or a commune in the district that
dared withstand this onslaught, though many protested at the
treatment and said the National Guard had no right to enforce
the oath upon loyal citizens.

"Loyal be d-damned," said Michel. "We'll soon s-see who's
loyal when we come to c-count the votes."

The opening meeting to discuss the Elections was held in the
church at Gault on the 26th of August. I was allowed to be present, though I kept myself well in the background. From the very
start of the proceedings there was trouble. By right of age and
precedence Monsieur Montlibert, mayor of Gault, was called to

preside over the assembly, to the loud protests of my husband and brother.

"He is an aristocrat," cried my husband, "he has no business to be here."

"It's m-men like him," shouted my brother, "who have b-brought the country to its p-present state. He's t-turned coat once, he'll d-do it again."

Michel's stammer, of course, was a handicap at such a meeting, and his temper was not improved by the murmur of laughter that rose from the benches all about us in the church. I at once felt hot with shame, especially as at this moment the curé of Gault, and those of Oigny and St. Agil, entered from the sacristy. Both Michel and François began waving papers above their heads and shouting, "No priests in this assembly. . . . Tell them to get out. . . . No priests in here."

The curé of Gault, a mild enough looking man in all conscience, stood by the chancel steps. "Those members of the clergy who have taken the oath have every right to be admitted," he answered.

"We don't want f-fools like you," shouted Michel. "Go suck your s-soup."

There was a moment's horrified silence. Then an uproar broke out. Some older members present began to protest, but the younger ones yelled and jeered, and within a few minutes the three curés retreated with dignity, afraid, no doubt, that their presence would provoke violence.

I was scarlet with embarrassment, and wished that Michel and François would hold their peace. Finally a Monsieur Villette was nominated instead of the mayor and, mounting a chair, rebuked "certain of those present who would drive good patriots from this assembly".

"There is no law forbidding a constitutional priest from becoming an Elector, or from voting," he announced, "nor for expelling any ex-member of the aristocracy."

There were cheers at this, and counter-cheers, or rather boos, from my brother and my husband and those who sided with them. Nevertheless, a show of hands decided upon the expulsion of the so-called former aristocrats, and the mayor Montlibert, with his son and a few others, left the church.

There was no further trouble until the bulletins, on which each man voting for an Elector had to write his name, had been dropped in the box provided. Villette, the president, was about to take the box to the scrutators to be counted when I saw Michel nudge my husband. François sprang to his feet and seized the box from the president.

"Your duties are finished," he cried. "It is not the business of the president to concern himself with the bulletins. This is the function of the scrutators."

He at once bore off the box to the sacristy, where the scrutators were waiting, all of them members of the National Guard, and I wondered how many of the bulletins they counted would find their way first to my husband and my brother. I sat silent, aghast at what I saw. The words "Liberté, egalité, fraternité" seemed far remote from the proceedings here. No one protested. Even the president Villette looked stupefied, and did not move.

"They deserve all they get," I told myself, to quiet my conscience. "Half of those who vote can't read or write, and some-one must do their thinking for them."

My husband returned and took his seat beside Michel. They consulted a moment, and then François called on Henri Dar-langes, from the parish of la Grande-Borde, to stand up and show himself. There was a shuffle of feet, and a frightened in-dividual stood to attention.

"We have information," said my husband, "that you are shel-tering two men in your house, former members of the aristoc-racy without passports, who have arms hidden."

"Not a word of truth in it," answered the man, a prospective Elector. "You are welcome to search my house and the whole parish."

Further consultation between Michel and François resulted in a demand for the return of Monsieur Montlibert, the mayor of Gault, to the assembly. I could see that it was my brother who was issuing the orders, and my husband who acted as spokesman for him.

"Citizen mayor," said my husband, "you have heard this man

Henri Darlanges deny all knowledge of strangers or hidden arms. As adjutant-general of the National Guard, Michel Busson-Challoir orders you to proceed at once to la Grande-Borde and search his house. The proceedings cannot continue here at Gault until this is done." When he had finished speaking the doors of the church were flung open and a great contingent of the National Guard marched in, about sixty of them, all workmen from le Chesne-Bidault.

I began to see what my menfolk were at. Suspicion, whether just or unjust, must be thrown on all prospective Electors of moderate views. Once tainted thus, no one would have the hardihood to vote for them. The way would be clear then for the progressives.

"By what right . . ." began the mayor, but Michel, leaving his seat and walking over to Henri Darlanges, cut him short.

"By the right of f-force," he said. "Fall in behind the Guard." And then, to Darlanges beside him, "G-give me your keys."

The keys were handed over without a word. François snapped out an order. Then he, and Michel, with the mayor and Henri Darlanges between them, marched out of the church, escorted by the National Guard.

The meeting broke up in confusion. Prospective Electors stood by uncertain what to do, most of them too scared to take any action. I saw one woman outside the church burst into tears and run to her husband, asking if everyone was to be put in prison.

I went and sat in the mairie, not knowing where else to go, waiting upon events. Some of our own workmen, in uniform, were on sentry duty outside. None of the inhabitants of Gault dared approach us.

Presently the procession returned. Henri Darlanges had his hands roped behind his back, and so had two other men with him, his lodgers, it appeared, looking even more frightened than he did himself.

A mock trial was set in motion, and the mayor Montlibert forced to interrogate the prisoners. It was obvious, even to someone like myself who knew nothing of the law, that none of the men had done wrong. No arms had been found in the house.

The men had no pretensions to being aristocrats. Monsieur Villette, who had presided over the proceedings in the church, spoke up in their defence.

"If you are in c-collusion with these men," said Michel, "have the c-courage to admit it, or keep silent."

I feared, from his gesture and his tone of voice, that the worst might happen and the wretched prisoners would be taken out into the street and hanged. They feared so too. I saw the expression in their eyes. Then Michel summoned the captain of his Guard, the workman André Delalande.

"Take these men into c-custody," he ordered, "and see that they are m-marched into Mondoubleau and handed over to the authorities f-first thing in the morning."

André saluted. The unfortunates were marched out of the mairie.

"That's all," said Michel, "no further questions. The meeting in the c-church will be resumed tomorrow morning."

The mayor Montlibert, the president Villette, and the other officials left the building without a word of protest. Then, and only then, did my brother wink at François.

"The scrutators are locked in the ch-church," he said, "and I have the keys. I suggest we walk across and f-find out if they are counting the votes correctly."

I returned alone that night to le Chesne-Bidault, except for six of the National Guard to act as escort. The next day I allowed the primary elections for the canton of Gault to continue without me. The proceedings, I was afterwards told, went smoothly enough until one official complained of the events of the preceding day, upon which he was informed if he gave further trouble the workmen of le Chesne-Bidault would be delighted to deal with him in their own fashion. The official was then silent.

I was not surprised, when the primary elections were over, to hear that both my husband and my brother had been elected for Gault. Whatever my own feelings in the matter, one thing was certain. Intimidation paid. "The destiny of the nation," said my brother-in-law, Jacques Duval, "depends upon the Elector's choice of deputies," and those who were returned for Loir-et-

Cher were all progressives. There was not a moderate man amongst them.

The fall of Verdun on the 2nd of September put the whole country in a state of alarm. If the enemy advanced one step further we were ready for them. I was prepared to fight beside the men in the foundry yard.

"Danger is imminent," wrote Jacques Duval from Paris. "The tocsin has sounded here in the capital. Let it do so in each département throughout France, so that every citizen can rally to the nation's defence."

The very day he wrote that letter the prisons were broken into by the Paris crowds, and more than twelve hundred prisoners were slaughtered. We never heard who was to blame for it. Collective panic was the excuse given. Rumour, passing from one man to another, had whispered that the prisons held armed aristocrats, awaiting their moment to break free and destroy the citizens of Paris. The "brigands" of '89 had been resurrected.

On the 20th of September the Prussian and Austrian armies were repulsed at Valmy, and a few days later Verdun was re-taken. The people's army had responded to the call.

The new Assembly—the National Convention—met for the first time on September the 21st. We hoisted the tricolour above the furnace-house at le Chesne-Bidault, and the workmen, all in their uniform of the National Guard, sang the marching song that had supplanted "Ça Ira"—the Marseillaise.

That evening, in the master's house, Michel, François and I set out the replicas of the original glass made twenty years ago for Louis XV at the château of la Pierre, and we toasted the new Republic.

FIFTEEN

"THE NATIONAL CONVENTION declares Louis Capet, last King of the French, guilty of conspiracy against the liberty of the nation, and of attempting to undermine the safety of the State.

"The National Convention decrees that Louis Capet shall suffer the death penalty."

There was not a home throughout the country, during January of '93, where the case was not argued, for or against the King. Robespierre had stated the matter with his usual clarity, when he declared in December before the Convention, "If the King is not guilty, then those who have dethroned him are."

There were no two ways about it. Either it was right to depose the monarch for summoning the aid of foreign powers against the State, or it was wrong. If right, then the monarch had been guilty of treason and must pay the penalty. If wrong, then the National Convention must dissolve, ask pardon of the monarch, and capitulate to the enemy.

"You cannot go against Robespierre's logic," said my brother Pierre. "The Convention must either accuse the King, or accuse itself. If the King is absolved, it is tantamount to saying the Republic should never have been proclaimed, and the country must lay down its arms against Prussia and Austria."

"Who cares about l-logic?" answered Michel. "Louis is a t-traitor, we all know it. One sign of weakness on the p-part of the Convention, and every aristocrat and p-priest in the country will be rubbing their hands with j-joy. They should g-guillotine the lot."

"Why not send the royal family into exile? Wouldn't that be punishment enough?" I asked.

A groan went up from my two brothers, and my husband too.

"Exile?" exclaimed Pierre. "And let them use their influence to win more support for their cause? Imagine the Queen in Austria, for example! No, imprisonment for life is the only solution."

Michel gestured with his thumb towards the ground. "One answer, and one only," he said. "As long as those p-people live, above all that woman, they're a menace to s-security."

As it turned out, when judgement was passed against the King and he went to his death on the 21st of January, we were in trouble ourselves.

A court of enquiry was held at Gault by the département authorities on the holding of the primary elections, and the part my husband and my brother had played in them. It seemed that the mayor of Gault, and other officials, had forwarded a complaint to the Minister of the Interior, Monsieur Roland, who then ordered the investigation. It did not surprise me when the various citizens of Gault and other parishes appeared as witnesses for the prosecution.

The enquiry was held on the 22nd and 23rd of January (the day after the King was guillotined in Paris). Whether the authorities of our district in Loir-et-Cher held a secret sympathy or not for the fallen Louis I do not know, but they certainly came out strongly against violence, and both Michel and François were severely reprimanded.

"This Court finds that Messieurs Busson-Challoir and Duval acted illegally in expelling the ex-aristocrats and the clergy from the primary elections the preceding August, that they acted with excess towards the president of the assembly, that the workmen from the foundry of le Chesne-Bidault threatened many peaceable citizens, that public tranquillity was disturbed, and that in the eyes of the law and justice such conduct is reprehensible, and Messieurs Busson-Challoir and Duval should be denounced before the tribunal and suffer whatever penalty the law pronounces against those who disturb public order."

So ran the indictment, and it was only the intervention of my brother-in-law that saved François and Michel from serving a term in prison. A heavy fine got them out of their scrape, and Michel lost his status in the National Guard as adjutant-general for the district. The incident, far from subduing his patriotism, made him more fanatical than ever.

During that winter of '93, as we read our *Ami du Peuple* and learnt of the continuing divisions within the Convention, with ministers like Roland—who had instituted the enquiry against Michel and François—relaxing controls and allowing grain-prices to soar, despite the opposition of Robespierre and his Jacobin associates, who warned them of the dangers of inflation, it was only persuasion on the part of Pierre that prevented Michel from leaving us and throwing in his lot with the extremists in Paris.

There were continuous riots in the capital through February and March, the people complaining of the price of sugar, soap and candles. Once again the journalist Marat acted as their spokesman, suggesting that the only way to bring down prices was to hang a number of grocers over their own doorstep.

"By heaven, he's right," said my youngest brother. "I don't know why all P-Paris doesn't rise and make that f-fellow a dictator."

Certainly our Republic, which we had toasted so hopefully in September, was beset with enemies, both beyond our frontiers and within them.

After February I gave up all hope of hearing from my brother Robert again. The Convention had declared war against both England and Holland, and Robert, if he were still in London, would not only be an émigré but perhaps actively employed against his own country. If so, he would be as great a traitor as those thousands of our fellow-countrymen who, at this moment of extreme danger to the Republic from the Allies abroad, chose to launch a revolt in the west and plunge us all into the horrors of civil war.

The priests were behind the insurrection. Resentful of the loss of those privileges which they had held for centuries, and the seizure of their lands and property, they had been playing for months past upon the superstitions of the peasants, who, slow to welcome change, mistrusted the decrees passed by the Convention. Above all the peasants feared the military call-up passed the last week in February, which summoned to the colours every able-bodied unmarried man between the ages of eighteen and forty who could be spared from his ordinary work.

The King's execution and this conscription were the two final factors to rouse the peasants in the west, spurred on by the non-juring priests and disgruntled ex-aristocrats. The rebellion, once alight, spread like a forest fire, or, worse, like a disease, infecting all those malcontents who, for one reason or another, had lost faith in the revolution.

By April the Vendée, the Basse-Vendée, the Bocage, Anjou, the Loire-Inférieure, all were in revolt. Thousands of peasants, armed with any weapons from ancient muskets to hatchets and harvest sickles, pillaging as they went, led by men of indomitable courage who had nothing but their lives to lose, pressed forward across the Loire, meeting no resistance at first save from the terrified inhabitants of the villages and towns, which they promptly sacked. The republican armies were engaged on the frontier, repulsing the Allied invaders, and only a few companies of the National Guard were free to withstand this new and appalling onslaught from the west.

The rebels triumphed, encircling Nantes, pushing on to Angers and Saumur, driving prisoners and refugees before them, escorted on their march by waggon-loads of women and children, peasant families and the wives and mistresses of the former aristocrats, all living off the country, robbing and destroying as they went.

Heaven knows we hated the Allied invaders, and the émigrés who inspired them, but we hated the Vendéans, as the rebel army came to be called, even more. The hypocrisy of their war-cry "For Jesus" and of the banners of the Sacred Heart which they brandished, as though upon some new crusade, was only surpassed by their brutality in action. Slaughter on a scale far greater than any attempted by the Paris mob was the portion of those village patriots who dared to resist them. Women and children were not spared, men were thrown, while still alive, into ditches piled high with corpses. Clergy who had sworn the oath to the Constitution were tied to horses and dragged on the dusty roads to a terrible death. Here at last, in flesh and blood, with no rumour about them, were the "brigands" we had feared in

'89. Wearing white ribands and white cockades, the royalist leaders urged their ignorant peasant armies forward, with the promise of more loot and further conquests, the priests in the rear summoning them to Mass before each battle. On their knees before the Crucifix at dawn, cutting their way through unde-fended villages at midday, drunk with slaughter and success by sundown, the conquering, ill-disciplined yet courageous rabble, calling themselves God's soldiers, marched on through April and May to what seemed victory.

It was a struggle, as my brother Pierre said, between the Te Deum and the Marseillaise, and through that agonising summer of '93 the singers of the Marseillaise suffered one humiliating defeat after another.

The Convention in Paris, torn by dissension within their own ranks, gave contradictory orders to those generals, hastily recalled from the frontier, who now found themselves faced with the task of quelling the rebellion. It was not until the Republican armies had been re-grouped, at the end of September, that the long series of Vendéan victories came to an end. Robespierre, now supreme in the Convention, and leading member of the Committee of Public Safety, was determined to crush the rebel-lion, and the generals were ordered to annihilate the rebels, giving no quarter, taking no prisoners.

On the 17th of October the Vendéans suffered a terrible de-feat at Cholet, in Maine-et-Loire, where two of their chiefs, d'Elbée and Bonchamp, were severely wounded. It was the beginning of the end for the rebel army, though they did not know it; and instead of retreating across the Loire, and making a stand on their own ground, they pushed on towards the north, with the idea of taking Granville, the Channel port, for the English were said to be preparing a huge fleet to help them. The people of Granville, to their eternal credit, resisted the rebels, and in mid-November the long retreat back to the Loire began, with the republican armies closing in upon the Vendéans from every side.

Work had come almost to a standstill at le Chesne-Bidault, for although the rebels were well to the west of us, in Mayenne, we could never be certain, living as we did on the borders of

Sarthe and Loir-et-Cher, that their leaders might not take it into their heads to strike across country into our own départe-ment. Michel and the workmen were in a constant state of alert, and in his capacity as captain of the National Guard of le Plessis-Dorin my brother was itching to be off with his men and in the thick of the fighting. Duty, however, constrained him to keep to the defence of the village, should it be threatened; and although I felt that he and his handful of workmen would do little against the Vendéan thousands, if they came our way, the very sight of them in their uniforms parading the foundry yard gave me confidence.

The preservation of life had become sweet to me once more, for my baby Zoë Suzanne, born on the 27th of May, was now six months old. Plump and healthy, she had shown more vigour from the first day than the two babies I had lost, and my mother, who had come up from St. Christophe to see us during the sum-mer, predicted a normal childhood. Once the Vendéans had been defeated, we might all relax—those of us who were patriots. Robespierre's stern rule, though it sent hundreds to the guillo-tine, including the Queen and Robert's one-time patron, Phi-lippe-Egalité, the duc d'Orléans, had not only saved the country from defeat but made day-to-day living easier for the people, with his Law of the Maximum limiting the price of food, essential goods and labour.

Our great concern during the autumn was for Pierre, his family and Edmé. The Vendéans, when they passed through Laval on their way north to the coast, were not nineteen leagues distant from Le Mans, and during the retreat, a month later, they traversed the same territory again. Mayenne, Laval, Sa-blé, la Flèche, each day we had the news of the progress south, the rebel army low in morale and riddled with dysentery, dis-cipline lax, and considerably hampered by the numbers of women, children, nuns and priests who followed in its train.

On Tuesday the 13th Frimaire (the 3rd of December) we heard that they had reached Angers, and were preparing to lay siege to the city. Jacques Duval was living with us at the time, and he brought the news from Mondoubleau, where he had gone to consult with the authorities.

"All is well," he said. "Angers will resist, our army under Westermann is in pursuit, and we shall trap them before they can cross the Loire."

Angers was twenty-two leagues south-west of Le Mans, more than a day's march from the city, and a wave of thankfulness came over me for Pierre and Edmé, Marie and the boys.

"This will be their end," went on my brother-in-law. "They will be caught there in a pincer movement between our armies. We can deal with the stragglers and the deserters ourselves."

I saw Michel look across at François, and I guessed what was coming.

"If the National G-Guard of every parish went off in s-strength," he said, "we could cut them to p-pieces if they dared march east again."

He crossed to the window, and, opening it, shouted to André Delalande, who was crossing the foundry yard.

"S-sound the alert," he called. "Have every man p-parade within the hour with f-full equipment. We're off in pursuit of the s-sacré brigands."

It was shortly after two when they set forth, three hundred of them, carrying the tricolour and beating drums, with Michel at their head. Had my father been alive he would have been proud of that youngest son of his whom, more than thirty years ago, he used to blame for his sullen ways and his stammer.

We were at the mercy of rumour during the rest of the week, except for the news that the Vendéans had been thwarted in their attack on Angers. The city, gallantly defended, had not fallen, and the rebel leaders were now trying to decide where and when they could cross the Loire before the republican armies attacked them in the rear.

I might have known that hearsay is never to be trusted, that rumour, in the past, had spoken of brigands when brigands were not there. This time it was the other way about. Victory was claimed before victory was achieved.

"We've been without news of Pierre for long enough," I said to François the following Monday, when we awoke. "I propose to have Marcel drive me to Le Mans today and spend the night with them, and, if all is well, return tomorrow morning."

He at once demurred, as husbands will, saying that if any harm had come to Pierre we should have heard of it long since. The roads were still unsafe, the weather threatening. Let Marcel go with a message if need be, but I must stay at le Chesne-Bidault. In any event, the baby would be restless in the night without me.

"We have had no broken nights with Zoë since she was born," I told him, "and she can sleep in her cradle beside Madame Verdelet. I shall be gone for half a day and a night, no more than that, and if Edmé and Marie and the boys wish to do so, I shall bring them back here with me when I return."

Obstinacy, no doubt, made me hold to my plan. I had seen my brother Michel march off the week before in pursuit of the Vendéans, and his courage had made me bold. Besides, had not Jacques Duval assured me that the "brigands", as we so rightly called them, were routed, struggling, as best they could, to make their way across the Loire?

Perhaps, and this I hardly admitted even to myself, I also felt that François lagged behind Michel. My husband, unlike my brother, had not volunteered to accompany the National Guard on their expedition. He could learn that his wife did not share his scruples.

Marcel and I set forth as soon as we had breakfasted. François, seeing that nothing would make me change my mind, said at the last moment that he would drive me. I would have none of it, however, and bade him stay at home and mind his daughter.

"If we do see any brigands," I told him as I said good-bye, "we'll give a good account of ourselves"—patting the two muskets strapped to the roof of the carriole. My words were spoken in jest; I little thought how near they would come to the truth.

Once past Vibraye I saw that my husband had been right about one thing—the weather. It turned bitterly cold, and started to rain and sleet. I was warmly wrapped, nevertheless, my hands and feet were soon numb with the cold, and Marcel, peering into the driving rain ahead, looked disconcerted.

"You haven't chosen a good day for your venture, citoyenne," he said.

We had been careful, ever since the September decrees, to

adopt the new courtesies. Monsieur and madame were things of the past, like the old calendar. I had to remind myself also that today was the 19th Frimaire, Year II of the Republic, and no longer the 9th of December, 1793.

"Perhaps not," I answered, "but at least we have a roof to the carriole and keep dry, which is more than our National Guard can say, closing in upon the brigands, perhaps at this very moment."

Luckily for my peace of mind I saw them jubilant, not outnumbered and in full retreat, as was the truth.

We reached Le Mans by early afternoon, but because of the weather it was already almost dark, and there were sentries guarding the bridge across the Huisne.

They came forward to take our passports, and I saw that they were not members of the National Guard but ordinary citizens, with armbands, armed with muskets. I recognised the leader—he had been a client of Pierre's—and at sight of me he waved his men aside and came to the carriole himself.

"Citoyenne Duval?" he called out, in astonishment. "What in the world are you doing here at such a moment?"

"I've come to see my brother," I told him. "I've been anxious about him and his family for the past weeks, as you may imagine. Now the worst is over I've seized the first opportunity to come and visit him."

He stared at me as if I had lost my senses. "Over?" he repeated. "Haven't you heard the news?"

"News? What news?"

"The Vendéans have retaken la Flèche and may well march upon Le Mans tomorrow," he answered. "There are nearly 80,000 of them, desperate with hunger and disease, preparing to strike east, with some wild talk of taking Paris. Almost every man here in the garrison has gone south to try and stop them, but they won't have much hope, some 1,500 of them, against that band of brigands."

I had thought it was the icy wind that had turned him pale from cold, but now I saw that it was fear as well.

"We heard there had been a victory at Angers," I said, my heart sinking. "What in the world are we to do? We've been half the day on the road from le Plessis-Dorin, and now it's almost dark."

"Go back there, if you have any sense," he answered, "or seek shelter for the night in some farmhouse out in the country."

I glanced at Marcel. The poor fellow was as white as the rest of them.

"The horse will never do the journey twice," I said, "nor will anyone in the country take us in, with this news. Doors and windows will be barred everywhere."

The citoyen Roger—I remembered his name, in a flash—stared up at me, the raindrops falling from his hat.

"I can't advise you," he said. "Thank God I'm unmarried. But if I had a wife I would not let her enter the city, not with this threat hanging over it."

My obstinacy was well-paid. What mockery it had been to leave le Chesne-Bidault without having waited for further news.

"If the brigands are coming," I said, "I'd rather face them with my brother in Le Mans than out here in the country beneath a hedge."

Pierre's client handed me back the passports and shrugged his shoulders.

"You won't find your brother in Le Mans," he replied. "The citoyen Busson du Charme will have left with the rest of the National Guard to defend the road to la Flèche. They had their orders at midday, just as we did."

To retreat now was impossible. The bleak countryside beyond the Huisne whence we had come, lashed with rain, grey in the gathering dusk, decided me. Also our dispirited horse, sagging between the shafts.

"We'll take our chance, citoyen," I said to Monsieur Roger. "Good luck to you and your men."

He saluted gravely and waved us on, and we entered a dead city, the houses shuttered, not a soul out in the streets. The hotel where we usually baited the horse was barricaded like the rest, and it was only after continued knocking that the landlord came, thinking we were the guard. Although he knew me, and the horse and carriole, he would not have stabled either had I not paid him triple his usual charge.

"If the brigands come, citoyenne, they'll burn the city down, you know that, don't you?" he said to me, on parting, and he showed me a pair of loaded pistols with which, so he assured me, he would shoot his wife and children rather than that they should fall into the hands of the Vendéans.

Marcel and I hurried through the streets to the quarter where Pierre lived, near the church of St. Pavin. As we walked, to be drenched by the rain within five minutes, I kept thinking of François and his brother, sitting contentedly at home at le Chesne-Bidault, knowing nothing of our plight. I thought of my baby too, sleeping peacefully in her cradle, and of poor Marcel's wife and children.

"I'm sorry, Marcel," I said to him, "you have me to blame for this adventure, no one else."

"Don't worry, citoyenne," he answered me. "The brigands may never come, and if they do we'll answer them with these."

He carried our two muskets over his shoulder, and I remembered the 80,000 Vendéans said to be starving in la Flèche.

Pierre's house was shuttered and barred like its neighbours, but here I had only to give two double knocks in quick succession, an old childhood signal, for the door to be opened forthwith and Edmé to be standing there. She might have been Michel in miniature, her brown hair ruffled, her eyes suspicious, a pistol in her hand which I had no doubt was loaded. At sight of me she put it down, and flung her arms about me.

"Sophie . . . Oh, Sophie . . ."

We clung to each other for a moment, and I heard my sister-in-law's anxious voice calling from the room beyond, "Who is it?" One of the younger boys was crying, a dog was barking, and I could imagine the pandemonium within.

I explained everything to Edmé in a moment, there in the entrance, then Marcel helped her bolt and bar the door once more.

"Pierre went off with the National Guard at noon," she said. "We haven't seen him since. He said to me 'Look after Marie and the children', and that's what I've done. We have food enough in the house for three or four days. If the brigands come, I'm ready for them."

She glanced at the muskets that Marcel had placed beside the door.

"Now we are well armed," she added, and, smiling at Marcel, "Do you mind serving under my command, citoyen?"

He was a lanky fellow of six foot or more, and he looked down at her sheepishly.

"You have only to give your orders, citoyenne," he answered.

I was reminded of our childhood at la Pierre, and how Edmé had preferred boys' games to dolls, forever asking Michel to shape swords and daggers. The chance to play the man had come for her at last.

"Troops cannot fight on an empty stomach," she said. "You'd both better come to the kitchen and fall to. It may have been foolish of you to leave le Chesne-Bidault, but I'll tell you one thing . . . I'm glad of reinforcements."

The boys now came running through from the inner room, Emile, the eldest, now thirteen, the youngest, Pierre-François, barely six, followed by a terrier bitch and a litter of puppies. My sister-in-law brought up the rear with the elderly widow and her daughter, permanent fixtures in this haphazard household, peering over her shoulder. I did not wonder that Edmé was glad of reinforcements. Her small community needed some defence.

We ate as best we could, bombarded on all sides by questions, none of which we could answer. The Vendéans were at la Flèche, that was all we knew. Whether they would now strike north, east, or west, nobody could say.

"One thing is certain," said Edmé. "If they try to take Le Mans, the city is virtually undefended. We have one battalion of Valenciennes quartered here, a detachment of cavalry, and our own National Guard; and they are now, all of them, somewhere on the road between the city and la Flèche."

This she told me later, when we were preparing for bed. She did not wish to alarm Pierre's wife, or the two boarders. She made me sleep on her bed, and she herself lay fully dressed on a mattress by the door. Marcel had elected to sleep in the entrance hall on a second mattress.

"If anything happens," said Edmé, "he and I are both prepared."

I saw she had a loaded musket beside her, and I had as much confidence in her capabilities to defend us as I would have had in Pierre himself.

We awoke to the same bleak sky and driving rain, and after breakfasting—eating as little as possible to save our rations—we sent Marcel out into the town to hear the latest news. He was gone more than an hour, and when he returned we could see at once by his face that the news was grave.

"The mayor and the municipality have already left for Chartres," he said. "All the public officials have gone with them, taking money, documents, papers, whatever mustn't fall into rebel hands. They've taken their families with them too. Whoever can find transport to get away has gone."

His words produced in me the old panic of '89. Then, the brigands had been legendary. Now they were real, not a half day's march from Le Mans.

"How many can the carriole hold?" I asked him.

He shook his head. "I called there not twenty minutes since, citoyenne," he answered. "The place was empty, and the stable too. That scoundrel of a landlord has taken carriole and horse to save himself and his family."

I turned desperately to Edmé. "What are we going to do?" I asked her.

She folded her arms and stood there, watching me.

"There's only one thing we can do," she answered. "Stay here, and fight it out."

Marcel moistened his lips with his tongue. I don't know who felt the more desperate, he or I.

"They were saying in the place des Halles that if the brigands enter the city no harm will come to those who don't resist them, citoyenne," he said. "It's food they want, nothing else. Women and children won't be made to suffer. They may take the men, though, and hang every one of them."

Edmé and I knew what he was after. He wanted permission to leave. He could still get away alone, and on foot. If he stayed with us, he might lose his life.

"Do as you wish, citoyen," said Edmé. "You don't belong here anyway. It's for the citoyenne Duval to say, not me."

I thought of the family waiting for him at le Chesne-Bidault, and I had not the heart to ask him to stay, though it meant leaving us defenceless.

"Go quickly, Marcel," I said. "If you reach home safely . . . you know what to tell them. Here, take your musket."

He shook his head. "I can travel quicker without it, citoyenne," he replied, and, bending low over my hands, he was gone the next moment.

"He meant," said Edmé, barring the door, "that he can run the faster. Are all the workmen at the foundry as chicken-hearted? If so, the place has changed. Can you fire a musket, Sophie?"

"No," I told her truthfully.

"Then I shall use the one and keep the second in reserve. Emile is old enough to use the pistol." She shouted for her nephew.

I had one of those strange aberrations of the mind when nothing that is happening seems true, and every action the sequence in a dream. I watched Edmé post the thirteen-year-old Emile at an upper window with the loaded pistol, while she herself, the muskets at her side, watched by the window of an adjoining room. Marie, the younger boys, the widow and her daughter were all locked up in the widow's apartment at the back of the house. The window there looked out upon rooftops but no street. It was the safest place.

"If they break down the door," said Edmé, "we can defend the stairs."

At this moment at le Chesne-Bidault Madame Verdelet would be giving Zoë Suzanne her mid-morning feed, lifting her from her cradle, propping her up in her high chair in the kitchen. Jacques Duval would be riding to Mondoubleau, perhaps, for news, and François employing the few men left about the foundry.

Just before midday I went down to the kitchen and prepared a meal which I carried up to the family in the back room. They had pushed the bed against the wall to give more floor space for the children's play. Marie, my sister-in-law, was mending the boys' socks. The widow was reading and her daughter threading beads on a string to amuse the youngest child. It was a calm, domestic scene, and the unusual peace more shocking to me than if the children had been crying and the others had shown fear.

I left them with their food and locked the door. Then I took a bowl of soup to Emile and a loaf of bread, which he ate as if half-starved.

"When will the brigands come?" he asked. "I want to fire this pistol."

The numb dream state that had been mine for the past few hours suddenly left me. What was happening was real. Edmé turned from her window on the street and looked at me.

"I don't want anything to eat," she said, "I'm not hungry."

Outside it was raining still.

SIXTEEN

I WAS SITTING AT the top of the stairs, resting my head against the baluster, when Emile called out, "There are some strange-looking people in the street. Some men who look like peasants, wearing sabots, and a lot of women, one of them with a baby. I think they must be lost."

I had been dozing, but his words startled me to action. I heard Edmé fumble with her musket, and I ran into Emile's room and stood beside him, peering through the chink of the shutters down into the street. When I saw them I knew. The Vendéans had entered the city. Here were some of the stragglers, who had found their way into our street, and were staring up at the houses for signs of life.

Instinct made me pull Emile back from the window.

"Stay quiet," I said, "don't let them see you."

He looked at me, puzzled, then suddenly he understood.

"Those ragged people down there?" he asked. "Are they the brigands?"

"Yes," I said. "Perhaps they'll go away. Keep still."

Edmé had crept into the room to join us. She had her musket with her. I questioned her with my eyes, and she nodded back at me.

"I won't fire," she said, "not unless we're attacked."

The three of us stood shoulder to shoulder looking down into the street. The first stragglers had gone ahead, and now others were coming, twenty, thirty, forty. Emile was counting them under his breath. They were not marching, there was no sort of order, these could not be the army proper, who would have gone by the main streets to the place des Halles. These were the followers-on, the rabble.

Now the numbers were growing larger, with more men than

women, many of them armed with muskets and pikes, some bare-foot but most in sabots. Some of them were wounded, and were supported by their fellows. Nearly all of them were ragged, ema-ciated, white with exhaustion, soaked and grimy with the mud and the rain.

I do not know what I had expected, or Edmé and Emile either. The beating of drums, perhaps, firing, shouting, singing, the tri-umphant entry of a victorious army. Anything but silence, the slow clatter of sabots on the cobbles and the silence. The silence was the worst of all.

"What are they looking for? Where are they all going?" whis-pered Emile.

We did not answer him. There was no answer to give. Like ghosts of dead men they passed beneath our windows and out of sight along the street, and as they passed more took their place, and then in the midst of them another band of women, and some half-dozen whimpering children.

"There won't be enough to feed them," said Edmé, "not in all Le Mans."

I noticed then that she had put down her musket. It was rest-ing against the wall. The clock in the entrance below struck four.

"It will soon be dark," said Emile. "Where will all these peo-ple go?"

Suddenly we heard a clatter of hoofs, and shouting, and what appeared to be a small body of cavalry came down the street, led by an officer. He wore the hated white cockade in his hat and a white sash round his waist, and flourished a sabre in his hand. He yelled some order to the straggling wretches ahead, who turned and stared at him. He must have spoken to them in patois; we could not understand a word of it, but we could see by the way he pointed with his sabre that he was directing them to the houses opposite.

Some of the people, dazed but obedient, began hammering at the doors. No one, as yet, touched ours. Another body of men, armed and on foot, came down the street. The mounted officer, at sight of them, shouted a command, directing them to the houses, and they scattered, taking a house apiece, hammering on the door, pushing the stragglers away. One of them came and knocked on our door too.

Then the mounted officer, raising himself and standing in his stirrups, shouted aloud, for all of us to hear.

"Not one of you who opens his door will be molested," he called. "There are some eighty thousand of us here in your city, and we must be fed and housed. Anyone who does not open his door will have that door marked, and the house burnt down within the hour. It is for you to decide."

He paused a moment, then, signalling to the mounted troops behind him, clattered off down the street. The armed foot soldiers and the peasants in the street went on knocking at the houses.

"What shall we do?" asked Edmé.

She had reverted to her rôle of younger sister. I watched the houses opposite. One of our neighbours had opened the door, and three wounded men were being carried inside. Another door opened. One of the armed soldiers shouted to a woman with two children, and motioned her inside.

"If we don't open," I said to Edmé, "they'll mark the door and come back and burn the house."

"It could have been a threat," she answered. "They can't spare the time to go round marking every door."

We waited. More and more of them were coming down the street, and since the officer had passed, giving his orders to knock upon the doors, the silence had been broken. They were now calling and shouting to one another in confusion, and it was getting darker as each moment passed.

"I'll go down," I said. "I'll go down and open the door."

Neither my sister nor my nephew answered me. I went downstairs and unbolted the door. There were some half-dozen of them waiting, peasants by the look of them, and three women and two children, and another woman carrying a baby. One of the men was armed with a musket, the rest with pikes. The man with the musket asked me a question—he spoke so broadly that I couldn't understand him, but I caught the word "rooms". Could it be that he wanted to know how many rooms there were in the house?

"Six," I said, "we have six rooms above, and two below. Eight in all." I held up my fingers. I might have been the patron of a hotel touting for custom.

"Go on . . . go on . . ." he cried to those about him, driving them ahead, and they filed into the house, the women and the other peasants. Following them was a man who seemed to have but half a leg; he was carried by two others who, though they walked, looked almost as ill as he.

"That's it," said the peasant with the musket, prodding his fellows like so many cattle, "that's it . . . that's it . . ." and he pushed them forward to the salon and to Pierre's small library that opened out of it.

"They'll fix themselves," he said to me, "they'll need bedding. . . ."

So much I understood, more from his gestures than his speech, and he pointed to his mouth and rubbed his belly.

"They're hungry. Doubled-up. What with that, and the sickness. . . ." He grinned, showing toothless gums. "All day on the road," he said. "No good. Everybody tired."

The man with half a leg was being stretched out on Marie's settee by his two companions. The women had pushed past me to the kitchen and were opening the cupboards. "That's it, that's it . . ." repeated the man with the musket. "Someone will be along directly to see to the wounded man." He went out into the street, slamming the door behind him.

Edmé came down the stairs, followed by Emile. "How many are they?" she asked.

"I don't know," I answered. "I haven't counted."

We looked into the salon, and there were more than I thought. Eight men, one with the injured leg, and two who seemed sick. One of these was already grasping his stomach and retching. The stench coming from him was appalling.

"What's wrong with him?" asked Emile. "Is he going to die?"

The other sick man raised his head and stared at us.

"It's the sickness," he said, "half the army has it. We caught it in the north, in Normandy. The food and wine there poisoned us."

He seemed more educated than the others, and spoke a French I understood.

"It's dysentery," said Edmé. "Pierre warned us about it."

I looked at her, aghast. "We'll have to put them in a room apart," I said. "They had better go in the boys' room upstairs."

I bent down to the man whose French I understood.

"Follow me," I said. "You shall have a room to yourselves."

Once again I reminded myself of some hotel patron, and a wild desire to laugh rose in me, instantly checked when I perceived the full state of the man with dysentery, whom his companion was helping from the floor. He had been lying, poor wretch, in his own filth all about him, and was too weak to walk.

"It's no use," said his companion, "he's too ill to move. If we could have the room yonder." He jerked his head at Pierre's library, and began to drag the sick man to it.

"Get a mattress," I said to Emile. "He'll have to have a mattress. The other one too. Bring down mattresses for both of them."

Surely, I thought, the sick man should be stripped of his things, and linen wrapped about him. The clothes he was wearing must be burnt . . . I went into the kitchen, and I saw that every cupboard had been flung open and every drawer turned out, and all the food remaining in the house piled high on the kitchen table. Two women were cutting up the bread, stuffing themselves as they did so, and feeding the children. The third woman stood by the stove, stirring the soup she had found there, suckling her baby at the same time. They took no notice of me when I entered, but went on talking to each other in their own patois.

I took some cloths and a pail of water into the salon to scrub the floor where the poor sick man had lain. And now the man with the injured leg was groaning; I could see the blood coming through his bandages. No one was looking after him. His companions had pushed past me and gone into the kitchen to search for food, and I could hear them cursing the women for feeding themselves before the rest.

There was a thumping on the floor from the back room above, and I called to Emile to tell his mother to keep the children quiet; the house was full of the Vendéans, some of them wounded and sick. He came running back again within the minute.

"The boys are hungry," he said, "they want to come down to supper."

"Tell them there is no supper," I said, wringing out the floor-cloth. "The Vendéans have taken it all."

Somebody thundered on the entrance door, and I thought it might be the man with the musket to see how his friends fared. But when Edmé went to open it six more of them pushed their way inside, five men and a woman, better dressed than our first peasants, and one of the men a priest.

"How many in the house?" demanded the priest.

He wore the Sacred Heart as an emblem on his breast, and a pistol thrust into his belt beside his rosary.

I shut my eyes and counted. "About twenty-four," I said, "counting ourselves. Some of your people are sick."

"Dysentery?" he asked.

"Two with dysentery," I answered, "one with a badly injured leg."

He turned to the woman beside him, who already held a handkerchief to her nose. She wore a bright green gown under a man's military cloak, and her feathered hat sat on a pile of curls.

"They've dysentery in the house," he said, "but it's the same everywhere. The house itself looks clean enough."

The woman shrugged her shoulders. "I must have a bed," she said, "and a room to myself. Surely the sick can all go in to-gether?"

The priest pushed past me. "Have you a room upstairs for this lady?" he asked Edmé.

I saw Edmé staring at his Sacred Heart. "We have a room," she said. "Go upstairs and find it."

The priest and the woman went upstairs. The other four men had already passed through into the kitchen. In the salon the man with the injured leg began shouting aloud with pain. In a moment or two the priest came down the stairs.

"Madame will stay," he said. "She is very exhausted, and hungry. You will please take some food up to her at once."

"There is no food," I said. "Your people are eating it all in the kitchen."

He clicked his tongue in annoyance and thrust his way past me to the kitchen. The uproar ceased. I heard the priest's voice only, raised in anger.

"He's threatening them with hell," whispered Emile.

The cursing changed to intoning. They all began saying the Ave Maria, the women's voices loudest. Then the priest returned to the entrance hall. He looked half-starved himself, but he had not eaten anything.

He stared at me a moment, then asked abruptly, "Where are the wounded?"

I took him to the salon. "One wounded," I said, "two in the further room with dysentery."

He muttered something in answer, and, unfastening his rosary, passed into the salon. I saw him glance down at the blood-stained bandage on the leg of the wounded man, but he did not examine the wound or touch the bandage. He held the rosary to the lips of the sufferer, saying, "Misereatur vestri omnipotens Deus."

I shut the door of the salon and left them alone.

I could hear the latest arrival, the woman, moving about in Pierre's and Marie's room above. I went up the stairs and opened the door. The woman had flung wide the cupboards and was turning Marie's clothes out on to the floor. There was a fine shawl amongst the clothes, a gift to Marie from my mother. The woman put it round her shoulders.

"Make haste with the supper," she said. "I don't intend to wait all night."

She did not bother to turn her head to see who it was at the door.

"You'll be lucky if you get any," I told her. "The women who were here before you have eaten most of it."

She looked over her shoulder at the sound of my voice, which was new to her. She was handsome in a disagreeable way, and there was nothing of the peasant about her.

"You had better watch your tongue when you address me,"

she said. "One word to the men below, and I'll have you whipped for insolence."

I did not answer her. I went out and shut the door. It was her kind that the Committee of Public Safety in Paris were rounding up and sending to the Conciergerie en route for the guillotine. As wife or mistress of a Vendéan officer, she believed herself of consequence. It did not matter to me. I passed one of the peasant women on the stairs bearing up a tray of food to her. "She doesn't deserve it," I murmured. The woman stared.

When I went into the salon once again the man with half a leg was crying softly to himself. The blood had come right through his bandages and soaked the material on the settee. Someone had shut the door leading to the inner room where the dysentery patients lay. The priest had gone.

"We'd forgotten about the wine," said Edmé, coming through from the hall.

"Wine? What wine?" I asked.

"Pierre's wine," she said. "There were about a dozen bottles in the cellar. Those men have found it. They have all the bottles on the kitchen table, and are knocking the heads off them."

Emile had crept past me and was listening at the door of the inner room.

"I think one of those men must be dying in there," he whispered. "There's a queer groaning noise. Shall I open the door and see?"

It was suddenly too much. The moment and the hour. Nothing that any of us could do would be of use. I felt my legs tremble under me.

"Let's lock ourselves in one of the rooms upstairs," I said.

As we left the salon the man with half a leg began to groan again. Nobody heard him. They were all singing and laughing in the kitchen, and just before we locked ourselves in Edmé's room we heard a great crash of breaking glass.

Somehow we slept that night, waking every few hours and losing all count of time, disturbed by continual treading in the rooms beside us, and by crying—whether of our own younger children from the back of the house or the Vendéans we could not tell. Emile complained of hunger, though he had eaten well at midday. Edmé and I had taken nothing since early morning.

We must have fallen heavily asleep, all three of us, in the small hours, for we were awakened about seven to hear the sound of the cathedral bells. Emile jumped off the bed and ran to open the shutters. The bells were pealing as they did on Easter Day.

"It's the Vendéan priests," said Edmé after a moment. "They're going to celebrate their entry into the city by singing Mass in the cathedral. I hope they choke themselves."

The rain had ceased. A dreary, fitful sun was trying to force its way through the pallid sky.

"The street's empty," said Emile. "None of the shutters are open in the houses opposite. Shall I go downstairs and see what's happening?"

"No," I said, "no, I'll go."

I smoothed my hair and straightened my clothes, and unlocked the door. The house was silent, but for the sound of heavy snoring in the adjoining room. The door was half ajar. I glanced in. The woman with the baby was asleep on the bed, and a man beside her. One of the other children was lying on the floor.

I crept downstairs and looked into the salon. The room was in complete confusion, with broken bottles strewn about the floor and men sprawled anyhow. The man with half a leg was still lying on the couch, but twisted sideways, his arms above his head. He was breathing loudly, half-snoring with each breath he took. He was probably unconscious. The door through to Pierre's library was still shut, and I could not go and ask after the men with dysentery because of the others sleeping on the floor.

The kitchen was in the same confusion. Wreckage and destruction everywhere, broken bottles and spilt wine, and the filthy litter of spoilt food. Four of them were on the floor here too, one of them a woman, with a child across her knees. None of them woke when I entered, and I felt they would lie here all the day. One glance about me, and in the larder, was enough to tell me there was nothing to eat.

Once, long ago when we were children, a travelling menagerie had come to Vibraye, and my father had taken Edmé and me to see the animals. They were penned in cages, and after staring at them awhile we came away, because of the reeking smell. The kitchen smelt as the cages had done that day. I went back again upstairs, and beckoned Edmé and Emile, and we went through to the room at the back to see Marie and the others. We found them desperate with anxiety, not knowing how we had fared. The children were whining and restless, asking for their breakfast, and the poor dog frantic to go outside.

"Let me take her," said Emile, "they're all asleep. No one will say anything to me."

Edmé shook her head, and I guessed her thought. If a dog was loose in the street, even for a moment, some passer-by might seek to destroy it instantly for food. The larder in our house was empty, others in the city would be the same. There were some 80,000 Vendéans in Le Mans, and somehow, through the day, all of their number must be fed . . .

"Have you anything to give our children?" I asked. My sister-in-law had four loaves left, and some apples, and a jug of milk half turned. The widow had three pots of blackcurrant preserve. They had water enough to brew coffee, and with this they must be satisfied. There was plenty of wood to keep the fire going.

The three of us drank coffee, knowing it might be all we should get that day, and then we locked their door and went back to our own room. We went on sitting there through the morning, keeping a watch on the window in turn, and about noon Emile, who was on guard, reported movement from the house opposite. Two Vendéans came out and stretched themselves, and presently a third, and then a fourth, and they talked amongst themselves awhile on the step, and then began walking up the street.

There was movement in our house too. We heard the door open below, and two of our "lodgers" went into the street, with the woman and the child who had been lying in the kitchen. They walked up the street after the others.

"They're hungry," said Emile. "They're going off to see if they can do better somewhere else."

"It's like watching a play," said Edmé, "and not knowing the ending. A play where the actors don't pretend any more, but come alive."

Suddenly we saw a carriage come up the street, driven by a man in uniform, wearing a white cockade. The carriage stopped before our door.

"It's that priest," said Edmé. "He's had a lift to save his feet."

She was right. The priest of the night before got out of the carriage and knocked on the door of our house. We heard someone open the door and admit him. There was a murmur of voices from below, and presently a stumping up the stairs, and knocking on the room at the end of the landing, Pierre's and Marie's room, where the woman in the green dress had gone.

"What's he going to do in there?" whispered Emile.

Edmé murmured something under her breath and Emile, halfchoking, stuffed his fist into his mouth.

In about five minutes' time the window of Pierre's room was flung open and we heard the priest shouting down to the soldier in uniform. The soldier shouted back, and then one of the peasants from below went and held his horse, and the soldier entered the house and came upstairs.

"Two of them?" whispered Emile, his voice high with hysteria.

Presently there was a sound of dragging and thumping from the room to the stairs, and peering from our window we saw that the priest and the soldier were hauling Marie's clothes-press into the street, helped by one of the peasants, and between the three of them they lifted it into the carriage.

"Oh no . . ." said Edmé. "No . . . no . . ."

I held her wrist. "Be quiet," I said. "We can't do anything."

Now the woman in the green dress was throwing things out of the window, shoes belonging to Marie, and a fur cape and several dresses, and, not content, she followed up with the blankets from the bed and the quilted bedspread that had been Pierre's and Marie's from their wedding-day. The woman found nothing else to her fancy, for soon we heard her coming down the stairs, and she went out into the street and stood talking for a moment to the priest and the soldier. Her voice carried, and it was not difficult to understand her.

"What has been decided?" she asked, and the soldier and the priest argued together, but it was impossible to hear them, though the soldier pointed towards the centre of the town.

"If the Prince Tallemont is for evacuating the city you can rest assured that is what we shall do," said the woman.

There was further argument and further talk, and then she and the priest climbed into the carriage and the soldier took the reins and they drove away.

"The priest didn't go in to look at the wounded man, or the men with the dysentery," said Emile. "All he could think about was letting that woman have my mother's clothes."

The priest's example must have fired the peasants, who had awakened from their drunken sleep below, for there now started a great racket throughout the house, up and down the stairs and in the salon and the kitchen, and the men began carrying things out into the street as well—pots and pans, and coats belonging to Pierre from the closet in the entrance hall.

I was reminded, all too suddenly, of the workmen from le Chesne-Bidault and their forays to Authon and St. Avit. What had been done to others was now done to us.

"Only surely," I said to myself, "it was not quite the same. Surely Michel and the workmen set about it differently?"

Perhaps not. Perhaps, in fact, it had been just the same. And there had been women and a young boy watching the National Guard from the windows of the château Charbonnières just as we now watched the Vendéans.

"We can't prevent them," I said to Edmé. "Don't let's look any more."

"I can't stop myself," said Edmé. "The more I watch, the more I hate. I didn't know it was possible to hate so much."

She stared down at the street below, and Emile called out in bewilderment and anger when he recognised familiar objects carried from the house.

"There's the clock from the salon," he said, "the one with the chimes. And my father's fishing-rod—what can they want with that? They've stripped the curtains from the window and rolled them into a bundle, and that woman with the children is making one of the men carry them on his shoulder. Why can't we shoot at them?"

"Because," said Edmé, "they're too many for us. Because, perhaps for this day only, luck is on their side."

I saw her glance at the two muskets still standing in the corner of the room, and I could guess how much it cost her to keep her hands off them.

"That's the finish," said Emile suddenly, his eyes filling with tears. "The woman has found Dadá in the cupboard below the stairs. She has given it to her child, and he's walking off with it."

Dadá was the wooden horse that had been Emile's childhood toy, prized all his thirteen years, and now the loved property of his youngest brother. Clocks, clothes, bed-linen, the theft of these I had accepted with resignation, but the bearing away of Dadá was the final outrage.

"Stay here," I said, "I'll get it back for you."

I unlocked the door and ran downstairs, and into the street after the woman and the boy. Neither Edmé nor Emile had told me, though, that the peasants had been piling their loot into a cart, and now, as I came out into the street, they had climbed up into the cart and were driving off. There were three or four of them in the cart, sitting on top of the stuff they had packed on to it, and the woman was there, and the boy clutching Dadá.

"We don't mind you taking the other things," I cried, "it's the horse. The horse belongs to the children in the house."

They stared down at me, astonished. I don't think they understood me. The woman nudged her companions, and broke into a silly cackle of laughter. She shouted something, which made all of them laugh, but what it was I could not say.

"I'll find your boy another toy if we could have back the horse," I said.

Then the man who was driving cut down at me with his whip, flaying my face. The shock of the pain made me cry out, and I backed away from the cart, and a moment later they were driving down the street. I heard the window above being opened, and Edmé called down to me, her voice half-strangled and unlike herself, "I'll shoot them for that . . . I'll shoot them for that."

"No," I shouted, "no, they'll kill you . . ."

I ran up the stairs and into the room, and as I entered it I heard the explosive shot of the musket. She had missed, of course, and the shot had hit a house at the end of the street. The peasants, startled, looked up at the sky and all about them, then drove on, turned the corner of the street and disappeared. They had not seen from where the shot had come.

"That was madness," I told Edmé. "If they had seen you, they would have sent soldiers back to shoot us all."

"I wish they would," said Edmé, "I wish they would . . ."

I looked at myself in the mirror on the wall. There was a great weal on my face where the man had laid his whip, and it was bleeding, too. I did not mind the pain, but the shock of what had happened made me feel faint. I put my handkerchief to my face and sat on the bed, trembling.

"Are you hurt?" asked Emile anxiously.

"No," I said, "no, it's not that."

It was what one person could do to another. The man driving the cart, not knowing me, cracking my face with his whip. It was Edmé, shooting wildly from the window. It was the crowd, in '89, before the Abbey of St. Vincent. It was the two men being butchered at Ballon . . .

"I'm going to see what's happening below," said Edmé.

I went on sitting on the bed, holding the handkerchief to my face.

When she came up again, and Emile with her—I had not noticed he had followed her—she said that the man with half a leg was delirious, moaning and thrashing about, his bandages loose.

"There's blood all over the settee and on the floor," said Emile.

"He'll die if a doctor does not see him," said Edmé.

I stared at her. "Perhaps we should try and clean the wound?" I said.

"Why should we?" she answered. "The sooner he dies the better. It would be one Vendéan the less."

She went over again to the window and stared down into the street.

Presently, when I felt better, I went downstairs myself to look at the injured man. There was no one else in the salon, all the others had gone. The man was muttering and moaning, and the blood had soaked right through the bandages to the couch and on to the floor. I went through the salon and opened the door of the inner room. The stench was unbearable. Instinctively, I clapped my handkerchief over my nose and mouth. One man lay on his back dead. I knew he was dead because of the stiffness. The other, the one who had spoken courteously the day before, lifted his head from his mattress as I entered.

"My friend is dead," he murmured. "I am going to die too. If you could ask the priest to come . . ."

I went out and shut the door. I went back to the wounded man and stared down at his bandage. At least, if I cut away the bandages and put a clean cloth on the wound, it might help to staunch the blood. I might have known, though, that the Vendéans would have stripped the linen closet too. It was empty. I found a white petticoat in Pierre's and Marie's room which the woman in the green dress had picked up and thrown aside. This I tore into strips to make a clean bandage for the wounded man.

When I tried to take away the soaked old bandage I found it stuck to the gaping wound beneath, and I was too sick to try and cut it away, so I put the new bandage on top of the old. Somehow, to my ignorant eye, it looked better, cleaner. I tried to give the man some water to drink, but he was too delirious to take it, and swept the cup aside.

"They'll have to have a priest," I remember thinking. "We can't do any more for these men. They must have a priest."

Edmé and Emile were still above, and the rest of the family shut away in the room at the back. Nothing any longer went by rule—I did not even know the time of day. I went out into the street to find a priest. The first I saw was in so great a hurry to attend a meeting of the Vendéan chiefs that he made a cross in the air above my head, after expressing his regrets, and went his way.

The second, when I told him men were dying, replied, "There are thousands dying, all asking to be shriven. Yours must await their turn. What is your address?" I gave it to him, and he too went his way.

Curiosity—for no one took any notice of me—made me walk as far as the municipality, and I saw, without surprise, that the Vendéans were serving it much as they had served us. Numbers of them were flinging things out of the windows into the street below, not to bear off as trophies, but for destruction. They had a fire burning before the building, and were feeding it with tables, chairs and rugs.

The crowds assembled were like nothing I had ever seen in Paris, before '89 or after it. There were peasants barefoot, with sabots looped from a string round their necks, their women hanging on to them, and soldiers too, wearing the white cockade, and ladies of the former aristocracy wrapped in military coats, their ringlets falling from beneath enormous hats. It was a masquerade of olden times, a scene from an opera. Had I not known their origin I should have said that these people had dressed up for the occasion, instead of fighting their way from the coast across the Loire to Normandy and back.

Suddenly there appeared two Vendéan chiefs riding in the midst of them, and the crowd fell apart, making way. They were fantastic, like engravings out of history, with great white plumes soaring from their hats after the style of Henri IV, and the broad white sash encircling their waists. Their breeches were the colour of chamois, their boots were buskin, and their swords were curved like scimitars.

No wonder that the peasants about me curtseyed, making the sign of the Cross at their approach.

"It's the Prince Tallemont," said a woman near to me. "It's he who wants us to march to Paris."

I continued walking, looking for a priest to come to the dying men, but everywhere people were piling carts and horses with the loot they had taken from the houses and the shops, and whoever I asked brushed my question aside, repeating the saying of the second priest that many people were dying, there was no time to attend to all of them, and anyway the city was to be evacuated the next day.

Here at least was something to cling to, even if we were left with dying men. I went back to the house without a priest, and we waited there through the rest of the day, but no one came, not even our peasant lodgers. They must have found more food and better quarters elsewhere.

When, just before dusk, I went into the little room through the salon, I saw that the man with the dysentery who had asked for the priest was dead. I found something to cover both their bodies, and shut the door. The man with half a leg was no longer delirious. He stared at me with hollow eyes, and begged for water. I gave him some, and when I asked after his wound he said it no longer pained him, but he had stomach cramps. He began to roll from side to side, gasping with this new pain, and then I saw that he too had dysentery. There was nothing I could do. I stayed with him a moment and left the water by his side, then shut the door and went upstairs.

Soon darkness came, and the long night. Nothing happened. Nobody came. Next day bugles sounded the alert, echoing from every quarter of the city, and, just as we had done the day before at the sound of the church bells, so we rushed again to the window, and flung aside the shutters.

"It's the call to arms," shouted Emile. "They're leaving us . . . they're going."

The Vendéans were running out of the houses opposite, some of them still barefoot, clutching their weapons. We could hear artillery in the distance.

"It's our army," said Edmé, "it's Westermann and the republicans at last."

Emile wanted to run out into the streets at once, and we had to hold him back.

"They're not here yet, Emile," I told him. "There may be heavy fighting in the city. We don't know which way the battle will go."

"I can at least help it to go our way," said Edmé, and she reached for the musket and took careful aim out of the window. This time, when she fired, she had an easier target, for she picked off a Vendéan standing in the middle of the road, uncertain which way to run. He fell instantly, his left leg kicking like a hare. Then he lay still.

"I've hit him," said Edmé, her voice unsteady. "I've killed him."

The three of us stared down at the doubled-up body in the street.

"There's another," cried Emile, jumping up and down. "Hit that one coming out of the door."

Edmé did not do anything. She just stared out of the window. The Vendéans came pouring out of the houses to the summons of the bugle. They took no notice of the man Edmé had shot. They shouted to one another distraught, asking which way to go. I heard one of them say, "The blues are attacking the city. The blues must have captured the bridge." They all started running up the street to the sound of the bugle, panic-stricken, in no sort of order, and out of the houses came the women too, some of them with children, running this way and that, like frightened geese. Then one of them saw the man Edmé had shot. She ran to his side and turned him over.

"It's Jean-Louis," she cried, "he's dead. Someone has shot him."

She began to scream, rocking backwards and forwards, and the child with her stared, his finger in his mouth. One of the peasants came and led them both away, the woman protesting, looking back over her shoulder.

"I'll go and tell them all in the back room," said Emile excitedly. "I'll go and tell them tante Edmé has shot a brigand."

He ran from the room, calling his news loudly. Edmé leant the musket against the window.

"I don't know why it had to be that one," she said, her voice unsteady still. "He wasn't doing anything. If it could have been the man who cracked his whip. . . ."

"It never is," I said. "It's never the right man. That's why it's so useless."

I turned away from the window, and went downstairs into the salon. The man with half a leg had fallen off the couch on to the floor. He was still breathing. He was not dead.

There was a great hubbub above. Emile had unlocked the door and told everyone that the brigands were running away, and Edmé had shot one who was lying dead in the street. The younger boys wanted to see. Even the dog came tearing down the stairs, barking excitedly to go out.

"No," I said, "go back, everybody. Nothing is over yet. They're fighting in the streets."

I saw the shocked white face of the widow staring down at the wounded man from the head of the staircase.

"Go back," I said. "Please all of you go back."

I shut the dog in the kitchen—the scraps and litter on the floor would quieten her. I could hear Edmé persuading the others to go back into their room until the fighting was over.

Through the rest of the day, all through the night, the battle continued, and next morning, about seven, we heard musket shots near to us in the street, and the sound of cavalry too.

Inevitably we went to our vantage point beside the window, and we saw that the Vendéans had come back to our street once more, but this time not as conquerors. They were running for their lives seeking shelter. Men, women, children, they were running down the street, their mouths open wide in terror, their arms outstretched, and our hussars were after them, cutting them down with their sabres, sparing no one. The women were screaming, and the children too, but our hussars were yelling and shouting in triumph.

"Get them . . . get them . . . get them . . ." cried Edmé savagely, and she picked up the musket once more and fired it blindly into the retreating crowd. Somebody fell, to be trampled in his turn by others.

The National Guard came running down the street behind the hussars, and they were shooting too, and suddenly I saw Pierre, carrying no weapon, his right arm in a sling, his uniform stripped and torn, and he was shouting at the top of his voice "No . . . no . . . stop the slaughter of the women and children. . . . Stop the slaughter. . . ."

Emile leant out of the window, laughing excitedly. "We're here, Papa," he called. "Look at us, we're here, we're safe."

Edmé picked off another Vendéan who had sheltered in a doorway, and the man's companion, firing blindly in self-defence, returned the shot, not looking, then ran on down the street.

The shot struck Emile full in the face and he fell backwards into my arms, choking, his face bespattered with blood.

He uttered no other sound, but from the street below came

the screams of the Vendéan women as they were cut down by our hussars.

Pierre did not see the shot that killed his son. He was still standing in the street, crying out to his companions of the National Guard, who took no notice of him, "Stop the slaughter! Stop the hussars from killing those women and children."

I knelt on the floor, clasping Emile to me, rocking backwards and forwards as I had seen the Vendéan woman do earlier in the day when she found the dead man in the street.

"Oh, Lamb of God," I said, "oh, Lamb of God who takest away the sins of the world, have mercy upon us. Have mercy upon us, have mercy upon us. . . ."

Somewhere, at the far end of the street, I heard a burst of cheering, and our men singing the Marseillaise.

SEVENTEEN

ALL RESISTANCE HAD ended before midday on Friday, the 13th of December, and the defeated rebel army fled in disorder south towards the Loire, leaving no Vendéans in Le Mans save those hundreds of women and children, the sick and the wounded, and their own dead.

If I do not speak of those first days following upon the battle it is because memory, mercifully blunted, contains few images. Our own grief for Emile, and the attempt to console his stricken mother and bring some sort of order back to the house, filled our hours. I remember that Pierre, when he knew that nothing could be done for his son, knelt by the side of the wounded man below and tended him until he died; and the knowledge that my brother could somehow assuage his own sorrow thus gave me courage to endure the days ahead.

The victory, though complete, held such an aftermath of horror that much of it is best forgotten. Our soldiers, outraged at their earlier defeats, returned measure for measure, not only when in pursuit of the fleeing enemy, but upon those Vendéan women and children remaining in the city.

The officials of the municipality had not yet returned from Chartres, and a body of citizens, my brother Pierre amongst them, formed a temporary administration to try and restore order. But they were not helped in their work by a large number of the population whose houses had been pillaged just as ours had been, and who saw, in those wretched prisoners left behind by the retreating rebels, a ready target for their feelings of revenge.

I thanked God I was not present when some twenty-two women and children who had been found straying on the roads outside the city were brought back and set upon in the place des

Jacobins by a crowd of Manceaux, who, so Edmé informed me afterwards, tore them to pieces, aided by the hussars. Such scenes could not quieten grief, or bring back the dead. They only added to the burden of sorrow. One of the sights that most sickened me, during the Saturday when I was in the town trying to buy bread for the household, was seeing a heap of bodies being tossed into a cart, preparatory to burial, like a load of dung, and on the top of them, spreadeagled, green skirts about her head, our red-haired lodger.

Michel appeared for a brief moment, on the Friday. It showed how all of us had lost count of the days in that he saw nothing strange in my presence in the city, or even questioned me. He and his men—he had lost some twenty of them in skirmishes with the Vendéans—had been lying in wait somewhere in the countryside the past few days, biding their time to join the republican armies. Now, with the Vendéans totally routed and in full retreat, he was returning in haste to Mondoubleau to tell the authorities of the rebel defeat.

"Nearly one hundred thousand of the brigands crossed the Loire two months ago," said Michel. "They may count themselves lucky if four thousand stragglers live to cross it once again. Those who do reach home will regret it. Our armies have orders from the Convention to raze every village to the ground. There will be no Vendée left."

It was a legacy of hatred to confer upon the west. Even those Vendéans who had not marched with the others, but had stayed peaceably in their homes, were as guilty as the rest. Not one of them was held innocent, no matter the age, no matter the sex. The oldest man must suffer with the youngest child. These were the orders.

Happily some of our generals, amongst them Kléber, who was to win greater fame in later years, protested against the severity of the decrees passed on to him, and the worst atrocities did not take place under his command. Others of the leaders were less humane. Like my brother Michel, they believed that the only way to crush a revolt for all time was to leave no one alive who could rebel.

I stayed a week with Pierre and his unhappy family, doing

what I could to help in the house. Then François came from le Chesne-Bidault to fetch me home, and we took the two youngest boys back with us, and the terrier and puppies. My sister-in-law, still prostrate, would not leave Pierre, and Edmé stayed behind to look after the pair of them.

My brother's chambers had been broken into by the Vendéans and more ruthlessly pillaged than his house. His furniture, his files, the documents of all his clients had been senselessly destroyed by a band of intruders who must have burnt whatever they could lay their hands on for the joy of seeing the flames.

Pierre's one concern was for the property of his clients. Some, poorer than their fellows, whose homes had been broken into in similar fashion and who had lost almost all they possessed, were not deprived for long. The necessities of life became theirs again; furniture, food, bedding was supplied by Pierre out of his own funds.

It was not until long afterwards that I heard the tale from Edmé. He all but beggared himself in the process, without a word to anyone but her, and was forced to sell his practice, a year later, and accept payment from the municipality as a public notary. I think, if anyone lived up to the principles of equality and brotherhood that had first inspired our revolution, it was my brother Pierre.

The "original" who, according to my father, would never make anything of his life, who refused to earn his living—returning from Martinique at seventeen with a trunk-load of coloured waistcoats and a parrot on either shoulder—was now, at forty-one, not only a leading patriot but one of the best-loved citizens in Le Mans.

Not so my brother Michel. Idolised by a section of his workmen, who admired his leadership and courage, and had shared in his exploits during the past few years, he was feared by a large number of them, and criticised for the ruthless discipline which he imposed upon the National Guard. The families of those who had lost their lives in the last campaign against the Vendéans murmured that their men had been sacrificed in vain. They had been enrolled to defend their parish, not to march for two days and attack against overwhelming odds.

The part Michel had played, and my husband too, in the primary elections to the Convention a year before was not forgotten amongst the various communes in our district. Busson-Challoir and Duval, so it was said, were favoured persons, not only because of their relationship to an ex-deputy but because of their high position as "acquirers of national wealth". This title, so popular in '91, had lost much of its prestige by '94. The poor were still poor, and those who had enriched themselves by the purchase of church lands were looked upon as profiteers, despite the initial act of patriotism.

If the civil war against the Vendéans was over, an aftermath of discontent remained, and this was very evident in our own neighbourhood and amongst our own workpeople. The millennium had not come about. Living was still dear. And, worst of all, conscription was taking away the youngest and strongest members of each family, very often the bread-winner.

"Why do our lads have to go?" This was the eternal question asked by the wives and mothers in our community. "Why don't they call up the officials first, and the acquirers too? Let them go off, and our lads follow afterwards."

As the wife and sister of both officials and acquirers I was hard put to it for an answer, except that the country, like the foundry, must be administered by men who were trained and capable. This reply would be received with a stare, or a grumble that the revolution had benefited those people who had been doing well in the first place, but as far as the workmen and peasants were concerned nothing had changed. Such statements were not true, but they made me feel uncomfortable all the same.

Another difficulty was that the Law of the Maximum, passed by Robespierre and the Convention the preceding autumn, put a limit, not only on the price of food and goods, but upon wages as well. This caused great discontent amongst workmen everywhere, and at our own foundry Michel and François were accused as if they were to blame for the decree, and not the Convention.

"Citoyen Busson-Challoir and Citoyen Duval can buy national property, but our wages must stay as they are," I would be told.

Throughout the winter and spring of '94 this spirit of dissatisfaction grew. News of the daily executions in Paris, not only of the former aristocrats but of the Girondin deputies who had helped to govern us the year before, and indeed of anyone who dared to lift a voice against the inner circle of the Convention, Robespierre, St. Just, and a few others, filtered through to us in the country.

Danton's death shocked all of us, even Michel. Here was one of our greatest patriots sent to the guillotine in his turn.

"We can't g-give an opinion," said my brother angrily, angry, I think, because his faith in the Convention had been shaken. "Danton must have been c-conspiring against the nation, or he would n-never have been condemned."

The war against the Allies progressed with successive victories for our republican armies, yet the numbers sent to the guillotine increased. François admitted to me that he believed Robespierre and the Revolutionary Tribunal had gone too far, but he dared not say so before Michel.

The excesses, and the severities, brought their own reaction throughout the country as a whole, and in our region too. Petty pilfering began in our own foundry, refusals to work, threats uttered against Michel.

"If this sort of thing continues," François told me, "either we must break up the partnership and Michel will have to go; or we shall have to surrender the lease, and leave le Chesne-Bidault."

The lease was due for renewal on All Saints' Day in November, or, as we now called it, the 11th Brumaire, and the decision what to do must be left over until then. Meanwhile, we should hope to see trade and tempers improved during the summer.

What distressed me most was that the goodwill amongst us all seemed lost. Hostility, for no good reason, could be sensed in the workmen's lodgings and on the furnace floor, and I could feel it with the women too. The camaraderie, instilled into the workmen when Michel first took over as master of the foundry, had vanished, and whether it was conscription, or the toll of the civil war, or the limit of their wages, nobody could say—these are things that are never put into words. Madame Verdelet, my usual informant, told me that the people were "fed up". This was the expression used.

"They've had enough," she said, "enough of the revolution, enough of fighting and restrictions, enough of change. It was better, so the older ones say, when your mother was in charge here and everyone felt settled. Now, nobody knows what tomorrow will bring."

Tomorrow, so far as the government was concerned, brought a struggle for power within the Convention itself, a treacherous assault upon Robespierre and his colleagues. On the 10th Thermidor, July 28th, the leader whose integrity and convictions we so much respected, however ruthless his methods, was sent to the guillotine within twenty-four hours of his arrest. The people of Paris, whom he had protected against invasion without and rebellion within for so many months, made no effort to save him.

The death of Robespierre and his friends was a signal for the relaxation of the many rules and restrictions without which the nation could never have survived. The moderates were back again. The Law of the Maximum was repealed. Prices and wages soared. Those with royalist sympathies began to talk openly of a return, before long, to the ways of the old régime and the restoration of the monarchy. The Jacobins everywhere lost their positions of authority, and this was reflected in the municipalities of the various districts throughout the country. "Progressives" were out of favour, not only with officials but amongst the workpeople too, and men like my brother Michel, who had openly supported the rigorous measures of Robespierre, were called the "enragés"—terrorists—and in some cases were arrested simply for this reason.

The halt in the forward movement of the revolution, and the fall from power of the Jacobins, profoundly shocked Michel. Just as his faith in human nature had been shattered when my brother Robert emigrated, so now his belief in the revolution received a similar blow. His pride suffered too. Michel Busson-Challoir had become someone of consequence in the district during the past few years, a figure to be reckoned with, possessing considerable power over his neighbours. Now, because of a switch in government policy, all this must be abandoned. He was suddenly no one—a master glass-blower whose business was not even flourishing, and about whom his own workmen muttered

spiteful slander behind his back. As the date for the renewal of
the lease approached I guessed, with a heavy heart, how it would
go.

"We're not only losing money," said François, "we're losing
the confidence of the trade as well. If we try to continue, under
present circumstances, we shall end as bankrupt as your brother
Robert, though for different reasons."

"What's the answer, then?" I asked. "Where are we to go?"

I could tell by my husband's face that he was not sure of my
agreement with his plans.

"My brother Jacques has been suggesting for months that I
should go into business with him at Mondoubleau," he said. "We
could share his house—there is plenty of room. Then, in a few
years' time, we could retire to our little property at le Gué de
Launay."

"What about Michel?"

"Michel must fend for himself. We've already discussed it. He
talks of going to Vendôme. There are several ex-Jacobins living
there with whom he is in touch, though they are lying low at
the present time. Whether he thinks of forming some sort of
society with them or not, I cannot say. Michel is not very com-
municative these days."

Once, had he admitted so much, François would have said
this with a sigh. Now he picked up our daughter Zoë, some fifteen months old, and jigged and danced her on his knee without
further thought of his associate and comrade. Time had come between them. Or perhaps the Vendéans. When my brother
marched his workmen off to war the year before, leaving my husband at home, something had been shattered.

"If this is how it has to be," I said to François now, "nothing
I can say or do will make any difference. I'll come with you to
Mondoubleau. But let it be, as you say, for a few years only."

I went out and stood in the orchard. It was a good year for
apples, and our old trees were laden. We had the ladder up
against one of them and a basket, half-filled, below. In my
mother's day the little apple-house at the far end of the orchard
would be stacked from one year's end to the other, and the apples
for the house chosen in strict rotation, so that the ones which

kept the longest would be eaten when the fresh fruit on the trees was ready to pick again.

Le Chesne-Bidault had been my home for over sixteen years. I had come here with my parents, my brothers and sister, when I was a girl of fifteen. I had continued to live here as a bride. Now, with my thirty-first birthday approaching, only a few days after the date when the lease for le Chesne-Bidault would be rejected, I must prepare myself to pack up our possessions and say good-bye. I stood there, tears pricking behind my eyes, and someone came softly behind me and put his arm through mine. It was my brother Michel.

"Don't fret," he said. "We've had the b-best of it. Nothing perfect ever l-lasts. I learnt that l-long ago."

"We've been happy here, the three of us," I said, "though I spoilt it for you at times by jealousy."

"I never n-noticed it," he answered.

I wondered, thinking how much my husband must have borne in silence in order to spare his friend. Men have strange loyalties to one another.

"Perhaps," I said, "when times become more settled again, and trade improves, we can start up all over again somewhere else."

He shook his head. "No, Sophie," he said, "once we've made the b-break, it's b-better to abide by it. François will soon s-settle down, either in Mondoubleau or le G-Gué de Launay, and help you raise your f-family. As for myself, I'm a l-lone wolf, and always have been. It might have been b-better had I been killed in a scrap against the b-brigands. The people of the district would have given me a hero's b-burial."

I understood his bitterness. He was now thirty-eight, the best of his life behind him. Trained in glass, he knew no other trade. He had thrown himself whole-heartedly into the revolution, and his fellow-revolutionaries had abandoned him. I could foresee no happy future for him in Vendôme.

When the time to leave came, I went before the others. I could not bear to see my home stripped bare. Some of our possessions went to le Gué de Launay, to be cared for by our tenant until we lived there; the rest we gave to Pierre. Saying good-bye to the families was like saying good-bye to my own youth, and to part of life that was now shut away forever. The older ones that I knew were sad. The others seemed indifferent. If they could earn a living under the new leaseholder, a relative of the proprietor at Montmirail, it mattered little to them who lived in the master's house.

As I was driven away, with Zoë in my arms, I looked back over my shoulder to wave at François and Michel; the last thing I saw was the foundry chimney piercing the sky, a wreath of smoke above it. And that, I thought, is the break up of our family; the Bussons, father and sons, existed no more. The tradition was broken. What my father created had come to an end. My sons, if I should ever bear them, would be Duvals, bred to a different trade in a different age. Michel would never marry. Pierre's boys, brought up in haphazard fashion without education, would not turn to glass. The art would be lost, the knowledge that my father bequeathed to his sons wasted. I remembered Robert, an alien and an émigré. I wondered if he were dead, and if that second wife of his had borne him children.

My daughter Zoë put her hand up to my face and laughed, and I shut the past behind me, looking forward, with some misgiving, to a house in Mondoubleau that would not be my own.

Nearly a twelvemonth passed before the four of us, Pierre, Michel, Edmé and myself, were reunited once again, and, when we were, it was not a moment for rejoicing, but for sharing a common grief.

It was on the 5th Brumaire, of the Year III (the 26th of October, 1795, by the old calendar), when we were sitting down to dinner—François, my brother-in-law, and I, with Zoë promoted to a high chair at the table and my infant son Pierre-François asleep in his cradle above—that we heard the peal of the entrance bell, and then the sound of voices. François rose to his feet to investigate. Within a few minutes he was back again, his face grave, his eyes searching mine.

"It's young Marrion," he said, "from St. Christophe."

Marrion was the farmer my mother employed at l'Antinière to look after the farm and her few acres. There were two of them, father and son. Instantly I knew the worst, and it felt like a cold hand touching my heart.

"She's dead," I said.

François came at once to my side and put his arms about me.

"Yes," he said, "it happened yesterday, very suddenly. She was driving out from St. Christophe to l'Antinière to shut up the house for the winter, young Marrion with her, and they were just turning down from the road to the farm when she collapsed. He called to his father, and between them they carried her inside and laid her down on the bed. She complained of violent pain, and was sick. Marrion sent his son for the doctor at St. Paterne, but the boy had hardly left the house when she died."

Alone there, with the farmer. Not one of us with her. And, knowing my mother, I could see what must have happened. She must have felt unwell earlier in the day, but told no one of it. Determined to keep to her routine of closing the farmhouse in the early autumn and spending the winter months in her other small house in St. Christophe—or Rabriant, as it had been renamed in '92, when the saints were out of favour—she had set out from the village to put everything in order.

Shock numbed my emotion, and it was still too soon for tears. I went into the kitchen, where young Marrion was having his dinner, and questioned him.

"Yes," he agreed, "the citoyenne Busson looked pale when she left the village, but nothing would deter her from driving out to l'Antinière. She said she must look round just once, before the weather turned. She was obstinate, you understand. I said to my father afterwards—it's as though she knew."

Yes, I thought, she knew. Instinct warned her that it was to be for the last time. But instinct came too late. There was no time to look about her, only time to lie down upon her bed, and die.

Young Marrion told us there was to be an autopsy. The health officer for the district was to go out to l'Antinière this very afternoon to discover the cause of death.

It was too late for us to drive down to St. Christophe that evening. We decided to send word to Pierre and Edmé at Le Mans, and to make a start early the next day. Someone, young Marrion said, had already gone from the village to tell my brother Michel at Vendôme.

It was one of those soft golden days that come sometimes in late autumn when the four of us gathered together at l'Antinière. Tomorrow the skies would cloud over and the wind come from the west, bringing the rain as it always did, stripping the last leaves from the trees and making the country all about us drear. Today everything was mellow, tender, and the yellow-washed farmhouse in the fold of the hills hazy under the sun.

It was the sort of day my mother loved. I stood on the rise of the hill above the farmstead, on the very spot where she had been taken ill, young Marrion told me, and I had the strange impression that she was with me, holding my hand as she used to do when I was small. Death, instead of severing all ties, made family feeling stronger.

The health officer was waiting in the house, Michel at his side. My brother had grown thinner and paler since he had left le Chesne-Bidault. Presently Pierre and Edmé joined us, and my sister, who had never shed one tear during our three days of terror in Le Mans two years before, now burst out crying at the sight of me.

"Why didn't she send for us?" she said. "Why didn't she tell us she was ill?"

"It was not her way," answered Pierre. "I was here only a few weeks past, but she never complained. Even young Jacques noticed nothing wrong."

Jacques was with one of our cousins, the Labbés, in St. Christophe, pending the decision about his future. It did not surprise me when Pierre instantly volunteered to be his guardian.

We stood in silence by my mother's body, while the health officer explained to us that the autopsy had shown the cause of death to be inflammation of the stomach, but of how long duration he could not say. He and his colleague had performed the autopsy in the farmer's lodging close by, and it was there that my mother's body lay, awaiting burial. The officer had placed his official seals on the doors of l'Antinière itself, but he removed them now so that we could go inside and see for ourselves that nothing had been touched.

I had not cried before, but I did so now. The imprint of my

mother was on everything we touched. Much she had given away to all four of us already, keeping for herself those things that reminded her most of my father and the life they had shared together.

St. Christophe might become Rabriant, Madame Busson a "citoyenne", kings, queens and princes go to their death and the whole country change; but my mother had held fast to her own timeless world. There was the old chest with the marble top, the walnut desk, the dozen silver plates she had served grand dinners upon when company came to the château of la Pierre. She had kept the eighteen goblets and the twenty-four crystal salt-cellars blown by Robert in his first days as a master, and in the writing-desk amongst her papers we found the closely-written copy of his procès for bankruptcy.

More intimate, as though she were with us still, was her easy chair before the fireplace, the card-table on which she played a solitary piquette, the music-stand—memory of days long past when we had our own choir at la Pierre and the workmen came to sing on feast-days—the dog-basket for Nou-Nou, the spaniel dead these many years, the parrot-cage for Pelée, one of the two parrots Pierre had brought home from Martinique in '69.

We went upstairs to the bedroom, and it was full of her presence—the bed with the green hangings which she had shared with my father, the tapestry on the wall, the fire-screen by the writing table. The clock on the chimney-piece, beside a silver goblet, my father's gold-topped cane and his golden snuff-box, given him by the marquis de Cherbon when he left Chérigny for la Pierre, her taffeta-silk umbrella, her bedside lamp . . .

"There is no such thing as time," whispered Edmé. "I'm back again at la Pierre. I'm three years old, and the bell is sounding in the foundry for the men to come off shift."

I think what moved us most was her wardrobe and the linen stacked neatly on the shelves within it. Linen that we had forgotten all about but that she had kept and treasured all these years, making do herself with a few worn sheets, the rest of it put away untouched that it might now form part of our inheritance. Embroidered sheets and napkins, table-cloths by the dozen. Petticoats, handkerchiefs, muslin bonnets of long out-dated fashion but exquisitely laundered and fresh, some hundred and twenty of them, laid on a shelf with rose-leaves.

These things, so unexpected and incongruous in our troublous times, were an indictment of our age that reverenced nothing past and hated all things old.

"If you have finished your inspection of the citoyenne Busson's effects," said the health officer from behind us, "the authorities will make a proper inventory in due course. Meantime, I must replace the seals."

We came out of our childhood world and were back again in Brumaire, Year III. Yet it seemed to me that I felt my mother's hand on both our shoulders as Edmé and I turned and left her room.

We buried her in the churchyard at St. Christophe beside her parents, Pierre Labbé and his wife Marie Soiné.

The five of us had an equal share in the inheritance, with the citoyen Lebrun, public notary for the département, representing young Jacques, in place of my émigré brother. These shares, drawn up into five lots, consisted of the various properties owned by my mother in the parish of St. Christophe. So that no one of us should own more than the other, the value of each of them was taken into account: whoever should find himself owner of Pierre Labbé's house in St. Christophe, for instance, would pay cash to whichever of us might hold the smaller properties. Then the notaries shuffled the names of the lots in a hat, and we all of us drew in turn.

Michel, who had no need of it, had the luck of the draw, finding himself possessor of my grandfather's house. He at once offered it to Pierre, who had drawn a small farm-outside the village, and my brother from Le Mans, with three hearty boys of his own, a newly adopted nephew, and another baby expected within the month, was glad of the exchange. It was shortly after this that he left Le Mans and brought his family to live in St. Christophe, for unrest had started again in the west and there was constant fighting against the royalist irregular armies, or "chouans", as they were called, and Pierre dared not expose his family a second time to the horrors of civil war.

I drew the small farm la Grandinière and Edmé la Goupillière, and the notary public held l'Antinière for Jacques. We continued to lease the properties, for the dwelling-houses were no use to any of us.

The personal effects were put up for sale amongst the four of us, and we bid for those things each one of us valued the most. I know that Edmé and I shared out the linen, that Pierre, because of his growing family, bid for all the chairs, for the dog kennel and the parrot's cage that had no parrot in it, and Michel, to my pleasure and my astonishment too, paid nearly 4000 livres for my father's golden snuff-box and his gold-topped cane.

"They're the f-first things I remember," he said afterwards. "Father would take the cane to Coudrecieux to church on S-Sundays, and when Mass was over stand outside ch-chatting to the curé, offering him snuff from that same snuff-box. It was the f-finest sight I've ever seen."

He pocketed the box, and smiled. Could it be, I wondered, that Michel, the son who had fought against parental authority from the beginning, was the one who all these years had loved my father most?

He looked across at Edmé, the other member of the family with no husband to consider. "What are your p-plans?" he asked her.

She shrugged her shoulders. The prospect of moving to St. Christophe did not attract her. If Pierre really intended to give up his position as public notary in Le Mans and live out there in a village, there would be no work for her. Domestic duties and a pack of boys might satisfy her sister-in-law, but Edmé Busson Pomard liked to use her brains.

"I have no plans," she answered, "unless you know of a new revolutionary party I could join."

Our mother's death, as it happened, had coincided with a fresh change of government in Paris. A royalist insurrection in the capital had been crushed a few weeks back by General Bonaparte, and on the very day my mother died the Convention wound up its sessions, and a Directoire of five ministers was given executive power. How they would govern the country nobody knew. The only men with any authority were the generals, Bonaparte above all, and they were too busy winning victories against our enemies abroad to sit in Paris.

"There're plenty of J-Jacobins in Vendôme," said Michel. "Hésine is there—he's to be c-commissaire under the Directoire. His idea is to work for the b-bringing back of Robespierre's Constitution of '93, and put an end to all these m-moderates and chouans. I know him well."

I could see a new light in Edmé's eyes. Robespierre had been her God, the Constitution laid down in '93 her breviary.

"He's going to p-publish a newspaper in Vendôme," Michel continued, "called *L'Echo des Hommes Libres*. Babeuf, the extremist, will write for it. He believes that all wealth, all p-property should be shared. Some men c-call it Communism. It s-sounds like a new faith, and one that I could believe in."

Suddenly he went to Edmé and held out his hands.

"Come to V-Vendôme, Aimée," he said, using the old pet name of childhood days. "Let's l-live together, and share our inheritance, and go on w-working for the revolution. I don't mind if they call me a t-terrorist, or an extremist, or a s-sacré Jacobin. That's what I always have b-been, and always will be."

"Me too," said Edmé.

They burst out laughing, and hugged each other like two children.

"It's a q-queer thing," said Michel, turning to me. "It must be something to do with l-living in a community all my life, but I'm lost without my own p-people about me. If Aimée comes to V-Vendôme it will be like living in the f-foundry once again."

I was happy for the two of them. The future, which had seemed so bleak and drear for both, now had a purpose. It was strange that my mother's death should have brought them together, the two who were lonely, the two most like in feature to my father.

"If our politics don't succeed," said Edmé, "we'll take another foundry and go into partnership. I can do a man's work. You've only to ask Pierre."

"I've always known it," replied Michel, quickly jealous. "I d-don't have to ask anyone."

He frowned for a moment, as if struck by a sudden thought, and heaven knows from what hidden depths within him came his next suggestion.

"We might rent the f-foundry at Rougemont," he said, "and reinstate it in its old g-glory. Not for ourselves, but to share the p-profits with the workmen."

He did not choose la Brûlonnerie, or Chérigny, or even la Pierre. He chose Rougemont, the foundry that had first brought ruin to Robert, and I knew that once again, without understanding why, Michel sought to atone for his brother's fault.

"That's the answer," he repeated. "If our political c-comrades fail us we'll go into partnership, Aimée, and d-develop Rougemont together."

As it turned out, it was not so much that Michel's comrades failed him as that their ideas of a people's sovereignty, with all things shared in common, displeased the corrupt Directoire to such an extent that some eighteen months later Gracchus Babeuf, the originator of these ideas, was condemned to death, and Hésine, the editor of *L'Echo des Hommes Libres*, imprisoned.

How Michel and Edmé escaped imprisonment themselves I never discovered. That both of them were deeply implicated in all that concerned Hésine and his associates was common knowledge in Vendôme, but François and I, with our growing family, were more concerned to keep out of politics and trouble than risk everything for a lost cause.

We settled in our small property at le Gué de Launay, outside Vibraye, in November 1799, just after Bonaparte's coup d'état in Paris and his subsequent appointment as First Consul. It was in this same year that Michel and Edmé, pooling their joint inheritance from my mother, entered into partnership at Rougemont.

The project was doomed to failure—we all of us knew it. Pierre, living in St. Christophe, his brood of boys enriched at last by the birth of a daughter named—so characteristic of Pierre —Pivione Belle-de-Nuit, warned both of them that any attempt to resurrect a glass-house the size of Rougemont, which had completely fallen into disrepair, would have small hope of success unless backed by vast capital sums.

Michel and Edmé would not listen to Pierre, or to anyone. A glass-house, where the workmen and the masters shared the profits, was their dream, and they pursued their dream for nearly three years, until, in March, 1802, they were forced to abandon it. Like other ideals, before and since, like the revolution itself and its spirit of equality and brotherly love, the attempt to put it into practice failed.

"He has ruined himself, and he has ruined your sister too," said my husband François, now the mayor of Vibraye and father of two sons, Pierre-François and Alphonse-Cyprien, besides our daughter Zoë. "Michel will be obliged to take some beggarly employment as manager of a small foundry, and Edmé either housekeep for him, or exist on a few acres in St. Christophe. They have thrown everything away, and are left without fortune or a future."

François had been successful; they had failed. Despite the happiness we enjoyed, François and myself, with our little property and our growing sons and daughter, there was something about our smug complacency that made me secretly ashamed.

It was a few months after this, when the First Consul had signed the Treaty of Amiens, so bringing about a truce at last between France and England, that I was in our garden with the children, seeing to the bedding out of some plants in front of the windows of the salon, when my eldest son, Pierre-François, came running up from the drive with his sister to tell me that a man was looking through the entrance gate, asking for Madame Duval.

"What sort of a man?" I asked.

We still had vagrants on the road from time to time, deserters from the remnant of the chouan armies, and as we lived some little distance out of Vibraye I did not care much for strangers when François was absent.

My daughter Zoë, now about nine years old, spoke for her brother.

"I can tell you he wasn't a beggar, maman," she said. "He took off his hat when he spoke to me, and bowed."

The gardener was within hailing distance should I need him, and I walked down the drive, followed by the children.

The stranger was tall and lean, and his clothes hung about him as though he had lost weight through recent illness. They had a foreign cut about them, as did his dusty, square-toed shoes. Spectacles concealed his eyes, and I could tell by the unnatural brightness of his reddish hair that it was dyed. I guessed him to be a travelling salesman, from the bag he had set down by the gate, who hoped to persuade me to buy trash.

"I'm sorry," I said, intending to drive him off by my severity, "but we have everything we need here for the household. . . ."

"I'm glad of that," he answered, "for I can contribute nothing. I have only one clean shirt in my bag, and my father's goblet, unbroken."

He took off his spectacles and held out his arms.

"I told you I'd never forget you, Sophie," he said. "I've come home to you, just as I promised."

It was my brother Robert.

PART FOUR

The Emigré

EIGHTEEN

THE FIRST SHOCK, so Robert said, came just five months after their arrival in England. Everything had gone well during the early months. His employers at the Whitefriars Glass Manufactury, known to him of old during the days when he had held the position of first engraver in crystal at the foundry in St. Cloud, and to whom he had written asking for work before leaving France in December '89, welcomed him with courtesy and kindness, and had arranged lodgings for him and his wife in Whitefriars close by.

The knowledge that he was free of debt, had no responsibility, and was in every sense starting life anew with his young wife, with whom he was much in love, made Robert ignore the small pin-pricks and irritants almost inevitably inherent in the position of anyone starting out to make a living for himself in a strange country. The language, the customs, the food, even the climate, which would probably have daunted Pierre and Michel, more tenacious in their way of life than their elder brother, he accepted as amusing, and a challenge to his own powers of assimilation. It delighted him to plunge immediately into English colloquialisms with a total disregard for grammar, to slap his fellow-workmen on the back, English fashion, to drink his grog and his ale, and to show himself in every way perfectly at home and quite unlike the frizzed and perfumed Frenchmen lampooned in the English newspapers.

Marie-Françoise, left alone most of the day in the lodgings, and obliged to do the household shopping without a word of English, was more overcome. But youth, good health, and a wide-eyed admiration for everything her husband said and did soon found her echoing his phrases, praising the Londoners for their good humour, and declaring that she saw more life on Thames-

side than she had ever done in her twenty-one years in Paris—
which, as almost all of them had been spent in an orphanage in
St. Cloud, was not surprising.

As far as his work was concerned—he was employed as engraver in crystal—Robert soon discovered that he had nothing to
learn from his associates. Equally, he could not boast of any
superiority in technique. The standard at the glass-works in
Whitefriars was high. It had been founded as long ago as 1680,
and the flint glass made there was famous throughout Europe.
There was no question of a Frenchman crossing the Channel to
teach his trade to English craftsmen; the contrary was the more
likely, and Robert was quick enough to tone down any little hint
of patronage that might have risen to the surface in his first attitude of bonhomie to all.

A lively interest, though much ignorance, about recent affairs
in France was shown by the cockneys, both at the glass-works
in Whitefriars and amongst his fellow-lodgers; and here Robert
was pleased to show himself supreme authority, once he had
mastered enough English to make himself understood.

"It takes more than a few months to set right the abuses of
five hundred years," he would declare, whether it was in a chop-
house near Thames-side or in his landlady's front parlour. "Our
feudal system was as out of date as your moated castles and barons
would be today. Give us time, and we may accomplish great
things. Providing our King adapts himself to the mood of the
people. If not"—here, he told me, he would pause significantly—
"if not, then we may replace him with an abler and more popular
prince."

He was referring, naturally, to his patron the duc d'Orléans,
whose arrival in England the previous October had contributed
largely to Robert's own decision to try his luck across the Channel.

He soon found, however, that Chapel Street was very different
from the Palais-Royal. The arcades of the latter had been my
brother's home and place of business; he had been free to come
and go at will, to exchange gossip and chat with the throng of
minor officials, busy-bodies, secretaries and personal aides that
went to make up the entourage of the duc d'Orléans. At the

Palais-Royal a whisper to the right person, a hint about favours given and received, would bring results. The very sense of being on the fringe of a society close to the most popular man in Paris had added enormously to Robert's self-esteem.

There was none of this in London. Laclos, Captain Clarke, the duc d'Orléans' valet and one or two others, including, of course, his mistress Madame de Buffon, were the only members of his personal circle whom the prince had brought with him to England. The servants in the furnished house in Chapel Street were English. Stately footmen answered the front door and stared blankly at any intruder upon the step. There was none of the coming and going, the free enter-as-you-will atmosphere of the Palais-Royal; and Robert, when he called for the first time soon after his arrival in London, was allowed to leave his card with the footman but was not invited within.

He called again, with the same result. The third time he wrote a personal letter to Laclos, and after a week or more received a laconic reply to the effect that, should the duc d'Orléans or his staff require any private business done for them during their temporary sojourn in England, Monsieur Busson would be informed.

Here was a rebuff, but Robert was undaunted. He took to frequenting the ale-houses in the immediate neighbourhood of Chapel Street, in the hope of meeting with someone or other, whether it was the valet or the barber, who might give him more definite news of the duc d'Orléans' intentions. He had some small success in learning that his patron was privately sounding the English Cabinet as to their objections or approval should he accept, if it were offered to him, the crown of Belgium. This, my brother insisted, was more than rumour. Full of optimism, as usual, he returned to Marie-Françoise with much talk of Brussels as a possible future home instead of London.

"If the duc d'Orléans becomes Philippe I, King of the Belgians," Robert told his young wife, "he will need a very large staff indeed. There is no question but that I shall obtain some sort of position."

"But can you leave the Whitefriars foundry so abruptly?" she asked. "Have you not signed papers agreeing to be employed by them for several months?"

He waved her question aside. "If I wish to leave Whitefriars I can do so tomorrow," he told her. "I only took on the work to tide over these present months. As soon as the duc d'Orléans has need of me he will send for me, and if it's a case of going to Brussels, to Brussels we shall go. There would be great possibilities in serving a new monarch, and our future would be assured."

The duc d'Orléans' expectations, and my brother's with them, were doomed to disappointment. The trouble in the Pays-Bas was short-lived, and the Austrians re-entered Brussels at the end of February.

Once again Robert presented his card in Chapel Street, and once again he was told that his prince and patron was at the races. The loss of a possible crown did not appear to have interfered with the duc d'Orléans' routine. The big shock came when, just as suddenly as he had left Paris for London in October the preceding year, so without warning, on the 8th of July, 1790, the duc d'Orléans quitted London for Paris, with, it would seem, nothing achieved politically between the two countries and little to show for his nine months' sojourn but plenty of entertainment and the sale of a number of race-horses. My brother was not even aware of the prince's decision to return home until he saw the news in a London newspaper.

He rushed to Chapel Street forthwith, and found the usual aftermath of departure—sheets already on the furniture, and the servants who had not already been paid off sweeping away the straw from packing-cases and grumbling at the master and mistress whom they had so lately served.

No, he learnt, there was no question of their return. The duc d'Orléans had left London for good.

This sudden departure had a profound effect upon my brother. He now realised, with a sense of finality, that neither the duc d'Orléans, nor any of his close associates, had any influence out of France, and that even in his own country the likelihood of the prince being appointed Regent or holding high office in the National Assembly was now remote. The temperament of the duc d'Orléans himself lacked fire and energy. He was not "cut out", as the English put it, to become a true leader of the French people.

Robert's adulation, almost idolatry, for his so-called patron turned to contempt. The qualities of amiability and generosity, so praised before, were now despised. The duc d'Orléans was a weakling, flattered by a self-seeking entourage, and those men he should have depended upon—amongst whom my brother included himself—had been spurned, their faith abused.

Robert, a confessed bankrupt in Paris, and likely to be imprisoned for debt if he set foot in the capital again, could not return to his own country. He must continue to build up what reputation he could for himself in London, and stay content as an engraver in crystal to his employers in Whitefriars.

As the months passed, and his young wife became pregnant, London no longer seemed an enchanted city full of promise. Promotion might come to his English fellow-craftsmen, but as a foreigner Robert must count himself lucky to be employed at all.

The first-born of his second marriage, a son whom they named Robert, was born in the late spring of '91, shortly before the flight of Louis XVI and Marie Antoinette to Varennes which shocked and outraged us all so much at home. In London, Robert said, the people were equally shocked, but for a different reason. Sympathy was for the injured French monarch and his Queen, forced to seek asylum beyond the frontier; and when they were apprehended and brought back to Paris there was scarcely a man in London who did not praise the dignity and resignation of the royal family, and hurl abuse against the French Assembly.

"It was impossible," Robert told me, "not to see the venture with their eyes. The account of the flight was in all their newspapers. People talked of nothing else in the ale-houses and at work, and, knowing where I came from, they accused all Frenchmen of treating their king like a common criminal. I knew nothing of the true circumstances. What could I do but agree? The Assembly, I explained, had got into the hands of hotheads and irresponsibles who were only seeking their own advantage, to which the cockneys countered, 'The more fools the French people to allow themselves to be so led. Such a state of affairs would never be permitted in England. In England there was too much common sense. The French were a nation of hysterics.' This was the attitude."

Almost immediately after the flight to Varennes came the flood of émigrés to England, all telling the same tale of goods sequestered, châteaux seized, clergy and aristocracy molested, a general persecution of all who had held any sort of position under the old régime. The English, always eager to hear anything to the detriment of their old enemy across the Channel, magnified each story of distress into wholesale condemnation of the revolution that had apparently convulsed all France.

"You must understand," said Robert, "that already in '91 the émigrés were painting a picture of desolation. It was not just Paris that had become impossible, but the entire country. There was no law, no order, no food; false money was floated to disguise economic failure, and the peasants were setting fire to every village. When you were peacefully giving birth to your daughter at le Chesne-Bidault, the one you have told me later died, and François and Michel were buying church lands and enriching themselves for the future, I saw the foundry in flames, and all of you in prison. My country, and you with it, had been seized by bandits. That was how we learnt to look at it from London."

These first émigrés, during the summer and autumn of '91, and on into the winter of '92, were mostly members of the former aristocracy and the clergy who could not, or would not, adapt themselves to the new régime. Fresh from his rebuff by Laclos and the Orléans faction, my brother hastened to make himself agreeable to the enemies of his former patron—persons close to Court circles, devoted to the King and Queen and to the King's two brothers, the comte de Provence and the comte d'Artois. As an émigré himself of more than two years' standing, Robert had some advantage over the newcomers. He could speak English, he knew the ways and customs, he was adept at acting as intermediary in negotiations between his bewildered compatriots on the one hand and the jocular cockneys on the other.

As courier, as inspector of furnished houses and apartments, as the friend-in-need who could arrange purchases at low prices without any difficulty, my brother was in his element. Marquises, countesses and duchesses, exhausted from fearful Channel crossings by way of Brittany or Jersey, would be enchanted to find a fellow-countryman who could so swiftly put them at their ease after their trials. His sympathy, his charm and his delightful manner made the ordeal of arriving in a strange country far easier to bear. Some small recompense might be forthcoming, of course, after they had settled down; meanwhile, possibly the people at the Embassy would take care of it. As to private arrangements, matters of percentages and so on, between the courier and the various London tradesmen and the vendors of furnished apartments, that was a matter with which the new émigrés need not concern themselves.

It soon became evident that to combine the work of an engraver in crystal at Whitefriars with his new status as courier to the élite of the former Parisian society would be a difficult, if not an impossible, task. My brother, with his gambler's instinct, chose to sever his connection with the Whitefriars foundry and throw in his lot entirely with the newcomers, or, as he put it to his employers, with his distressed fellow-countrymen. This was, like almost all Robert's ventures, a mistake, and one which— within a few years—he was profoundly to regret.

"I chanced my luck," he said, "and my luck lasted just as long as the funds the émigrés brought with them. When, instead of finding themselves in London for six months or a year, fêted by the English and treated as heroes and heroines, they discovered that they were paupers forced to accept English charity without any prospect of returning to their own country, their luck ran out, and so did mine. I was not to know in '91 that in January '93 the Assembly in Paris would give place to the Convention, that the King would be condemned to death, and that the Allies, in whom all of us in England had put our faith, would be repulsed by that citizen army we had been laughing at for months."

The émigrés, my brother amongst them, who had lived in almost daily expectation of a triumphant Allied invasion—the entry of the duke of Brunswick's forces into Paris, followed by the overthrow of the Convention, the restoration of Louis and the mass punishment of every revolutionary leader—found, to their horror and consternation, that none of this came about. The

Republic, threatened on all sides, stood firm. The King went to the guillotine. Any émigré who dared to set foot in France would suffer the same fate, as a traitor to his country; and unless they chose to join their fellow-royalists in the Prince de Condé's army, the émigrés must accept their status as refugees in a country that, by the spring of '93, was actively at war with their own.

"The honeymoon was over," said Robert. "Not my own—that had ended after the first year—but the honeymoon of the French émigrés with the English people. We had not only killed our King—we were accused of this just as though we had voted for his death in the Convention—but we were members of the enemy. Any one amongst us might have been a spy. The favours, the generosity, the courtesy, the welcome, all this went after the declaration of war. We were no longer part of London society, except those notables who really had a foothold amongst the first English families. The rest of us, as I have said, were refugees, with little money left, no prospect of employment, obliged to give an account of ourselves whenever questioned, and treated as a general nuisance by all concerned."

The manufacturers of Whitefriars Glass regretted that they already had more than enough engravers in crystal on their books, and Robert's place had long ago been filled. In any event, times had changed. French craftsmen were no longer popular with the English workmen.

"I walked the streets as many of us did, looking for work," confessed Robert. "My English helped, and after several weeks I managed to obtain a place as packer in a glass and china warehouse, in Long Acre—the sort of work I used to give to porters when I had my laboratory in the rue Traversière. In the evenings I taught English at a school in Sommerstown, Pancras, founded by one of our émigré priests, the Abbé Carron. We had moved lodgings several times, and were by this time housed at 24, Cleveland Street, with a crowd of other émigrés. The parish of Pancras was full of French families; it was almost like living in the Bonne-Nouvelle or the Poissonnière, and we had our own schools, and our own chapel in Conway Street, off Fitzroy Square."

Marie-Françoise, despite her lack of education—she still could not sign her own name—adapted herself to changing circumstances as gallantly as Cathie would have done, perhaps more so, for her upbringing in an orphanage had made her hardy, and used to restrictions.

"She kept reminding me of Cathie," Robert admitted, "not only in her looks but in her ways as well. Sometimes—and you won't understand this, Sophie—I would find myself living a fantasy, a recreation of the past, and Cleveland Street became St. Cloud at the time when Cathie and I were living there together. In '93, when our second son was born, we called him Jacques. It made the fantasy more real."

He never told Marie-Françoise about her predecessor, nor of the other Jacques, some twelve years old by now, living with his grandmother at St. Christophe. The lie that Robert was a bachelor, without ties, started as a jest, had developed into a supreme deception, and along with it grew a mounting fabrication of untruths, with so many devious strings that they could not be unravelled.

"I myself began to believe what I had told her," Robert said, "and those fantasies were a consolation in times of trouble. The château between Le Mans and Angers to which I was heir, owned by an elder brother who detested me, became as real to me, and to her, and presently to our growing children, as if it had existed in reality. It was a mixture of Chérigny and la Pierre, the places where I was happiest as a boy, and of course had its glass-house beside it, for otherwise I could not explain my work as an engraver."

As the tide of emigration increased, with not only the aristocracy and the clergy seeking the safety of the English shores, but merchants and traders and members of the bourgeoisie as well, so my brother's fantasy took shape. In their parish of Pancras, or "Little Paris", as they called it, it seemed imperative to him, as one of the first-comers, to hold his status as a fervent loyalist to the King who had been dethroned, and later to the comte de Provence, whom the émigrés called Louis XVIII. His old patron the duc d'Orléans, self-styled Philippe Egalité when he took his seat in the Convention, and one of the deputies who voted for his cousin's death, was perhaps the most hated man in Pancras.

Robert was careful to impress upon his wife that she must never mention his earlier connection with the Orléans entourage and the Palais-Royal.

"In any event," he told her, "I only moved on the fringe of that society. I was not deeply involved. Their politics were suspect from the start."

This was a volte-face which must have surprised even Marie-Françoise, and to make up for it he would embroider afresh upon his own past, dwelling upon the beauty of his birthplace, the tranquillity, the peace, all of which had been denied him so long because of the hostility of the mythical brother.

It was providential that nobody with any knowledge of Busson l'Aîné, the bankrupt of Villeneuve-St. Georges and the debtor and fraud of La Force prison, should be amongst those who had fled from France to England. As it was, Busson l'Aîné was no sort of designation for one who declared himself a member of the aristocracy, and Robert, following the example of his true brothers, Pierre and Michel, who had many years before taken the names of du Charme and Challoir to distinguish themselves from him, decided that it would increase his stature in the eyes of his fellow émigrés, and amongst the Londoners as well, if he too took a suffix.

He chose the name of his birthplace, the farmhouse Maurier, and on moving to 24, Cleveland Street, at the end of '93 signed himself thus—Busson du Maurier. His wife, and his neighbours also, understood "le Maurier" to be a château. As the months passed, and tales of "Robespierre's Terror" were wafted by spies across the Channel, with all the exaggerated horrors of innocents mounting the guillotine in thousands not only in Paris but in the provinces as well, my brother suited his fantasy to the times, and suddenly declared to his wife, and an admiring audience of horrified émigrés, that the château had been attacked by an army of peasants, all within it murdered, and the château itself burnt to the ground.

"I had to do it," Robert said. "It was becoming an encumbrance. And a danger too. I had not realised there was a real château Maurier in the parish of la Fontaine St. Martin, near la Flèche, belonging to the family d'Orveaux. One of this family,

an officer who later joined the Prince de Condé's army at Coblenz, appeared in London, and on hearing my name called to
claim relationship. I had the greatest difficulty in shaking him
off. He might have exposed me. Luckily, we moved in different
circles, and a few weeks later I heard that he had left the
country."

The myth of belonging to the former aristocracy, the fantasy
of the burnt-down château, these extravagances may have flattered my brother's egoism during the early wartime years when
the émigrés of Pancras saw themselves doomed to many months
of exile. But as one year passed and then another, with no sign
of a break in hostilities, and the French armies winning victory
after victory, the plight of the refugees in London worsened, and
their sufferings became very real indeed.

"Our daughter Louise was born in '95," said Robert, "and another boy, Louis-Mathurin, in November of '97. That made four
young mouths to feed, six counting ourselves, and seven with
the young servant that Marie-Françoise had to help her with the
children. We had the whole of the second floor of our lodging-
house, and the old couple below us, the Dumants, used to complain of the children's noise. I would leave the house early, to
go to my work in Carter's warehouse in Long Acre. I was away
all day, and—as I told you—would teach in the Abbé Carron's
school in the evenings. Even so, I did not earn enough to keep
us all or pay the rent. We had to accept assistance. There was a
fund, an allocation for us émigrés, arranged between the English Treasury and our own officials. I was given £7 a month,
starting in September of '97, just two months before young
Louis-Mathurin was born. But it did not go far, and at times I
was almost desperate."

My brother had an advantage over many of his fellow-émigrés
in that he had been born to a trade, and had worked in glass from
the age of fourteen. As foreman in the warehouse in Long Acre
his talents were wasted, but at least he knew what he was about.
Others were less fortunate. Counts and countesses, who had
never worked in their lives, were now glad to pick up a few ex-
tra shillings by tailoring and dress-making, and one of the most
popular "trades" in Pancras and Holborn was the fashioning of

straw-hats by the émigrés for those Londoners who cared to patronise them.

"It became quite the thing," Robert said, "to walk from Oxford Street to Holborn to see where straw was cheapest. The pavements would be crowded by the marquis de this and the baron de that, all with bundles of straw under their arms to take back to their wives, who waited with bunches of ribbons and velvet flowers to decorate the finished article, after their husbands had twisted the straw into shape.

"Marie-Françoise was no modiste. Her talent lay in laundering, something she had learnt at the orphanage in St. Cloud. There was a wealthy middle-aged spinster called Miss Black, who lived round the corner from us in Fitzroy Square—she stood as godmother to Louis-Mathurin—and all her finery came to Cleveland Street to be washed and pressed and mended. Marie-Françoise did it herself, and then sent it back in a basket by the maidservant—it did not do for Madame Busson du Maurier to be seen carrying laundry in the street. The worst of it was, when I came to be away from her and the children for seven months, from July '98 to February '99, she had to arrange for friends to collect our allowance from the authorities, as she understood nothing of finance, and still could not sign her name. This added to her troubles."

When my brother reached thus far in his story he became purposely vague. He talked of "other business" that had concerned him during these months of absence, and avoided questions. No, he had not left the country, he had remained in London, although at another address. It had nothing to do with the war or with espionage or with any matter concerning the émigrés. I let it go, trusting he would tell me in his own good time. It was not until one evening a few days later, after he had shown the family goblet to my daughter Zoë and the boys, and I had put it away in a cabinet for safekeeping, that I learnt the truth.

"Those seven months," he said, "when I was absent from Cleveland Street, came about for the sake of that same glass."

He paused, watching my eyes.

"You had it copied," I suggested, "or worked on copies yourself, and this meant taking up employment in some foundry the other side of London?"

He shook his head. "Nothing so simple," he said. "The fact is, I was so pushed for money that I sold the glass to George Carter, my employer at the warehouse in Long Acre, and regretted doing so the instant I had sold it. It was no use buying it back, for the money he had given me in exchange went immediately on food, rent and other necessities for the children. There was only one thing to do, and with the keys of the warehouse in my possession it was the simplest thing in the world to achieve. I knew where the glass was packed, ready to dispatch to some firm in the north of England, in Staffordshire, and I returned to Long Acre one evening when the building was locked for the night, and let myself in. It took me only a matter of minutes to secure the glass, nail down the packing-case as though nothing had been disturbed, and let myself out again. Unfortunately I had mistimed the hours of the night-watchman. I understood that he came on duty at eleven o'clock. Instead, it was half-past ten. I walked straight into him as I left the building."

" 'Anything wrong?' he asked.

" 'Nothing at all,' I assured him. 'I had some business to do for Mr. Carter.'

"The fellow knew me, and accepted my tale, but when I went to the warehouse next morning I was summoned into the office by George Carter himself, and he had the empty packing-case on the floor beside him.

" 'This is your work, isn't it?' he said.

"It was no use denying it. The glass had gone. I had the keys of the building. The night-watchman had seen me.

" 'I shall summon you for trespass and theft,' he said, 'and to ensure that there is no chance of your giving me the slip I have the Sheriff's officer waiting to apprehend you. You will either return the glass or pay me the sum of £135 that I gave you for it.'

"I told him I would keep the glass and return the £135 as soon as I could raise it amongst my friends.

" 'Your friends?' he said. 'What friends? A bunch of émigrés like yourself, fed and clothed by the charity of the English government. I'm afraid I haven't much respect for you or your friends, Mr. Busson Morier. If you can't produce the glass today, or its value in cash, you will be taken into custody and committed for trial. As to your wife and children, your so-called friends must take care of them.'

"There was no question of raising the money, no question of returning the glass. I could not even raise the money for bail, for not one amongst us could muster more than twenty pounds. The worst part about it was returning to Cleveland Street and breaking the news to Marie-Françoise.

" 'Why not give him back the glass?' she asked me, bewildered that I would rather be arrested for debt and theft than surrender it. 'Robert, you must, for my sake and for the children's.'

"I would not agree. Call it sentiment and pride, and cursed obstinacy, but I kept seeing my father's face and the day he put the glass into my hands, and God knows I had let him down often enough in after years. I saw Michel, and you, Sophie, and Pierre, and my mother, and dear dead Cathie, and I knew that whatever happened to me I must not let the glass go."

Robert looked across the salon at the glass, safe at long last in the cabinet at le Gué de Launay.

"My father was right, you know," he said. "I misused my talents, so the glass brought me ill-luck. Endeavouring to sell it was the final insult to his memory, and to a perfect work of art. I had time enough to think about that during seven months in jail."

He smiled, and despite the lined face, the spectacles, and the dyed hair there was something of the old Robert in that smile.

"I should have been deported," he said, "but the Abbé Carron intervened. It was he who had my sentence reduced to seven months, and finally raised the money for my release in February of '99, about the time your General Bonaparte was winning victories against the Turks, with all of you applauding him here at home. Winter in Cleveland Street was bad enough, with the children ill with whooping-cough, and Marie-Françoise pregnant again and doing the laundry for Miss Black in Fitzroy Square. Yet to live as an alien debtor was harder still, confined in a cell about six by four, knowing that it was my own pride and my own folly that had brought me there."

My brother glanced about him, at the familiar furniture he had known at l'Antinière and le Chesne-Bidault.

"First La Force in Paris," he said, "and then King's Bench in London. I've become an authority on prisons on both sides of the Channel. Something, I might add, I have no desire to hand down to my children. Nor will they ever know of it. Marie-Françoise will see to that. When I returned to Cleveland Street we told them that I had been on business in the country, and they were still too young to question further. She will bring them up to believe that their father was just, upright, a devoted royalist, and indeed the very soul of honour. She believes it herself, and is hardly likely to tell them otherwise."

He smiled again, as though this new image of himself was an excellent jest, as worthy in its way as that of the impoverished member of the former aristocracy.

"You talk," I said, "as if Marie-Françoise were already a widow, and you in your grave."

He stared at me a moment, then took off his spectacles and wiped them.

"She is a widow, Sophie," he said. "Officially I'm dead. The sick man with whom I voyaged across the Channel died just before we reached Le Havre. He died with my papers upon him. The authorities will notify our committee in London, who will break the news to Marie-Françoise. Bereft, with six children to rear and educate, the Abbé Carron and his helpers will do far more for her than I ever could. Don't you see, Sophie, it was the only way out? Shall we call it—my final gamble?"

NINETEEN

I WAS THE ONLY one to know my brother's secret, and I kept it even from my husband. François believed, and so did the others when they came to hear of his return, that Robert was a widower once more, his second wife having died in childbirth, as Cathie had done, during his first years as an émigré in London. It was bad enough that he had emigrated, thus forfeiting all respect and honour; but to have been imprisoned in London for debt, and to have left his wife and six young children to the mercy of others, was something that I knew very well my husband would not stomach, or my two brothers either.

Robert's action in allowing another man to be buried as himself was, I felt certain, a criminal one which—if it should be discovered—would mean yet a further term in prison, perhaps for years. I could not condone his crime, neither could I condemn him. His lined face, the pouches beneath his eyes, even the tremor of his hands, a disability that had come upon him after leaving King's Bench prison, proved to me how much he had suffered.

The dyed hair, an attempt to make himself look young but failing in its purpose, made me the more compassionate. I saw him as he was, a broken man, yet remembered the lovable boy, my mother's first-born. For the sake of her memory alone I could not betray him.

"What do you intend to do?" I asked him when he had been at home with us little more than a week, and François and I were still the only ones to know of his return. "Did you have anything in mind when you left London?"

"Nothing," he confessed, "only a profound desire to get away from England and come home. You don't know what it is, Sophie, to have mal du pays. I did not once. London, for the first few years, was almost as much of an adventure as Paris used to be when I lived there with Cathie. It was only when the war started and the people turned against us, followed by the horror of those seven months in prison, that I came to long for my own country—not Paris, but this."

We were in the garden at the time. It was summer, and the trees about us were in full leaf. Rain, during the night, had made the earth smell rich, and raindrops glistened on the petals of my roses and on the long grass below the gravel walk.

"Looking out through the bars of King's Bench at that sooty London sky," he said, "I would dream myself back at la Pierre and become a boy again. You remember when I was sworn in as master, and we processed from the glass-house to the château, and my mother wore her brocade gown and had powder on her hair? Looking up at her that day was the proudest moment of my life, and the time when she came to visit me at Rougemont. Where do they go, Sophie, those younger selves of ours? How do they vanish and dissolve?"

"They don't," I said. "They're with us always, like little shadows, ghosting us through life. I've been aware of mine, often enough, wearing a pinafore over my starched frock, chasing Edmé up and down the great staircase in la Pierre."

"Or in the forest," he said. "It was the forest I missed most. And the smell of charcoal from the foundry fire."

When Robert was released from prison no one would employ him, nor did he blame the Londoners for this. Why should they give work to an enemy alien, and a convicted thief? The Abbé Carron put him to sort library books in the schools, and this, with the allowance from the Treasury, kept Robert and his family from greater poverty still. Another baby, a girl, to whom he gave Cathie's second name Adelaide, was born when he was still in prison, and a son, Guillaume, eighteen months later.

"I tried to keep the children French," my brother told me, "but, although they lived in what was virtually a French colony, they were hybrids from the start. Robert became Bobbie, Jacques James, Louis-Mathurin liked his name to be pronounced Lewis when he was little more than four years old. And Marie-Françoise, her looks gone and her hopes for my ultimate success blighted forever, turned to religion for comfort. She was always on her knees, either in our lodgings, or around the corner in the French chapel in Conway Street. She had to cling to something, and I had failed her."

It was too late to reinstate himself in the eyes of his fellow-émigrés. They pitied him, but they despised him too. Anyone who could sink to trespass and theft when existing on foreign charity could never again rise to a position of trust amongst them. My brother's one salvation was that the Abbé Carron did not despise him too.

"As Marie-Françoise and the children became more reconciled, or it would be more truthful to say more resigned, to our drab, hopeless future," Robert said, "so I yearned the more for France, for home. I began to feel a contempt for our émigré princes, for the comte d'Artois holding a petty court in Edinburgh, and for our King in Poland. Secretly I rejoiced in Bonaparte's victories—he was the leader we had needed all the time. The country which I had believed finished when I came to London was by now the strongest in Europe, and the most feared. Had I been younger, and more courageous, I believe I should have escaped somehow and crossed the seas to follow him."

As soon as the Treaty of Amiens was signed, and the amnesty granted to returning émigrés, my brother determined to come home. He had no thought then of deserting his wife and children. His idea was to seek me out, take counsel with Pierre and Michel, obtain some promise of employment, and then return to London to fetch his family home.

"Even as I said good-bye to them," he told me, "there, in our cramped lodging in Cleveland Street, I reverted to the old fantasy of the burnt-down château, of the splendours lost and gone. 'We'll rebuild,' I assured them, 'on the site of le Maurier, in the park, and found another glass-house where you, Bobbie and James, and Louis-Mathurin can work.' I half believed it myself as I told them this, and, although inwardly I knew it could never be, it might still be possible, I thought, when the time came, to create some sort of a home for them and so make up for the deception.

" 'I'll see you,' I told them, 'in six months or less. In just as long as it will take me to arrange matters on the other side.' And, God forgive me, when I left Cleveland Street and mounted the coach for Southampton I felt all the burden and the trouble of the years slide away from me. Their faces dimmed almost as soon as I sniffed the salt air of the Channel, and once aboard the packet I had only one thought in my mind, and that was to feel French soil under my feet once more."

Even then Robert still looked upon his journey as an experiment. He had no other purpose but to explore the possibilities of settling in France again. It was not until the evening before landing that temptation, swift and instant, came to him when, in the small cabin that he was sharing, his fellow-passenger was seized with a sudden heart attack and died before a doctor's help could be sought.

"He lay there in my arms," he said to me, "this sick man, an émigré like all of us on the boat, known to nobody except by his papers. To change those papers, replacing them with my own, was a moment's work. To call for help, to report the death, to acquaint the port officials when the boat docked and to leave the burial arrangements to them, all that was easy. I left Le Havre a free man, Sophie. Free to pick up my old life again without ties or responsibilities. Not perhaps as a master glass-maker, but as something else, it does not matter what. I'm ambitious no longer, I only want to make up for the years I've missed. Above all, I want to see my son."

This was what he had been leading up to from the first. Once he had settled down under our roof at le Gué de Launay, his story told, his secret shared with me, it was Jacques who was foremost in his mind. His mother's death he had expected. Grief for her soon passed. Jacques had become the symbol of everything precious in that old life laid aside.

"I've already told you," I said, playing for time, "Jacques is a conscript in the republican army. He was called to the colours in April, on his twenty-first birthday, and he is attached to an infantry regiment, I don't know where. Not even Pierre could give you his exact whereabouts at the present time."

"But tell me about him," protested my brother. "How has he developed, whom is he like? Does he often talk of me?"

The first two questions were easy enough to answer.

"He has your eyes," I answered, "and your colouring. That much you know. He has Cathie's build, he is small, below middle height. As to his nature, I've always found him affectionate and loyal. He is much attached to Pierre and to Pierre's boys."

"Is he intelligent and quick?"

"I would not call him quick. Conscientious would be the better word. He's taken to life in the army, judging by his letters home, and the officers speak well of him."

Robert nodded, pleased. I knew that for him Jacques was still a merry boy of eight, clamouring to help with the harvest in the fields of l'Antinière that summer of '89.

"If he is like Cathie in nature we shall get on famously," he said. "Surely now we are at peace they might let him home on leave, on compassionate grounds, to see his father?"

I was silent. Had my brother's desire to see his son blunted perception?

"You forget," I said after a moment, "that the republican army has been fighting England, the Allies and you émigrés for nine years. A sudden peace may suit the Consul and his government, but it doesn't make the soldiers who fought the battles the less bitter. You can hardly expect the commanding officer of Jacques's regiment to send a conscript home because of you."

Now it was his turn for silence. "You're very right," he said at length. "Now that I'm home I forget I was ever away. I must be patient, that is all."

He sighed and turned to go indoors, and I noticed, not for the first time, how humped his shoulders had become in these last years; he had the stoop of an old man, and he was not yet fifty-three.

"Besides," I called after him, "it would not do to call attention to your presence here, since you are officially dead."

He gestured, as if this did not concern him.

"Dead to those in London, perhaps," he said, "and to the port officials at Le Havre. Nobody else is likely to interest himself in another broken-down émigré come to end his days amongst his family."

The meeting with Jacques was thus postponed, for I was not lying when I told Robert that neither Pierre nor I knew where the battalion was stationed. Jacques might be anywhere—Italy, Egypt, Turkey—and the signing of peace treaties would not guarantee his return home.

"If I can't see my son," said Robert, "I can at least see my brothers. Are you not going to write to them and tell them that the prodigal has returned?"

Once again, I felt that he lacked perception. My welcome, because I loved him, was no surety for the feelings of the rest of us. François was noticeably cool, which Robert accepted because he had never known him well. As for my children, they were too young to form opinions, and seeing my fondness for this sudden long-lost uncle they took their lead from me.

But Edmé and Michel. . . . That was another matter. The pair of them, their inheritance and savings sunk in the Rougemont foundry and so lost, as I have said, were at present living on the borders of Sarthe and Orne, not far from Alençon. Michel had a position as manager of a small foundry there, and Edmé kept house for him. How long this would continue we did not know. Michel already showed signs of bronchial trouble, the dread disease of every glass-blower, which would, before very long, put an end to active work, if not to his life as well. I had seen too much of it in old days amongst our craftsmen at le Chesne-Bidault not to recognise the symptoms—the unhealthy pallor, the shortness of breath, the tight dry cough. Once the disease took hold, the end came quickly. It did not bear thinking about. I used to put it from my mind, and so did Edmé, but we were not deceived.

A letter, warning us of their approaching visit, came in the last days of July. Edmé had heard tell of a good doctor in Le Mans who was knowledgeable about chest diseases. The summer weather, with the warm winds blowing grass and pollen, had increased the severity of Michel's cough and his shortness of breath. Edmé had persuaded him to take a few days' absence from work, and they were to proceed to Le Mans, and would spend the night with us on their return.

"What shall I do?" I asked François. "Shall I be blunt with them and tell the truth? That Robert has come home?"

"They won't come here if you do," he answered. "I have not forgotten, if you have, what Michel said about his émigré brother. He told me once that Robert would be better dead, and that was the end of it. Certainly warn them, so that they may make a change in plans. I don't want a fight under my own roof. As it is, I find myself in considerable embarrassment because of your brother's presence here. It's hardly becoming in the mayor of Vibraye to house an émigré, relative or not. I think you don't always realise what is due to my position."

I realised too well. The years that had dealt so kindly with my husband's face and fortune had not graced him with humility or compassion. I loved him still, but he was a world away from the young man in the uniform of the National Guard singing "Ça Ira", who used to follow Michel on forays in '91.

"I'll write to Edmé," I said, "and to Michel too. It's best that they should know Robert is here, and so keep away."

The letter was dispatched. A week passed, and also the date that Edmé and Michel were due to visit the doctor in Le Mans. I expected to hear the result of the visit on their return to Alençon, with comment, perhaps, on Robert's presence. I did not expect the sound of wheels on our gravel drive one afternoon, and the sight of the hired 'chaise outside the windows, with first Michel and then Edmé descending from it.

Robert, who was reading, laid down his book and spectacles.

"Were you expecting visitors," he enquired, "or does monsieur le maire perform his duties at home as well as at Vibraye?"

There was little love lost between him and my husband, but the pinprick did not rouse me on this day. I was too much concerned about the others.

"It's Edmé and Michel," I said quickly. "I'll greet them, you stay here."

His face lit up, and he rose to his feet. Then, seeing my expression, his smile vanished. Slowly he sat down again.

"I understand," he said, "you don't have to tell me."

He was not so lacking in perception after all. François, perhaps, had been more explicit than I had realised.

I went out of the salon and into the entrance hall. Edmé was there before me. Michel was still without, paying off the driver.

"You didn't expect us," she said at once. "You were right, we had decided otherwise. Then, after seeing the doctor, Michel changed his mind."

I looked at her. The question was in my eyes.

"Yes," she answered, "what we feared. He can't get better. . . ."

She showed no emotion on her face. Only her voice betrayed her.

"It may be six months," she said, "or even less. He took it well. He insists that he will go on working until the end, and it's better so."

She said no more, for at this moment Michel came into the hall. I was startled by the alteration in his appearance since I had seen him last, a few months back. His face was grey and pinched, and he walked with little shuffling steps. When he spoke the breath came short, as though the effort hurt him.

"We can p-put up at Vibraye if you have no room for us," he said. "My f-fault, as Aimée will have told you. I ch-changed my mind."

I put my arms round him. The square stalwart figure had become suddenly small.

"You know there's room for you," I answered, "tonight and always, should you want it."

"Only t-tonight," he said. "Tomorrow I must get b-back to work again. Is Robert here?"

I glanced at Edmé and she nodded, then dropped her eyes.

"Where are the children?" she asked. "Shall I go and find them?"

My sister, no great lover of young people under the age of twelve, must have needed the excuse. Michel might have changed his mind about coming to le Gué de Launay, but she had not.

"As you please," I told her. "They are somewhere in the garden. Come, Michel."

I put my arm through his and opened the door of the salon. On the instant I was back again to that moment, thirteen years before, when he and I had walked out of the laboratory in the rue Traversière.

Robert, standing by the window of my salon, nervous, watchful, ready to match his mood to his brother's whatever it should be, whether mocking or aggressive, was not prepared, in fact, for what he saw. The angry fanatic with his shock of dark unruly hair had gone forever. The sick man, who stood with his arm in mine, had lost his fire.

"Hullo, mon b-brave," said Michel.

This was all. He shuffled towards Robert, holding out his arms. I went out of the room, leaving them alone, and shut myself upstairs until my tears had dried.

François was kept in Vibraye that day until after we had dined, and I was glad of it, for it meant that the four of us could be together. It was only Pierre we lacked to make my family complete.

Edmé, cool at first, holding out a stiff formal hand to Robert, which he kissed in mock solemnity, then flung aside to take her in his arms, soon found it hard to withstand the old gaiety, the old forgotten charm. She followed Michel's lead, through love of him, I think, more than anything else, knowing as I did that the occasion was almost certainly unique, never to be repeated. As to Michel, whether his own death sentence had blotted out resentment I do not know; but remembering how he had felt, and spoken too, during the years since Robert left us, it was a miracle this day to see how he had mellowed.

They say death does this to us once we are warned. Unconsciously, we strive not to waste time. Pettiness falls away, with all those things of little value in our lives. Could we but have known sooner, we tell ourselves, it would have been otherwise; no anger, no destruction, above everything no pride.

At dinner Robert kept us entertained with stories of cockney London, mocking the city that had sheltered him, along with its inhabitants and his own fellow-émigrés, in merciless disregard of any help they may have given him. But as we moved back into the salon afterwards he suddenly said, "But why, mon vieux, are you killing yourself as manager in a scrubby little foundry near Alençon when you might have taken the lease of some place like la Pierre? You could surely have done so, with our mother's inheritance, and what you had made besides out of church lands?"

My heart sank. This topic might lead us to the drama I had dreaded before they came. There was no time, though, to leave the room on some excuse. Robert had firmly shut the door behind him as we entered.

Michel walked slowly to the hearth-rug, and stood with his hands behind his back. He had taken wine at dinner, and two spots of colour showed on his grey, sick face.

"I had n-no alternative," he replied at last. "Aimée and I went into p-partnership together in the Year VII. We lost everything we p-possessed."

Robert raised his eyebrows.

"Then I'm not the only gambler in the family after all," he said. "What in the world induced you to take the risk?"

Michel paused a moment. "Y-you did," he said.

Robert, bewildered, looked from him to Edmé.

"I did?" he asked. "How could I have possibly done such a thing when you were over here and I in London?"

"You m-misunderstand me," answered Michel. "It was the th-thought of you which induced me, that's all. I wanted to succeed where you had f-failed. I did not d-do so. I think the answer is that we both of us, you and I, l-lack not only our father's t-talent, but his courage as well. I shall leave no children, but your J-Jacques may pass on both qualities to p-posterity."

Not necessarily Jacques, I thought. There were the children abandoned in London, who might do the same.

"Where did you lose your money?" asked Robert.

"At R-Rougemont," answered Michel.

I shall never forget the look on Robert's face. Incredulity passed to admiration, then to pity, then to shame.

"I'm sorry," he said. "I would have warned you had I known."

"Don't be sorry," answered Michel. "It was all experience. I've learnt my l-limitations, and the country's too."

"The country's?"

"Yes. Our p-plan was to share our p-profits with the workmen. Perhaps you haven't heard of Gracchus B-Babeuf, who killed himself rather than be g-guillotined? He believed that all wealth and p-property should be shared amongst the people. He was a f-friend of mine."

Our émigré, spectacles in hand, stared back at his youngest brother open-mouthed. It was not just thirteen years that stood between them, but a century of ideas as well. King's Bench prison might have taught him some humility, but his world was still the world of '89; Michel's and Edmé's belonged to a future we should never live to see.

"In other words," said Robert slowly, "you gambled on a dream."

"P-put it that way if you like," replied Michel.

Robert crossed to the window and looked out over the garden. The children were chasing butterflies on the lawn.

"Come to think of it," he added, "my gamble was also a dream. But a different one from yours."

We were all of us silent for a while, until Michel's cough, stabbing the air, made us suddenly conscious of what lay ahead for him. He sat down, gasping, waving his hand to draw attention away from himself.

"Don't be alarmed," he said, "it c-comes and goes. Sophie gave me too good a d-dinner." Then, smiling at his brother, he asked, "What happened to the g-glass?"

"The glass?"

Robert, startled into the present, was nonplussed for a moment only. Then, with a glance at me, he went to the cabinet. "It's here," he said, "the only thing I brought home with me from England. I nearly lost it once, but that's another story."

He opened the cabinet and took out the glass and showed it to Michel. "Not a scratch upon it, as you see," he said, "but I won't let you handle it, you say it brings bad luck."

"Not any l-longer," answered Michel, "my luck ran out some t-time ago. I'd like to hold it now."

He put out his hands and took the glass and turned it this way and that. The light from the window caught the engraven fleur-de-lys.

"They were c-craftsmen, I'll say that for them, both my f-father and my uncle," Michel said. "I've t-tried to copy this a hundred times, and always f-failed. Is Sophie going to keep it?"

"Until Jacques takes it from her," Robert answered.

"He won't d-do that," said Michel, "he belongs to B-Bonaparte. Jacques will f-follow the First Consul to the S-Siberian steppes and beyond. You ought to have bred more s-sons. I'm sorry your s-second marriage ended as disastrously as the f-first."

Robert did not answer. He took the glass from Michel and put it back in the cabinet. I was still the only one to know his secret.

"Too late for you and me to enter into p-partnership, mon vieux," said Michel, "the p-plain fact being that I may not live six months. But I'd welcome your c-company, even though you are a s-sacré émigré. You don't m-mind, do you, Aimée?"

"Not if you want him with you," answered Edmé.

"You can come back to S-Sophie and the comfort of the mayor's establishment after I'm g-gone," continued Michel. "How about it?"

This time it was Robert who was thinking of the parting at the laboratory in the rue Traversière. What bitterness he may have suffered then was now forgotten, extinguished forever by his brother's words. They made a strange contrast: Robert, the one-time dandy, now stooping, with his clothes hanging about him, his dyed hair streaked with grey, spectacles on nose; and Michel, no more a terrorist of the district of Mondoubleau ready to fight the world, but a dying man, facing his last battle.

If they had known then, I kept repeating to myself, if they had known then, would they have acted differently, would they have never quarrelled? Why the loneliness, the resentment, the anguish in between?

"I'll come with you," said Robert. "I'd be proud to do so. As to your six months' sentence, we might wager on that too. I give you at least a year. If I win, so much the better for both of us. If I lose, I shan't have to pay my debt!"

One thing was certain. Neither the London rain and fog, nor the gloom of King's Bench prison, nor Michel's approaching death, could quench my eldest brother's sense of fun or his gambling instinct.

TWENTY

My ELDEST BROTHER lost his wager. Michel died seven months later, in February, 1803—thank God, without much pain. He was working until the day before he died, and the end came suddenly, after a paroxysm of coughing. He was talking to Edmé one moment, and the next was dead. We brought his body back to Vibraye and buried him in the cemetery there, where I shall lie one day, and my sons as well.

None of us could have wished him to live longer. His strength had gone, and he would never have taken to an invalid's life, humped in an easy chair. His last months were made the easier by the presence of Robert, who, Edmé said, was gentler with Michel than she was herself. He made his bed for him, helped him to dress, and sat by him at night when his cough worsened; and all of it was done with ease and gaiety.

"I grudged his coming," Edmé admitted, "but after two weeks relied on him completely. Without him I think I could hardly have faced the end."

So the youngest of my brothers was the first to go, and, never having lost my faith, I liked to think of him when he was no longer with us, walking in some celestial glass-house with my father, reconciled at last, his stammer gone. Sentiment can turn after-life into a fairy tale for children, and I prefer this to Edmé's theory of oblivion.

She herself was so much moved by Michel's death that she lost all purpose for a while. He had been that purpose for more than seven years, and without him her roots were severed. They had shared the same beliefs, the same fanaticism for so long, and even in failure, when their dreams had shattered, their mutual loss became their consolation.

"She should marry again," said François bluntly. "A home and a husband would soon put her to rights."

I thought how lacking in intuition men could be in persuading themselves that mending some stranger's socks, and attending to his comfort, could content a woman of thirty-eight like my sister Edmé, who, with her quick brain and passion for argument, would—had she lived in another age—have fought for her beliefs like Joan of Arc.

For Edmé the revolution had come to an end too soon. Bonaparte's victorious armies might be a cause for pride, but in her view, and in Michel's also while he lived, the glory was all an empty mockery to make the generals shine—the mass of the people did not participate. The new aristocrats were the First Consul's friends, be-feathered and be-ribboned, jockeying for favours just as the courtiers had done once at Versailles. Only the names had changed.

"I've outlived my time," she used to say. "I should have gone to the guillotine with Robespierre and St. Just, or else died for their ideals in the streets of Paris. Everything since has been corruption."

A few weeks with us at le Gué de Launay were enough. She was plainly restless, bored. She packed her things and went off to Vendôme in search of any of the former clique of "Babouviste" adherents who might still be living there, and when next we heard from her she was writing articles for Hésine, Babeuf's friend and associate, who was once more at liberty, and agitating against the conscription laws.

I always said she should have been born a man. Her brains and her tenacity were wasted in a woman.

When the spring came Robert and I went down to St. Christophe to see Pierre, who, of course, had come earlier to Vibraye for Michel's funeral, so the pair of them had already seen each other. I had had no fears about this encounter. Pierre had welcomed the émigré as though he had never been away, and immediately presented him with that share of my mother's inheritance which he had carefully kept apart from the portion of it that had gone to Jacques. The rent from the small farm property, with the produce from the vines, though not in any sense a considerable sum, was at least enough to keep my eldest brother in the future, with enough over for investment.

"The question is," said Pierre, "what do you want to do with it?"

"I propose to do nothing," answered Robert, "until I can discuss the matter with Jacques. I don't understand this business of conscription. Isn't it possible to buy him out of the army?"

"No," said Pierre, "and even if it was . . ."

He left his sentence unfinished and glanced at me. I knew very well what he was thinking. Jacques, whether a soldier or civilian, was nearly twenty-two, and believed his father dead, or so we supposed.

"I think you should know," said Pierre, "that Jacques has never mentioned your name to me in all the years he has lived with us here at St. Christophe. My boys have told me the same. He may have talked about you to my mother, when he lived with her, but never to us."

"Perhaps not," Robert replied. "It does not mean he never thought about me."

I could tell that Pierre was disturbed for both their sakes. There was nothing he would have liked more than to bring father and son together, but Robert refused to see that the position was unusual. It was not as though he had returned as a colonialist might do after long absence. He had deserted his son, deserted his country, and lived as an émigré in England for thirteen years. He must not expect to find on his return the same affectionate lad that he remembered.

"What about his other grandparents?" persisted Robert. "Has he lost touch with them? I suppose so."

"On the contrary," said Pierre, "he writes to them very regularly, and sees them too, or did until he was conscripted. It was part of the arrangement I made for him when I became his guardian. I understand that when the old Fiats die everything they have will go to Jacques. It may not amount to much—the house in Paris and the old man's savings—but it will certainly be something, and a pleasant addition to a conscript's pay."

Robert was silent. After a while he said, "I hardly think the Fiats have any great opinion of me."

"Would you expect otherwise?" asked Pierre.

"No, no, very naturally not. Is it possible they may have poisoned Jacques's mind against me?"

"Possible," answered Pierre, "but improbable. They are a good old couple, and more likely left your name alone. The word émigré would hardly be used in front of Jacques."

Robert's face set in hard lines, unlike his usual expression. It was strange that he should learn from Pierre what he had not heard from Michel.

"Were we so much despised?" he asked.

"Frankly, yes," said Pierre, "and don't forget you were one of the first to go. In your case there was no persecution."

"Only the threat of a prison sentence," answered Robert.

"Which again is hardly likely to win admiration from your son," said Pierre.

Pierre, himself the most compassionate and forgiving of men, had the faculty of seeing straight where this whole question of emigration was concerned, and he wished to spare his brother humiliation. He did not reckon with Robert's powers of fantasy, nor suspect, as I did, with my knowledge of the London years, that Robert could fabricate whole images to quieten his conscience.

The test came sooner than we had expected. We were in the last days of our visit when Pierre-François, aged sixteen, Pierre's third boy and namesake to my own son, came running into the house, breathless and excited, to say that the 4th battalion of the 93rd regiment of foot had been reported in Tours.

"They've halted there, on their way north to the coast," he said, "and likely to be in the garrison three days. Without a doubt Jacques will ask permission to come and see us, if only for an hour or two."

Jacques was attached to the 5th company of this battalion, and if the report was true, if they were indeed in Tours, it was likely that he would be granted leave of absence.

"We must set out for Tours immediately," said Robert, in a fever to see his son. "What is the sense of waiting here?"

"Let us first discover if the report is correct," answered Pierre.

"It is doubtless the 93rd regiment, but not necessarily the 4th battalion."

He went off to track the rumour to its source, while Robert, more restless and impatient than he had ever been since his return from England, and reminding me of old days, paced up and down the untidy living-room of Pierre's house, littered as it always was with puppies, kittens, pet-hedgehogs in home-made cages, books—too many for the bursting shelves—heaped in corners, and the startling, very lifelike drawings by Pierre's daughter, the enchanting, seven-year-old Pivoine Belle-de-Nuit, already a favourite with her uncle.

"If Pierre causes me to miss Jacques now I shall never forgive him," said Robert. "Tours is barely an hour-and-a-half from here. It is now two. We could hire a conveyance and be there by four o'clock."

I sympathised with his agony, but with Pierre's caution too. We none of us wanted the disappointment of a fruitless journey, nor, on arriving in Tours, the possibility of Robert's entering into heated argument with Jacques's officers.

"You can trust Pierre to do what is right," I said. "You must know that by now."

For answer he pointed at the disorder of the room. "I'm not so sure," he answered. "What is all this due to but muddled thinking? Those lads of his may be fine fellows, able to put a kitten's paw in splints, but they can barely write their own language. I suppose my son has suffered the same lack of education because of Pierre's theories."

I let him rave. Anxiety was the reason for it. He knew as well as I did that Pierre's ideas on the upbringing of children mattered not at all, his integrity was what counted. But for Pierre's fore-sight, Robert himself would now be penniless.

"I'm sorry," he said after a while, "I'm not blaming Pierre. I don't think he understands what this meeting means to me."

"He understands very well," I told him. "That's why he is taking such pains about it."

Pierre returned within the hour. The report was true all right. The 4th battalion had arrived in Tours.

"I suggest," said Pierre, looking at his watch, "that we wait to see if Jacques travels on the diligence from Tours to Château-du-Loir, which is due here at five o'clock. If he is upon it, and I think he very well may be, then we shall see him in two hours. One thing I beg of you. Let me meet the boy alone, and tell him you are here."

"For the love of God, why?" Robert, at the end of his patience, shouted his question, to the alarm of little Belle-de-Nuit, scribbling by the window.

"Because," said Pierre patiently, "this will be an emotional moment for you both. You don't want people watching you in the street."

The next two hours were a strain upon us all. If Jacques was not on the diligence Robert's disappointment would be intense, and a fresh plan must be made. If Jacques was upon it . . . I was not sure of the answer, nor was Pierre.

Five minutes before the hour Pierre walked to the mairie, where the diligence was due to unload its passengers. He went alone. Pierre-François and the other boy, Joseph, remained in the house with their mother and Belle-de-Nuit, at Pierre's express orders. The children ran upstairs to watch the expected arrival from the upper windows. Robert and I sat in the living-room, or rather I sat, whilst my brother paced the floor. My sister-in-law, from discretion, kept to the kitchen.

Presently I was aware of Belle-de-Nuit standing in the door-way, a puppy under either arm.

"Papa and Jacques are walking up and down outside," she said. "They've been doing so for ten minutes or more. I don't think Jacques wants to come inside the house."

Robert was making for the entrance immediately, but I seized his arm.

"Wait," I said, "perhaps Pierre will explain."

A moment later Pierre came into the room. His eyes sought mine and I understood the message. Then he turned to Robert.

"Jacques is here," he said briefly. "He has only an hour, and must take the returning diligence to Tours. I have broken the news to him that you are with us."

"Well?" My eldest brother's anxiety was pitiful to watch.

"It's as I feared. He was very much shaken, and only consents to see you for my sake."

Pierre went out into the entrance hall and called for Jacques. Robert himself moved forward, hesitated, then waited, uncertain what to do. His son came into the room and stood beside his uncle at the door. Jacques had grown no taller since I saw him last, but was broader, more thick-set; no doubt he had filled out with army rations. He looked well in his uniform, if a trifle over-burdened with it, and a little clumsy. I thought what a different figure he cut from his father in old days as an officer in the Arquebusiers, who took greater interest in the fit of his coat than he ever did in soldierly activities.

He stood there staring at his father, pale and unsmiling. I wondered which of the two suffered the most—Jacques, at the sight of his elderly father, nervously twisting his spectacles in his right hand, or Robert, at the sight of his hostile son.

"You've not forgotten me, have you?" Robert said at last, summoning a smile.

"No," said Jacques, his young voice harsh and abrupt. "It might be better if I had."

Pierre beckoned to me from the door.

"Come, Sophie," he called, "let's leave them together."

I was about to cross the room, but Jacques held up his hand.

"No, uncle," he said, "stay where you are, and tante Sophie too. I should prefer it. I have nothing to say to this man."

It would have been kinder had he walked up to his father and hit him across the face. I saw the agony of disbelief in Robert's eyes, then the recognition of defeat. Undaunted, he made a final effort to overcome the situation with bravado.

"Oh, come, my boy," he said, "it's too late for drama. Life's too short for that. You're a fine man, and I'm proud of you. Come and shake hands with your old father, who's loved you devotedly all these years."

Pierre laid his hand on the boy's arm, but Jacques shook it off.

"I'm sorry, uncle," he said, "I've done what you asked. I've come into the room. He sees that I exist. That is enough. Now I would like to go and see tante Marie and my cousins."

He turned on his heel, but Pierre still barred the way.

"Jacques," he said softly, "have you no pity?"

Jacques swung round and looked at all of us in turn.

"Pity?" he asked. "Why should I have pity? He didn't have any pity for me nearly fourteen years ago, when he deserted me. All he could think of was getting out of the country as quickly as possible, fearful for his own skin. Now, because of the amnesty, he thinks it's safe to return. Well, that's his affair, but I wonder he had the face to do so. You can pity him if you like. I can only despise him."

It is a disadvantage to see the past as clearly as the present, and to carry a picture in the forefront of one's mind which is as vivid today as on the day it happened. For my part, I was sitting in the carriole leaving l'Antiniére, and Jacques was a sunburnt little lad in a blue smock, kissing his father good-bye.

"That's enough, then," said Robert quietly. "Let him go."

Pierre stood aside, and Jacques went out of the room. I heard little Belle-de-Nuit call him from the stairs, and her brothers too, and one of the puppies began barking excitedly. They took him into their world, and the three of our generation were left alone.

"I was afraid of it," said Pierre, whether to Robert or to me I do not know. Deep in thought, he repeated it once more. "I was afraid of it."

Presently Robert went upstairs to his room and shut the door. He stayed there until the time came for Jacques to mount the diligence for Tours. Then he stood on the landing, in the hope that his son might relent and come up to bid him good-bye. We pleaded with Jacques, but he was firm. Neither Pierre, nor Marie, nor I could make him change his mind. He had spent his hour of absence sitting with his cousins in the old playroom above, telling them, so we learnt afterwards, of his experiences as a conscript, and, judging by their laughter, making a joke of it. Never once did he speak about his father, and they, taking their lead from him, let it alone.

As he set forth for the diligence accompanied by Pierre-François and Joseph, having kissed us all, and we heard the door into the street slam behind him, the sound echoed from above.

It was Robert, who had waited until the last moment, shutting his bedroom door.

That night I spilt his secret, and told Pierre about the family left in England. He heard the whole wretched tale through without comment, and, when I had finished, thanked me for having told him.

"There's only one thing to do now," he said, "and that is to bring his wife and children over here. Whether he goes to fetch them, or I go, is immaterial. Without them he will become a broken man, because of what Jacques has done to him today."

The relief of having unburdened myself to Pierre was very great. We talked at length about the procedure necessary to bring Robert's wife and children from London across the Channel. She believed herself a widow, and would be receiving assistance from the authorities in England. No one must know in that country that Robert was not dead, for the penalty, as I had imagined, would be severe. Pierre, for all his knowledge of the law, was uncertain how it would be applied. The fraud was a peculiar one, and he would have to take counsel, discreetly, amongst his legal friends.

"Surely the best way to set about it," I said, "is for you, or for me, to write to Marie-Françoise, offering her a home over here, and saying that we have Robert's inheritance to offer her?"

"And if she doesn't want to come?" replied Pierre. "What then? She may prefer to live in London amongst those émigrés who have no wish to return. It would be better for one of us to go in person and persuade her. If she once knows Robert is alive, there will be no question but that she will come."

I remembered how Robert had told me that his wife had turned very religious during his term of imprisonment. It might be that she would have scruples about keeping the fraud secret, and would want to tell the Abbé Carron, who had been so good to them.

There seemed no end to all these problems, but I knew Pierre was right. The only way for Robert to make restoration for the past, and for what he had done to Jacques, was to become reunited once more with his second family. He had committed the same crime twice. There was no other word to describe it. It was only a matter of time before guilt for the first crime would merge into guilt for the second, and when that happened . . . Pierre looked at me expressively.

"What are you afraid of?" I asked him.

"I'm afraid he might kill himself," answered Pierre.

He went upstairs to his brother, and stayed with him for a long time. When he came down again Pierre told me that Robert had agreed to do anything that was suggested. Jacques was lost to him, doubtless forever. He realised now the irreparable damage he had done to a sensitive boy. The idea that it was still possible to become reunited with the children left in England would prove his salvation.

"Can you delay your return home for a few days?" asked Pierre.

I told him I could. Charlotte, niece of dear old Madame Verdelet who used to cook for us at le Chesne-Bidault, was quite capable of looking after my family for a little longer.

"In that case," answered Pierre, "I shall go to Paris tomorrow. I shall learn there what are the possibilities of one or other of us travelling to England. Meanwhile, stay here with Robert. Don't let him out of your sight."

He was away the next morning before Robert had even risen, and during the days that followed I did as Pierre told me, and, with the boys and Belle-de-Nuit, kept Robert company.

He was strangely quiet and contrite, and had become, during the twenty-four hours since Jacques had departed, a much older man.

The shock had been profound, not only to his emotions but to his self-esteem. During those long hours alone in his bedroom, after Pierre had spoken with him, I think he must have realised, at last, just what had happened in the years between. The stigma of having been an émigré, and all that it must have meant to Jacques, the son of an émigré, brought up in a household of patriots, was now made clear. We—Pierre, Michel and I, and Edmé to a lesser degree—had been able to accept him; our middle years made it easier for us. The young are less forgiving.

While we waited for Pierre's return from Paris Robert talked, at first with some hesitation, later with eagerness, of the possibility of seeing Marie-Françoise and the children once again.

"She will soon get over the deception," he said. "I can make up some story or other of the papers becoming mixed, it's of no great consequence. And once here, with the money from the inheritance, we can find a place to settle. The children, anyway, will speak both languages, always an advantage for their future careers. My little girl Louise is almost the same age as Belle-de-Nuit. They will be great companions."

He took his niece on his knee as he said this, and she, being an affectionate child, clung closely to him.

"Yes," he said, "yes, I see now I was mad to do what I did. It would have been so simple to come to you, as I planned first, and make arrangements to bring them over. At the time, of course, I knew nothing of the inheritance, I did not even know that I should find any of you alive. I acted on impulse. I've done so all my life."

I encouraged him to think and to plan for the future. It seemed the only way to pass the time, and it prevented him from brooding over Jacques.

After five or six days he had almost recovered his spirits, and was becoming restless for Pierre's return. At last, just a week after he had left us, and we were in the dining-room, about to sit down to dinner, Belle-de-Nuit called out, "I can hear my Papa in the hall." She struggled to get down from her chair, but Robert was there before her. I heard him greet Pierre, there was a quick exchange of questions and answers, and then silence. I felt that something was wrong. I got up and left the table, and went into the hall.

Pierre was standing with his hand on Robert's shoulder.

"There is nothing to be done," he was saying. "Hostilities have broken out again between the English and ourselves, and the Channel ports are closed to traffic. I understand now why Jacques's battalion was marching north. They say Bonaparte is preparing to invade England."

The truce that had lasted for fourteen months had ended, and the war, which had started up anew, was to continue for another thirteen years. Pierre's plan had been formed too late. Robert had lost not only his eldest son, but all chance of reunion with his second wife and family. He was never to see them, or to hear of them, again.

TWENTY-ONE

WE HAD BECOME so used to Bonaparte's success that we looked upon the renewal of war between France and England as a temporary set-back to our personal hopes and plans. It would all be over in a few months. Bonaparte would invade England, march upon London, and force the English government to accede to his terms, whatever they should be. As to the émigrés living under English protection, they would very naturally be sent home to their own country; therefore Robert's desire to be reunited with Marie-Françoise and the children could not be long deferred. Since we reasoned thus, the outbreak of war was less of a shock than a frustration, or so I argued, supported by Pierre. It was Robert himself, calmer and more resigned than we expected, who warned us not to expect an early victory.

"You forget," he said. "I've lived amongst these people for thirteen years. A continental war may not rouse them, but if you threaten their own shores they'll turn tenacious. Do not count on any quick result, and if Bonaparte launches an invasion, it may misfire."

The months that followed proved my brother right. The great army gathered at Boulogne waited in vain for a chance to cross the Channel, and when summer turned to autumn, with the onset of bad weather, their hopes of success faded, and so did ours.

Robert, who was living with us once more at le Gué de Launay, admitted to me one evening during the worst of the winter, in February, 1804, that even when spring came he did not believe Bonaparte would risk invasion.

"The chances of a defeat at sea would be too great," he said. "I think we must make up our minds to a long-drawn-out war between ourselves and England, no matter what success Bonaparte may have elsewhere. This means, from my own point of view, that I must stop thinking of Marie-Françoise and the children. I'm dead to them, and have to face the fact they are dead to me."

He spoke without bitterness, but with decision, and I realised that he must have been turning the matter over in his mind for some while.

"Put it that way if you will," I told him, "but not if it's just to quieten your conscience. They are alive in London, growing year by year, just as Pierre-François, Alphonse-Cyprien and Zoë are growing here, and Pierre's brood at St. Christophe. Accept the fact that they are living and you cannot help them. It will be easier for you to hold to the truth if you have the courage."

"It isn't a question of courage," he answered. "I mean they are dead to me emotionally. It's a strange thing, but I can't even conjure up their faces any more. They've become like shadows. When I think of Louise, who was always my favourite, her features turn into those of little Belle-de-Nuit. Perhaps it is because they are the same age."

Here was a perplexity. I know that if I had been separated from my children, no matter for how long, their faces, and their voices too, would become more vivid. I wondered whether the disastrous encounter with Jacques had shocked some part of Robert's brain, affecting his memory. Or could it be that he conveniently forgot all things that troubled him? I doubted if the thought of Jacques had bothered him much in London, and the decision to name his second boy Jacques could have been pure perversity, and part of the fantasy-life. I could not help remarking, though, his genuine affection for my children, and for Pierre's also. He had a natural way about him, gay and light-hearted, that won their response, despite his age, and I noticed that my two sons would run to him with some problem of grammar or arithmetic sooner than to their father. After all, it was Robert who had tried to teach me Latin in the old days at le Chesne-Bidault before he married, and during those last few years in London he had helped the Abbé Carron with the émigré pupils in the Pancras school.

"You've wasted your time as a master-engraver," I said one

day, after I had found him with my two boys on either side of him, with a volume of Latin grammar in his hands. "You ought to have been an instructor in a school."

He laughed and put the book aside. "I was glad enough of the work in London for the money it brought in," he said. "Here it passes the time and stops me thinking, which—you will agree— is an achievement."

Once more he spoke without bitterness, but although I knew he was content with my company, and happy to be amongst us, I sensed the void within. A year ago he had been building in imagination a future with Jacques; now that was over, but the days had to be filled all the same. My brother was fifty-four. His inheritance from our mother was untouched. Somehow he must maintain himself and have a raison d'être.

"You have only to say the word," Pierre wrote to him, "and I will join forces with you in any undertaking you care to suggest, with one exception. The glass-trade must be barred to us. For one thing, we haven't the resources. For another, your creditors in Paris have forgotten you, but any attempt to bring your name forward again in circles familiar to the trade might fetch them about your ears. Here, in the Touraine, you are unknown." We were many years distant from Busson l'Aîné and his influential friends.

In early May Pierre told us that Jacques had written him to say his grandmother, Madame Fiat, had died, and he was on leave in Paris receiving the inheritance due to him. His grandfather, old Fiat, was also ailing, and Jacques confirmed that when he died the house and its contents would belong to him.

"Which means," said Robert, "that Jacques now knows himself to be independent. He will be able to sell the house and invest the proceeds, leaving the capital untouched until he quits the army."

"In other words," I replied, "he will never need your help. When you saw him last year you could not be sure. Now you know."

"He would not have come to me direct," said Robert, "but he might have approached Pierre. Even that last hope is now denied me."

It was not until news came that Jacques's regiment had embarked at Toulon for service in the Mediterranean, and was likely to be out of the country for at least two years, that Robert finally decided what he wanted to do with his own inheritance. He asked Pierre to come to le Gué de Launay for a family conference, and when the three of us were together—François preferring to take no part in the discussion, and Edmé too deeply involved with her Jacobin friends in Vendôme to attend—he put his proposal to us.

"I want to devote my life, what remains of it," he said, "to the young. I want to try and do, heaven knows in a much smaller way, what I watched the Abbé Carron achieve in London. He chose a crowd of fatherless boys and girls from the poorest amongst the émigrés, housed them, fed them and clothed them, and gave them an education into the bargain. It could be that this is what he is still doing for my family there. In any event, I want to do it here."

I think we were too surprised at first to make any comment. My remarks to Robert that he had wasted his talents as an engraver had been spoken in jest. I had never for one moment considered they would bear fruit. As to Pierre, he had his own strange ideas on education; let a child alone and it would teach itself was the method he had employed with his own boys, much to the disruption of his household, good-humoured though it was. Now, with Robert's pronouncement exploding amongst us like a cannon-ball, I wondered what the effect would be on Pierre. An occasion for argument, perhaps, with the theories of Jean-Jacques claiming us until midnight. Instead, Pierre's enthusiasm took me by surprise. He leapt to his feet and clapped his brother on the shoulder.

"You've got it," he almost shouted. "You've got it absolutely. I can think of at least six boys straight off, sons of my old clients in Le Mans, who would come to us as pupils. I could teach them philosophy, botany and law, and leave the rest to you. We would charge practically nothing, of course; we don't want to make money out of them. Just enough to cover the cost of food and rent. Sophie, you will give us Pierre-François and Alphonse-Cyprien. I'm not so sure about my own three, they'd be better working on a farm. But it will mean letting the house in St. Christophe and moving to Tours. Tours must be our centre. I wonder if we can persuade Edmé to quit Vendôme and give lectures on political freedom? Perhaps not, her ideas are too advanced, and we must do nothing to offend the Code Civil."

Pierre's enthusiasm was infectious. He had all of us inspired. Two days later he left for Tours in search of suitable quarters for the proposed pension, and, more important still, to obtain permission from the authorities for "les frères Busson" to found a "maison d'éducation" for fatherless children. Even François, who had prophesied some fresh speculation on Robert's part with its inevitable loss, had to agree that the new idea was commendable, if hardly profitable, but insisted that our own boys, having a father living, could not qualify for positions in the school.

It took six months or more before the pension was ready to receive its first pupils, and when it opened in early December, 1804, at No. 4, rue des Bons Enfants, Tours, I remember that our own family celebrations coincided with that of the whole nation. The city was beflagged, the crowds were out in the streets, for Napoleon Bonaparte, the First Consul, had been crowned Emperor.

How much the general excitement contributed to my two brothers' sense of dedication I did not know, but the occasion was a moving one. As they stood side by side, welcoming their twenty pupils, in the square oak-beamed room on the first floor of the ancient house in the centre of Tours which they had taken for their pension, it seemed to me that the wheel had somehow come full circle, and the Busson brothers were together again in a community. This community life was what they had known as children in the glass-houses of Chérigny and la Pierre; it was something to which they had been born and bred, and although here in Tours there was no foundry chimney, no furnace, no product made with hands, fundamentally the spirit was the same.

My brothers were the masters, imparting knowledge and a way of life to these children, just as my father and my uncles had bequeathed the knowledge of their craft to my brothers when they were apprentices at la Pierre. Here, in the rue des Bons Enfants, were no molten glass, no rods, no pipes; the glass-blowers did not stand before the fire, blow-pipe in hand, breathing life into the slowly expanding vessel. Instead there were children, their personalities malleable, awaiting development, and my brothers must guide them as surely and as steadily as they had once shaped liquid glass, bringing to fullness and maturity a rounded and balanced human being.

Pierre had the ideals and the selflessness to put those ideas into practice, Robert the powers of persuasion, the necessary charm and inventive ability to turn a history lesson into an adventure.

I watched the eager expectant faces of those orphaned boys, and the one girl amongst them, little Belle-de-Nuit, twenty-one in all staring at my brothers, who, each of them in turn, made a short speech of welcome. Pierre, his blue eyes, so like my mother's, afire with enthusiasm, and his white hair en brosse, bore small resemblance to those professors of education whom I had seen elsewhere in Tours.

"I am here," he said, "not to teach you, but to be taught. I've forgotten all I ever learnt, except a smattering of the law, which I applied in my own fashion when I was a notary in Le Mans. I know nothing about buying and selling, and if you ask my brother about this it won't help—he lost everything he possessed in speculation. What I do remember is where to look for wild strawberries in early summer, and the most likely trees to climb to find the nests of buzzards—for this, you must go to the forest, and we will do it together. Buzzards are predators, that is to say, they rob the nests of other birds and eat their young. This is anti-social, and for this reason they are mobbed by their fellows. People who follow their example in the world suffer likewise. We might also examine together the life-cycle of butterflies and moths. You are all of you, at this period of your life, grubs and caterpillars; the fascination of growing up is to see what you become.

"I don't intend to make any rules here that I won't keep myself. If you make any amongst yourselves I will keep them too. My wife has one request, that you don't throw your food upon the floor. Food, mixed with dirt, encourages rats, and rats breed plague. Nobody wants plague in Tours. This evening, if any of you care to listen, I shall be reading the first few chapters of Rousseau's *Emile* aloud. If nobody turns up it does not matter. I enjoy the sound of my own voice, and shall not be offended. Afterwards, I shall start building an aviary for two birds with broken wings that my daughter, Pivione Belle-de-Nuit, brought with her from St. Christophe, and helpers will be welcomed. Now, perhaps you will have the courtesy to hear my brother. He is the elder by three years, and has all the brains."

Pierre sat down, amid bewildered though polite applause, and François, at my side, whispered that the pension would surely be closed down by the authorities within the year.

Robert rose to his feet, his hair, newly dyed for the occasion, contrasting a little oddly, if spectacularly, with his new plum-coloured coat. He carried a sheaf of papers to steady the tremor in his hands.

"There was once a lad," he said, "who went to Martinique to seek his fortune. He returned empty-handed, having given away whatever he possessed, save for an embroidered waistcoat and two parrots. That lad, now middle-aged, has just been speaking to you. He knows little more of life now than he did then. If you want to learn how to gamble for vast sums and lose them within the year I can teach you, but don't expect either my brother or myself to bail you out of prison afterwards.

"The English poet Shakespeare said that life is 'a tale told by an idiot, full of sound and fury, signifying nothing'. But he put these words into the mouth of a Scottish chief who had murdered the king sheltering beneath his roof, so it need not apply to you at the moment—unless you rise up and murder my brother and myself in our beds. Life, on the contrary, is at its most intense when it is silent; the silence of a prison cell, for instance, which gives every opportunity for thought, or when sitting beside the dead body of a loved one to whom you never bade good-bye.

"The sound and the fury, nevertheless, you will experience all in good time as obedient conscripts fighting for the greater glory of the Emperor and France. But whilst you are here, at No. 4, rue des Bons Enfants—which name, by the way, is quite fortuitous, for we came upon the street by chance—I shall endeavour to imbue your reluctant souls with a desire for stillness. Restless as a caged lion myself, I can never stay motionless for more than five seconds at a time; hence my respect for those who can. I was forced to remain still at certain periods of my life, which I may tell you about one day—it will depend upon how much I have had to drink.

" 'Pitchers have ears'—another quotation from Shakespeare, *Richard III* this time, for I am an English scholar—and if you keep yours alert you may hear a great deal to your ultimate advantage, on the wiles of men and princes. For I speak as one who saw the heyday of Louis XV and his unfortunate descendant, and now bows the knee to the Emperor Napoleon. History, literature, Latin, grammar, arithmetic, I'm a qualified professor in all five subjects—in my own opinion, if not in my brother's—and before you go out from here in a few years' time to shed your blood on the battlefields of Europe, I suggest you obtain some sort of grounding in these matters, along with gathering wild strawberries with my associate, so that dying you may murmur, 'Virtuti nihil obstat et armis,' which may be some consolation in the circumstances.

"In my own youth I held to the precept, 'Video meliora proboque, deteriora sequor', which is the reason my hands tremble today and I dye my hair—I do not ask you to follow my example.

"Meanwhile, my life is yours. This is your home. Trample on both to your hearts' content, and be happy."

Robert shuffled his papers, replaced his spectacles, and gave a signal for dismissal. The children, conditioned after the first speech to applause, clapped their hands loudly, led by Belle-de-Nuit. Only my husband, the mayor of Vibraye, shocked beyond measure, stared firmly at his feet.

"I think it only fair to tell you," he said to my brothers as soon as the children had clattered down the stairs and across the small inner court to their own quarters, "that, despite our relationship, I shall have to erase the name of the pension from my list of recommendations. These children won't have a chance

under your care. They will grow up either scoundrels or buf-
foons."

"We are most of us either the one or the other," replied Robert. "In which category do you class yourself?"

This was no moment for a family quarrel, and I laid my hand
on François' arm.

"Come," I said, "you must see the dormitory where the boys
will sleep. Pierre has contrived it with great cunning, and par-
titioned it into two."

My tact was wasted, for at this moment Edmé, who had come
over from Vendôme for the occasion, approached us.

"I liked both your speeches," she said in her usual forthright
fashion, "but you neither of you said anything about tyranny.
Surely one of the first lessons a boy should learn is how to distinguish between the oppressors and the leaders of the people?
Nor did you as much as mention the Rights of Man."

Pierre looked astonished. "But I gave an explicit description of
tyranny when I spoke about buzzards," he said. "And as to the
Rights of Man, I intend to hammer the point home when we
find our first clutch of eggs and leave them intact. Birds have
their rights as well as human beings. Little by little these children will discover the facts for themselves."

Edmé appeared relieved, though not entirely convinced, and
as we made a tour of the house I saw her frowning at the en-
thusiastic "Vive l'Empereur" that one of the students had already
scrawled in enormous letters over the entrance to their dormitory.

"That," she observed quietly, "should be removed straight
away."

"What would you put in its place?" questioned Robert. "Children, like adults, need a symbol."

" 'Vive la nation' would be preferable," she said.

"Too impersonal," answered Robert. "You can't have the
nation seated on a white horse, with the tricolour in the background against a stormy sky. When these lads scrawl 'Vive
l'Empereur', that is what they see. Neither you nor I will ever
dissuade them."

Edmé sighed. "Not you, perhaps," she replied, "but if I was
allowed to speak to them for twenty minutes about conscription,

and what it will mean for them, they would never scrawl 'Vive l'Empereur' again."

I could not help being relieved, for the sake of both my brothers, that my sister had not been invited to lecture at the pension in the rue des Bons Enfants, for if she did the place would close, not in a year as François prophesied, but within three months.

As it turned out, the pension Busson remained open for nearly seven years, though not quite as my brothers intended it. The laws on education became much stricter as the months passed, all part of the Code Civil, which the local authorities throughout the country were bound to enforce. Boys were obliged to attend the State schools and be taught by qualified teachers, and so the unorthodox and original theories of my brothers were never fully put into practice. The pension remained a pension for fatherless boys, a place in which to eat and sleep, but they went daily to the State schools.

As time went by, and the children grew older and left, their places were taken by those homeless or down-on-their luck individuals so dear to my brother Pierre. Needless to say, they never paid for their bed or board, but looked to him for charity. The pension, started with such high hopes, deteriorated into a kind of lodging-house where all were welcome, with Pierre acting host, and Robert endeavouring to make up for his brother's lack of money sense by coaching private pupils before they sat for examination.

The decline, so François said, was only to be expected; indeed, it was a wonder the place was kept going at all. It saddened me to see the house grow shabby from want of care, the walls unpainted, the stairs unscrubbed; and when I went to stay in the rue des Bons Enfants, as I did from time to time, I would miss the laughter and the clatter of those children of the first year, when the pension opened. Instead I would hear a rasping cough from some semi-invalid in the room adjoining, or meet a grumbling individual as I walked down the stair to the inner court where the children had once played.

Neither Robert nor Pierre seemed aware of dilapidation or decay. They had chosen to live thus, and it seemed to suit them.

The light of both their lives was Belle-de-Nuit, whose radiant presence turned the otherwise drab pension to a place of joy.

This enchanting child, doomed—though thank heaven neither her father nor her uncle lived to see it happen—to die of tuberculosis before she was twenty years old, had all the family gifts and none of their faults. Selfless like Pierre, she possessed more application and discernment. Intelligent like Edmé, she was without rancour, and envied no one. Her talent for drawing was such that had it matured she could have excelled as a professional artist. As it is, I keep the best of her drawings, filed away in my cabinet in le Gué de Launay.

She was the only one of Pierre's children to profit by Robert's teaching. The boys, after military service, drifted into various trades, Joseph starting up as a saddler in Château-du-Loir and Pierre-François, my own son's namesake, becoming a hairdresser in Tours.

"The inevitable result of deliberate neglect," François used to say. "Those boys, with proper upbringing, might have entered a profession."

Even so, what talent they possessed came from their hands. I have seen leather-work stitched by Joseph with all the loving care that a fine engraver would put upon his glass, and wigs dressed by Pierre-François that the Empress herself would not have scorned to wear. Nothing is degraded that is bequeathed with love. My father handed down a passion for craftsmanship to the grandsons he never saw.

"Let each one work to the best of his ability," Pierre used to say. "I don't care what they do as long as they do it to extreme."

He spoke his own epitaph. Fishing one Sunday on the banks of the Loire, he saw a dog leap from the opposite shore to retrieve a stick, thrown by its master. The dog faltered in midstream and pawed the water, frightened, at which my brother flung off his coat and plunged in after him. The dog, seeing his rescuer, gained courage and turned for the shore, but Pierre, shocked by the sudden cold and hampered by his clothes, was seized with cramp, and sank. The owner of the dog gave the alarm and a boat was launched, but it was too late. Pierre's body was recovered three days afterwards.

The impulse which brought him death, and so much grief to his family, had its consequences, one of which might never have occurred had he lived. Because of it, I like to think that his impulse was not in vain.

The tragedy happened in April, 1810, a few days before Pierre's fifty-eighth birthday and Jacques's twenty-ninth, and during the time when the Emperor was holding the celebrations in Paris for his second marriage, to Marie-Louise of Austria. Jacques's regiment had formed part of the Grande Armée since 1807, he had campaigned in most of the countries in Europe, and his company was amongst those doing duty in the capital for the marriage celebrations.

I wrote to him instantly, upon learning of the accident, so that he could send a message of sympathy to his aunt and cousins. I did not imagine for a moment that he would obtain leave of absence.

François and I and our daughter Zoë, now seventeen, went down to Tours for the funeral, and we delayed our return for a day or two, with the intention of taking my sister-in-law Marie and Belle-de-Nuit back with us.

The child, who was now fourteen and had adored her father, had stifled her own grief in attending to her mother. It was during their preparations for departure, when I was with her in her room, that she suddenly turned to me and said, "I don't know if I did wrong, tante Sophie, but I wrote to Jacques to tell him what has happened."

"So did I," I reassured her. "No doubt you will be hearing from him, and your mother too."

She looked at me in her steadfast way, then said, "I've asked him to come here. I told him he was needed."

This news disturbed me. We did not want a repetition of the encounter of seven years past. Pierre's death had greatly shocked my brother, and he was in no state to suffer a second rebuff.

"It wasn't wise, Belle-de-Nuit," I said. "You know Jacques does not care to speak to his father, or to see him. That is why he refuses to come on leave to Tours unless your uncle is away."

"I know that very well," she answered, "and it was always

Papa's wish to bring them together. It seemed to me that the time had come to try just that. We will see."

I did not know whether to warn Robert or to say nothing. I felt certain Jacques would not be able to get leave of absence because of the celebrations, but I was wrong. I never discovered what special pleading Belle-de-Nuit put into her letter, but it brought a response, which mine would never have done. That evening, I was descending the old staircase into the inner court, with Robert by my side, and as I paused a moment, my hand on the carved balustrade, I heard Belle-de-Nuit's cry of welcome in the archway leading to the street beyond.

Instinct told me who it was, and I made to turn.

"What's the matter?" Robert asked. "If it's another caller, the child will deal with him."

They came through the archway together, Belle-de-Nuit in her black mourning dress and Jacques in his uniform of caporal fusilier. The boy had developed into a man, still short but broad and thick-set, with powerful shoulders, and I should hardly have recognised him but for his blue eyes and his shock of fair hair.

The pair of them stared up at us, and I saw that Robert beside me had turned white. He must have shared my instinct, for he turned to make his way back up the stairs once more, stumbling as he did so.

"No, uncle, don't go." Belle-de-Nuit's voice rang clear like a command. "Jacques has permission from his company commander for two days," she said, "after which they will rejoin the battalion for service in Spain. He has come to say good-bye to you."

Robert hesitated. His hand on the balustrade trembled.

"I was decorated last year at Wagram," said Jacques. "If it would interest you, I should like to show you the medal."

The voice was no longer harsh and arrogant. It held respect, and a certain shyness too. Robert turned again, and looked down the stairs at his son. His hair was no longer dyed these days. It had gone white, as Pierre's had done, and he looked all of his sixty years.

"I heard about the decoration," he said. "I should like to see your medal more than anything else in the world."

Jacques started up the stairway towards us. I kissed him quickly, and then joined Belle-de-Nuit in the court below. Our presence was not needed at this encounter. Looking back over my shoulder, I saw father and son silhouetted a moment at the turn of the stairs; then Robert put his arm through Jacques's and led him up to his room beyond.

The rest of us left the next day for le Gué de Launay, and Jacques spent the remaining twenty-four hours of his leave alone with his father. I could only guess what the reconciliation meant to both of them.

There is little left to tell about my brother Robert. Despite my entreaties that he should give up the pension and come to live at le Gué de Launay, he would not be persuaded. I think he felt that Pierre would have expected him to stay.

"I shall keep the place open," he told me, "just as long as I can afford to do so."

But once Pierre's widow had departed back to St. Christophe with Belle-de-Nuit, unable to face life at the pension without him, the little joy remaining went out of the poor shabby building, and with it my brother's will to live.

He became very frail and shaky during the succeeding winter, and, like Michel before him, complained in his letters of shortness of breath. He continued to coach pupils before examinations, for young faces were his one delight, reminding him, not only of Jacques and Belle-de-Nuit, but of that family of his across the Channel, of whose existence I alone knew.

He spoke of them to me the last time I saw him, which was in May of 1811, little more than twelve months after Pierre's death.

"If he still lives," Robert said to me, "my second Jacques will now be eighteen years old, Louise, like Belle-de-Nuit, approaching sixteen, and Louis-Mathurin in his fourteenth year. I wonder if they have become entirely English, disliking all things French, even their own language."

"I doubt it," I said, "and one day, ten, twenty, thirty years hence, they will come home."

"Perhaps," he answered, "but not to me."

He waved good-bye to me from the upper window of his room

at No. 4, rue des Bons Enfants, for I would not let him walk with me to the diligence that would take me back to Vibraye, in case it strained his heart.

I left him with an unhappy feeling of premonition. There were not more than half-a-dozen persons living in the pension, none of whom knew him well, or would be able to take care of him if he became ill.

A month later, on the 2nd of June, at about three o'clock in the afternoon, he was climbing the stairway from the inner court to the landing above when a clot of blood must have blocked a vein of his heart, for he fell, and was found there by two of the lodgers, dying, a moment or two afterwards.

They carried him to his room and laid him on his bed and stood there waiting, uncertain whom to send for or what to do. He tried to speak but could not, and they thought he wanted air, and opened the window. It troubles me still, after thirty years, to know that my brother was with strangers when he died.

EPILOGUE

MADAME DUVAL laid down her pen on the 6th of November, 1844, the day before her eighty-first birthday. It had taken her a little over four months to write the story of her family, and during the telling of her tale she had lived again, in memory, many incidents she had thought forgotten. Their faces were very clear to her: her father Mathurin and her mother Magdaleine, her three brothers, Robert, Pierre, Michel, and her sister Edmé.

She had outlived them all, even her nephew Jacques, who, severely wounded in January, 1812, had died the following June, shortly after leaving hospital, thus surviving his father by only twelve months.

Edmé, poor Edmé, whose dreams of a life where there should be a "communauté des biens", equality and happiness for all, were shattered forever by the restoration of the monarchy, continued to lead a lonely and frustrated existence in Vendôme, telling all who cared to listen to her of the great days of the Revolution and the Constitution of '93. Passionate for reform, forever scribbling ideas for a future political system that no editor in Vendôme dared to print, she died in her early fifties, "sans fortune et sans famille", a republican to the end.

François Duval had the satisfaction of seeing his son, Pierre-François, succeed him as mayor of Vibraye in 1830, and his daughter, Zoë, married to Doctor Rosiau, former mayor of Mamers, before he was laid to rest in Vibraye cemetery, near to his one-time partner and comrade, Michel Busson-Challoir.

The glass-houses founded and developed by Mathurin Busson nearly a century before had continued to flourish, though no member of his family had any connection with them.

On her eighty-first birthday, despite the lateness of the season and the threat of rain, Madame Duval induced her son, the mayor, to drive her the short distance to la Pierre, so that she might descend from the carriage awhile, and look through the park gates at the château and the foundry beside it.

The château was shuttered, its owners away in Paris, but smoke came from the foundry chimney, and the familiar bitter tang of charcoal filled the air. Workmen were wheeling barrows to and from the sheds to the furnace-house, a two-horse waggon waited to be loaded, and three apprentice-boys, laughing and joking to one another, came out of one of the sheds bearing a crate between them.

Across the greensward were the workmen's cottages, and one or two women stood in the open doorways, staring at the carriage. They had taken advantage of the meagre sun to spread their linen on the grass to dry. The foundry bell sounded for the midday change of shift, and the men came out of the furnace-house and from the sheds, and gathered in little groups. Like the women, they stared at the waiting carriage.

"Haven't you seen enough?" asked Pierre-François Duval, mayor of Vibraye. "We are drawing attention to ourselves, standing about like this."

"Yes," answered his mother, "I have seen enough."

She got back into the carriage, and looked for a moment through the open window. Nothing had changed. It was still a community, a little body of craftsmen and workmen with their families, indifferent, even hostile, to the world outside, making their own rules, abiding by their own customs. What they created with their hands would go out across France, through Europe, to America; and surely each object would carry upon it some stamp of the first masters who long before had worked here with pride and love, passing on the old traditions to their successors.

Madame Duval's last glimpse of her childhood home la Pierre showed the furnace-house, with the buildings grouped about it, caught momentarily in the pale glimmer of a November sun, the whole shrouded and protected by the tall forest trees whose strength and durability fed the furnace fire.

That night she made a package of all the papers she had

written, tied them with ribbon, and gave them to her son for dispatch to her nephew Louis-Mathurin in Paris.

"Even if he does not read any of it aloud," she said to herself, "or suppresses those parts that show his family, and especially his father Robert, to disadvantage, it will not matter. I shall have done my duty and told the truth. Most important of all, his son George, the boy he called Kicky, will keep the glass."

She went over to the window and opened it, listening to the rain falling upon the garden below. Even here, in her own house at le Gué de Launay, it seemed to her that the community she loved was not far distant. The men would be going on night-shift at la Pierre and at le Chesne-Bidault, and the women preparing coffee; and even if she herself no longer lived amongst them, the spirit of the past was with her still.